Praise for the Painted Souls Series

for *The Swordsman of Venice*

"Rob Samborn has crafted a thrilling stand-alone adventure sure to propel readers to his longer novels, *The Prisoner of Paradise* and *Painter of the Damned*. Delivering excitement and romance in abundance, *The Swordsman of Venice* helps keep swashbuckling alive."

- Bruce Leonard, author of *Quilt City Murders*

"An unforgettable tale of redemption and danger in the New World. A thrilling continuation of a masterful historical saga."

- Gary McAvoy, bestselling author of the Vatican Secret Archives series

for *The Prisoner of Paradise*

"The city of Venice soaks into your bones in Rob Samborn's *The Prisoner of Paradise*. As the painting comes alive, so does every word on the page in this gripping and transportive read."

- EJ Mellow, bestselling author of *Song of the Forever Rains*

"Rob Samborn's gift for vivid narrative, world-building and edgy suspense is brilliantly showcased in this immersive, time-traveling thriller infused with Gothic horror, supernatural danger and twisty suspense."

- Jayne Ann Krentz, *New York Times* bestselling author

for *Painter of the Damned*

"From 16th century Venice to modern Madrid, Painter of the Damned splashes bright history, dark arts, crimson action, and shape-shifting twists onto an epic canvas to create a genre-bending masterwork."

- David L. Robbins, *New York Times* bestselling author

for *Master of the Abyss*

"Rob Samborn is an effortless storyteller. I slipped right into this story like a warm jacket on a cold day. With characters you'll fall in love with and a plot that will keep you turning the pages, never sure what twist or turn is coming next, it's utterly enchanting, totally unique, and simply unputdownable. I've never read anything quite like this, which meant I had no clue what was coming and I was here for it. My advice: crack open this book and prepare to devour it!"

- Kiersten Modglin, bestselling author of The Arrangement Trilogy

The Swordsman of Venice

The Complete Novel

Rob Samborn

Lost Meridian Press

THE SWORDSMAN OF VENICE

by Rob Samborn

Published by Lost Meridian Press
www.lostmeridianpress.com

ISBN: 978-1-965946-78-7

Address permissions and review inquiries to author@robsamborn.com or lostmeridianpress@gmail.com.

For media or rights inquiries, please contact Kimberly Brower of Park, Fine and Brower Literary Management at kbrower@parkfinebrower.com.

Editor: L.A. Mitchell
Cover Design by Damonza

Connect with the author at www.robsamborn.com.

First Edition
Printed in the United States of America.

Books by Rob Samborn

The Prisoner of Paradise

Painter of the Damned

Master of the Abyss

Content Warning

This book is intended for mature audiences only. It contains many period-accurate scenes and themes that some readers may find triggering. If it were a movie (fingers crossed), it would be rated R on the MPAA rating scale.

Sensitive readers should take note.

To the people.
Never stop fighting.

PART I

OUTLAW

"All our knowledge has its origins in our perceptions."

\- Leonardo da Vinci

I

Republic of Venice

1589 A.D.

Seawater sprayed over the gunwale of Angelo Mascari's skiff and drenched his horsehide boots. He cared not, for the ordeal had defiled far more.

Muscles burned. Blood drenched his lacerated, scorching right hand. Rest was a luxury he didn't have.

He yearned to let the wind guide him, but he feared his enemies would spy his sail in the full moon's light. The spiteful celestial orb leered at him, a glaring reminder of this worst of nights. He blamed himself. How could he not? Perhaps he should surrender and allow them to do what they would. Is a sealed destiny more favorable than a life unknown?

"Never," he cried. He swallowed the pain, drove the oars into the inky lagoon, and continued his excruciating task of paddling to the coastline.

A glimmer bounced off the silver crucifix dangling over Angelo's blood-stained shirt. He gazed up, his anger boiling. "It was for love," he whispered.

Sweat drenched his filthy clothes as he labored in the overbearing humidity. A rank stench accosted his nose, but it emanated from his pores, not the lagoon. He was desperate to dive into the water, not to cleanse himself of the grime, but of all he'd seen. And all he'd done. He glanced behind as he rowed. No boats tailed him.

Small flickers of lanterns bobbed on the city's bank. Venice's darkened silhouette was a sight to behold. Its splendor was surpassed only by its power and wealth—of the few who controlled it.

Catch, drive, release.

Harder, faster, repeat.

Splinters rooted in his skin.

Venice was all he knew. He had never set foot on the mainland and was now forced to flee. Far from his home. Far from all the territories of the Republic. How could he save his beloved by traveling away from her? A most uncertain future lay beyond the horizon.

The horrific vision of Isabella couldn't be shaken. He squeezed his eyes shut, attempting to remember the image of the radiant eighteen-year-old beauty. But her face flickered and dissipated, like the hearth's ashes thrown into a canal. If only he hadn't gone to his enemies' ritual.

What choice did he have? Had he a choice in anything?

Forcing his mind to less unsettling thoughts, he silently thanked the one who had aided him, God rest his soul. Somehow, his unnamed collaborator knew of Angelo's predicament. The old nobleman provided the skiff and instructed Angelo journey to Palos on the western edge of Spain. Along with the boat and a pouch of coins, he was given a sealed letter for a man named Sebastiano Cadamosto, who'd provide Angelo passage across the Atlantic to New Spain.

That was moments before an untold number of Protectors of the Order rushed them. Angelo disarmed one on the *fondamenta*, but there were too many. An assailant had shot a crossbow with remarkable aim, tearing the flesh from Angelo's stronger fighting hand. Against such odds, he had no choice but to take the skiff and row furiously as additional arrows struck the craft.

"Death is but the first consideration," the nobleman had said.

Fearing his words fulfilled by the Order, the man slid a dagger across his own throat.

Angelo's fate now lay with a stranger hundreds of leagues away. His collaborator never revealed how fleeing to the New World might lead to his beloved's salvation. Reaching such a far-off destination seemed impossible, but he owed it to Isabella to try. He did not know how to find Cadamosto, but that problem was secondary. First, he needed to make his way across Europe with nothing but the rags on his back and the money in his doublet.

The notion of never returning home singed his heart, but his sorrow was fleeting. His love, Isabella, was the true victim. *Her unimaginable agony.* Angelo prayed he could've taken her place, that he could've received the torment.

One day, he vowed for the tenth time in as many minutes. *One day, her captors will feel a pain far more severe.*

II

Venice

Paulina Cicogna couldn't fathom it. No, fathom was too strong a word. She couldn't *accept* how the men bickering in front of her were blind to the most obvious solutions. Though she was the only one present with a brain, it was a privilege for her to be in this room, and her father had instructed her not to speak.

She didn't want to speak; she wanted to scream. She wanted to shake each man by the shoulders, slap the demons clouding their impotent minds from their heads, and brand the solution on each man's forehead—even her father's—so they wouldn't forget.

The men droned on, arguing over how best to solve their problem.

Fools. Ignorami.

In the corner of her father's office, propped as if a living sculpture to be unnoticed, she drilled her fingernail into her wrist to divert her anguish. The pain wasn't intense enough, so she clamped down on her inner cheek with her molars and ground the flesh until it bled. The coppery nectar soothed her spirit and calmed her rising pulse. She wiped her brow, brushing away a strand of her long, brown hair that her servant braided the evening prior. Her father preferred she wore a netted bonnet and brighter dresses than her favored black and gray, but the headwear constricted her brain, and any dress of color was suited for children.

Truth be told, Paulina was thrilled to be there. Her father's office was the grandest in all of Venice, as it should've been, since Pasquale Cicogna was the ruler of the Republic. The Doge's Palace was her *father's* palace. When she turned sixteen three months back, he allowed her to attend certain meetings. This was her third. Though he was grooming her for a position of power, she knew a girl could never become dogaressa without marrying a doge.

She'd change that.

Her father sat on his high-backed chair in the center of the room, listening to his men. He stroked his thick, dark gray beard and mustache that accentuated sharp cheek bones on his angular face.

Three advisors, all in their fourth or fifth decades of life, along with two Protectors of the Ancient Order of the Seventh Sun, both just in their third decade, stood before Doge Cicogna. The Protectors, Ivan and Vito Uccello, were renowned for their cunning, loyalty, and swordsmanship. Along with their dark eyes, Vito's hulking stance and stark gaze beneath thick, shoulder-length flaxen hair, and Ivan's raven-colored hair topping a perpetual tight scowl, had earned the men the nickname the Bird Brothers. They reveled in the moniker, as they fancied themselves birds of prey. Yet here they stood, unable to remedy their failings. Ivan's recently broken nose served as a glaring reminder of this fact. Paulina was fond of Vito, but the brothers should've been groveling for their lives.

Her father had been home for three minutes before they knocked on the door, informing him that sleep would elude him; he had pressing business to attend to. She'd been up waiting for him and thus was privy to the news: spies had been discovered.

She made herself known and asked to go. The doge pondered, but in his sleepy state, he honored her request. Her twin sister and younger brother still slept, though her father never would've brought them to this meeting. It didn't matter that her sister wasn't there, for Paulina would tell Maria everything later anyway. She loved her sister dearly and confided in her multiple times a day. She was Paulina's verbal diary, and Maria would never say a word, for Paulina's loving sister had been dimwitted since birth.

As the men debated the next course of action, she scratched her aquiline nose before shielding a yawn with her hand. Boredom, not lack of sleep, had compelled the involuntary movement. She gazed about the room. Inlaid wood paneling took up the bottom half of the walls, underscoring the wraparound fresco above it illustrating many of Venice's triumphs in the Republic's six-hundred-year history.

Knocks rapped on the large wooden door before it opened.

Two additional Protectors entered, both dressed in black hooded cloaks. The smaller man had a severe bruise on his left cheek. They dragged a third man by the arms, his black noble attire dripping water and blood. They dropped him on the middle of the floor and flipped him over. Count Pietro Stefanetti. And he was dead. Paulina pursed her lips when she noticed the method of the traitor's demise: a slit throat.

Oblivious that her father's Persian rug had just been sullied, Vito Uccello stared at Paulina as if she'd trespassed in the holiest of sanctuaries.

The other men in the room gazed at Stefanetti with grave expressions. She was unsure why they were so despondent. Every man there had seen a dead body, many by their own hand. Apparently, they were unfamiliar with the concept of treason. Had they forgotten the cause of Caesar's demise? Or Jesus's? They should've been elated that Stefanetti lay at their feet.

Vito continued to stare at Paulina. "Most Serene," he said to her father, "with all due respect, is it wise the signorina be present?"

The question incensed Paulina. Vito hadn't complained about her presence on a prior occasion. Quite the opposite.

"Do not question my judgment," said the doge.

The Protector bowed in acquiescence.

"That said," the doge continued, "Paulina's attendance is unusual, but rest assured, my daughter is an asset. She's my balance, an old soul, who may offer a more... *creative* insight than us men."

"And what insight do you have, my dear?" Vito asked Paulina.

Paulina's eyes lit up, but her father raised a finger, barring any response.

"I've instructed Paulina to observe for now. She and I shall convene later. That is the last you and I"—he glanced at the others—"or any of you shall discuss my daughter or her presence at this or any future meetings. Let's get back to the situation at hand."

Paulina smiled at her father.

An old soul.

He'd often referred to Paulina as such. She used to consider it a compliment. 'One wise beyond her years,' he'd say. In recent months, she'd grown tired of the appellation. She was a *young* soul, with *young* blood and *young* thoughts... swimming in a sea of fetid milk.

Again, the men resumed their discussion. Though the doge ruled the Republic and had the final say on who advised him, when it came to affairs of state, he was the first to remind anybody that Venice was a republic, so he listened to the others with genuine earnestness. Vito and Ivan Uccello argued for an operation to ferret out traitors, spies, and conspirators. The doge's three advisors—two members of the Council of Ten and Senator Quattrone—thought it more prudent to tread stealthily, so they could learn more before taking definitive action.

The discussion moved to the facts at hand, so the two soldiers recounted their tale of catching Stefanetti. There had been another man, Angelo Mascari, but he'd escaped. For Paulina, Mascari's name fit like a linen glove. Pietro Stefanetti was the fraternal uncle of the recently deceased Isabella Scalfini, collaborator and lover of Angelo Mascari, and thus a conspirator in the murder of Councilman Renzo Scalfini.

As such, by aiding one who had killed a member of the Council, Isabella's uncle had attacked the Republic itself. Yet, death would not have been an appropriate sentence for such a crime by association.

As they continued their story, Paulina's lower abdomen quivered when it was revealed that Stefanetti had slit his own throat. A most interesting turn of events. The coward had feared a trial.

Or perhaps her arousal came from Vito. For despite the doge's command and Vito's apparent displeasure, the Protector continued to throw glances at Paulina that lingered on her full, rosy cheeks and large brown eyes.

She gazed back at the husky Protector with a coquettish smile and fluttered her long eyelashes.

He looked away and cleared his throat.

Though she'd yet to choose a new suitor, she knew what men desired, for she shared those same desires. When her husband died in a church fire two weeks after their wedding day, she was uncharacteristically distraught. Vito's arms—and body—draped her in comfort. That was nearly a year ago.

He wasn't the most handsome in her father's employ and far beneath her station, but that didn't prevent her from teasing the man, which she often did before their one night together. Of late, she found the game played both ways. In the rare moments when she and the Protector were alone in the courtyard or royal gardens, she'd marvel at the girth of his arms and the way his blonde hair draped over his colossal shoulders. Or perhaps sneak a lightning bug-kiss.

The doge knelt and examined Stefanetti's throat. "A pity he took his life. What of the swordsman, Mascari?"

Senator Quattrone cleared his throat. "As I said, Most Serene, my Protectors did not have a boat—"

"You do not need to repeat yourself." Paulina's father rose and straightened his *corno ducale*, the gold-linen horn-shaped hat unique to the doge. "It's *our* Protectors. Remember the covenant, *Exalted Master*."

Senator Quattrone nodded his agreement.

"Regardless," continued the doge, "the question was to the Bird Brothers."

"We will formulate a contingency plan, Most Serene," Vito replied.

"We're beyond the formulation stage, no? If Stefanetti was working with Mascari and committed suicide to protect him, then clearly, Mascari is also part of the Guild. They need to be stopped before they do more damage. The criminal cannot get far without a horse. Gather squadrons and send them to all the towns on the mainland accessible from the Rio della Sensa. Find Mascari and bring him back alive. He *will* expose his collaborators."

All the men in the room bowed to the doge.

Paulina loved when her father assumed an authoritarian position. Yet she didn't bow. Not because she wasn't required to, but because she disagreed with his solution.

In *her* mind, the answer couldn't be simpler: gather anyone who's ever uttered a single question of the doge... then cut out their tongues and stick their heads on pikes in Piazza San Marco.

III

Mestre

The incoming tide aided Angelo's aching muscles and sleep-deprived brain as he lugged the skiff onto the rocky beach.

Though the shore was a faint outline from his island city, he had seen this town while at sea when he apprenticed as a bird's nest lookout on a fishing vessel. The captain was kind enough to grant his uncle's request for the training, as Angelo's father had recently succumbed to the plague.

Angelo burrowed deep into the recesses of his mind for the town's name, for he was nine when he last saw it. The town and lands beyond were part of the Republic but looked and smelled alien. Water lapped the beach; seagulls squealed on their hunt for food.

Across the Venetian Lagoon, obscured by twilit fog, lay Angelo's beloved Isabella, along with his past and a once-promising future.

The apprenticeship on the fishing boat had lasted only a few weeks, since his mother needed him at home. A life off the water led to a misspent youth filled with odd jobs around the neighborhood, doing whatever he could to earn a ducat for his family. Fights were frequent, as was being on the losing end of them. His fortune—nay, his fate—changed when he stole an oak dowel from a shipbuilding yard.

An innate gift for swordplay brought certain notoriety to Angelo. Local bullies who'd previously pummeled him left him alone. A few befriended him. Others came from adjacent neighborhoods, challenging Angelo with their sticks and, sometimes, swords. It didn't matter who or what he fought against. He always stood his own. Word of Angelo's victories spread, and by fifteen, he was accepted into Master Salvator Fabris's renowned school of swordsmanship. The education did not come cheap, and his master forbade him from entering circuit bouts. Angelo earned a meager wage in underground prizefights, but the winnings scantly covered food for himself, his sisters, and his mother, who had become bedridden with consumption. As his mother's condition dwindled, so did his finances. Before long, his troubles had reached unwanted ears.

He'd never forget the day Ivan and Vito Uccello—the Bird Brothers, as they were more commonly called—confidantes and Protectors of the Doge, approached him. Though he had no idea how they knew he existed, they offered to pay his debts for a single task: seduce Isabella, the wife of Councilman Renzo Scalfini, and once in their bedroom, steal a book filled with untold secrets.

Angelo loathed taking the contract. He was neither a deceiver nor a thief, but his creditors were growing impatient.

Nobody had anticipated the outcome of the job. The love between Angelo and Isabella was immediate, undeniable, and unbreakable. He couldn't betray her and reneged on his agreement. Their love also blinded them to the risks of their affair. When her husband caught them, the brute beat and raped Isabella. Angelo came to her defense, and in the struggle, Renzo met his demise.

They were interrupted by the Bird Brothers, who witnessed the lovers driving a letter opener into Renzo's heart. Unarmed and outnumbered, Angelo fled out the window. Isabella was detained.

Shortly thereafter, from a furtive nook in the largest room in the Doge's Palace, a gruesome scene unfolded before Angelo's eyes. Shackled to a chair before Tintoretto's half-completed *Paradise*, out of pure vengeance, his enemies drained Isabella's essence from her body.

In the flesh yet flesh no more.

Now, standing on the opposite bank of his home, all the air in Angelo's lungs discharged with a long sigh. A tightness spread from between his shoulder blades to his lower gut. He would've retched if he'd eaten or drank anything in a day. Swallowing the bile, he pressed both hands to his lips and blew a kiss across the water.

"Adio sani, 'mòre mio. Goodbye, my love." He uttered the words to both Venice and Isabella. But it was not truly goodbye, for he knew, one day… one day, he would return to them.

His throbbing right hand reminded him of immediate concerns.

Retrieving his rapier from the skiff, he wiped the moisture and blood from the blade and sliced off the bottom of his shirt, which he wrapped around his hand. Blood continued to seep through the makeshift bandage, but it appeared to slow. He scratched the mucky rag on his ear—an earlier wound borne by the affair.

Hundreds of boats emerged, moored along the coastline in the dawn's welcoming rays, already strong for late July. Fishermen prepared for the day's work. He had steered clear of them on his way and now wanted to collapse into a deep sleep. Despite his utter exhaustion, he had to move forward. The fishermen would hopefully provide a boost for his next step. The nobleman's skiff was a gift that saved his life, but it wouldn't carry him to Palos.

Using his rapier, he pried out an arrow lodged in the craft's side before sliding the sword into the scabbard hanging from his hip.

He kicked his dinghy back into the water, jumped in, and rowed past the first three boats he came across. None of those were what he searched for, as they all used dinghies similar to his to haul supplies to their larger vessels.

At the fourth fishing boat, two ginger-haired boys, neither older than twelve, one lugging ropes, the younger carrying buckets, trudged through the water to their boat. An older version of the boys followed.

"A pleasant morning, my good sir," Angelo said to the barrel-chested fisherman with a red beard wrapping half his face.

The fisherman adjusted the rolled net hoisted over his shoulder and nodded a fair enough reply.

Angelo paddled to the beach and hopped out. Broken shells and pebbles crunched under his boots. "I see you're in need of a skiff."

"Are you giving me yours?"

"It's for sale."

"Not interested. I have two strong sons."

The older son had climbed aboard their boat. The father threw the rope, which the boy caught with deft hands.

"Surely a skiff would aid your work, sior," Angelo said. "I no longer need it, so you can have it for the best price."

"What price is that?"

"A skiff like this is worth at least thirty ducats."

"Ha, where?"

"La Serenissima, of course."

"You're not in Venice, boy. Here a skiff like that is sold for ten. I'll give you eight."

"Eight? The sail alone is worth four."

"Then sell it to someone else."

Angelo exhaled. He craned his neck at the boats down the line. None of them would do. "What's the name of this town, sior?"

The fisherman laughed. "Be gone, boy. I can't be flubbing the dub now."

The restless hands of time needled Angelo's back. Though he'd evaded the Order, they knew where he was headed. The fisherman's gaze fell like a netting as Angelo scanned the sea for incoming boats. The coast was clear; the same could not be said for his anxiety.

"Sì, sior. I'll take your offer," he said. "If you include some bread and salted pork."

The fisherman eyed Angelo's bandaged hand and ear. "The town's Mestre," he said. "Now my price is seven."

"You said eight not a moment ago."

"Information has a cost, as does time. As does food. In the next moment, my price will be six."

"Give me seven, then," Angelo replied through gritted teeth.

The man waded over and inspected the skiff. He reached into his smock for his coin purse, counted off seven, and handed them to Angelo.

"Grassie, sior." Angelo pocketed the money. "Could you be so kind as to tell me how to get to Palos?"

"Is that a town?"

"Sì, in the Spanish Kingdom."

The man coughed out a phlegm-filled hack, which he spat into the sea before resuming his laughter. "Are you jesting me?"

Embarrassed, Angelo squinted across the water toward Venice. His home felt further than anything. "I'm not."

"Then it's a pity you sold your skiff. Head west, I suppose. Walk a long time, then swim a long time."

Angelo gazed west. The beach extended to a low dune. Could the journey take weeks? Months? A year? That was just to Palos.

The fisherman shook his head. "The fish won't wait for me all day, boy. There's a path there." He pointed past the dunes. "Go to town and likely you can find a carriage heading to Genoa. That's the best I can offer you."

"Thank you for your kindness," Angelo said. He lowered his head and slogged away, remembering his Maestro Fabris's advice on goals: *'To reach the top of a ladder, one must step on all the rungs.'* Genoa was Venice's rival. He'd need to enter enemy territory to reach Palos and, ultimately, the New World. He spoke adequate Latin and *la lingua italiana* but prayed the Genoese wouldn't recognize his accent.

"Boy," the fisherman called.

Angelo turned.

"Never negotiate when desperate. Or at least hide your desperation, else you'll never win."

"I've nothing to lose."

"Every man has something to lose. Especially a desperate man."

The words hit home. Angelo *was* desperate. But if he had nothing, how could he have something to lose? With that despondent thought, he headed for the dune.

"You forgot something," said the fisherman.

Angelo turned again to find a bundle flying toward him. He caught it and unwrapped it. Inside was a wedge of bread and a slab of salted pork.

He smiled broadly at the fisherman.

"How did you know we had salted pork?" the man asked.

"All fishermen have salted pork."

"All too true. You'd think we'd eat fish." He chuckled. "Remember what I said. Also remember I'm the kindest man you'll meet."

IV

Mestre

A twenty-minute walk led Angelo to the town's outskirts. Though not distant from the sea, he guessed he was already farther from water than at any point possible in Venice. The tranquility of the stroll gave him pause but soothed him. He stretched his arms wide. Finding solitude in his birthplace—a cramped island city constructed entirely by man's hand—was a castle in the sky. He'd heard about other lands, of course, and had seen paintings and read children's stories with his limited literacy, but to experience it first-hand felt like a miracle.

Now, forced to flee to New Spain, all he wanted was to return home. Unfortunately, he'd be arrested the moment he stepped into the city and likely handed the same fate as his beloved. Or worse, if such a sentence were possible. He'd be discovered in Venice or throughout the Veneto, but his collaborator had said they'd also find him anywhere in Europe. Could that be true? Did his enemies have that far a reach? Surely, he could hide in Rome and disappear with a new identity. Running to the other side of Earth must have been an overreaction. The nobleman had also said Angelo was 'a liability to the Guild, to the cause at large.' Unless that guild's cause was saving Isabella, he wanted no part of it.

The calls of ducks and frogs emanating from reeds segued to sparrows and squirrels searching for food amid cypress trees.

The more Angelo contemplated the situation, the more he realized there was another reason to travel that distance. There must've been someone in New Spain who had the wherewithal to free Isabella and 'the others,' as his collaborator put it. The man never had a chance to explain.

Who could it be in such a far-off land? Never mind a guild. Angelo would need an army to defeat his enemies. Even if someone had such strength or persuasion, why would that person aid him? No, he didn't need to find someone. He needed some*thing*. Was there a tool or key hiding in the New World, something that could help him complete the impossible? Tales abounded of ancient cities paved in gold and filled with mystical artifacts. Whatever he needed, he'd find it, return to Venice, and liberate his beloved.

With a mission firmly planted in his heart and mind, Angelo returned his thoughts to the splendor of nature enshrouding him. He marveled at the buzzes of flies and bees and the chirps of crickets in the brush. More foliage existed in that short space than in all of Venice. The air was different too. Gone was the ever-present stench of decaying fish and canal sewage, replaced by the scent of trees, flowers, and... *life*.

Entering the town of Mestre through the city walls returned him to the familiar feeling of civilization, albeit on a quainter scale. The architecture resembled that of Venetian homes and palazzos. Angelo wandered the town, searching for a carriage house, but couldn't find one. His search led him to Piazza Ferreto, the town's main square, which, he was pleased to discover, differed little from the piazzas of Venice. When nine o'clock struck on the castle-like clock tower, its bells reminded him of how precious little time he possessed.

Realizing he couldn't find a carriage to Genoa on his own, he asked five people. None knew, but one suggested he ask at an inn on the edge of town, backed against a wooded area.

"You're a fine mess," the gelatinous innkeeper said while sweeping the tavern floor in the two-story building. "Did someone drop you in a sausage grinder?"

"I feel that way, siora."

A spattering of guests sat at long tables drinking ale. It had taken a minute to get the innkeeper's attention and more minutes to provide relevant information, but she warmed up to him.

"Don't we all, sometimes," she replied. "One carriage makes the trip to that filthy place and the driver shall return in three days' time. You can ask your questions to him direct. He usually stays in Mestre for some days before departing again."

"That's almost a week," Angelo replied.

"I see you can count."

In her fourth decade, the innkeeper's matronly bosom looked as if she were smuggling two piglets in her dress. She was kind to answer Angelo's questions, but he didn't appreciate her sarcasm in his time of need.

"What am I to do until then?" Angelo asked, more to himself.

"I know an inn where you can stay." She gestured to the tables and benches behind her. "The taverna serves the best mussels in Mestre, and the wine flows all night long."

"It sounds wonderful. Where is this inn?"

The innkeeper grinned at her new guest.

The boisterous dining hall was a welcome respite from Angelo's recent travails, despite the heat of the place. A summer rain brought a sizeable crowd of mostly fishermen into the taverna, making the place feel like a ship's hold jammed with pilchards. Angelo sat near the hearth, which doubled the temperature. An odor of free-flowing ale, wine, and sweat permeated the stale air, but before him, a fragrance of anise danced on the ocean's bounty. Mussels lolled in a broth kissed by the Lord's divine chef, satiating his previously empty stomach.

Earlier in the day, Angelo had prepaid the two-ducat fee for a week's bed and dinner. Staying so close to Venice concerned him, but with the carriage not departing for Genoa in that time, he had little choice. He figured he'd stay the entire seven days, stashing bread from each supper for the following mornings.

After providing Angelo with a comparatively clean shirt left behind by a delinquent guest, along with a needle and thread, the innkeeper had shown Angelo to the second-floor sleeping quarters, an open room with twelve narrow beds, six of which were presently occupied. A door in the rear, at which Angelo's bed was situated, led to an outside staircase for access to the outhouse and for the guests to empty their chamber pots, which was not part of the service. Given that the inside staircase led directly into the taverna below and passed the innkeeper's room, she insisted all guests use the backdoor if needing to relieve themselves.

Each bed had a small locking armoire, but he owned nothing short of the clothes on his back and his rapier, which was forbidden in the dining hall. He deposited the sword in the wardrobe. As an afterthought, he also locked away the letter for Sebastiano Cadamosto.

The innkeeper washed Angelo's clothes with no extra charge nor questions and managed to erase the bloodstains from his doublet with some sort of blessed soap. He used the needle and thread to stitch his hand. The sleeve from his old shirt sufficed as a new bandage. He also removed the bandage from his ear. It was ugly but healing.

Before long, revelry from the taverna drifted through the floorboards. Days of hardship left Angelo with a single desire: to get lost in a haze of pot-shotten camaraderie.

As the wine wench brought flagons and his companions continuously refilled his thick, etched green glassware before it was empty, his knowledge of time disappeared with the dorona wine. Similar states of inebriation walloped his cohorts. Across the long table sat the innkeeper. Leaning on her was her husband, a male version of the jocund woman. Both wore wide, perpetual grins.

A bearded Milanese monk relaxed to Angelo's right, and a bespectacled Englishman conversant in Italian enjoyed the gaiety on Angelo's left. Both were on their way to Venice, and though their reasons for visiting the city of sin were diametrically opposed, their paths crossed in the middle of a wine barrel.

While the monk took his imbibing as seriously as morning prayer, the Englishman was loose with his words and fast with his hands. They clinked their pewter chalices in front of Angelo, splashing a rogue golden wave onto his shirt and causing the whole table to laugh, including the innkeeper, who couldn't contain herself. Angelo appreciated her respect for humor, as she'd given him the clothing a few hours prior.

"Angelo," the Englishman spat, as he leaned into him, "come back to Venice with us. We need a guide."

"I wish, my friend." Angelo heard himself slurring his words, but his brain couldn't be bothered to correct his speech. "But I'm afraid they've locked me out and tossed the key."

"Oh no," the innkeeper said in a severe tone. "What have you done?"

"Looks like they slammed the door on your hand too," said her husband.

"Pray tell it's not something that can't be absolved," the monk said.

"It's a sin, indeed," said Angelo. "One that perhaps can be absolved yet not explained."

"With as vague an answer as that," the innkeeper's husband said with a chuckle, "you are thus obligated by the rules of this inn to spin a yarn that rivals one of Dante's."

Angelo doused his tongue with wine, letting the spicy, dry flavor of the dorona grapes seep in. His new friends sipped their drinks while anticipating the tale. There was too much they wouldn't believe, for he scantily accepted it himself. Seven months of magical bliss with Isabella Scalfini, the love of his life, his soul mate. It was more a dream than a tangible experience. Yet, her taste lingered on his tongue, overpowering the wine; her touch bristled his skin, overtaking the tavern.

How he yearned to be with her. How he would do anything at that moment to be with her, naked, as they'd been on his cousin's boat, lying beneath the open sky, planning a life together. It all came crashing down in a cataclysm. If only her ruthless husband had returned to her bedroom five minutes later. If only he could've done more to save her.

If only.

Angelo took another swig, then briefly closed his eyes.

"There was a girl."

"There always is," the other three men said in unison before laughing and toasting each other.

"You better believe it," the innkeeper chimed in. She held her head proudly, as if representing all of humanity's better half.

"This was no ordinary girl," Angelo continued. "She was the loveliest, wittiest, cleverest, strongest, most radiant person I've ever met. Present company excluded, of course." He winked at the innkeeper, who blushed. "I shall never forget her smiling eyes. When Isa—*Ismeralda*—gazed at me, it was as if her eyes beamed with joy." Despite the alcohol sloshing in his head, Angelo silently exhaled relief that he didn't let Isabella's name slip. His new friends were strangers. Protectors could've arrived before dinner. It was unlikely the people at the table were part of the Order, but that didn't mean they wouldn't talk, especially if plied with drink... which was exactly what they were doing to him.

"Sounds like quite the bird." The Englishman pursed his lips and cocked his head as if coaxing Angelo to divulge information.

Concern accosted him. Angelo glanced at the surrounding tables. Other patrons were all stuffed as ticks, drinking and laughing; none minded him. Relaxing, Angelo's thoughts skipped to Isabella. He yearned to talk about her. He *needed* to talk about her. Doing so would keep her alive, at least in his memory.

"She *was* a bird. An injured and caged bird, who I freed, and we soared to the sky together." He gulped some wine and exhaled before continuing. "Our love was taken from us. Ripped out like an Oriental rug from beneath our feet. We shared a love for the ages. A love poets would've killed to write about. Minstrels would have sung our song from the mountaintops. Alas, it was not to be."

"*Was* a bird?" the innkeeper asked.

Angelo paused before responding. Even if they were family, he couldn't tell the truth. He didn't know the truth. He'd witnessed the ritual. Could he trust his eyes?

"I meant she was a sweet songbird," he said, staring into his wine. "Before she was taken."

"Who took your love?" the monk asked.

Again, Angelo considered his companions. Were they genuinely interested in this tale of lost love? Or were they spies? Their heads swayed toward him and back. Or was that his? Angelo didn't care anymore. He needed to tell his story but commanded himself to avoid details that would lead to his undoing.

Another flagon was dropped onto the table. In a fluid motion, the monk snatched it and refilled everyone's cup. Angelo wondered how many drinks he'd consumed and how much he owed. He assumed the wine wench kept track, though it seemed impossible since his glass was never empty. On only one occasion had he drunk this much. It was before a duel, when his opponent had challenged him to a drinking match. The other man won, but it turned out it was a ruse to avoid facing Angelo's blade, as neither could stand. Master Fabris was not pleased. Angelo forgot his limit then but sensed he approached it. He nodded his thanks to the monk and downed a healthy gulp.

"Men." He swept his hand out, knocking over the Englishman's chalice. Wine gushed across the table. Unbothered, the Englishman replenished his drink. "Immoral men who used me and Isa—*Ismeralda*—for their devious schemes." Words and thoughts collided in a murky cloud. He tried recalling what he told himself to do moments prior, but the memory didn't come. Instead, his beloved occupied his mind. "We were caught in the middle, treading waters into which we dare not wade, but a love that powerful blinds you from dangers lurking below the surface. Now she's... she's..."

"Does your mangled ear affect your tongue?" the innkeeper's husband asked. "Spit it out, boy."

"She's locked away."

"In prison?" asked the Englishman.

"No. Yes. No. I think, yes."

"She's either imprisoned or she's not, lad. Which is it?"

"She's in a prison... of sorts."

Refusing to cry, Angelo choked back his tears. He bit his bandaged fist.

The innkeeper grasped his left hand from across the table. "You poor devil." She turned his hand over, uncurled it, and studied it, tracing her finger over the lines on his palm.

"You're a palm reader?" he asked.

"The shrewdest in the Veneto," her husband replied.

"Hush," the innkeeper said to her husband. She turned back to Angelo. "How old are you?"

"Twenty."

"Your soul is young," she said, scrutinizing his hand. Her touch sent small ripples of electricity up his arm. "You have much to do and much to learn. There is pain, but also happiness and love."

"So we'll be reunited?"

"It's a rocky road, but there's an end. Love waits at the destination."

A ping of hope in Angelo triggered a smile. "I cannot live without my soul mate."

The Englishman raised his glass. "'Love is composed of a single soul inhabiting two bodies.'"

Angelo shot a glance at the Englishman. "Yes, yes. That's exactly what we are. You are right, my friend."

"I'm the opposite. One body containing myself and a certain Greek philosopher."

"You said a prison of sorts?" the monk asked Angelo. "In the top of a tower?"

"No." Angelo laughed. "Not a tower."

"Let me guess," the Englishman continued. "Your Ish... merlda—that name doesn't roll off the tongue, does it—is being held by a jealous suitor who lays a firmer claim to your lady."

Angelo offered a half-hearted wobble of a nod.

"I knew it," said the Englishman. "It's a modern-day Tristan and Isolde, yet you, my young Tristan, will have a happy ending. You shall free your Ishmel—can we call her Isolde? Let's call her Isolde. And you shall spend the rest of your days with her."

"I... I've been told it's possible to free her, but I can't. Not now. I don't know. Not now. Maybe later." He chugged his wine and slammed his glass on the table. The room tilted. "I cannot return to Venice. Not now. Not now."

The Englishman emptied his chalice down his throat. "Nonsense," he said as he beckoned the wine wench. "Do you love her?"

"More than the days of life itself."

"Would you do anything for her?"

"Of course, but—"

"But nothing. Come with us. We'll help you free her." He reached over and slapped the monk's back.

"You will?"

"Thou shall help save thy new friend's true love," the monk said. "It's the unspoken eleventh commandment."

Angelo smiled, not admitting he'd broken three commandments with Isabella. "Yes. Yes, you're right," he said. "Why am I running? I will fight, and I will free her. Her soul cannot wither for another day. Thank you, my friends. Tomorrow, we'll… we'll…"

The room spun in vivid swirls before his head hit the bowl, splashing the remaining broth onto the table. He was less cognizant of the strange sensation of his feet dragging over steps he wasn't climbing.

V

VENICE

~ Three Months Prior ~

IT HAD BEEN TWENTY-ONE days since Angelo laid eyes upon Isabella. After bringing her home from the doctor under cover of darkness, he had watched the Scalfini residence from afar, praying to glimpse his beloved, but to no avail. The doctor had instructed Isabella to tell her maidservants that her cycle was unusually severe. Angelo suspected she followed orders; he feared the warning was valid.

Those twenty-one days had been torture, and Angelo couldn't wait any longer. Without Isabella, a part of him had been ripped out. He needed to know she was healthy and recovering. That morning, at great risk, he gave a wax-sealed note to an errand boy to deliver to her. Angelo's literacy was minimal, so he focused on his penmanship and kept the message brief. He also worried the note would be intercepted. He didn't possess a seal, so he used Master Fabris's, which was an engraving of a castle atop an elephant. Without time to melt the wax, he exhaled hot breath on it and pressed it closed. Unfortunately, it was such a poor job that anyone with a finger could have opened and resealed it, or worse, given it to her husband.

'Lady Scalfini, the Berico-Euganeo ham you ordered will arrive by skiff this A.M.'

He underlined and embellished 'A.M.' so she'd realize he did not mean ante-meridian, but his initials, Angelo Mascari.

A note of an ordered ham, personalized to the lady of the house, was likely strange, but it referred to their meeting at the market. She had purchased a ham that day, which he helped carry to her home, before the first time they made love. He chuckled at the notion of a ham preceding their intimacy. The skiff referred to his cousin's dinghy, which they often used for their interludes. She'd know where it was docked.

The errand boy appeared at the doorway of the Scalfini residence. He bowed to the Moor butler and scurried to Angelo, who had been surveilling the scene from behind an onion cart on the *fondamenta*.

"What did she say?" Angelo towered over the boy, who must've been no more than six. His brown clothes were near rags. The scamp reminded Angelo of himself at that age.

"I don't know, sior."

"How could you not know?"

"Because I didn't see her. I gave the letter to the butler. He told me wait a moment, then sent me away."

It was a scenario Angelo should've expected. He handed the boy a half-soldo coin and shooed him off.

Angelo realized he had just put Isabella in potential danger. Should Renzo—or any of the staff—inquire about the ham and discover there was no such purchase, Renzo would demand more information. His demands would be physical. Angelo also cursed himself for not including a meeting time. Should Isabella come, it could be at any hour, any day. He'd sleep on the skiff if need be.

Not two minutes later, she emerged from the doorway. He made the sign of the cross, thanking Mary for answering his prayer.

Isabella seemed in good spirits, wearing his favorite sky-blue gown, her auburn hair plaited down her back. Her complexion was far rosier than he'd last seen that fateful night. She waved off the butler and skipped onto the *fondamenta*, joining the masses going about their business.

Though he longed to follow her, Angelo had to arrive at their meeting location ahead of her to ensure it was safe. He bolted from his spot and dashed through the winding *calle*.

Arriving out of breath on the Fondamenta de la Sensa, Angelo crouched in a doorway of a striking pink house within sight of his cousin's white skiff. This part of the Cannaregio Sestiere was one of the quietest neighborhoods in Venice. Children sat on the canal's edge, their feet dangling over the water. Three homes down, workers unloaded a dining table from a small barge. There were no potential spies, advertent or inadvertent. He worried more about someone following Isabella, so he positioned himself at a strategic vantage point.

When she strolled past as casual as can be, Angelo longed to reach out and embrace her, but he resisted. Instead, he observed their surroundings. It appeared she was alone, but he couldn't take chances. When she stopped in front of the skiff, Angelo walked by briskly.

"Conceal yourself under the blanket," he whispered and kept going without acknowledgment. After a minute, he did an about-face and changed his pace, still observing. No one paid him any heed.

He casually untied the skiff, hopped in, and rowed away.

"'Mòre mio," Isabella said from beneath the wool. "It's been too long."

She lowered the material to unveil her radiant face. Those smiling eyes almost compelled him to drop the oars and kiss her on the spot. He kept his wits and continued rowing.

"You have no idea how I've missed you, cara," Angelo said. "Are you well? I feared for your health."

"I've had a full recovery, caro. The bleeding ceased a week ago. I feigned continued illness as Renzo was home every day. Providence must have guided the timing of your note, for he departed to Bologna this morning."

The corners of Angelo's mouth rose. "It seems the hand of Providence touches everything we do."

As Angelo rowed to the Venetian Lagoon, he raised the sail and let the wind pull them from their serene city.

Using the canvas sail to shield her, Isabella popped up from the blanket and tackled Angelo, locking her lips to his. He couldn't resist. With one hand on the rudder, he placed the other on the small of her back and let his tongue join hers. She broke free and continued her journey up his neck to his ear.

"You bathed today," she whispered.

"These days, I always want to bathe for you. Though I never want to wash away your scent."

She untied his tunic and kissed his chest.

"My sweet." Angelo's voice caught in his throat. Her lips on his skin were like being touched by a deity. "Are you sure you're ready?"

"Worry not. I am fine."

An unwanted frown crossed Angelo's face. "Are you not sad... for what we did?"

Isabella raised her head and met his gaze. "Of course I'm sad. I'm sad for us, for our situation. Who knows who Renzo would've killed had we been discovered? I'm sad, but I'm also angry. I know my place in this world, and it isn't just. I curse my father and the day he sent away an eleven-year-old girl to be the grindstone and mattress of a monstrous swine more than three times her age." She wiped a tear and squeezed Angelo's hand. "I wish we could walk the streets arm-in-arm, free of peril, free to make a family of our own."

Fantasies of joy bubbled behind Angelo's eyes. "A dream."

"Perhaps not. Perhaps we can make it so, even if it means leaving Venice."

He brushed a stray lock of hair from her eyes. "Nothing would make me happier."

She caressed his cheek. "Then let's make it happen. Someday. But please. Today, our happiness is short-lived. I cannot be gone for too long. I need our bodies to be one."

"I will be gentle, 'mòre mio."

He matched the passion of her kiss.

VI

Mestre

A boot heel in the ribs jolted Angelo from his slumber and back to his present reality. He didn't know why he'd been kicked, but his cough and subsequent pain quashed his arousal; dreams of Isabella would need to wait. His half-sleep wine fog, combined with filtered moonlight slicing through the shutters, prevented him from identifying the prowler looming over his bed.

"You leave a trail like a slug with syphilis," the man said in a whisper loud enough to be heard over the pitter-patter of raindrops pelting the inn's roof.

Even in hushed tones, Angelo identified the voice's owner. Ivan Uccello. The man was a Protector of the Order and half of the Bird Brothers. His sibling, Vito, was likely not far.

Angelo flexed to bolt upright. He froze when the sword's tip found his throat. The Mongolian short sword had a small, intricately carved hilt and a razor-sharp, foot-long blade. Though an unusual weapon in the Veneto, Angelo was all too familiar with it—and the crooked nose behind it.

"A sword at the throat sobers a man like nothing else. How's your face, Ivan?"

A recent memory flashed in Angelo's mind. When the Bird Brothers apprehended Isabella, Angelo had cracked Ivan's nose. The Protector seemed to think of the same moment as he stared down. He flicked his wrist, slicing Angelo's cheek. Angelo winced and wiped the blood away.

"Still attached," Ivan said. "Unlike half your ear."

In the skirmish, Ivan's brother, Vito, had sliced off Angelo's earlobe with a broken mirror shard.

"Now shut up and tie this around your wrists." Ivan tossed a leather strap onto Angelo's chest.

Angelo didn't touch it. "How am I supposed to tie something around my own hands?" he asked at full volume.

"Lower your voice," snarled Ivan. "Use your teeth."

"What's going on there?" a groggy voice asked from the bed across the room. The other lodgers continued their snoring.

"Mind your business," the Protector snapped, his eyes fixed on Angelo. "You've seen and heard nothing, lest you value your eyes and ears."

The man fell silent. Angelo wrapped the bind around his wrists and tightened it with his teeth, careful not to disturb his stitching or bandage.

"Get up."

Again, Angelo followed the instruction. Ivan pointed the sword across the bed. He motioned for Angelo to go to the rear door, which he did, while the Protector pressed the blade against the back of his neck.

Realizing he was fully clothed and wearing his boots, Angelo couldn't recall how he ended up in bed, but he silently thanked the Lord he hadn't been undressed. A pounding headache and a still-spinning room reminded him of his night with his new friends in the tavern below. A realization dawned on him: the wine had loosened his lips. Somebody was not his friend.

"Let's go," Ivan said. "Out the door and down the stairs. Slowly."

Angelo elbowed the door open and stepped under the awning at the top of the staircase. A light but persistent sprinkle created a small waterfall trickling down the moldy wood.

"Where are we going?" he asked before taking another step, wishing he had his rapier, or at least a banister, to brace himself.

"Venice." Ivan shut the door. "Where you'll be sentenced for your crimes."

"No trial?"

"Isabella was already tried, and she confessed on your behalf."

"You lie."

"It was difficult to understand her amid all her screaming, but she admitted guilt, nonetheless. Now move."

"It's just us out here," Angelo said. "Let's have a duel. Finish this like men."

"We already did that."

Angelo laughed. "I was without a sword and one against two. And *still* won."

"Hardly. Besides, I only accept duels with gentlemen, not gutter bleeders." He nudged his prisoner forward.

The steps were slicker than Angelo expected. He steadied himself against the inn's wall and glanced down behind him at Ivan's feet. His captor wore a similar, albeit newer, pair of boots fashionable in Venice, and he'd likely be experiencing the same sense of unbalance. Horsehide boots were treated with wax and pitch to make them waterproof. But they were slippery, especially when new.

At the middle of the staircase, Angelo jumped off, rotating his body, so he faced the building when he landed in the mud. He reached up with his bound hands, grabbed Ivan's ankle, and yanked it forward.

The Protector skimmed down the stairs. The force of the impact ricocheted his head back into the wood.

Rushing over, Angelo kicked the sword away. He raised his boot to jab Ivan's gut, but the Protector caught it and twisted, forcing Angelo to stumble backward. Ivan pounced up and clocked Angelo in the jaw. Sucking up the pain, Angelo blocked the next blow, but his opponent gripped his throat and shoved his head into the mud.

Angelo squeezed his thumbs into the Protector's eyes. Ivan recoiled, releasing his hold to defend against the assault. Snapping his torso upward, Angelo head-butted Ivan's nose. The man rolled off and Angelo scrambled away. His bound hands landed on a fist-size rock.

Ivan scrabbled to all fours and charged. Angelo awkwardly chucked the stone, striking Ivan in his already broken nose. Stunned and wavering, the Protector managed only a grunt.

Diving from his knees, Angelo battered his shoulder into Ivan's chest, forcing his attacker to the ground. He flipped the man over, grabbed a fistful of hair, and buried his face in the dirt, pressing it with all his strength. He crawled on top of the Protector and jammed his knee into his foe's back. Ivan struggled, flailing his arms and legs, desperate for air, like a giant, dirty fish, until he fought no more.

Angelo raised Ivan's head. The man slurped in air.

"Leave me be," Angelo hissed. "I've done nothing to you."

"You murd—"

A face plant in the muck cut off the next word. Again, Angelo held him to the point of suffocation before lifting his head.

"Will you leave me be?"

"Yes!" Bloody dirt sprayed from Ivan's mouth.

Angelo released Ivan's head and collapsed off him. He rested in the mud, letting the rain cool his skin as he caught his breath.

He crawled to his feet, retrieved the sword at the bottom of the stairs, and positioned it to cut through his bind.

A blow to his legs toppled him over. He narrowly missed smashing his face against the bottom step. Ivan clutched his feet and clawed up his body.

Angelo stretched for the sword until his fingers touched the metal. With his palm protected by the bandage, he gripped the blade and jammed the hilt into his assailant's face, further damaging the man's obliterated nose.

Ivan screamed and clutched his injury.

Scurrying away, Angelo flipped the sword, caught it with his bound hands, and swung, slicing through Ivan's thigh. The Protector cried out again.

Angelo jumped to his feet, kicked Ivan in the jaw, and slammed his foot on the man's chest. He connected the end of the blade with Ivan's throat.

"You call yourself a Protector?" Angelo spat on the shriveled cur beneath him. "Of order? You're a bringer of chaos and evil."

"We gave you promise. A future. You kissed away everything, Mascari. All your own doing." He coughed a crimson bubble of saliva. "Yet you blame *us* for providing debt relief and the love of your life."

"You took her from me!"

Ivan grinned. Blood stained his teeth. Mud covered his face. "In a fitting manner. I always thought she was a work of art."

Angelo tightened his grip around the hilt. The Protector was all but asking for death. Angelo had already killed one man and hoped there wouldn't be another.

He owned no guilt for Renzo's demise, but the man was a noble. Should he kill a Protector, they'd send an army for him, led by Ivan's brother.

Digging his fingers into the mud, Ivan heaved himself away from the sword. Angelo pressed the tip into his adversary's windpipe, a hair from puncturing it.

"She suffered," Ivan said through gritted teeth.

"I know."

Angelo drove the sword into the Protector's throat.

Neither Ivan's last breath nor his expression was expected. The breath was curt, and his eyes froze in surprise. Angelo anticipated the man would continue fighting, but it was as if Ivan never imagined a lowly swordsman from the slums would finish the job.

It may have been an involuntary muscle reaction, but an additional breath and eye blink prompted Angelo to ram the blade through Ivan's neck and into the ground, ensuring a quick end to any suffering.

A shiver and nausea swelled through Angelo. After a moment, he steadied his breathing, as instructed by Maestro Fabris. Then with a shaking, bloody hand, he retracted the weapon and wiped it on Ivan's shirt.

The second man Angelo had killed in a week lay at his feet. A repugnant trend was developing. The first was an unfortunate result of a misplaced five minutes. An accident, one could call it. How five minutes can change a life so. Ivan's death, though a by-product of the first, fell into the category of self-defense. He closed the dead man's eyes. Justified or not, Angelo vowed he'd never kill again. He kissed the silver crucifix Isabella had given him and tucked it back into his shirt.

A snort snapped him back to his present situation. He sliced the bind off his wrists before peeking around the building's corner to find a majestic chestnut-brown mare tied to a ring. A thin white stripe ran down her snout. Two bags were strapped to the embroidered leather charro saddle, hanging gracefully on the horse's back. Undoubtedly the animal belonged to Ivan, as the guests' horses would've been sleeping in the stable. Horses were transported across the lagoon regularly, though not typically at night.

The hour stood high. Angelo's pursuer would not have traveled alone.

He hoisted Ivan's legs and dragged his body into the woods, ten paces beyond the outhouse.

Rummaging through the Protector's clothes, he liberated the dead man of a coin purse. He also took the scabbard, engraved with Latin and symbols he knew not but guessed were Oriental.

Angelo hurried back to the inn, sheathing the sword as he ran. He climbed the stairs and crept into the sleeping chamber. Snores rose from the beds. The rain likely drowned out the commotion of the fight.

A quick turn of the key in the armoire resupplied him with his rapier and the letter for Cadamosto, which he tucked into his filthy doublet.

"I'd recognize that scabbard in moonlight," the monk whispered from his bed.

Angelo spun around.

"Carried by a specific few. Divini protettori dell'ordine. The Divine Protectors of the Order."

The man's knowledge was a surprise, but there was no time for a history lesson. Angelo rushed to the monk's bedside. "Did you betray me?"

"I am but a man of God. I know not your crime, but it could not be worse than what the Ancient Order of the Seventh Sun has done. *Now* I understand your answer about your love's imprisonment."

"You're with the Guild?"

The clop of horse hooves precluded the monk's response. Angelo hustled to the window and inched the shutter open. Four men on horseback arrived at the inn. Two dismounted while the other two remained on their steeds.

"Awake, innkeeper," one of the men ordered.

From his vantage point, Angelo could only hear the conversation.

"Return in the morning," the innkeeper's husband replied. "I'll call the constable."

"The constable sent us here."

"What business do you have at this hour?" the innkeeper asked.

"You're harboring a fugitive called Angelo Mascari."

There was a brief pause before the innkeeper's husband spoke again. "There is no guest here by that name."

"Think again. Harboring a criminal is a crime itself."

"I do not know of a Mascari," said the innkeeper. "There was a guest named Angelo. He dined here, then returned to Venice."

Apparently, the men heard enough. The inn's door burst open.

Angelo dashed to the rear of the room.

"There's a path that will circumvent the town to the main road," the monk whispered. "Take it south to Bologna. Beware, the Order's tentacles are everywhere. Godspeed, my friend. Your secret is safe with me."

"You have my eternal gratitude."

Angelo hustled down the stairs, nearly slipping.

Peering around the back corner, he sensed Ivan's horse had yet to be discovered. He stroked the animal's nose. "You're a beautiful creature," he whispered. The mare snorted in thanks.

Angelo untied the rope and guided the horse behind the inn as fast as he could in the mud. It wasn't long before he located the back path. He had a best guess as to the direction of south, though he was far more concerned about the horse.

He'd been on one a handful of times. Master Fabris insisted his students practice the art of equine sword fighting, not because it would be useful in a bout, but because it required supreme balance and awareness. If one could fight on a horse, one could fight anywhere. Of course, Angelo had never ridden a horse beyond the stable nor faster than a trot.

Memories of Venice conjured snippets of his drunken conversation from hours prior—talk of accompanying the Englishman and the monk back to his city to free his love. His strongest desire was to do just that, but it was far too dangerous, and he refused to put another soul in harm's way. Staying alive had become the task at hand. He yearned to save Isabella with all his heart, but his collaborator in Venice had been right. He couldn't do it dead. And death was but the first consideration. Angelo would follow the nobleman's advice, journey to Palos, and then to the New World. It would take years, but he'd save Isabella one day.

With not a minute to waste, he tucked Ivan's Mongolian short sword into a saddlebag and mounted the horse, which pranced nervously. Scratches behind wet ears relaxed her. Angelo slapped the reins and trotted away in the clouded moonlight.

VII

Veneto to Romagna

THE JOURNEY TO THE papal state of Romagna had been an uncomfortable, yet mercifully uneventful, two days with an overnight stay in an unwitting farmer's barn. Angelo's hand and ear were healing nicely, but the blisters on his aching buttocks and inner thighs seemed to be incurable, second to the sunburn covering his face and neck. Having previously only voyaged by boat or foot, he had fantasized about horse travel. Now, he loathed the thought of mounting the animal again. He needed a day, if not a fortnight, to recover.

After fleeing Mestre, Angelo rode until dawn's break. He arrived in an unnamed town before the residents woke, enabling him to water his horse from the piazza's well. Reclining on a stone bench carved with cherubs, he assessed his present situation, along with Ivan's belongings. In addition to his recently deceased assailant's sword and coin purse, he discovered practical treasures. Ivan's saddlebag was loaded with three maps of the Venetian Republic and adjacent Florentine and Papal territories, a compass, a wrap of dried salt cod, two loaves of bread, a dozen carrots, five apples, and goatskins of red wine and water.

The most valuable prize was a letter authorizing diplomatic passage for Ivan Uccello as the doge's envoy.

Spirits lifted, Angelo replenished his belly and fed the horse, whom he dubbed Linguini. After his new friend devoured a third of the rations, Angelo discovered a second document rolled behind the letter. The ducal seal of a winged lion had been stamped in red over perfect calligraphy. With his limited literacy, it took time to decipher all the words in the dim morning light.

By decree of Doge Pasquale Cicogna
A Warrant for his immediate Arrest is hereby issued to and against Angelo Mascari, citizen of Venice, the Republic of Venice, La Serenissima, wanted for his complicity in Crimes of adultery, murder, and Offences against the State as a culpable individual, convicted by the Council of Ten, authenticated by His Serenity Doge Pasquale Cicogna.
Mascari must be captured alive and returned.
A bounty of 500 Ducats will be furnished to the Captor.

The warrant didn't surprise him. The size of the bounty and demand for a live capture were revelations that churned conflicting feelings of pride and anxiety. A reward for his head wasn't the type of notoriety he'd sought. He wished to God he could've lived his days with Isabella and achieved fame as a swordsman. Burning the warrant crossed his mind, but a plan hit him: use the warrant and Ivan's credentials. By assuming the Protector's identity, he'd have free passage. It was a gamble but less perilous than being a fugitive. He tucked both documents back into the saddlebag.

For a moment, he considered reading the letter for Cadamosto but decided against it. If the Spaniard was willing to provide Angelo a means to reach New Spain, then surely he was part of the Guild and willing to help. But if Cadamosto realized the seal had been broken, it could be the end of Angelo's road.

Combining the money given to him by his collaborator, the eight ducats he received for the skiff, and the mix of Venetian, Roman, Florentine, and Genoese currency from Ivan's coin purse, Angelo had a total of forty-three gold pieces and eighteen silver. More wealth than he'd ever possessed, yet his gut warned him the sum was likely insufficient for his journey.

While Ivan's supplies presented a windfall, Angelo couldn't muster a shred of joy. As a fugitive, his once-bright future had darkened to eternal night. Alone in the world, other than his new four-legged walking torture chair, he was unable to follow the immediate path he so yearned to trod: save Isabella and exact revenge on those who took her.

"I promise, my sweet, I will return to you as soon as possible."

I know.

Angelo jutted his head up. He glanced around, but he was alone. He chuckled. Lack of sleep had him hearing voices.

How he'd return to Isabella was another question entirely. The current priority was to reach Palos alive. Still, as dire as the situation was when he stepped back and analyzed it, though he'd killed a member of a formidable and relentless group, he was in a more advantageous position than he was the previous day.

You've done well, 'mòre mio.

Again, Angelo checked his surroundings. The piazza was devoid of people, and Linguini didn't say the words. Yet, he recognized that voice as pure as honey. *Isabella's voice*. He knew it was in his head, brought on by sleep deprivation, stress, and injuries, but he welcomed it.

The town's early risers opened their shutters and tossed their chamber pots. He quickly gathered his things and guided Linguini out of the square. The townsfolk would remember any stranger.

VIII

VENICE

DOGE PASQUALE CICOGNA CONTEMPLATED the body of Ivan Uccello in devout silence, as if praying. Yet he didn't kneel or clasp his hands.

Other than in actual prayer, it was the quietest Paulina recalled seeing her father. Even when eating, he always had something to say. He always uttered a sound.

She hovered over the corpse along with three advisors and three Protectors, including Vito Uccello, who had returned from Mestre with his recently murdered brother. Vito remained silent but suppressed tears of dark rage.

She pitied the man. The brothers were famously close. Losing Ivan in such a despicable way must've felt like a knife in his back. Angelo Mascari was a rogue indeed. One who'd pay. She tried to make eyes with Vito, share his pain and anger, and offer *him* comfort, but the Protector refused to meet her gaze.

Her family's personal medico crouched over the deceased, whose clothes, skin, and hair were caked in dried mud. He'd been laid on a quilt crested with St. Mark's Winged Lion, resting on the floor of the Four Doors Room. As a child, when she and her sister were permitted to play in the palace on Sundays, the *Sala delle Quattro Porte* was her favorite room for hide-and-seek, so named because the southern and northern walls each had two doors that led to one of four rooms. As the formal foyer for more important chambers, ornately chiseled marble framed each entry, with small allegorical sculptures of the virtues that government officials should embrace. Paintings depicting Venetian governance decorated the walls, and bas-reliefs on the ceiling symbolized the Republic's grace under Heaven. Though small compared to most rooms in the complex, leaving through any of the doors gave one the sense of entering greatness.

Tonight, Paulina wondered if they were portals to Dante's Inferno.

"The Protector is dead, Most Serene," the doctor said.

Senator Quattrone drew in a sharp gasp that could've cut his throat. He reacted not to the statement but to the medico's audacity of declaring the obvious to the smartest man in the Venetian Republic.

All the men cleared their throats and stifled retorts, staring at the gaping hole in Ivan's throat. Paulina wondered if the doctor would soon meet a similar end. He deserved it for such insolence. He'd been summoned there to offer insight on the situation, not exclaim that the sky was blue.

"Grassie, Medico." The doge flicked his hand.

The physician nodded and exited through the southwest door.

A silence fell over the space again as the doge continued to regard his departed confidante. After a moment, her father's genuine emotions betrayed his facial features. He clenched his jaw. He narrowed his eyes. His nostrils flared. Then he emitted a low guttural growl.

The corners of Paulina's mouth rose.

"Who is this scoundrel, this criminal, this Angelo Mascari, that he can murder my most devoted and skilled Protector? My friend?"

Vito made the sign of the cross.

"Mascari is the best swordsman in Venice," a Protector mumbled under his breath.

"Silenzio!" The doge's scream reverberated off the walls.

Paulina gazed at the paintings surrounding the group. It was as if the men in the artwork stared down at the scene, emboldening and supporting her father's fury.

"My *Protectors*," the doge said in an angry, nearly inaudible whisper, "are the best swordsmen in Venice." Then he screamed, "Or at least they're supposed to be!"

The force of his words impelled everyone to step backward. Even Paulina.

"It's one thing to do well in a judged tournament on a stage," the doge said. "It's another in *real* battle. Mascari does *not* have military training." He took a breath. "Vito Uccello."

Vito bowed. "Sì, Most Serene."

"This is the second of my closest friends killed in a week. Besides murdering Renzo Scalfini, I had originally doubted whether Mascari was worth pursuing." He exhaled another throaty sigh. "Your brother must be avenged. Return this rogue to Venice. Alive. He'll reveal his collaborators. Then, he'll pay for his crimes. The bounty has been doubled. Spare no expense. However far you need to go, however much you need to spend, however many men you need."

Vito offered an unforgiving grin. "We will leave at once, Most Serene."

"Good. Now everyone out. Prepare Signor Uccello's funerary gondola."

The men carefully lifted Ivan's body and filed for the southwest exit. Paulina followed.

"Except you, Vito," said the doge. "And Paulina."

Paulina froze. Did her father suspect something between them? With her head low, she silently turned back. If he knew, she'd be chastised, but Vito would land in the *pozzi*, rotting out his days behind iron bars in the dungeon beneath the palace. With a reluctant exhale, he released his brother. He allowed the other men to carry the body out before he closed the door.

"How is it possible," the doge said, "that such a love affair occurred?"

Simultaneously, Paulina and Vito exchanged a glance and swallowed.

"Father—" Paulina started.

Vito raised his hand. "Most Serene, I can explain."

"Good," said the doge. "Because I want to know how Mascari, an indebted swordsman, was in a position to meet Isabella Scalfini, a noblewoman, let alone manage to seduce her in her husband's bedroom."

Upon hearing the question, Paulina allowed herself to breathe again.

Vito cleared his throat before speaking. "I believe they met at Signor Balbi's Christmas ball."

"Daughter? Have you something to add?"

"I gathered the same." Paulina's voice came out a half-octave higher than intended. She adjusted to her normal tone. "I heard this from her friend Violetta, who also met the rogue."

The doge paced the room. "There is zero doubt Mascari is a member of the Guild." He stopped at a painting of an angel blessing La Serenissima. "Clearly he seduced Isabella with the intent to steal the book. *My* journal. One I consigned to her husband's safekeeping because I was worried about it in this very palace." He turned to Vito. "Yet you and Ivan claimed he did not have it in his possession at the time of Renzo's murder."

Vito shifted his stance, staring straight ahead. "Forgive me, Most Serene. Is it not best we speak about this in private?"

The doge narrowed his eyes. "You try my patience, Vito. Paulina is an extension of myself." He sighed. "That said, the two people I trust most in our earthly realm are in this room. It *was* three if you count your dead brother. Trust cannot be built with secrets."

"Grassie, Most Serene." Vito bowed his head. "I will not question you again."

"So, if Renzo didn't have the book that day, and it wasn't in his strongbox when you and your men searched the house, there are few options. Either Renzo stashed it somewhere else, which I do not believe he would, you and Ivan took it that day, which is impossible, Isabella took it and hid it, which is possible but unlikely, or a servant took it. Again, possible but unlikely. Or the most likely of scenarios: Mascari took it a previous day but wanted to continue copulating with the lovely Isabella. Let's be honest, who'd blame him for that?"

Blood rushed to Paulina's cheeks at her father's statement.

"I concur," Vito said, ignoring the doge's lewdness with an expression that looked like glee or perhaps... relief.

Paulina, too, was relieved. Let her father concern himself with issues more pressing than her daughter's indiscretions. Though she wondered about this curious book.

"Should my journal fall into the wrong hands," the doge continued, "it could topple the Republic, the Papacy, everything we hold dear. Am I clear?"

"Yes, Most Serene." Vito bowed.

"We need to know if Mascari found it. You will also have the opportunity to avenge your brother. Keep this part of the mission to yourself. Do not even mention it to Quattrone. The man can't be trusted."

Vito widened his eyes. "Sior?"

"Exalted Master or not, he has his own designs. Bring Mascari back. Get it done. Come, daughter."

The doge headed for the northeast door. Paulina didn't immediately move as she let the conversation sink in. Not only was her curiosity about the book doubled, but so was her hatred of Angelo Mascari.

It wouldn't be long before the swordsman would be hanged in St. Mark's Square along with the other traitors. And she'd have a front-row seat.

Upon the welcome news, Vito met Paulina's gaze. In that moment, they shared an unspoken desire for more than righteous vengeance.

IX

Romagna

The ride to Bologna's outskirts took longer than expected, partly because Linguini was in no mood to walk—or talk. Neither was Angelo, so he couldn't fault his equine friend.

Though Bologna was more a trading partner with Venice than a rival like Genoa, Angelo suspected arriving in any large city at nightfall would be a risk not worth chancing. He knew nothing of the place, inns would be closed, and ruffians hostile to outsiders may well be on the prowl. Sleeping on the street with Linguini was not a tempting proposition.

Thus, shortly before dusk, when he came upon a vineyard in the hills of Romagna outside the city, he took the chance of encountering an angry vintner by entering the gate and walking Linguini to the villa.

Weeds blanketed the path. Crows landed on desiccated grapevines, and flies buzzed all around. Brittle ivy dangled from the two-story villa's pink stucco. The vineyard was in such a sorry state Angelo wondered if the property was abandoned.

An unnatural scream and thump came from behind the villa.

Moments later, a gray-haired, bearded man greeted Angelo halfway up the path. A beeswax lantern lit his leathery skin. His blood-soaked right hand carried a matchlock rifle.

"Stop where you are, stranger," the man said.

Angelo obeyed. Considering the gun needed two hands, he assumed the weapon was already loaded and cocked. The reason for blood on the man's hand was another concern.

"Good evening to you, signor. I'm in need of lodging and hope that you may oblige."

"This ain't an inn. You're on private property, vagabond."

"I can pay."

"You'll find lodging in the city. Best be on your way."

"Would you accept a scudo for a night in your barn for myself and my horse?"

The man lowered his rifle a bit. "In the barn? With the horses?"

"All I need is some hay. For me to sleep on. And her to eat." Angelo smiled as he stroked Linguini's nose.

"You'll be gone by Prime?" The man remained stoic.

Angelo shrugged. "Or Terce. I'm a late riser. Worry not, I'm eager to reach Bologna."

"From where do you hail?"

"Venice, signore."

"What business do you have in Bologna?"

"None, signore. I'm passing through to Genoa."

"Your purpose there?"

This man cannot be trusted.

Isabella was right. Angelo considered his words. "Official business, signore, on behalf of Doge Cicogna."

The man raised an eyebrow. He studied Angelo's tattered attire in the pale light. Angelo straightened and widened his shoulders. The man eyed Linguini, a gorgeous creature in the orange glow of the setting sun.

"You'll be gone by Terce?"

"Gone by Terce," Angelo replied with a wide grin.

"You'll need to leave your sword in the villa. Remove it slowly and toss it to me."

Do not give him your sword.

"What choice do I have?" Angelo mumbled to the voice in his head.

"None, if you want to stay," the man said.

Angelo unbuckled the scabbard and tossed it over.

The man retrieved the rapier. "Any other weapons?"

"None," Angelo replied without hesitation, but a half second later, he remembered Ivan's Mongolian short sword tucked in the saddlebag. He opened his mouth to declare the weapon but opted against doing so.

"Well, you look harmless enough. Any extra money helps these days." The man gestured to his withering, fruitless vines. "Four years of blight." He extended his bloody hand to Angelo. "Diego Venturi."

"Glad I came along," Angelo said, shaking Venturi's hand. "Ang—er, Uccello, Ivan Uccello." He wiped his hand on his pants.

The man raised his eyebrow at the slip of Angelo's name. "Apologies for the mess," he said. "You caught me preparing supper. Come. I'll show you to your quarters. Prepare for luxury."

He led Angelo and Linguini up the hill to the villa and then to the large barn behind it.

A headless chicken lay on a stump.

Inside the barn were eight stalls but two horses. "The back stables have been cleared out, so take your pick." His eyes saddened. "Food for the family comes first. There's a trough behind the barn. We have some reserve Barbera. For one more scudo, you can have a flagon."

Angelo didn't respond. He already well overpaid for a night in a barn and wasn't in a position to purchase the most expensive wine he'd ever taste.

Venturi raised his hands as if offering communion. "Two flagons, then."

"Your wine must be fit for a king at that price."

"It is. I'll throw in a hot chicken dinner and breakfast."

Never negotiate when desperate. It seemed like a moon's age since the fisherman spoke the words to Angelo. The vintner was indeed desperate, but what did he have to lose? Some wine? Blight and hunger were no way to live. Angelo had lived most of his life on the edge of poverty. The worst of destitution is fear. The fear of not knowing when or what your next meal will be. Angelo did not possess a coin to spare, but then again, the money in his pocket had come easily to him.

"Your wife and children are inside?" he asked.

Venturi raised an eyebrow, then relaxed. "Ah, I mentioned family. You're an observant fellow. I see why you're in the doge's employ despite your"—he looked Angelo up and down—"appearance."

Angelo smoothed his clothes and assumed a commanding tone. "My appearance is none of your concern. Where is your family?"

"Wife's inside. My two daughters are grown. Went to Bologna for work."

The man's gaze swept the floor, flashing a hint of shame.

"Two flagons, dinner, and breakfast sounds wonderful." Angelo handed Venturi the coins.

The once-lavish two-story Venturi villa was a skeletal abode, with bare walls and floors, lacking furniture other than necessities. Venturi introduced Angelo to his wife, who apologized for her home's state before saying hello. Also in her sixth decade, her long, gray hair framed her tanned, oval face. Cracks lined her eyes. The couple had sold most of their belongings, of which she told Angelo about each one. Their footsteps echoed off the marble floor.

"Falling on tough times must be worse than being born into poverty," she reasoned.

Angelo considered the notion, but at least the Venturis were fortunate to have experienced wealth at one point.

Over dinner, Signor Venturi acknowledged that despite the hardships, they were still able to eat well. This was partly due to over twenty chickens that feasted on the vineyard bugs, horsemeat that had lasted all winter, and herbs and vegetables unaffected by blight. They traded eggs and their remaining wine for wheat, salt, and other items, but mostly they dined well, thanks to Signora Venturi's skill in the kitchen. Angelo complimented her with every bite of his four servings. Pasta stuffed with egg and seasoned with lavender and sage had his tastebuds dancing the bassadanza. Isabella had told him of tortellini, but he had never tasted the Bolognese specialty. Signora Venturi told a story of how Venus's navel inspired the creation of the ring-shaped pasta.

The tale prompted Angelo to drift into visions of Isabella and her divine umbilicus. So lost in thought did he wander that he failed to respond when they called him Ivan and inquired of his business. He recovered after an unknown number of utterances of the Protector's name.

"Apologies," he said. "I'm quite fatigued from my journey. I'm searching for a Venetian rogue."

"Rogue?" Signora Venturi asked. She exchanged a glance with her husband.

"He committed crimes most foul. Have you heard of such a man in these parts?"

"Fortunately not," she replied. She downed her glass. "You're quite young to be looking for him alone, are you not?"

"Signora," Angelo said, "if you have issues with the doge's men or his decisions, you are welcome to make your position known by submitting a petition through the proper channels." He smiled, quite pleased with his response.

"What should we do if we encounter this rogue?" asked Signor Venturi.

"Come directly to me, of course."

He smiled politely. "We'll do just that."

Not wishing to repeat his drunken night in Mestre, Angelo consumed only two glasses of Barbera and excused himself. The Venturis offered an empty room in the villa, but Angelo insisted on his agreed-to accommodations.

X

Venice

~ *Six Days Prior* ~

Isabella's light touch skimmed the stubble on Angelo's chin. A small smile played at his lips, but he didn't want to open his eyes. Not yet. The late afternoon bustle from the Grand Canal below intruded through the window, but it didn't spoil the moment. It was rare that he spent time with his love. Once awake, it would mean his imminent departure.

He loathed leaving her.

In the distance, the clock tower rang three times. They had overslept and were at significant risk, but he cared not. He opened his eyes. As always, her dark beauty captivated him. Her skin was flushed, and damp auburn hair at her temples fell to frame her almond eyes. He loved her eyes so. Even closed, they beamed with intelligent contentment as if pondering the most exquisite dream.

A silk mosquito net draped her oak bed, trapping the humid summer air within the space. He preferred a breeze, but at this moment, the conditions comforted him. He was certain their activities, not the temperature, illuminated her face's glow. The room smelled of them now. Satin sheets, damp from their commingled sweat, stuck to his shoulders. Compared to his own bed—a straw mattress in a room he shared with his mother and youngest sister—the luxuriousness of Isabella's chamber heightened this forbidden slice of paradise.

Opening her eyes, she beamed before curling a finger around his hair. "Buongiorno, caro."

"Mia bella Isabella," he said, bringing her other hand to his lips. "My beautiful Isabella."

He pressed his lips to hers. She returned his embrace, the kiss growing more passionate.

Angelo had always thought himself a righteous man. His mother taught him from an early age to treat others as he wanted to be treated. He sparred with dignity and humility while dueling in underground prizefights for a trickle of ducats. He never supposed he'd be the type to bed another man's wife. Though his father was taken when Angelo was nine, he was aware the man had been unfaithful to his mother. Seeing the grief she carried thereafter, Angelo had sworn off infidelity.

From the moment he met Isabella, everything changed.

Intense and undeniable love for her justified the indiscretion, and Angelo longed to ease her misery. He knew of her husband's temper, his brutality. He tried not to think about it too often, as it torched his veins. Though a fighter by trade, Angelo was not an angry or violent person by nature. Still, he held himself back from seeking out Renzo and taking matters into his own hands when Isabella divulged the things her husband done. Angelo wanted to do right by her. Today was the day.

He couldn't yet offer her the comforts and finer things of the upper class, but he could give her something infinitely more valuable. True love.

Leaning back, he brushed a lock of hair from her face. "It's unwise for us to continue in this manner. It's becoming far too perilous."

"I agree." Her voice wavered. "No, no, I do not truly agree. I know of the hazards, but I worry not of the ramifications. Do you... Are you saying you do not want to continue... this?"

"Of course I do. That was not the intent of my words." He kissed her on the forehead. "What I meant was..."

"Tell me." She touched his lips.

Angelo pulled himself to a sitting position, and she did the same. He took her hands. "Isabella, do you love me?"

"Now and forever. Your heart sets mine ablaze."

For the first time in his life, Angelo's eyes welled with bliss. He took his love's hand and pressed it against his heart to feel the heat emanating from within. Heat she ignited. "Then run with me," he said, giddy from a mix of anticipation and apprehension. "We can start a new life beyond Renzo's grasp. Grow old together, have children. Be happy. This life is torture for you, and to be without you is torture for me. I can no longer stand idle, knowing what that brute does to you."

Her eyes widened, and for a moment, he thought she might refuse. She threw her arms around his neck. "Oh, Angelo."

"Is that a yes?"

She pulled back and clasped his face. "Sì, sì, dio cantante!"

He kissed her hard, ecstasy flooding every nerve of his body, invigorating his soul. "I'll make arrangements. My cousin will lend us his boat. This time tomorrow, meet me where we left for our day on the water."

Her arms tightened around his back. "I'll be there."

"But for now," he said, reluctantly pulling away. He kissed her once more and slipped out of the bed.

Angelo grinned as she watched him dress with an appreciative eye. He raked his fingers through his curls, tousled them, then smoothed them back.

"You like doing that."

"A feather must be ruffled before it's straightened." Her radiant smile made him feel as though his heart would burst. Oh, to be with her forever.

"This will be the longest day of my life."

"One day. Before a lifetime together." He jumped onto the window frame, showing off his athleticism and cat-like gracefulness in the face of danger.

Angelo peered out the open window. Spotting no unwanted observers, he blew his lover a final kiss and rolled out, finding a familiar foothold. He shimmied down the building's side, using the rails and masonry until he landed in the alley.

At the corner of the Scalfini residence, he joined the stream of pedestrians with a spring in his step. As he rounded the corner onto a busy *fondamenta*, he bumped into a stout man walking with a limp.

"Mascari," growled the man. "A wingless pigeon has more grace."

The apology Angelo was about to offer resiled in his throat. He instead offered a curt nod. A man half a head higher and a full body wider stood before him. A landscape of small pocks dotted the man's forehead over deep-set eyes, and thinning brown hair covered his head. It was none other than Renzo Scalfini, senior councilman—and Isabella's husband.

Two other men in their early thirties flanked Renzo. Vito and Ivan Uccello. The Bird Brothers.

"Why are you in San Polo?" Scalfini asked Angelo. "Shouldn't you be somewhere offending someone? Perhaps gaping at another man's wife with lecherous eyes?"

The Bird Brothers chuckled, each displaying a set of yellowed, crooked teeth. Angelo withdrew from Renzo's sour breath.

"I had business here," Angelo said, ignoring Renzo's reference to the night they met at a Christmas Ball. "I must be off. Adio sani, siori."

"Ciao," said Ivan.

Vito stood statue-like, never taking his eyes off Angelo.

Scalfini grunted a reply, but Angelo did not stay to hear it. Though acutely aware he needed to be cautious, something compelled him not to hurry. He realized he was famished. As he strolled away from the trio, he grinned, remembering how he worked up such an appetite.

Salivating at the delectable fragrances wafting from street vendors along the canal, he strode to an outdoor cook and ordered *baccalà alla vicentina*.

While paying for his meal of salted cod and polenta, he sensed the curious need to glance toward the Scalfini house, though it was a block away and obscured by other buildings. A distant shriek reached his ears.

Angelo froze. Was it a startled horse? A moment later, he recognized the tone of a second cry. The shout came from the top floor of the home he left not ten minutes prior.

Fear stabbed his chest. He raced back for Isabella, ignoring the vendor's angry protests.

Love guided him up the front steps of the Scalfini home. Having only entered through the front once, he was nervous but had no other choice. Angelo stealthily opened the door and let himself in.

The Bird Brothers sat in the parlor. A dark-skinned female house servant, no older than Isabella, unwittingly distracted them with glasses of grappa. Startling these men would be a grave mistake. After crossing himself, Angelo held his breath, slipped through the foyer, and hopped up the steps.

His gut instinct drove him to the master bedroom.

Angelo shoved open the bedroom door with such force that it smacked into the wall. The doorknob shattered the plaster.

A grotesque display of humanity's worst revealed itself to him.

Purple handprints disfigured Isabella's neck. Her top lip and nose oozed blood. She was naked, bent over the wooden marriage chest at the foot of the bed, her breasts flattened against it by Renzo.

XI

Romagna

"Signor Uccello, Signor Uccello..."

The name birthed a grumble of maggots that enveloped Angelo's skin. He blinked his eyes open. Dawn's rays poked through the barn's open-air windows and cracks in the ceiling.

"Signor Uccello..."

The Uccellos were directly responsible for Isabella's fate. Rage burned through him. Though he'd sworn never to kill again, he now had no remorse for Ivan's death. The man deserved it. His brother, Vito, deserved to die. No. Angelo shook his head. He wouldn't stoop to their level. He'd keep his vow.

The call of the name continued, accompanied by rooster cackles he'd apparently slept through.

The barn doors creaked open. Light flooded the space. Linguini whinnied. A mélange of hay, dirt, and manure wafted into Angelo's nostrils. He crawled to his feet, stretched his back, and brushed off his clothes.

Venturi stood at the barn door beckoning. "Breakfast is ready, Signor Uccello. Fresh eggs. Same as every morning. Come."

Cracking his neck, Angelo walked slowly out of the barn and up the slope to the imposing villa. Crows cawed overhead. Chickens ran about, nearly tripping him.

"Sleep well?"

"Well enough." Angelo yawned. "Much gratitude for your kindness. How long of a ride to Bologna?"

"With a horse like yours, just over an hour."

They entered the villa and headed for the dining room. A single plate of two fried eggs and a sprig of fried rosemary waited at the table.

"Where's your wife?" Angelo asked, raising an eyebrow at the solitary setting.

"In the garden."

"You're not dining with me?"

"Oh, we ate already. Us old folk eat quite early, you know. Sit. Please."

He pulled the chair out for Angelo, who sat and shoveled a forkful of the now-cold eggs into his mouth, followed by a morsel of rosemary for flavor and texture.

Signora Venturi entered the dining room. "Good morning, *Angelo*," she said with a wide grin, emphasizing his name.

"Pleasant morning to you, signora."

Angelo stopped chewing, recognizing his blunder. He placed the fork on the table and raised his gaze. The couple stood not five feet away, the husband wielding Angelo's rapier, the wife holding Ivan's Mongolian short sword and the doge's warrant.

"I knew it," said Signora Venturi. "I can *smell* a liar. Five hundred ducats. I can't believe it."

"He must've killed Uccello, too," said the husband. "Surely the reward will be higher." The two of them flashed mouths of wine-stained teeth.

I told you they couldn't be trusted. The wife's even worse.

Angelo swallowed, wiped his mouth, and stood.

"Sit down," the vintner said.

"No."

"Force our hand, and we'll slice you to pieces," said Signora Venturi.

"You need to keep me alive for the reward. You've read the warrant. You know what I've been accused of. And... of what I'm capable of."

Their smiles perished. Glancing at each other, they retreated two steps and raised the swords in defense. The husband held the rapier with enough poise that led Angelo to presume the man had some training, if not military experience. The wife, on the other hand, wielded the short sword like an axe. She was a wild card and would likely hack away with no control.

Angelo took his last bite of eggs. While chewing, he snatched the plate and whipped it at the vintner. The porcelain ricocheted off the man's cheek, stunning the couple. Angelo threw the fork at the wife, who blocked it with the sword. He jumped on the table, sliding across it as he ducked under the wife's swing. He grabbed the blade's crossguard and twisted, disarming her.

With a quick toss, he caught the sword's hilt. Hooking his foot behind the woman's ankle, he shoved her backward. She tripped over his boot and tumbled to the floor. She cried out, clenching her back.

Angelo parried a thrust from Venturi, calculating his longer reach. He'd never dueled with a short sword before. Besides the inadequate length of the blade, the weapon was unnecessarily heavy. It was an interesting exercise. He defended two other blows, then hit with a riposte, striking the rapier just above its swept hilt. The sword flew from Venturi's hand and landed on the floor with a clatter. Angelo brought the tip of the Mongolia short sword to his opponent's throat.

"Sit. Next to your wife."

"Are you hurt, my sweet?" Venturi asked his wife. He sat beside her and aided her into a more comfortable position.

"My back," she said. "The whoreson broke it."

"You're fine." Angelo retrieved his rapier and targeted both swords at his assailants. He briefly assessed his rapier, pleased to find it was undamaged. Assaulting his own sword had made him cringe. "Where's the matchlock?" he asked.

"In the kitchen," Venturi replied through gritted teeth.

"Stand."

The two obeyed. As they entered the kitchen, Angelo stepped behind them, his two swords at their necks. Two matchlock rifles leaned against the wall, prepped for action.

"Sit. Center of the floor."

The couple submitted again.

"Please, sir," Venturi begged. "They're our means of defense."

"Then you should've used them."

Keeping an eye on the Venturis, Angelo rested his swords on the counter. He emptied the rifles of their bullets and pocketed them.

"Where are the other bullets?"

"Those are the only two we have," the woman said, inching toward the door.

Angelo smirked. He scanned the kitchen and found a small metal bucket on a shelf. Inside were a half-dozen bullets, which he pocketed, as well. He tossed the rifles on the floor, then retrieved his swords, pressing the tips against the back of the Venturis' necks.

"Stand."

They did as instructed.

"Now walk. To the barn."

When they arrived at the barn, Angelo commanded them to lie in an empty stable. Though irritated, he channeled no wrath. He bore considerably more pity, as he couldn't fault them for their actions. They knew not of his situation, so the possibility of him being an actual criminal was strong, and they tasted the promise of a life-changing reward. Still, there was a strong chance they'd follow him or contact the authorities.

He freed the two horses and slapped their rears. The animals bolted. Though it would take some time, Venturi could corral them.

Keeping one eye on the couple, Angelo prepared Linguini's saddle. He stowed the short sword and mounted the horse. He pointed his rapier down at the couple.

"Two daughters, working in Bologna, yes?" Angelo asked.

Signora Venturi glared at her husband.

"It shouldn't be hard to find their brothel. The beautiful daughters of the failed Venturi vineyard." Angelo's taunts were met with gasps. He continued. "Worry not. No harm shall come to them... should you stay mum on this encounter. You've read the warrant and have seen my skills. Should you inform the constable, neighbors, or anyone, I cannot promise I'll be as lenient with your girls as I've been with you. Capito?"

They nodded, chins tremoring with fear.

"Desperation is a powerful thing," Angelo said. "It can get you killed."

"We're near death anyway," the husband replied. Tears welled in his eyes.

"From death comes rebirth," Angelo said. He gestured to the fields. "These insects, they feed on the dying vines. Kill the plants. Rip them up. Then wait some time for the pests to die, and you can harvest again."

"Ave Maria," Signora Venturi said, crossing herself. "Like Jesus. The resurrection."

"If you say so," Angelo replied with a kind smile. "You may need to wait more than three days."

"You're a Venetian," the husband said. "How do you know so much about farming?"

"I know nothing of farming. I know of scavengers. Of death and… the prospect of rebirth. Stay in the stable until Vespers. Arrivederci."

Angelo nodded his head and rode Linguini out of the barn. As he passed the chicken coop, he scattered the bullets in the pen before galloping away.

XII

Bologna

"Bless me, Father, for I have sinned. It has been... some time since my last confession."

"Tell me your sins, my son."

Tears welled in Angelo's eyes. His throat gripped the base of his tongue. Knotted rows bubbled in his gut. He *had* sinned, but he'd also been sinned against.

No, the actions of others are an excuse for the weak.

Isabella was right, of course. Tracing the events back in his mind, though he'd been wronged, his decisions led him to every sin and his current predicament.

The journey from the Venturi vineyard was an early morning pleasure through rolling hills, the likes of which Angelo had only seen in paintings. Linguini matched Angelo's spirits. He wasn't surprised, as her previous owner undoubtedly treated the horse like cattle. Angelo watered and fed Linguini frequently and spoke to her on their ride. It felt like months since he had a friend. Trotting along briskly, they arrived at Bologna's city walls in less than an hour, just as the day's heat rose.

Papal guards in full armor inspected a long queue of merchants and their goods. It hadn't occurred to Angelo that he likely crossed the Venetian Republic boundary long before he reached the Venturis. Now, on the precipice of entering Bologna, the capital of Romagna, it set in. Leaving his home city had brought about a profound sadness. Entering another country sparked uncharacteristic anxiety. He'd either be permitted entry, turned away, or arrested for illegally possessing a diplomatic missive.

An answer soon arrived. As he had no wares and arrived by horseback, two guards ushered him to the front of the line, skirting a mother with three young children.

"Halt," called a voice. Two additional guards on horseback galloped up.

Angelo's heart seized.

Without explanation, the guards grabbed a hooded man ahead of the family and dragged him away, much to the man's terrified protests.

On his turn, Angelo took control of his nerves and presented the doge's official passage for Ivan. The guard reminded Angelo that Bologna was not part of the Venetian Republic. Angelo wiped the sweat bubbling on the back of his neck. He expected an entrance fee, but the guard directed him to the cardinal legato's office at the cathedral for governmental business.

Though half Venice's population, with its wide streets and squares, Bologna felt significantly larger. After losing his way, he asked a passerby for directions to the city center, who curtly pointed to the Piazza Maggiore, where Angelo marveled at Neptune's Fountain and the facade of the massive Salaborsa Library. But it was the Basilica di San Petronio that commandeered his focus. The imposing Gothic cathedral was grander, darker, and less ornate than Venice's Basilica di San Marco and cast a gloomy shadow rather than a welcoming aura. Still, he headed for the entrance, though he had no intent to see the cardinal. It wasn't the architecture that drew him in like a fish on a line but angelic voices.

Though the interior contained few decorations or paintings, the colossal space was the most glorious house of God he'd ever had the privilege of entering. The marble-chilled air was a respite on his skin. Singing echoed off the walls. In Venice, the choirs were all adults, mixed of men and women. Here, the chorus was comprised of young boys. He'd never heard the madrigal before; its tones and words compelled him to sit on a pew. Many of the benches were filled, but he found a spot in the back.

The lyrics, about a bereaved widow who wandered the countryside as a pilgrim, moved him to tears. What would Isabella have done if their situation were reversed? He shuddered, thinking of her in any hardship, let alone what would've happened had she been caught by Ivan in Mestre. Tears flowed down Angelo's cheeks. Ivan deserved to die. Renzo deserved to die. Though even as a swordsman, Angelo wished he hadn't been the one to take their lives. Not only had he lost his love and caused the nobleman's death, but he had snuffed out two lives with his hands.

An overwhelming need to talk to someone consumed him—the need *to confess*.

"Your secrets are safe here, my son," the priest said. "Confessions are confidential."

"A conversation between God and me?"

"Precisely. You must speak aloud, in His house, for Him to hear."

"Is there no boundary for absolution? No crime too severe?"

"That is for God to judge, not I. You carry the world on your shoulders, but clearing your chest is the second step in the release of burden. First you must ask God for forgiveness. Then, forgive yourself. And forgive those who've wronged you."

Angelo snapped his eyes up. Though the small confessional box was confining, the aroma of the oak invigorated him. Through the lattice screen, the priest's obscured features seemed elderly and kindly, as was his soothing voice. How could he fathom any forgiveness?

"I'm on the run," he whispered.

"Who chases you?"

"Ghosts. My conscience. You see..." Telling the truth to a stranger, even a priest, did not feel wise.

"You are protected here, my son."

Angelo inhaled and exhaled deeply. As he did, his sorrows toppled forward. "I am the reason for my love's... death." In actuality, he wasn't sure if she was dead or alive. He'd seen what happened. If that was not death, then it was *worse* than death. But the nobleman said there was a way to save her. "She's the love of my life. And I hers. The notion that we were soul mates was never a question, but plain *fact*, from our first gaze into each other's eyes. Alas, she was married. Her husband was a cruel, vicious man, who beat her, raped her, and used her. She longed for a better life, a life of happiness. I couldn't dream of providing the wealth he had, but I gave her love, respect, and kindness."

"That is a noble endeavor, my son. Surely God will forgive your trespass."

The priest waited while Angelo digested his words. He prayed such absolution was possible.

"Neither the cause nor the scheme worsens the sin of adultery," the priest continued. "Marriage is a covenant in God's eyes, but the Lord values love, true love, over all else."

Angelo cracked a smile. He wiped the tear from his eye. "Our true love was discovered. In the heat of the moment, her husband was killed."

The priest remained silent. A disclosure of murder likely erased any good will.

"That's quite the tale, my son. Where are you from? Your Latin has a pronounced accent. And forgive me, but a rudimentary command."

Angelo paused. He had told himself he wouldn't lie to a priest. He respected the man of the cloth. Doing otherwise would be distrusting God. Truths of this world had been revealed to him. Told by the Lord himself. Yet the men who guarded those truths lied. How far would their deceit extend to protect their secrets? Could he trust this man behind a screen and admit he was from Venice? Lying to a priest was far less grave than other sins he'd committed.

"You are safe here," said the priest. "It is forbidden to break the sacred seal of confession."

The law was known among all Catholics. Should the priest recount what was said, he'd be excommunicated. But as the monk said, the Ancient Order of the Seventh Sun had committed far more serious crimes.

Angelo rubbed the stubble on his jaw. "Milan."

"I see. Adultery and murder—"

"Self-defense." He gazed at the priest's blurry silhouette. "Out of love. Tell me, Padre, you speak to God, do you not?"

"We all do, mio fio."

"I don't think he hears me. Can you... can you ask him something?"

"Of course."

Angelo wiped a tear from his eye. "Is Isabella alright? Can she truly be saved?"

The priest whispered silently to himself. "My son," he finally said, "life is a series of gifts, obstacles, and choices. Do not squander the gifts you're given. Rise to the challenges you face. Most importantly, choose wisely. Everything you do in life, every step you take, is a choice. You will not always make the right choice, but every now and again you're offered a gift in the face of a challenge. That gift is *time.* Time to think about a decision. Rarer still, time for a second chance."

"That doesn't answer my question."

Of course it does, 'mòre mio. Trust your heart.

The priest's and Isabella's words lingered in Angelo's head. She may not have been alright, but he was sure in his heart, as sure as his breath... *she could be saved*. He had been offered a gift for a second chance—the nobleman's aid. With that notion cemented in his head, he accepted his gift. He would travel to far-off lands, align himself with this shadowy Guild, find what he needed to free his beloved, and return to do just that.

At any cost.

For the next hour, he wandered the streets on foot, leading Linguini along until his appetite beckoned. A beefsteak, a bowl of rabbit-stuffed tortellini, and a carafe of chianti had him thinking for a moment to yield to simple comforts and settle in Bologna.

Satiated, Angelo found the carriage house, where a Genoa-bound driver waited for two additional passengers to fill his four-person buggy. The four-day, three-night journey cost ten gold pieces, including meals and nights at the waystations. The driver at first refused Angelo due to the slim likelihood of booking another solo passenger. Unable to find another carriage leaving soon, Angelo offered fifteen. They settled on eighteen. Despite Angelo's request, the driver refused to leave that day. They'd go in the morning, when the clock tower struck seven times. Angelo paid in full, in advance.

He had saved his next task for last, as he loathed completing it.

Angelo looked Linguini in the eye and rubbed her nose.

"It's been a pleasure to know you, my friend. You were a treasure."

The horse snorted and rocked her head.

"Don't look at me like that, Linguini. I don't have a choice in the matter. You're far better off here, in this beautiful place. There's no future with me."

Initially, Angelo had asked his driver if he needed a new horse. He didn't but he directed him to an untidy man at the rear of the carriage house who possessed one horse on a two-horse hitch. Linguini's new partner was a ragged beast that looked more pitiful beside Angelo's mare.

The man couldn't believe his luck. Angelo knew nothing of horse prices, let alone one of Linguini's stature; though he sensed the man duped him at twenty-five scudi, Angelo had limited alternative.

He'd only known the horse for a few days, but a profound sadness rippled through his body. Traversing the continent to Spain on Linguini's back was not an option; the poor thing would never make it. Angelo sighed and handed the reins to the new owner.

"Bottle your frets. I'll treat her like I'm riding the pope." The man smiled, displaying a set of decaying teeth. "Well, in a manner of speaking."

"Adio sani, sweet friend." Angelo kissed Linguini on the nose, scratched her ears, and departed forthwith, not stopping until he found a guesthouse.

The following morning, after waking at dawn, Angelo relaxed in his room until the clock tower rang seven. He lazily made his way to the carriage house, arriving before the departure time. The driver secured Ivan's two saddlebags to the hood and suggested a street vendor selling lime juice and bread.

A distressed whinny and angry yell preempted Angelo's breakfast.

The unease in his gut confirmed his worries. At the rear of the carriage house was Linguini's new owner, whipping and punching his friend as he attempted to set the yoke around the horse's neck.

"Signore," Angelo yelled as he approached the unkempt driver, "stop hurting that horse at once."

"This horse is my property, and I shall do as I please," the man replied.

"Then I shall buy her back from you." Angelo removed his purse.

The driver laughed and waved Angelo off. He yanked Linguini's mane as he raised the yoke. Linguini rocked her head, causing the driver to lose his grip. The yoke fell into his chin. Enraged, the driver grabbed a prodder leaning against a post and swung.

Angelo caught the man's hand, the metal rod inches from Linguini's ear. He positioned his body in front of his equine friend.

His action infuriated the driver. He whipped his hand from Angelo's and took a menacing step forward.

Angelo narrowed his eyes. His palm gripped his rapier. The man's sour breath was so repugnant that Angelo gagged, but he held steady. The guilt of killing Renzo and Ivan—two men he loathed—still weighed heavy, yet he longed to drive the tip of his blade through this barbarian's heart.

Instead of drawing his sword, Angelo's peripheral vision and gut surveyed his vicinity. A dozen stablemen watched the scene for their morning entertainment. His concern was not that he had an audience but that this audience would remember him.

Eyeing Angelo's hand on his sword, the driver adjusted his composure before flashing a smile of six yellowed. He stepped back and spat on the floor before placing the prodder against the post.

The stablemaster approached. He was a man who tried to make himself presentable, with long, gray hair and an upright posture, but his filthy clothes and rotting mouth belied any sense of respectability.

"What's the trouble here?" he asked Angelo.

"No trouble, Stablemaster," the driver said. "This man wishes to buy *my* horse. Well," he said to Angelo, "a horse such as this is worth fifty scudi."

"I shall give you thirty," Angelo said through gritted teeth.

"Forty, and you have a deal."

Angelo unfastened the breeching strap from Linguini, letting it fall to the ground.

"So we have a deal then?" The man drooled.

Angelo nodded and counted out the money. Seeing all was well, the stablemaster turned and went back to his business.

"Here is thirty." Angelo dropped the coins into the filthy driver's hand.

"I said forty."

"You'll be happy with thirty. You rob me of five, but I spare your life." Angelo lifted his sword halfway out of the scabbard. The man backed up and bowed in defense.

"Come, my friend." Angelo led Linguini by the reins back to his carriage. "I'll be right back," he said to his driver.

"How soon?" the man asked. "We depart without delay."

"How much time do I have?"

"Fifteen minutes. The other passengers shall be here shortly."

"I need more time. I must sell this horse before we leave."

"I cannot possibly wait that long, signore. We must make the waystation by nightfall."

"I will return shortly. Do *not* leave without me."

Angelo mounted Linguini bareback and trotted out of the carriage house.

Visions of the downtrodden merchants entering the city flashed into Angelo's mind. One group remained at the forefront of his memory—a mother and her three sons, none over ten, lugging cured hams over their tattered clothes.

He rode eight blocks to *Il Mercato dell Erbe*. It took several minutes to search the market before he found the family. He dismounted, nearly knocking over an herb stand in his haste.

"Where is your husband?" Angelo asked the mother, a haggard woman in her third decade.

She smoothed down her wavy blonde hair. "Died two years ago, signore. Are you in need of a ham?"

"I'm not. I wish to sell you this horse. I shall give you an excellent price."

The woman seemed stunned.

"Would you like to buy her?" Angelo asked.

"I have no need for a horse. Nor do I have the money if I did."

"Five scudi," Angelo said.

The woman stared, astonished. "Signore, clearly that is charity and most unexpected, but we have no means to care for it."

The kids sat on the street with their hams presented on a quilt. They watched Angelo with sad yet curious eyes. Caring for a horse was no simple task; Angelo hadn't considered they didn't have the means.

"Signora," Angelo said, "my friend's name is Linguini."

"Who names a horse Linguini?" the eldest boy blurted out.

The woman smacked the back of her son's head. He scowled and rubbed it.

"The man who names a horse Linguini," Angelo said, "is the man who offers her *free of charge* to strangers."

"Are you jesting us, signore?"

"Can we eat him?" the boy asked.

His mother smacked him in the back of the head.

"What? He's named after a pasta," he blurted out with a grin.

Angelo glared at the child. He gambled Linguini's life with this family, but it would be better than with the despicable driver at the carriage house. "I'm not jesting you," he said. "This is a mare. I shall gift *her* to you on three conditions. One, you care for her and treat her with kindness. Two, should you choose to sell her, you shall do so only to a person who will show her equal compassion and that you sell her for no less than fifty scudi."

"Fifty scudi?" exclaimed the eldest.

"That's right. Linguini is a fine specimen worthy of a duke."

"What's the third condition?" asked the mother.

Angelo drew his sword. He pointed it at the ground but looked each in the eye as he spoke. "Should you even think about eating this horse or consider selling her to a slaughterhouse or anything of the sort, then you shall know the feeling of a slaughterhouse yourselves. Capito?"

"Ave Maria." The mother crossed herself. "My son was jesting."

You're a good man, Angelo Mascari.

Nodding, he sheathed his weapon.

"Why are you doing this?" the mother asked.

Angelo glanced in the direction of the carriage house, then spoke quickly. "Do you accept my conditions?"

"Sì, signore, of course. Grazie, thank you, thank you." She rose and hugged him.

"Farewell, Linguini." Angelo gave the horse a final pat on her nose and bolted away.

Out of breath and panting, he rounded the corner to find his carriage gone. He raced onto the square and caught sight of the buggy, rolling away.

"Wait!"

Angelo burst into a full sprint. Two dogs barked and gave chase. He reached the carriage just as it exited the piazza. His fingers gripped the panel, giving him enough of a hold to jump onto the rail. The dogs gave up their noisy pursuit.

"I told you to wait!" Angelo shouted to the driver.

"And I told you we must arrive at the waystation by nightfall. Get inside."

Pulling the carriage door open, Angelo ducked into the small compartment.

"I gather you've had a better morning than I?" he asked the two startled young men on the bench.

XIII

Bologna

Bellezza snorted upon seeing Vito. He'd always loved his brother's horse. The mare nuzzled his flaxen hair, knocking it off his shoulder, bringing a smile to his face and unwanted tears that he forced back. At least she lived. When Vito had discovered Ivan's body behind the inn in Mestre, he so overflowed with rage and sadness that he hadn't thought to search for the horse. After he left the Doge's Palace, rationality returned. He'd put himself in the fugitive's boots. He didn't know Mascari's destination; the rogue likely didn't have one. Chances were, he was trying to put distance between himself and Venice. If Vito were doing the same, he'd know the doge's mare would be a target, so he'd ride to the nearest city and sell the animal to an unscrupulous—or unwitting—buyer.

Tracking down the horse in the market and then to the carriage house, where he now stood, was child's play.

The only surprise was the presence of children. A mother and three boys caressed Bellezza as if she were a family member. Vito watched from the carriage house door, the mid-afternoon sun roasting his hat.

"Wait outside," he said to his men. Five Protectors were overkill. He longed to pursue Mascari alone, but the doge convinced him to leave nothing to chance; it could not be denied that the swordsman's right arm was very threatening when wielding a blade.

Vito strode over to Bellezza. Ignoring the family, he stroked the mare's nose. "We shall have our revenge," he whispered into her ear. She exhaled a snuffle of agreement.

"Do you wish to buy her, signore?" the mother asked.

"My, you're big," the eldest son said. "You're like a giant eagle."

Vito threw a sideways glance their way, then assessed the horse from snout to tail. She was in good health and spirits. Mascari may have been a criminal, but he fed and cared for this animal.

"Do you lay claim to her?" Vito asked the mother.

"Sì," the boy replied, gawking at his frame. "Linguini's ours."

Vito chuckled. "Linguini? Who names a horse Linguini?"

"That's what I said," exclaimed the boy.

The woman smacked the back of his head. "It's the name we gave her years ago. Been in the family for years."

"That's right," said the boy, rubbing his head. "You can have him for fifty scudi."

The mother glared at her son. "*Her*," she hissed through clenched teeth.

"Scusa," the boy said. "*Her*. She's a fine specimen, worthy of a duke."

Vito returned a knowing grin. "I suppose that explains the ducal brand."

The family stared at him, mouths agape.

"Ducal brand?" The mother said, barely a whisper.

Stepping to Bellezza's right hindquarters, Vito revealed a faint outline of a winged lion. "This horse is the property of Doge Pasquale Cicogna," he said. "I am reclaiming her."

The children protested. "That's not fair," said the eldest. "He was gifted to us."

"*She*. I suppose your benefactor was a wiry man. About yay tall?" He held his hand to his chin. "Two decades in age. Dark eyes, dark unkempt hair. Likely in a rush?"

The family nodded in unison.

"As pompous as an ape on a throne?" asked the eldest son.

Vito smiled. "That's the one."

The mother glared at her offspring. "That man gave us charity," she hissed through clenched teeth.

"This mare was never a gift to give," Vito continued. "Only the Doge of Venice has that right."

"We're not in Venice," said the boy.

"Do you want to start a war over a horse?"

The boy sucked air. "Please. He's all yours. A beautiful specimen. A wondrous—"

"Be gone." Vito shooed the family. The mother grabbed her children and scurried away with them but not before spitting on the muddy floor.

Vito surveyed the stable until he found what he searched for. "You there," he called to the stablemaster.

"How may I help you, signore?" An older man with scraggly, thinning gray hair and a decrepit smile sat at a cluttered desk.

"Do you know how those people came upon this horse?" Vito asked as he approached.

"I do."

"Are you going to tell me?"

"I will."

Vito narrowed his eyes. Typically a patient man, the Mascari affair had tried his nerves. He already had enough to worry about with Paulina and the doge's book. He took a swig from his wine flask, fished out a ducat from his purse, and tossed it onto the desk. The stablemaster smacked it before it rolled off.

"The man you seek," he said, "took a carriage to Genoa."

"He caused a ruckus here," another man said, approaching the desk. Dressed as a driver, this one had worse teeth than the stablemaster. "He tried to sell me that horse. I knew it had the doge's brand. When I refused, he almost beat me to death with my prodder. I would've cared for the mare. I would've returned her to her rightful owner."

"He speaks sincere," the stablemaster said.

"How long ago did he leave?"

"Yesterday morn."

It was all Vito needed to hear. His suspicions were confirmed. Mascari headed to the coast. Vito exited the carriage house and found his men standing in the shade of a walnut tree.

"Zanca." Vito beckoned his most steadfast Protector, a man who only went by his surname. Though under the doge's employ, Vito had only learned Zanca's Christian name once and since forgot. The men walked over to the side of the building, away from prying ears.

"I need you to deliver a letter to the doge."

"Of course, signore. Right away."

"I know I can rely on you, Zanca. I'm correct, right?"

"With my life, signore."

With pitch-black hair and a dark complexion, Zanca had Sicilian ancestry but was dependable. Of late, Vito wondered if the same could be said for himself. An ocean of guilt had been threatening to swallow him whole. The doge put his faith in him, yet he'd deceived his lion. Twice. It was hard to say which deception was worse.

Technically, he'd done nothing wrong with Paulina; she was a widow and no longer a virgin. They'd only been together once, but the bond he felt with her solidified by the hour. While his affection for her strengthened, so did the odds of discovery. Despite being favored by Doge Cicogna, above all else, the doge despised treachery. When he learned his sister had been basket-making with a Protector, he had the poor sap tied to the Column of San Todaro for a week before sentencing him to the *pozzi* for life. The doge's sister was in her fourth decade at the time. Vito shuddered, thinking what the doge would do to the man who lay with his sixteen-year-old daughter. Given that Vito wasn't of noble rank, marriage would never be an option.

He had disclosed his transgression to his brother. Vito wanted to confess, but Ivan convinced him the doge wouldn't be forgiving. Eventually, he'd find out, and they needed leverage.

That was why he stole the doge's ledger from Renzo Scalfini's strongbox.

Once they knew the book was in the councilman's possession, the plan to manipulate Angelo into stealing it came about swiftly. In a matter of minutes, everything went awry and then impeccably resolved. When Vito and Ivan took it, it was as if Destiny had presented him with a reward. Now, the book was stashed safely away, and Angelo was the perfect scapegoat. He'd be tortured for knowledge he didn't possess and hanged for Ivan's murder. With Vito's love for Paulina intensifying, he needed that leverage more than ever.

"Your loyalty is unparalleled," he said to Zanca. "I'll have a second letter for you to deliver to someone else."

XIV

The Journey to Genoa

The distance between Angelo and Venice grew. His injured hand had healed enough to remove the bandage, and his body felt rested. Isabella continued to speak in his head, but her visage receded into his mind's fog, like waking in a half-sleep state in which the dream was still happening but crumbled with the slightest disturbance. He often closed his eyes and pictured her—dancing at the ball, laughing in the market, or the throes of ecstasy beneath him, rocking on his cousin's skiff. He remembered Isabella's fondness for music and poetry, her sense of humor and justice, her warmth, her love. He thought of her so frequently, the images were not limited to those of happiness. Her tears, hatred for her husband, bruises, and blood were prominent fixtures in his mind's eye.

As the physical gap between them increased, his heart pounded more intensely for her. It killed him that traveling farther away was the route to saving her. He'd find that mysterious solution in the New World. It could be years before he returned to Venice, but sobeit.

The horses soldiered on, dragging the carriage toward Genoa, yet another stop on his strange journey that was thrust upon him without notice and against his will. Though he yearned to free his beloved, a reluctance to pursue this venture lingered. Until the ride from Bologna, he had spent little time contemplating his situation, but four days and nights in a carriage and stable waystations with strangers gave him ample time to do so. Was reaching the New World *his* goal? Or was it the goal of others?

On the fourth day, as they neared Genoa, the Ligurian Alps rolled by in the distance, blurring into waves of greenish-beige. Angelo gazed out the window at the monotonous, albeit gorgeous, landscape, a far cry from the island city that was his home. A new thought occurred to him: though his collaborator died before his eyes, why was the man so desperate for Angelo to leave Venice? Was he working for the Order? Could Cadamosto be waiting for him in Palos simply to kill him?

Angelo considered these notions for a moment. No, his collaborator took his own life while enabling Angelo's escape. Moreover, it would have been a simple task for the nobleman to be the bait, and they could have trapped Angelo on the spot. He couldn't think of a dubious reason why he'd been supplied with coin and a boat, though his collaborator's motivation to aid Angelo continued to elude him.

He'd learn the answer soon, he supposed, so there was no use in racking his brain. Between thoughts of Isabella, he focused on pragmatic musings and the ride.

Angelo's traveling companions in the carriage were two Genoan brothers, aged twelve and thirteen, both rail-thin, with the fairest complexions he'd ever seen. They'd been attending the seminary school in Bologna and were returning home for their summer recess. They hadn't taken a vow of silence but spent most of each day acting like it, burying their noses in their studies and the Bible. On the rare occasions when one felt the desire to converse, it was always with the other and invariably about God or the meaning of specific Biblical passages. Angelo attempted to engage them in discourse, hoping to glean useful information about furthering his journey, but the boys had only been to Genoa and Bologna, and conversations about their hometown soon shifted to something about angels or whatnot. Despite his name, the topic never interested Angelo.

As such, he spent much of the journey in the rider's box.

"Seven and thirty years," the driver said.

Angelo had thought the man's age was closer to fifty-seven. A beard peppered with gray spots obscured much of his face, but deep grooves carved his weathered skin beneath sunken brown eyes.

The driver chuckled at Angelo's reaction and puffed on his pipe. "Been outdoors all my years. Driving this carriage for twelve of them. The wife forced me to wear this hat just a year ago."

He pulled his tripoint so low that Angelo wondered how the man could see the road.

"And you?" he asked Angelo.

"Twenty."

"I thought you were ten."

Angelo laughed. The driver joined in.

"Twenty is awfully young to be traveling to Genoa on business, is it not?"

The question was peculiar. Angelo didn't recall stating the purpose of his journey. It could've been an assumption. Still, if he were to engage with answers, it was best to avoid topics he knew little of.

"I'm not on business. I'm a pilgrim."

The driver glanced askew at Angelo but nodded his acceptance.

Three sparrows flew inches over the horses' heads.

"Do you live in Genoa or Bologna?" Angelo asked.

"Genoa, but I'm Bolognese. I wish we lived in Bologna, but the wife is Genoan, and you couldn't get her to leave her city if, well, her husband drove a stagecoach." He laughed again. "That and my twelve kids."

"Twelve?"

"Six boys, six girls. Alternating."

"Really?"

"That's what happens when you sit down with God and plan your whole life out."

The man's response brought a smile to Angelo's face—one that quickly reversed course as the creaky wheels bounced over some rocks.

As the dirt road smoothed again, Angelo continued the conversation. "Twelve years on the road, twelve children. Coincidence?"

"It's only coincidence I have twelve offspring in each city."

Angelo's jaw fell open. The driver swatted his shoulder before he had the chance to contemplate such an accomplishment.

"I'm playing, of course. With a wife like mine, who welcomes me home with open arms and open legs, I have no need to look elsewhere. Though we won't be having a thirteenth, I can tell you that. My meager living is scant enough to support my brood. The eldest boy'll be setting up his own routes in a few years.

Though the driver had been riding the same route for a dozen years, he'd also taken travelers north and west, through France and Spain. He'd never been as far as Palos, but he knew it was on the coast of the Strait of Gibraltar. The man didn't know the precise cost and travel time, but estimated land travel at roughly two months and a sea voyage at about a week. He figured Angelo had more than ample funds for either choice.

On the fourth day, with a light shower pattering the roof, they arrived at the carriage house in Genoa. Despite the inclement weather, the manager was duly impressed with the driver, arriving on schedule at eleven o'clock in the morning.

Since he was so known for his punctuality, the boys' mother waited for them in a separate carriage. Dressed in all black, she showered her sons with hugs and kisses. Angelo was surprised by the show of affection from such a pious family. His envy must've been quite noticeable as he stood in the doorway, the drizzle serving to moisten rather than clean the mud and horseshit caking his boots.

The driver appeared at Angelo's side. "The upper crust won't get out of their carriage for fear of sullying their silk stockings," he said. "Dream clients."

Knowing the family possessed both love and wealth heightened Angelo's jealousy.

"You'll have your own family one day. Just keep practicing." The driver clapped him on the shoulder.

"Tell me, signore," Angelo asked with a smile, "which way to the docks?"

"Docks? I thought you were a pilgrim. Do you not want to visit the Cathedral of San Lorenzo?"

Angelo swallowed. He sensed the driver didn't buy his lie. "Of course. And I will. As I mentioned, my true destination is Palos, and I wish to find a ship and secure passage before nightfall."

"A pilgrim in a rush."

"The Lord created the Earth in just six days."

The driver laughed and provided directions. The men exchanged pleasantries before the driver bid farewell to Angelo, as he yearned to return home, citing his own need to hurry. Angelo wished his new friend well in his pursuit of expanding his business. The man then retreated to the stable, where his horses had been eating.

After thirty minutes of trudging uphill, Angelo realized either the driver's directions were incorrect or he had taken a wrong turn. Rain created waterfalls that rolled down the narrow cobblestone streets, making walking difficult. The docks wouldn't be at an elevation. Fortunately, from his vantage point, he spied the large, circular harbor in the Ligurian Sea, turned cobalt from the weather.

Venetians were birthed with an innate hatred of Genoa as the two rival sea powers fought for dominance of the Mediterranean. He recalled Venice triumphed in 1381 after nearly 130 years of war, but there were still constant skirmishes two centuries later. Despite the animosity, Angelo found the townsfolk to be welcoming as they aided him with directions.

The port brimmed with sailors and merchants coming from or going to cities around the world. Though engrossed in their job, two courteous dockworkers directed him to a trading vessel bound for the west coast of Spain.

The galleon was a beauty with three decks and four masts. The name painted on the stern was an auspicious sign: *La Signora Fortuna*. It was precisely what he needed. *The Lucky Lady*. A sailor dangled from a rope on the ship's side, scraping off barnacles.

"Signore," Angelo called to the man, "I understand your ship is bound for Palos."

The sailor threw a glance Angelo's way. He raised an eyebrow over a bearded face, then returned to his work without answering. Seagulls squawked overhead, speeding for shelter in the weather.

"Signore," Angelo tried again, "where would I find the captain?"

The sailor's voice was as gruff as his cracked skin. "The captain's a busy man," he said. "We all are."

"I just need a moment of his—"

"Have you cargo bound for Spain?"

"Sì." There was no need to reveal the facts.

With a grunt, the sailor hoisted himself up and over the ship's taffrail. Moments later, as heavier drops landed on Angelo's head, an older man with a long gray beard and a black tricorn hat poked his head over the side.

"I am Captain Franco Doria. I'm told you have cargo," the man said. He glanced up and down the dock. "I've never seen you. Who do you work with?"

Angelo flashed a wide smile. "I'm honored to meet you, Captain Doria. It seems I've found the right boat."

"What are you shipping, boy? I transport the finest of luxuries."

"You're looking at it. The finest luxury in all of Italy." Angelo extended his arms and bowed with a flourish. He felt foolish putting on a show before this grizzled captain in the rain, but for a reason he couldn't pinpoint, he sensed the man appreciated humor. He straightened to find the captain staring at him, dead-faced.

Then the man released a grumble that may have been a reluctant laugh. "We take passengers. Five denari each way."

"I only need the outbound passage."

"Very well. If the weather clears, we depart at dawn."

An uncontainable grin stretched on Angelo's face. He was nearly there. "Can I sleep on the boat, capitano?"

"We're not an inn, boy. You can find the Villaggios' just up the road there. Three blocks straight, make a right, then a left. Look for a red and blue sign with a picture of a village. Nice place. I've known the family for years. What's your name?"

"Uccello, signore." Angelo didn't love lying to the captain, but he couldn't chance anything at this stage. "Ivan Uccello. I shall see you at dawn."

Angelo bowed and turned.

"Uccello," the captain called. "Don't forget to bring food and wine. If you want to eat and drink for eight days."

"Grazie, capitano."

With a quick prayer that the markets would be open at dawn, Angelo nodded and headed in the inn's direction.

After an additional thirty-minute meandering walk through worsening precipitation, he finally found the place, a three-story building one block from Piazza de Ferrari, which he assumed was the city's main square.

He reached the inn soaking wet, but the innkeeper scant took notice and was quite obliging. The portly man introduced himself as Samuele Villaggio, proprietor of the Villaggio Pensione. Roughly Angelo's age, Villaggio had shaggy, light chestnut hair with an equally disheveled beard. A stack of leather-bound books sat on the desk. Behind the desk, a nearly camouflaged brown cat slept on an additional pile of books. A bookcase stood in the sitting area, apparently for guests.

Feeling quite comfortable in the place, Angelo didn't bother to negotiate or seek alternative accommodation. Perhaps he'd take time to practice reading. He removed his purse from his satchel and opened it to pay.

The gold pieces were missing.

Genoa

A PANG OF FEAR undulated through Angelo as if his body were a pond and a boulder had slammed into it.

"M-m-m-my coin," he stammered. "They're gone."

"Perhaps they fell into your bag," Villaggio said, expressing what appeared to be sincere concern.

Angelo nodded, unable to tell if his forehead was wet from rain or sweat. He dug through a saddlebag to no avail. He checked his second satchel, which was also devoid of money. All those coins, vanished. All that remained in his purse was one measly silver coin.

Through all the toil of his journey, he'd not felt so defeated as he did now.

"I had the money," he said to the innkeeper with a dumbfounded stare into space. "More than enough."

"Were you robbed?"

"Of course I was fucking robbed! What do you think happened? The coins grew wings and flew home to their goldmine?"

"Peace, signore!"

Angelo composed himself and breathed. He combed his fingers through his wet hair, tangled it, then smoothed it back. "My sincerest apologies, Signor Villaggio. That outburst was unacceptable."

"Worry not. I understand your alarm."

Angelo couldn't imagine the seminary schoolboys stole his money.

"I know who did this," he said with a snarl, cursing the driver under his breath.

Carrying the saddlebags over his shoulders, he raced to the carriage house in the increasing downpour. As he rounded the corner a block away, he slipped and landed on his tailbone. Instant pain ricocheted up his spine to the base of his neck.

"Merda!"

He grabbed his bags and staggered to his feet, gritting his teeth. Pure rage persisted in his head. The driver may *never* make it back to his family.

Upon reaching the carriage house, Angelo burst inside like a famished dog looking for a rabbit that had evaded his jaws. Ignoring the questioning looks from the other drivers, he hurried to the stable but did not find the driver or his horses. After searching the rest of the place, he found the manager sitting at a large table by the entrance.

"Where is he?" Angelo demanded.

"Who?" the manager asked.

"The driver. The cutpurse who brought me here from Bologna."

"Do you have a quarrel with him, signore? He arrived on time. A minor miracle, being it was his first route."

"First route? So th man's a thief *and* a liar. Do you know where he lives?"

"I do, and he said he wanted to get a head start on getting there, though I was quite surprised he left in such a hurry in this weather."

"I don't care about getting wet. I'll find him in his home."

"Not today, you won't."

"Why is that?" Angelo raised an eyebrow.

"Because he lives in Bologna."

It wasn't the first time Angelo had been duped. As he trod the streets, soaked and shattered to his core, he vowed it would be the last.

The carriage house manager pitied Angelo's situation and promised to seek reparations when the driver returned. Angelo scoffed at this notion. The bounty the driver stole was worth more than a hundred roundtrip routes. He'd never return.

To compound the dreadful circumstance, no other driver would give chase in the weather, and Angelo couldn't pay them, regardless.

He cursed the thief. When he had spoken with the captain of *La Signora Fortuna*, Angelo had felt more hopeful than he had in weeks. Finding Sebastiano Cadamosto—and more importantly, the answer to how traveling to the New World could save Isabella—was in his grasp. *La Signora Fortuna*. He spat on the muddy cobblestones and cursed Lady Luck.

If the journey took eight days, assuming the ship departed in the morning, arrived on time, and stayed two days before returning, it would be back in eighteen days. Who knew when it would depart again? Angelo estimated he had three or four weeks to earn enough for the voyage, no easy task given he didn't know a soul and also needed money to eat. On clear days, he could sleep outside. Begging for food was not beneath him. He could also sell his meager belongings. At this point, the two saddlebags contained nothing but the maps, the letter authorizing Vito passage, the warrant, and the Mongolian short sword. The bags would fetch enough to cover some meals, but the other items would leave a trail. The doge's warrant—a much bigger issue—loomed over him, darker than any cloud. It was a matter of time before they found him. He loathed to sell his rapier and, worse, only possess the short sword. No, he needed protection. He'd keep both swords for the time being but sell the saddlebags.

Angelo shoved his worries to the side of his mind. At this moment, he needed a bed. Preferably a dry one.

When he returned to the inn, Villaggio helped with the bags and provided a beige linen towel, which Angelo graciously accepted.

"Did you find the thief? Did you get your money?"

"Already on his way back to Bologna," Angelo replied, drying his hair.

"Bologna?" Villaggio opened his guest register and wrote in it. "I would've expected the villain to hail from Venice. Thieves and liars, the entire city. The whole Republic."

Angelo swallowed hard. It had been nearly two hundred years, but old wounds let grudges fester.

"It doesn't matter where he's from. I haven't the money to pursue him."

"How much do you have?"

"What's your rate?"

"Two silver per night, inclusive of breakfast and dinner. How long do you need to stay?"

Angelo laughed inwardly at his pathetic situation, releasing a snort through his nose. He didn't have coin for one night. He wondered if he could beg the captain to let him sleep on the ship but then dismissed the notion; he'd be kicked off in the morning, likely never allowed on board again.

Genoa should've been just another stop on his journey into the void, like a stepping stone in a bridgeless canal enshrouded by dense fog. With money, at least he knew he'd reach the other side. Now, the stones in front and behind him vanished. He was trapped on a single step in the middle of a lagoon, with the water rising over his feet. Soon, it would be up to his knees, then his neck, and before long, engulf him entirely.

"How long do you intend to stay, signore?" Villaggio asked again.

What was the answer? A lifetime? A minute? Angelo clenched his jaw. Money didn't matter. He'd walk across southern France and the heart of Spain if he had to. He'd sleep in forests and on the streets. He'd beg for food. Steal it if necessary. One thing was certain: he'd reach Palos and save Isabella.

Angelo snapped out of his trance. Right now, he needed a bed. "You said two silver per night, yes? Would you consider a discount rate for a pilgrim in need?"

Villaggio eyed him suspiciously. "Pilgrim? Where are you from?"

"Rome."

"How much do you have?"

"A single silver."

The innkeeper exhaled and shook his head.

"Please, signore," Angelo said. He sensed kindness in the man's eyes. "I have nowhere to go and cannot sleep on the street in this downpour."

"I'll tell you what," Villaggio said. "We have some vacancies, so I can cut your rate in half for the night. After that, assuming there's still space, we might barter for something of value or negotiate a work exchange. There's always work to be done, and I'm alone here."

Angelo brightened. A work exchange wouldn't get him to Palos, but he could find additional work on the side. *La Signora Fortuna* was a puzzling one. He silently thanked her for this offering and promised never to get angry at her again. "Grazie, signore. I cannot thank you enough for your generosity."

Villaggio waved him off. "What's your name?"

"Mas—Stefanetti. Angelo *Stefanetti*," he replied, placing his silver piece on the counter. Though he hadn't pondered it for more than a second, Stefanetti was the safest choice. It was Isabella's maiden name, so he'd easily remember it. Should the Order come looking for him, it would be unlikely they'd inquire under that name.

A wise decision, caro.

Villaggio led Angelo to his room on the second floor. It had two beds, with the other unoccupied. While the accommodations pleased him, he was dismayed by the solitude, despite his recent travails with a supposed friend.

"Dinner is at seven," Villaggio said, handing Angelo the room key. "You'll hear the bells downstairs."

"Thank you again, Signor Villaggio. Should I come early to help prepare?"

"That won't be necessary. You can help clean afterward. And please, call me Samuele."

The innkeeper smiled and closed the door.

Needing light, Angelo opened the shutters to a wondrous view of the port, backdropped by the Ligurian Sea. *La Signora Fortuna* rollicked on the waves, taunting him as if beckoning him to come, though he'd much rather be on land in this storm. Rain continued to fall, but the eave protected him, allowing him to avert his gaze from the galleon and admire the sea.

The sight brought him back to Venice. It had been days since he'd seen water, and he truly longed for it. Never a day went by in Venice when he did not see it. He closed his eyes and inhaled the ocean air. Despite the hardships and setbacks, he'd already accomplished more than he'd thought possible.

You traversed the whole of the Italian peninsula. Pride tinged Isabella's voice.

Angelo laughed aloud. "Without dying."

XVI

Genoa

Angelo woke fully engorged, unsure if the ring he'd heard was an actual bell or Isabella's moan of passion in his dream. Not stirring, he continued fantasizing about her until he recognized the innkeeper's chimes resounding from the first floor. Dinnertime.

With his love's naked body still riding him in his mind's eye, Angelo had no inclination to lose the vision, yet he didn't want to be late, especially after Samuele's kindness.

Sliding off the thin bed, he stretched his stark-naked body, his fingers grazing the low ceiling. Before passing out, he'd taken the opportunity to wash his stained clothes in the rain and drape them on the interior shutters to dry. To his dismay, he found it was still drizzling, and everything was exceedingly damp. Without an alternative wardrobe, the cold, wet fabrics smothered his body heat. He massaged his beard. Though the room lacked a mirror, he could feel the growth was unruly and longer than he typically allowed, but he liked it; it fit the part of a poor pilgrim. After donning his boots, he sleeked back his hair and headed downstairs with a ravenous stomach.

Samuele waited at the bottom of the staircase.

"Right on time, Signor Stefanetti. This way," he said.

"It's Angelo, my friend."

With a nod and a smile, Samuele led the way through a door to the left of the small reception foyer.

They entered a dining room with eight unoccupied tables, one with a book haphazardly placed on it. Surprised none of the other guests were on time, Angelo raised an eyebrow but shrugged it off. Samuele brought him to the table closest to the kitchen and gestured to a chair, which Angelo took. The cat mewled and wound its way through Angelo's legs.

"Care for some wine?" Samuele asked. "We have a tasty Colline di Levanto."

"Never heard of it, but absolutely."

"Ah, you'll love it. A Ligurian white."

Angelo sat alone for a few moments before Samuele returned carrying a large jug and a glass, which he placed on the table and filled for Angelo. He waited for his guest to taste it, seemingly impatient for an appraisal.

"Delicious." Angelo downed the wine.

"It's made from Vermentino grapes," Samuele said, refilling the glass before disappearing into the kitchen again.

Do not consume too much.

Angelo nodded at Isabella's words of wisdom in his head.

Before any additional guests arrived, Samuele returned, carrying two wide-brimmed bowls, a large plate, and a second glass. "Apologies," he said, placing the dishes down, "but we won't be having a first course tonight. Mind if I join you?"

The request took Angelo aback, but he jumped at the opportunity for companionship. He pulled out the chair next to him. "By all means."

"Grazie." Samuele took his seat.

"This looks delectable," Angelo said, eyeing the dishes. "What do we have here?"

Samuele pointed to the bowls containing chopped meats in a green sauce. "Cow's tripe in pesto"—he gestured to the large plate—"and bell peppers, tomatoes, and mushrooms, stuffed with ground lamb, mushrooms, and cheese, respectively."

Angelo had never seen cuisine like this, let alone a green sauce. "Pesto?" he asked, taking his first bite. The tripe was succulent and the sauce savory, with a nutty sweetness.

"It's made of basil, pine nuts, and olive oil. Do you not have it in Rome?"

"I wish." Angelo stuffed another bite in his mouth, praying they didn't have pesto in Rome. "This is divine. My compliments to the chef," he added, hoping to change the subject.

"Thank you." Samuele bowed his head.

"*You* made this?"

The innkeeper replied with a proud smile.

"So, you're the manager and chef?"

"Along with housekeeper, repairman, bookkeeper, librarian, and everything else you can think of. As I said, I'm alone here. Animal caretaker, too." He fed a small piece of tripe to the cat, who gobbled it up.

"Speaking of which"—Angelo glanced around the still-empty room—"where are the other guests?"

"I'm afraid you're the only one at the moment. Business has been slow since the war broke out."

Angelo had taken a cheese-stuffed mushroom but left it on his fork. If a new fight erupted between Genoa and Venice, it would be his ruin, should his origins be discovered. "War?"

"Have you not heard? Henry III was assassinated, and the Bourbons are disputing Henry IV's succession."

"Who are these Henrys?"

"You don't get out much, do you? Henry III is—*was*—the king of France. Most of my guests are travelers coming to or from France. I'm a waystation of sorts."

Angelo's mind reeled. Civil war in France? He'd already resolved to walk across France to Spain. He didn't have the funds to backtrack to Bologna to find the driver. Even if he went by foot, the Order was likely hot on his tail. He needed to go away from Venice, not the opposite. With no money and his only route forward cut off, his predicament grew more dire by the minute.

"Are you okay, my friend?" Samuele asked. "You look like you've seen Alberti's ghost. Is Paris your destination?"

Angelo's good mood evaporated. Gulping the bile that had accumulated in the back of his throat, he dropped his fork on the plate and glared at his dinner companion. "Why are you asking me so many questions? Why are you being so nice to me?"

The outburst startled the innkeeper. He chewed his food, gently put his silverware down, and placed his hands on his lap. He seemed incapable of meeting Angelo's gaze. A confession of complicity dangled over the table.

"Sometimes..."

"Sometimes *what*?" Angelo's fingers lighted on his knife.

"Sometimes you just need a friend." Samuele said the words meekly, then looked at Angelo like a sad dog.

Angelo snatched his hand away from the knife and rubbed his beard. "Tell me, friend, why are you alone here? Have you no staff or family to work with?"

Eager for conversation, Samuele's family history dominated the remainder of the meal, though tension lingered. When they finished, the innkeeper cleared the plates and returned with a thin green bottle, two small glasses, two small plates, and a pale-yellow cake in a frying pan.

"If you've never had pesto, I'm assuming you've never tried Genoa's other delicacies. Sciacchetrà, a dessert wine from Cinque Terre." He poured two glasses, then served the cake. "And our famous Torta alla Genovese, a sweet pie filled with almonds, hazelnuts, pine nuts, apples, raisins, and dates."

Angelo took a sip of the wine. His eyes lit up on the sweetness. He couldn't help but finish it. Samuele promptly refilled his glass.

"They say it's a white wine, but it's really more of an amber," he said with a content tone. "And you're supposed to *sip* it."

Angelo toasted him and tasted the cake, which was the perfect complement to one of the most delicious meals he'd ever had. He had trouble believing this scraggly innkeeper was such an inspired chef. Though he dearly missed Venice and its cookery, food this good would help ease his homesickness.

"So," Samuele said, "enough about me. Where are you headed? Genoa is clearly not your destination."

Samuele's face was flush from drink, and Angelo assumed the same for his own. Needing to curtail his inebriation before he revealed too much, he nudged his glass aside and wiped his mouth before he spoke. Though he was not in the business of lying, he'd become quite practiced at it since Vito and Ivan engaged him. Angelo learned the best lies are those that are most verifiable.

This is a man you can trust, caro. A man who can help.

Angelo nodded to Isabella's words in his head. "My original destination," he replied to Samuele, "before I was made destitute, was the Port of Palos, in Spain, where I intended to secure passage to the New World."

"The New World? Are you a pilgrim or a crusader?" The innkeeper seemed genuinely interested, if not a tad envious.

"Samuele," Angelo said, feeling his cheeks burn with shame, "I apologize for my outburst. Since my money was stolen, my new plan was to travel through France, but with war, that's not possible." He sighed, needing to repent. "I'm afraid I also deceived you when we first met. I'm no pilgrim."

Samuele laughed and waved his hand. "A blind man could see that. I'm assuming you're neither a crusader. Tell me, what will bring you across the ocean?"

Now comes the next lie. Best to keep it simple and impossible to challenge. "Adventure and glory, of course."

Leaning back in his chair, Samuele grinned. "I had two guests last year who were on their way to do the same. They spoke of vast riches in exotic lands." He stared at his wine a moment. "I long to travel in the footsteps of our eminent Christopher Columbus. One can dream, eh?"

The innkeeper broke the silence that followed.

"What will you do now, with no money?"

"Excellent question, my friend."

"Can you not return to Rome?"

"If I had the money to return to Rome, I'd have the money to continue my journey."

"True." Samuele picked at the crumbs on his plate.

Raindrops pelted the windows in the worsening storm.

"You mentioned you have work to do," Angelo said. "I can work for you. I can help clean, fix things, anything."

"That offer still stands in exchange for room and board. I won't have anything extra to pay you with the lack of guests." He snickered at his misfortune. "You'd be cleaning up after yourself, really. I know many people in town, and I can inquire on your behalf. Have you a trade? Any specific skills?"

"I'm a swordsman," Angelo replied, again thinking it best to be candid.

"A soldier?"

"A swordsman for sport. A fencer. I trained to compete in the European circuit before this opportunity presented itself to me."

Samuele's eyes lit up. "Genoan sailors have an expression: 'The weather is a great bluffer.'"

The conditions outside told another story. "What's that supposed to mean?" Angelo asked.

"It means you should come with me tonight."

XVII

Venice

Though small, the *Giardini Reali* was one of the few places with trees in Venice. All citizens were allowed to visit the Royal Gardens, but as the doge's daughter, Paulina Cicogna had always thought of it as her family's. As a child, it was her playground. A minute walk from the Palazzo Ducale, she'd now often visit the gardens to read, practice her maths, or simply contemplate the infantile nature of man.

Undisturbed by prying eyes, she sat on a wooden bench and removed Vito's envelope from her dress. Delivered by the Protector Zanca, she knew nobody had seen the letter, but there was still severe danger. Of course, her father would only yell and scream at her. Vito would most surely find himself in the *pozzi*.

She scanned the area again before breaking Vito's wax seal, an image of two birds gazing away from each other. Nymph-like fantasies of a 'My Dearest Paulina' salutation had bounced in her head, but alas, the letter was addressed to: 'Paulina Cicogna, Venerable Daughter and Trusted Advisor to Doge Cicogna.' Vito began the missive stating a similar update had been sent to her father and then continued all business, apprising her of the Angelo Mascari situation. Vito had tracked the murderer to Bologna and now pursued him to Genoa. He feared the rogue had stolen Ivan's money and may set sail to parts unknown, but Vito was confident he'd find Mascari first. They'd return the criminal to Venice. Justice would be served.

That was it. Short and to the point. The back was blank. She held it up to the sun, thinking maybe he'd written a hidden message in light-sensitive ink, but the paper held no such markings.

Paulina wondered why Vito would've sent her the same update he'd sent to her father instead of love poems. She reread it, and on the third reading, one sentence popped out as if it were part of an illuminated manuscript: 'The distance grows, as does the desire.'

Another sentence later in the letter had the same effect: 'The figs are in season in Bologna. I long to take them with me.'

Vito had written the first line in the context of seeking vengeance for his brother's death. The second referenced his travels. Neither was in the message to her father. Then she realized that the letter itself was Vito's expression of love and desire. It was as if he were confiding to her in private. He longed for her the farther he traveled. She was his fig. Could he have been indicating that he wished she were there with him, to pursue the outlaw together, then rip out his heart, hand-in-hand? No, that was impossible. Her father would never allow it, and despite her ingenuity and resourcefulness, it was far too perilous for a girl to travel alone.

She gazed out to the water. Among the hundreds of vessels entering and exiting the Grand Canal, a warship departed the city, voyaging toward the Adriatic Sea.

XVIII

Genoa

Never had Angelo seen anything like the venue nor the contenders. The victor loomed over his defeated opponent and discharged a guttural cry, to which the crowd of men encircling the swordsmen roared their approval with near-feverish enthusiasm. A stench of tang and sweat permeated the thick air. The loser, gripping his bloodied bare chest, spat a dollop of blood onto the dirty floor. He retrieved his rapier, stumbled to his feet, and bowed to the winner before visiting the medic—a relic of a man who may have only been able to see his wine flagon in the candlelit cellar.

An hour prior, Angelo and Samuele departed the inn, each with a lantern in hand, and walked fifteen minutes through the streets. The storm had finally tapered off, and though the sun had set, the air remained hot. Moisture rose from the ground in spectral vapors. Their candle lanterns had glass housings and a reflective backing, but the candlelight provided just a few steps of visibility in the mist.

Samuele led Angelo off the main street and down two alleys, at which point he stopped at an old wooden door and smiled.

"Here we are," Samuele said. "I think you'll be quite pleased with this evening's entertainment."

He knocked, and a metal slot slid open. Untrusting eyes narrowed at Angelo but widened upon seeing Samuele. The door creaked open. A man a head taller than Angelo, with a thick beard and shoulders the size of watermelons, greeted them. He vigorously shook Samuele's hand, then quickly ushered them down a dim stairwell.

Though the sight was commonplace for anybody outside of Venice, to Angelo, opening a door and stepping downward was so alien that he hesitated. He'd never been below the surface of the Earth before.

"What are you waiting for?" Samuele called. "They already started."

Excited voices rose from below, like some sort of party. Angelo followed Samuele down and entered a large space with a low ceiling. Rank air, stained with the odors of ale, sweat, and other bodily fluids, engulfed him. Banners with St. George's cross and griffins hung on the rough-hewn stone walls. At least fifty men, all soused, cheered on something in the center of the room.

Angelo followed Samuele through the crowd to see what caused the tumult. Upon getting his first complete look, he grinned, feeling right at home. Two men were in a square of dirt, dug a few inches below the floor. These men presumably had just finished a fencing bout, as the victor, still holding his sword, stood over his defeated opponent, whose rapier lay four feet away. The man on the floor had a thin slice across his chest.

Seeing Angelo's grin, Samuele slapped him on the back.

"You see? I knew you'd like this."

Having participated in dozens of illicit prizefights, Angelo was not surprised to see the fight in a square rather than the long, rectangular *piste* used for the dueling area in proper fencing. He was amazed that both men were bare-chested. In Venice, leather sparring doublets were required in all bouts. Though a doublet would not shield a mortal wound, it certainly helped.

As the injured loser walked with dignity to the medic, the winner released another scream of victory. The man was two or three fingers shorter than Angelo and so thin that he looked emaciated. Rather ugly, with a button nose and pinched eyes, he had long, straight black hair that draped his shoulder blades. Though a slight man, he was quite imposing. His pale, bone-white skin glistened with sweat. Angelo, too, perspired from the warmth of the place. Breathing was also an arduous task in the ventless room.

"That's Draco," Samuele said, catching Angelo's gaze. "He's undefeated."

"Undefeated?" Angelo asked.

Samuele didn't have time to respond, as a blond bar wench wearing double braids and a red frock brought them two clay mugs of ale.

"Ah, my darling, Melissa. You know me too well." Samuele squeezed the girl's butt. She shifted away and bumped Samuele with it. He laughed.

"You're lucky I'm holding these mugs, Samuele."

"If I were truly lucky, we'd be doing something else," Samuele replied, taking the two mugs.

Melissa smiled and tapped Samuele's cheek. "You can be lucky in your dreams tonight."

"How long did this bout last?" Angelo asked.

"Less time than it took to fill these mugs," she said before walking away.

Samuele handed a mug to Angelo. "Draco's damn good, though an incessant prick."

"Grazie," Angelo said, taking the ale, "but I haven't a coin to pay."

"On me, my friend."

"New round! Do we have a challenger?" a sharp voice bellowed from the side of the room.

All eyes shifted toward the source.

"The bet maker and owner of this fine establishment," Samuele said, pointing to an older man sitting at a table. Two larger, muscular men stood on either side of him.

"I challenge," a heavily accented voice replied. A bald and bearded man, a head taller and twice Draco's weight, marched to the edge of the ring. "Deiter Schön, from Munich."

Schön removed his shirt, and the crowd cheered. The man was an ox on two legs. Draco offered a sly smile.

"A Bavarian comes forth," the bet maker called out, articulating each letter and rolling the R sounds. "Now we have a duel."

"It shan't matter where the man's from or how big he is," Draco shouted, turning in a circle to the room for all to hear. "I've defeated men of all sizes from the four corners of the Earth."

The crowd laughed and applauded, appreciating the showmanship of the boast.

"The Earth doesn't have corners," Samuele yelled back. "Or did the bats not teach you that in your cave, Draco?"

The room erupted in hysterics. Nearby men slapped Samuele's back. It seemed everyone in the place knew each other.

A hush quickly descended. Draco raised his blade at Samuele, glaring at him. The stare in the swordsman's eyes terrified Angelo as if Draco were ready to commit murder for a simple jest. "Ah, jolly Samuele, the town boil. How's your mother?" Draco asked with a hiss.

Samuele clouded. He looked to the floor without a response.

"Your fight is with me," Schön declared. He unsheathed a curved cutlass as long as Draco's rapier but three times as thick.

"Overcompensating for something?" Draco asked.

Many of the men laughed.

"Enough talk," yelled a man on the far side of the room. "What are the odds?"

The bet maker stood and walked to the ring, adjusting his feathered maroon cap. Long, curly gray hair bounced on his forest green cape, which hung over yellow and red checkered hose. While the attire was extravagant, it was faded and worn, as if the man were a noble fallen for grace—or always yearned to be one. The bet maker examined Schön, walking around the giant and his sword. "A win by the Bavarian pays... two-to-one," he announced.

"Two-to-one?" Draco scoffed. "Just because he's a big oaf with a clumsy weapon? Have you lost all faith in me?"

The bet maker ignored Draco and returned to his desk. "Taking wagers now," he called.

An air of excitement resumed as many of the men went to the desk to place their bets, which the bet maker recorded in his blotter.

"Thanks again for the ale," Angelo said. "It tastes like fir bark and thyme." He'd consumed such drink many times on the Venetian docks.

"Not my favorite," Samuele replied, his good mood returning, "but the house banned wine here two years ago after three men ended up dead in a drunken side bet dispute."

"They allow side bets here?"

"Not at all. The dispute was with the house."

Angelo nodded. He eyed Draco again, who stretched and practiced moves. Upon closer inspection, he wasn't skin and bones but sheer muscle, without a drop of fat on him.

"How much does the winner earn?" Angelo asked. Should he duel, a win would ease his financial situation.

"Twenty-five percent of the pot."

"And the loser?"

Samuele laughed. "Is that a joke?"

"In tournaments on the European circuit, the loser will also receive a percentage of the pot, should he perform well."

"You mentioned you were preparing for competition."

"I can handle a blade," Angelo said. A vision of his fight with Ivan flashed in his mind and reminded him of his pursuers. Dueling here was a tempting proposition, but one that would get him noticed.

Samuele gestured his head toward the Bavarian, who also practiced. "Would you bet on him? I'd love to see that fungus sack finally lose."

"I wouldn't bet on anybody without first seeing their skills."

"Sage advice. But one needs to dream, eh?" Samuele shrugged. "I dream of shitting down Draco's throat." He headed over to the betting desk.

While Angelo sipped his ale, he studied Draco. The Genoan's moves were nimble. Even while practicing, the swordsman possessed remarkable speed. His footwork was balanced, but as Draco lunged, it appeared he hadn't a target in mind, as if he relied on his speed too much. Angelo raised an eyebrow, continuing to observe the man and ignoring the Bavarian altogether.

Samuele returned a few moments later. "Let's see if I can make some money tonight."

"How much did you bet?"

"Five silvers. It was going to be a gold piece, but then decided to semi-heed your advice."

Angelo smiled.

"All wagers are in," the bet maker announced. He stepped back into the ring, and everyone fell silent. "In times immemorial"—he addressed the establishment, flourishing his hands for dramatic effect—"there was a glorious battle commanded by the Germanic barbarian Arminius and the distinguished general of the Roman legions, Publius Quinctilius Varus. Do we have the makings of a rematch?"

The patrons roared their approval. The bet maker raised his hands and waited for absolute silence before continuing, accentuating each syllable as if addressing a royal court.

"As is the custom in our illustrious venue, we state the rules before every duel. Step out of the boundary thrice, and you are the loser. The fighter who draws first blood from the man's front torso is the winner. Cuts on the limbs, back, or face, no matter how many you may inflict or receive, are inconsequential to the verdict. Should you receive a fatal incision, well... you lose. Begin!"

He shuffled out of the ring.

The fight between the Bavarian and Draco did not disappoint. The Genoan's fluid muscles moved with speed, grace, and unexpected power. Schön's strength disguised his skill, and he easily parried Draco's onslaught of attacks. The Bavarian's longer reach aided him, as well. At one point, Schön punched Draco in the face, causing his opponent to spit blood, but Draco didn't hesitate. He took the hit, continued to spin, and ducked, slicing Schön in the calf. The Bavarian screamed in pain. Draco popped up and cut an 'X' on the Bavarian's back. Draco moved with demon-like speed; his showmanship did not best his concentration.

Schön advanced and twisted just as Draco thrust toward the man's arm, causing Draco to miss.

The Bavarian lunged back, but Draco's damage had already been done. Schön slowed. Draco dodged the blade and sliced his opponent's chest.

The crowd exploded in a mix of cheers and boos.

"A turd in my teeth," Samuele said, with a glower far worse than it should've been for five silvers.

"You don't like losing, do you?" Angelo asked.

Samuele exhaled through his nose. "Especially when it's all I had." He cleared his throat. "I owe the house far more."

Angelo pitied his new friend, especially after he'd been so kind. He wished he had something to offer, but they were in the same boat. Or in Angelo's case, no boat at all.

As winnings were distributed and the doctor aided Schön, Draco wiped himself clean and chugged an ale the maiden had brought.

When the banter died down, the bet maker again called out, "Who is the next challenger?"

He was met with silence.

Temptation tugged at Angelo's sword arm. The money would come quickly. So would the notoriety. He stilled his twitching fingers.

"Is there no beardsplitter here man enough to face me?" Draco shouted. His sweaty chest heaved as his scowl crossed the room. With his sword pointed outward, he spun around, searching for an opponent. His long black hair danced over his white shoulders like wings.

"Usually Draco's facing a man's *ass*," said the bet maker.

The crowd erupted in hysterics. Draco pointed his sword at the man. "You wouldn't be funny without a tongue, old man."

"Lighten up, Draco."

"Can you beat him?" Samuele whispered.

"I'm not sure," Angelo replied honestly. Though he hadn't found a flaw in Draco's approach, Angelo sensed he was the better fighter. Either way, the notoriety that would come from the fight posed too great a hazard. "It matters not. I don't have my sword."

"You want to go to Palos, don't you?"

"Yes, but—"

With a huge grin, Samuele shouted to the room, "We have a new challenger!"

Draco rolled in laughter. "Cut back on the ale, Samuele."

"Not I." Samuele grabbed Angelo's wrist and held it up. "This man."

Angelo snatched his hand back. "I told you. I don't have my sword."

"Not to worry, my friend."

The crowd backed away from Angelo. Three dozen men of all ages, social classes, and varying stages of inebriation scrutinized him. Melissa handed three mugs of ale out and a fourth to the bet maker, who walked over. "You are?" he asked.

A win would be a godsend for Angelo if the bounty covered the sea passage. If not sufficient, word about Draco's victor would spread quickly. A loss would be devastating altogether. Then again, if he didn't try, where would he be? Biding his time in Genoa, penniless until Vito found him. Angelo steeled his nerves. He'd risk anything for Isabella. "Angelo Stefanetti. From Rome."

"A Roman comes forth! Perhaps to avenge the fallen Bavarian?"

"I don't have my rapier with me."

"Did gladiators bring their own weapons in Ancient Rome?"

"I believe so."

"Well, not always. There's a reason this magnificent arena is known as the Coliseum of Genoa."

The crowd laughed. The bet maker clapped his hands twice. Moments later, a bodyguard carried over a wooden box, which he set on the floor. He lifted the lid, displaying six swords, including two rapiers.

Angelo had never expected to participate in an underground fight, but it was the chance he needed. He exchanged eyes with Samuele, who nodded. They glanced at Draco, who watched with eager anticipation. Short of a lethal wound, there was little downside to the bout. Squeezing a fist, Angelo tested his injured hand; he had full flexibility and the stitching held tight.

Crouching, Angelo lifted the rapiers and appraised them. Surprisingly, they were straight, sharp, and well-balanced. Both were equal in size, about an arm's length. He chose the one with the simpler swept hilt. It was a design similar to his own, one that protected the hand without added weight that would sacrifice wrist movement.

He rotated the blade, tapped it on the floor, and practiced a lunge.

"This rapier will do," he said.

Triumph for me, my love, Isabella whispered in his head.

"Magnifico," said the bet maker with giddy excitement.

Angelo removed his doublet and shirt, exposing his lean chest. The bet maker sized him up.

"You're a wiry fellow. Moderately attractive. Easier on the eyes than our house ghoul." He scowled at Draco, then squeezed Angelo's bicep. "You have some muscle, but you look unpracticed. Do you have experience?"

"Some."

"Who is your fencing master in Rome? I'm familiar with many of them." He whispered into Angelo's ear, "Some intimately."

Angelo ignored the remark and gazed around at the faces staring at him. "I'm self-taught."

"Well, then." The bet maker offered the crowd a wicked grin. "The odds are set at fifteen-to-one in favor of Draco."

Excitement again filled the room as men rushed to the betting desk.

"You should make it a thousand-to-one," Draco shouted. "Not a chance this gutter rat prevails."

Samuele's eyes grew wide. "Do you really think you can beat him?" he asked Angelo.

"We'll learn soon enough."

At the words, Samuele headed over to the money desk. While men placed their bets, Angelo practiced his moves. Draco stood stock-still, studying him. The action reminded Angelo of Master Fabris, who'd often do the same with his students.

A commotion came from the desk. "I cannot let you do this, Samuele," said the bet maker. "I've known your family for decades."

"It's my property, my choice," Samuele replied.

Angelo headed over. "What's going on?"

"Your friend neglected to bring his brain tonight. He wishes to wager his inn on you," the bet maker said, animating his hands.

"What?" Angelo turned to Samuele. "Absolutely not."

Samuele pulled Angelo aside and spoke in hushed tones. "This is my decision. I have faith in you."

"You barely know me."

"So what? What am I to do? Continue running an inn with no guests? I spend more than I make every month. If I lose—if *you* lose—so be it. If we win? I'll have more than enough to repay my debts, and you'll have enough to go to Palos."

The extra pressure was an unwanted addition, but the innkeeper was right. "I'll do right by you," Angelo said.

The innkeeper shook his hand and headed back to the money desk. After all the wagers were in, the crowd dispersed around the ring, and the bet maker stepped between the swordsmen.

"Gentlemen," he said, beginning his rehearsed speech, "as is the custom of our illustrious venue, we state the rules before every match."

"We know the rules," Draco said, staring straight at Angelo. "Step out thrice, you lose. First to draw blood on the torso wins. Capito?"

The bet maker looked to Angelo, who nodded his understanding.

"Good," Draco said. "Let's get on with it. My pizzle's getting peckish."

The bet maker exited the boundary and raised his hands. "Begin."

Angelo took an en garde pose. Draco did not. Before Angelo had a sense of place and balance, the Genoan was on him like a force of nature, each stroke controlled and deliberate. Angelo managed a few parries before stepping out of the ring. He collided with Samuele, who rubbed his shoulders.

"What's going on?" his friend asked. "I thought you said you're the best."

"One foul to the Roman," the bet maker said.

Half the crowd applauded. The others leered at Angelo as if they wanted to fight him themselves. He sensed that if he lost, they might just do that. Though he was bare-chested, the heat of the room increased. He wiped his sweaty palm on his pants and took his position.

"Begin," the bet maker announced.

This time, Draco stood with his rapier at his side, watching motionless. In an en garde pose, Angelo held himself as stony as possible, waiting for the perfect moment. Draco blinked. Angelo lunged. His opponent parried, stepped aside, and kicked Angelo, landing a boot in the thigh. Again, Angelo stumbled into the crowd, who voiced their mix of approval and dismay. As hands jostled him, he found his way to Samuele, who took him aside.

"What was I thinking?" the innkeeper said with rapid-fire desperation. "The pensione has been in the Villaggio name for five generations."

Angelo didn't answer. Breathing came in short spurts. His hand trembled and felt wet. He realized blood seeped from his wound. Never had he been on the cusp of losing a bout so quickly. In Venice, he'd dreamt of participating in the European circuit. Now, his first officiated duel outside his city, and he was about to lose everything... again. And he'd inadvertently take Samuele down with him. Palos was months away, after all. That would give the doge's men ample time to find him, and what then? Would he meet the same fate as Isabella? His beloved would indeed be lost forever.

"You can beat him," Samuele pleaded. "You *need* to beat him."

"Fight, Roman," someone shouted.

Another man nudged Angelo from behind. "Get back in there," he said.

Warm ale splashed on his sweat-drenched back. The pong of it made him gag.

Ignore them. Isabella's voice echoed in his head. *Remember your training. You are the better man.*

Her words soothed his frazzled nerves. He eyed Draco, who continued to match his stare. "He's too fast," he said to himself. "I don't think I can win. The man has no weakness."

"Then look for a strength," said Samuele.

Angelo caught his breath and turned to his friend. "What?"

"Look for a strength and exploit it."

The advice made sense. Angelo could use Draco's speed against him.

The crowd continued to shout for Angelo to fight, but he paid them no heed.

Some months prior, he defeated another swordsman with blazing quickness, one who dubbed himself the Whip Snake. Angelo had won by startling his opponent with a full-speed assault. Despite the victory, Master Fabris was furious with Angelo's clunky effort, claiming it embarrassed Fabris's fencing school. The master instructed him on how to complete the move gracefully the next time, though Angelo had never used it in a judged tournament. More importantly, if not executed properly, an adversary could implement a potentially fatal counter-strike.

With a reassuring nod from Samuele, Angelo entered the ring and took his stance.

"Begin," the bet maker announced.

Angelo suspected Draco wanted to finish the bout quickly. He was right. A flurry of swings and footwork accosted him. As the Genoan charged, Angelo performed a passata sotto. He evaded the attack by dropping his body beneath Draco's weapon. With his free hand on the ground for support, Angelo thrust up, but his adversary arched his back and parried. With Draco looming over him, sure defeat was inches away. Angelo pulled his support hand from the ground, and as he fell, he rolled into Draco's legs. Momentum propelled Draco out of bounds.

Samuele and half the room erupted in cheers.

Whenever victory was in Angelo's grasp, a tingle originated at the base of his spine, working its way up to his mouth, causing an involuntary smile and, more importantly, confidence. Master Fabris would've admonished Angelo for his wretched passata sotto, but he got to his feet, feeling that tingle.

Draco returned to the ring and glared. The man was not used to defeat.

The swordsmen took their positions. Again, the bet maker called for the start. And again, Draco's move was predictable. Angelo retreated two paces, aware his heel grazed the ring boundary. He accosted Angelo faster than before. Angelo's parry was late. Draco's blade nicked Angelo's forearm, but he spun and shouldered his opponent, knocking him from the ring.

An onlooker screamed. The others stared aghast, then hooted praise. Draco had carelessly stabbed a man in his right shoulder.

"You half-wit goat," the man cried.

"Get out of the way next time," Draco replied.

He extracted the sword from the man's flesh and smiled at the blood. He didn't bother cleaning it. Clutching his injured shoulder, the man stumbled over to the medic.

Draco returned to the ring and stared at Angelo. The crowd resumed their cheers, loving the duel as its climax approached.

Yet he didn't attack. Instead, he matched Angelo's stony pose. Impatience murmured in the crowd. Angelo didn't want to make the first move, but the men surrounding him started yelling and heckling.

"Nobody paid to see statues," the bet maker declared.

Angelo sidestepped to his left. Draco did the same. When Angelo shifted his arm, Draco followed, mirroring each move. As the house favorite, the Genoan controlled the board. He could stand there all night. Eventually, the crowd would turn on Angelo. But he could play his opponent's game.

With the tip of his rapier aimed squarely at Draco's windpipe, Angelo inched forward. Draco matched the move, the two swords slowly approaching what would be a sure death if the other flinched. The men stopped. Razor-sharp steel hovered a hair from Angelo's throat. One half second of hesitation, one wrong breath, would be his undoing.

Sweat trickled from Angelo's forehead, but he dared not blink. His heart pounded, but instead of his own body, he focused on Draco, who was in the same position. Angelo met his opponent's gaze, waiting for a reaction. All he had to do was flick his wrist, and he'd slice open his windpipe.

The game was not finished.

Angelo retreated a half step. As expected, Draco did the same. In that motion, Angelo struck. Draco parried. Onlookers burst into yells.

Steel scraped steel. Sweat flew from bodies. Footwork shifted on the muddy floor. Draco attacked, lunging for Angelo's sword hand. He shifted, parried, and riposted, returning the same move, but Angelo's aim was true. He struck Draco's wrist. His rapier dropped to the floor.

Blood dribbled down the Genoan's hand. He didn't utter a cry, but the injury was severe.

The crowd clamored for a finale.

Angelo wouldn't end the fight this way. "Pick it up."

With his eyes planted on Angelo, Draco did. He grimaced when he attempted to hold the rapier. He shifted the weapon to his left and lunged. Angelo easily parried, knocking the sword out of Draco's hand.

"You fight dirty," he said. His face turned beet-red. "If you cannot fight with honor, then you cannot win with honor."

The words infuriated Angelo. He flicked his wrist and carved a small incision in Draco's chest, ending the bout.

"Yes!" Samuele yelled. He rushed to Angelo and bear-hugged him. Elated from their winnings, others in the room rushed over, slapping his back.

"This man is a cheat!"

Draco's shout silenced the space. Blood dripping from his chest and arm, he stood before Angelo, rapier in hand. The crowd backed away. Draco snapped the tip of his blade at Angelo's throat. "You're from Rome, are you? Then you must know Edoardo Vezzalli."

"Get your sword out of my face," Angelo said. A defeated man could be more dangerous than one in a bout, but he kept his wits. Fortunately, he still held his sword.

"Do you know Edoardo Vezzalli?" Draco demanded. "It's a simple yes or no question."

"No."

"I thought not." He spoke to the crowd. "Why would you know the top fencer in Rome if you're not from there?"

The onlookers voiced their dismay.

"What are you talking about?" asked Samuele.

"Your friend lied to you," Draco said before turning his attention back to Angelo. "But you know Salvator Fabris, don't you? For the passata sotto is taught by him. To his students... in *Venice*."

Angelo held his tongue.

"Is this true?" Samuele asked.

"Listen to his diction," Draco continued. "Look at his clothes. Of course, it's true."

Angelo nodded.

"You lied to me?" Samuele asked.

"I can explain."

"You see?" Draco shouted with zeal, slicing his sword in the air. "The man is a liar, and thus the win should be voided. *I* am the winner."

"Hold on," Samuele said, "I'm sure Angelo has a good reason for his fib, but what difference does it make if he's from Venice or the moon? He bested you." He whispered to Angelo, "You *better* have a good reason. For *all* the lies."

"I do," Angelo said. "Please believe me."

Samuele clinched his jaw but nodded.

The crowd shouted their differing opinions. It was impossible to hear anyone.

"The man is a deceiver," Draco yelled above the voices. "He's a Venetian spy, come to Genoa to learn our fighting techniques."

This statement riled the crowd, especially those who had lost their bets.

"I am no spy," Angelo yelled, drawing away from the angry men.

"Enough," called out the bet maker, entering the ring.

"Samuele's right," called someone. "It shouldn't matter where he's from."

The men parted, with those who squandered their money shouting at the winners. Unfortunately, there were far more losers. The bet maker glanced around at the angry faces. He raised his hands to quiet them.

"Friends. Calm yourselves. Though the pious of Genoa would say this is a house of ill-repute and look down on our activities, you all know we have a code of honor. It is true that this man lied about his origin. It is also true that none of us share any love for Venetians, who are well known to be liars from a city of crooks. This man proved that today. While they are liars and swindlers, Genoans are not. During the bout, the swordsman of Venice broke none of the rules. Therefore... all bets shall be paid."

The men who won cheered, but the losers weren't quelled. Some threw their mugs on the ground and approached the winners. The bet maker's guards stood between the two groups. The door guard rushed down the stairs and joined in.

"If any of you wish to return here in the future," the bet maker said, "you'll leave the fighting to the duelers. While I cannot control what happens outside these walls, I shall remind you that all contenders are welcome to fight again." He glanced at Angelo and Draco. "I've yet to set the odds for a rematch, but if one man is injured on our streets, there may be no way for you to win your money back."

Though they craved more blood, the men grumbled and dispersed. The last to move away was Draco. He pointed his sword again at Angelo.

"You and I are not finished." He stormed off to the medic.

Angelo finally breathed again. He relaxed his grip on his rapier and handed it to a guard.

With a smile that consumed his face, Samuele slapped Angelo on the back. "Grazie, mio amico, I'm debt-free! And you won a quarter of the pot! Now you can make it to Spain."

Angelo glanced about the space. Despite the bet maker's words, dozens of eyes glared at them. "If we make it out of here alive."

"A tremendous idea," Draco exclaimed to the room, silencing everyone. Seething with vitriol, he met Angelo's eyes. "Let's have a rematch. To the death."

Angelo chuckled nervously at the suggestion. The man was genuinely insane. He shook his head and walked away.

"I expected as much," Draco shouted. "A swordsman who's afraid of dying."

The statement cut Angelo deeper than he would've expected. The art of fencing required one to contemplate mortality frequently. Master Fabris often asked his students the same question. Angelo didn't fear death, but he didn't want to die. After seeing Isabella's demise, he knew there were outcomes *worse* than death. Then again, ridding the world of bugger like Draco would be charity. He turned back to his adversary.

Do not forget your promise. Isabella was right; Draco wasn't worth it.

"I'm not afraid of dying," Angelo said. "But I vowed I'd never kill *again*."

The room hushed. Even Draco's eyes widened at the word 'again.' Angelo seized the moment. He grabbed Samuele's arm. As they made their way for the exit, the silence was short-lived. The men resumed their shouts, demanding money and blood-sport entertainment.

Neither Angelo nor Samuele could contain their excitement as they climbed the stairs and exited into the open air. Mist rose from the cobblestones in the hot, humid night. With his coin purse replenished and the clouds breaking, La Signora Fortuna was on Angelo's side again.

She opens doors, but one must step through themselves. If such a thing as luck exists.

"Right you are. As always," Angelo replied to Isabella's voice in his mind.

"And you just met me," Samuele said.

Angelo clapped his friend's shoulder. "How did you know that about a strength? To look for one and exploit it?"

A rat dashed past, chased by two alley cats.

"Your strength is your cunning. Your ability to observe a situation—or a person—and make it work for you. Why did you lie about being Venetian?"

"We're a city of liars, remember?"

"A self-fulfilling prejudice." Samuele snickered and stopped walking. "I sense that your fib, and your quest to go as far as you can, if for gold and glory or not, stems from some ulterior reason."

The fog dispersed indistinct voices, making it difficult to discern where or from whom they came. Angelo also stopped, glancing up and down the narrow street. Faint shadows flickered on the walls. Though the buildings were shuttered, and they were seemingly alone, unsettling worries tensed his spine.

"Come," he said. "Voices carry here."

Angelo reclined on a wooden chair in the entrance room of the Villaggio Pensione. He sipped his Sciacchetrà, a Ligurian sweet wine that Samuele had opened to celebrate their victory. It was time to provide an honest explanation to his new friend. Or at least a bit of honesty.

"Truth be told, I'm a wanted man."

The innkeeper dragged a wooden chest over to the bookcase. He dropped it and took a half step away at the confession.

"Not to worry, amico," Angelo said. "It's nothing like that. You see, there was a girl."

"I'm told there always is."

"I've heard the same. Except this girl was married to a nobleman. Let's just say this nobleman had powerful friends whom I may have... angered."

Samuele sat on the chest. He drank his wine, which he'd placed on the bookcase. "They'll pursue you to Genoa? Or across the ocean?"

"I pray they do not, but they're unyielding."

"Come now, Angelo. I've never been to Venice, but I suspect groping for trout in another man's river is no worse there than here. What did you do?"

Angelo sighed. He detested lying to his friend, but honesty had led to disaster too many times. "Everything I did was in self-defense or to protect my beloved. These men are zealots. Fanatics. They claim I am the root of their troubles, yet I am but a pawn caught in the middle. That is the truth." He crossed himself. "Hand to God."

"'Impossible loves. I am very much afraid they can become an addiction.'"

Angelo threw a glance at the innkeeper. The man was certainly insightful. "You've had such loves?"

Samuele chuckled, motioning to the bookcase. "With my friends here. And some guests. Cesare Borgia said that, not I." He laughed again. "And no, he was never a guest. Having lived in an inn my whole life, I've met many people. I think I'm a fairly good judge of character. I can tell you're a good, sincere person."

Angelo beamed at the sentiment, though he wished Samuele hadn't mentioned sincerity amidst so much deception. "Now your turn," he replied. "How did you know about exploiting strengths?"

His friend raised his palms as if proselytizing. "'Find a strength and exploit it.' More perception from Cesare Borgia. The man was a ruthless reprobate, but sometimes you must be ruthless in this world."

"Says the man with a heart of gold."

"One can dream, eh?"

"Trust me, my friend," Angelo said, reclining further. "It's far greater to be kind than ruthless. After all, you were kind to me as a stranger. You had faith in me without knowing my skill, and look what it got you."

"Very true."

Samuele opened the chest, which was empty. After a few moments, he returned, his arms loaded with bundles and bottles. He placed them carefully into the trunk, then chose books, which he also put inside.

A nervous sensation grew in Angelo's gut. He suspected what Samuele was doing but asked anyway. "What are you doing?"

Samuele selected another leather-bound tome and placed it on the growing pile. "My faith in you will let me realize my dreams of adventure. Let me come with you. To the New World."

For some time, Angelo had been craving companionship, but he didn't want to put his friend in danger. He sighed. He also couldn't delay his trip. Samuele couldn't possibly make arrangements for his inn by morning.

"It'll be dangerous," Angelo said.

"I'll have the best swordsman in Italia by my side."

"Flattery will get you nowhere."

"It'll get me on a ship."

Angelo laughed. The friendship would be good for his spirit. And how dangerous could the voyage to Palos be? Samuele could easily return to Genoa from there if need be.

"I'll have your back, of course," Samuele said. "After all, I'm not entirely debt-free."

"You owe me nothing."

"But I do." He motioned to the chest. "I have plenty of food and wine for the journey. I can pack a few extra bottles of that Sciacchetrà."

"Maybe instead of all those books."

"It's a long trip," Samuele replied with a wide grin.

Angelo gestured to the inn around him. "You're willing to leave all this behind? It's your legacy."

"It's not what's behind us that matters, but what's ahead. I'll visit my cousin tonight. He'll manage the inn in my absence. He's done it before. Though I'll kill him if he drinks all the wine again."

The past shaped Angelo's life, but he knew nothing done could be changed. So why dwell on it? Only the future mattered. He smiled at his new friend, glad for the camaraderie.

"Okay, okay." He stood and clinked his glass to Samuele's. "I was going to ask you, you know."

The innkeeper's eyes lit up. "Really?"

"No."

XIX

Genoa

Amid dozens of other boats in the busy harbor, *La Signora Fortuna* glimmered in dawn's rays, lifting Angelo's heart. Pelicans skimmed through a perfect westward breeze. After all the hardships, all the violence, all the setbacks and rotten hands, there she was—Lady Luck, opening a door that would bring him one step closer to Isabella. He patted his doublet, ensuring his coin purse was tucked safely inside. Nothing stood between him and that boat, short of losing his money again.

Angelo and Samuele smiled at each other. His friend, too, would achieve a dream. With his saddlebags over his shoulders and his rapier sheathed at his side, Angelo used his free hand to help carry Samuele's trunk along the quay and to the center of the dock extending over the water. They set it down at the gangway. Sailors loaded the ship with final supplies, while those on board prepped the vessel.

Pipe clenched in his teeth, Captain Doria greeted Angelo and his companion with a blustery chortle.

"Good of you to help Signor Uccello with his chest, young Villaggio," he said.

Samuele raised his eyebrow at Angelo, but he ignored the name. "This is *my* chest, capitano. I'm joining the voyage."

"We won't be back for almost a month. You can leave your inn for that long?"

"And then some."

"Have you coin?"

"And then some." Samuele grinned. He presented a handful of coins.

The captain counted them and nodded. "Very well. You there," he called to two sailors. "Help our passengers with this chest."

The men did as instructed and carried it to the deck.

"What are you lingering for?" Captain Doria asked as he climbed the plank. "We raise sail forthwith."

Angelo and Samuele turned back to the city. They didn't need to exchange words as they silently bid farewell to their homeland.

"Come, mio amico," Angelo said. "Adventure awaits."

They turned for the gangway.

A gallop of hooves on the stone quay broke through the peaceful morning.

An arrow struck Angelo's saddlebag.

He shoved Samuele down as a second arrow flew over his friend, embedding itself in the galleon.

Shouts erupted from the horsemen and the sailors.

"What's the meaning of this?" the captain called from his ship.

"Run," Angelo said. He grabbed Samuele's arm. The two of them stumbled for the gangway.

"Hoist the plank," the captain yelled out.

As Angelo and Samuele reached the board, two sailors snatched it from their feet and pulled it onto the ship.

"No," Angelo called. "Wait!"

"Andiamo, raise anchor!" Captain Doria ordered. "Raise the main sail!"

Hooves clopped where the quay met the dock. Angelo turned to find Vito atop Linguini. Behind Vito were four additional Protectors on horseback, all wearing armor adorned with St. Mark's winged lion. Two of them loaded their crossbows.

"Buongiorno, Linguini." Angelo winked at the mare, who snorted in response.

"Her name is Bellezza, fool," said Vito.

"What's going on?" Samuele asked. "What is this?"

"This," said a familiar voice, "is justice."

Draco appeared from behind the horses, a wicked grin plastered on his face.

"You see, signore?" he said to Vito. "I told you the vagabond would be here. On a silver platter with nowhere to go."

"Quiet." Vito dismounted. "Whatever happens, guard any escape routes," he ordered his men. "If Mascari boards another ship, follow him on."

The men bowed and spread out a bit, remaining on the quay.

Vito left Linguini and confidently walked the dock toward Angelo, drawing his sword.

Angelo did the same. "Step behind me," he said to Samuele, but his friend didn't move.

Wrath fueled Vito's eyes. "Angelo Mascari," he said. "By order of Doge Pasquale Cicogna of the Most Serene Republic of Venice, you are hereby under arrest for many crimes, all of which you will pay for."

Shouts from the ship continued. Men raised the main sail.

"You'll have to take me back alive," Angelo said.

"Oh, that we will. Very, very wounded."

Angelo raised his rapier, standing en guard. The odds seemed impossible against five men, plus Draco, with no retreat.

"Bastardo," Samuele said to Draco. "How could you do this?"

Draco advanced, his rapier in his left hand. His right hand was heavily bandaged. "The man is a fugitive. A murderer."

"He's my friend. This has nothing to do with you." Samuele seethed.

"It's okay," Angelo said. His gaze shifted between Vito, Draco, Samuele, and *La Signora Fortuna*, which began to move. Once again, he had pushed his luck so far that it now dangled from a cliff.

"No," Samuele said. "This ignoble vermin has ruined everything." He clenched his fist and approached Draco.

"You two can quarrel elsewhere," said Vito, his gaze locked on Angelo. "Mascari, on your knees."

A way out eluded Angelo. Could he defeat all these men? Draco or Vito would be hard enough alone. Would they harm Samuele in the fight? He glanced at his friend. The innkeeper burned with anger. That fueled Angelo's rage. He wasn't a criminal. He was wronged, time and again. He and Isabella were the *victims*.

The ship slowly creaked away. If he reached out and touched it, the vessel would glide past his fingers. Isabella's salvation was in his grasp yet sailing away.

He got to his knees. "You need five men to apprehend me?" he asked Vito.

"Just one," the Protector replied. "You wish to duel, here in Genoa? You'll be tried whether you can walk or not."

Fury boiled in Angelo. "The crimes are yours. Everything that happened commenced when you propositioned me."

Draco laughed. "How easily Angelo goes down."

"Bastardo!" screamed Samuele. Fist raised, he charged Draco.

With a flick of his wrist, Draco plunged the tip of his sword into Samuele's gut. The innkeeper cried out.

Angelo gasped.

His friend was severely wounded.

"No!"

In a frenzy, with months of injustice brimming to the surface, Angelo let loose an assault. Wrongs would be righted. *Finally*.

He hurled a saddlebag at a surprised Vito, then turned his attention to Draco, who smiled gleefully at his sword impaled in Samuele's stomach. Before Draco had a chance to react, Angelo swung, slicing through the villain's wrist. Draco screamed at his severed left hand, still attached to the hilt.

Angelo spun and parried a blow from Vito. He followed with a riposte and a quick lunge, which met its mark in Vito's right bicep. The Protector cried out and dropped his weapon. Angelo readied his sword for a death strike to the throat. The fiend more than deserved it.

But he remembered his vow. He would not kill again.

Instead, he released a guttural cry and tackled Vito, shouldering him off the dock. The Protector landed in the water with a splash.

Vito's men dismounted.

Angelo rushed to Samuele and kneeled by his side.

"One can dream, eh?" Samuele whispered.

"Mio dio," Angelo said. "I'm sorry." He removed the blade from his friend's gut. Samuele winced and gritted his teeth. Angelo chucked Draco's own hand at the crying man.

"I'll live," Samuele said. "Your dreams are still alive too. Go."

The four Protectors dashed for them, two with swords, two with crossbows.

"Arrivederci, my friend." Angelo squeezed Samuele's shoulder.

He popped up and sprinted the length of the dock, sheathing his sword as he ran. *La Signora Fortuna* picked up speed. It was too far, too fast. But he pushed himself harder, stronger. Isabella's fate was on that ship. He reached the dock's end and leaped, catching the tail of a rope with one hand. His body hammered the ship, rippling sharp aches down his side, but he held tight. An arrow struck the boat. Another ripped through his pantaloons, grazing his thigh. Hand over hand, he climbed until he made it to the top.

He hauled himself over the taffrail and collapsed on the deck.

Eyes closed, chest heaving, Angelo lay there, thinking of nothing, doing nothing. Seagulls squawked overhead. Waves lapped against the ship as a gentle breeze caressed his skin beneath a warming sun.

"The fare has doubled." The gruff voice waylaid Angelo's ears.

He opened his eyes to find Captain Doria and two other sailors staring down at him with contempt.

"Or do you wish to swim back to your pursuers?"

Angelo fished his coin purse from his doublet. He dropped it on the deck. A sailor snatched it and handed it to the captain, who counted out the fare, before tossing the small bag onto Angelo.

"I'll have no violence on my ship, boy," said the captain. "You and I shall talk later."

Isabella's crucifix dangled on Angelo's neck. He pressed it to his lips, then tucked it into his shirt.

When he caught his breath, he got to his feet and stumbled to the stern. He gazed back to the quay, where Vito and his men watched the departing ship. Draco sat on the dock, clutching his handless arm. Samuele lay next to him—another casualty in the wake of Angelo's actions. He prayed that his friend survived. Angelo bit his hand until he drew blood. He never should've allowed the innkeeper to join him. The risks were far too severe.

It's a fault not yours, my love.

Once again, Isabella's reassuring words calmed him.

The mission did not change. He accomplished the first goal.

Even if Vito commandeered another boat and pursued him, Angelo finally had the upper hand; they'd never have time to catch him. Moreover, the Protector could learn he was headed to Spain, but he hadn't a clue of Angelo's final destination.

With that reassuring thought, he strode to the ship's bow, nodding at the crew as he passed. Before him lay the expanse of the Mediterranean Sea. Eight days to Palos and he'd find Sebastiano Cadamosto. He'd finally learn why the nobleman told him to go to New Spain.

And you can free me.

Angelo turned to his right. In his mind's eye stood the memory of the most spectacular girl he'd ever seen. The auburn-haired beauty. His undying love. His Isabella.

The two returned their gaze to the sea ahead.

He'd reach that distant land and find the mysterious artifact that would save Isabella. And he *would* save her.

However long it took.

And my captors will feel a pain far more severe.

PART II

BLADE FOR HIRE

"There are more things to be explored and conquered within the soul of man than on the surface of the earth."

- Hernán Cortés

explorer, conquistador, genocider

24 YEARS LATER

XX

Republic of Venice

1st of January, 1613

"*Bon an, mio amici,*" the doge said, his gravelly voice leaning on every syllable as though each were a crutch. "Happy New Year, my friends."

Vito Uccello dipped his head, his response in Venetian polite and steady. "And to you, Most Serene. May the Lord grant you continued health, happiness, and prosperity." Around him, his comrades echoed the sentiment, each tone measured but curious as they stood in the doge's wood-paneled office. Doge Marcantonio Memmo, glossy-eyed with a stoic demeanor that belied his advanced age, was the fifth doge Vito had served. Yet in forty years of loyalty, he had never been summoned on the first day of the year.

Inquisitive unease marked each of his colleagues. Standing to his left was Senator Benito Grimani, who hovered in his third decade of life and bore an intensity Vito loathed. On Vito's right stood his second-in-command, Leonardo Ponte, whose alertness mirrored Vito's apprehension. Across from them, settled in a crimson-velvet chair beside the doge, was Senator Marco Quattrone, the Exalted Master of the Ancient Order of the Seventh Sun. Quattrone's mouth held a smug hint of knowing, his posture confident, wearing his superiority as if it were a cloak.

The doge's lack of haste was notable, piquing Vito's curiosity further. Morning's chill seeped through the Palazzo walls, matching the frost-tinged canals just beyond, and weighted the silence with anticipation. Vito adjusted his stance, his breath visible in the cold air. Given that the men present were members of the Order, he surmised the gathering was not one of official Republic concern.

"You are no doubt wondering why I asked you here today," the doge began as if reading each man's thoughts. "To call you away from your families on such a hallowed day."

Grimani bowed. "To be in your gracious presence, Most Serene, is an auspicious beginning to the year."

Vito kept still but threw a sideways glance at the senator. Benito Grimani's bootlicking manner never failed to curdle his stomach. His sycophantic, honeyed words were the unctuous pretense of a man who would—if he could—butter the doge's ass and devour his shit with a spoon. Only too well did Vito know the true nature of Grimani, a man who betrayed his compatriots with a smile. It was but one reason his wife felt no remorse for her adultery.

While Vito was larger and knew he could best the senator despite being twenty years his senior, Grimani had been an officer in the Venetian Armada and trained in sword fighting under Salvator Fabris, the same fencing master who had instructed Angelo Mascari years prior.

"Your flattery never ceases to amaze, Senator Grimani," the doge responded with an aged, wheezy voice that caused the cracks in his skin to undulate. Wispy strands of white hair fluttered out of his tight-fitting red linen cap like cobwebs clinging to an ancient relic.

"It never ceases, period," Quattrone murmured, earning a quick snicker from Vito. The Exalted Master's remark was a rare confirmation that others saw through Grimani's thin veil.

Vito's thoughts drifted to Grimani's wife, who regrettably knew the man better than anyone. For twenty-five agonizing years, Vito and his beloved Paulina had managed to keep their relationship a secret, each feigning devotion to their spouses. Years of familial obligations had dulled their trysts to fleeting encounters, but his misguided hope that one day they could be together was a quiet fire that could not be diminished.

"Sit, siori." Doge Memmo motioned to a series of stately chairs typically reserved for the Council of Ten.

In another first in his long career, Vito had never been invited to sit in the leader of the Republic's private office. Grimani and Ponte took their seats, also guarded in their movements. The chill in the air sharpened as Vito settled his oversized physique into the stiff, high-backed seat. Once in their places, the doge lifted a sheaf of frayed papers off his lap.

"This is the reason for today's meeting," he said, a sparkle in his cataracted eyes. "I have come to possess the chronicle of an expedition to find something truly priceless. One could say this account is second in value only to the treasure it describes. A treasure located in the New Kingdom of Granada."

Grimani's posture straightened with interest. Quattrone, however, looked supremely unsurprised, his fingers steepled as though savoring the moment, his mouth a flat smile.

"The brave souls of this expedition," the doge continued, "never found it and perished. Led by Don Alonso de Cáceres in 1548, their fate was previously unknown. This unearthed chronicle survived the ordeal and was delivered to me through the generosity of our esteemed ally, King Philip III of Spain, who is quite familiar with my desire to find this treasure."

Vito wondered why the doge held any interest in the New World, let alone possessed the journal of a deceased conquistador. In part due to the doge and his predecessors' policies, Venice had famously steered clear of the Americas, vexing enterprising explorers and financiers. Vito assumed the supposed treasure was an untapped gold or silver vein.

After letting the words sink in, the doge continued. "Based on Cáceres's journal and Indian accounts, we believe this is our best opportunity to claim a treasure that defies imagination."

"Riches, Most Serene?" Grimani's voice held a note of greed.

"In a manner of speaking, Senator." The doge stood, his frail frame belying the spark that blazed in his eyes. With creaky legs, he paced before Vito, Grimani, and Ponte, capturing each man's gaze as he passed. "*Intangible* riches. The kind most men fantasize about. But we, members of the Ancient Order of the Seventh Sun, know certain truths about this world."

Vito leaned forward, surprised by the intensity in the doge's tone. "Sior, is there another Sun Crystal?"

"No, my Protector." A wide smile exposed his remaining yellowed teeth. "There is a spring. One of crystalline water. Hidden deep in the jungle. If you drink from this fabled pool, it is said your essence will be rejuvenated, prolonging life beyond its natural span."

Silence descended over the room, save the doge's steps as he hobbled back to his chair. He sat, exhausted from his brief journey. Vito exchanged a glance with Leonardo Ponte, whose usually impassive face revealed a glimmer of disbelief. The man made the sign of the cross, seemingly perturbed by the tale, despite his knowledge of the Order and its secrets. Ponte smoothed back his thick, black hair. A pang of envy struck Vito. What little he had remaining of his once-flaxen hair was now stone gray. Ponte shifted in his seat, which Vito knew was uncomfortably tight for the man, for their frames were equally large.

The young Protector was the first to respond, doing his best to smother a chuckle. "Most Serene, you speak of... the Fountain of Youth?"

The unprofessionalism was cringe-worthy, but Vito had to admit—he felt the same amusement at the absurd notion.

Senator Quattrone raised his hand, offering to respond on the doge's behalf. "You laugh. Truth be told, I did the same when I first heard of Cáceres's chronicle. Yet consider secrets our Order knows. We've seen the existence of souls. Moreover, we have harnessed them, torn them from their earthly forms. What makes the idea of a spring of youth so unbelievable?"

The verity of the statement quieted the naysayers. It still seemed far-fetched, but the implications of such a discovery would be enormous. His eyes drifted to the fresco that illustrated Venice's triumphs. He wondered if this could be another. Grimani and Ponte did the same, also contemplating Quattrone's statement. Vito shook his head. This was the flight of fancy of aging men. Wishful thinking, nothing more.

"You raise a valid point, Exalted Master," Vito said, "but many such myths have endured since time memorial. The soul is *not* myth. Our Lord Jesus Christ tells us so." He crossed himself, as did the others. "Our Order merely discovered a method of extracting one's soul from the corporeal form."

"And our Painter?" Quattrone asked, a wry smile curving on his lips. "The Sun Crystal? The truth of seven lives across one soul?"

Vito nodded. These were indisputable facts. While the Sun Crystal could be classified as a tool used to extract and preserve souls, Jacopo Tintoretto was in his ninth decade yet looked as though he were in his fourth, imbued with its power.

"We have obligations," Doge Memmo interjected with renewed vigor on his brittle frame. "We are the stewards of *Paradiso*. Those who have eyes on my seat are laughingstocks. An embarrassment to the Republic, and none are in the Order." He motioned to Quattrone. "We have no possibilities to replace our Exalted Master, should he pass. Think of it. *All of us* could live beyond our years. There are some in this world who may not wish for that. Others say it is sacrilege. I say we owe it to our Order. If there's even a hint that the Fountain is real, is it not worth seeking?"

Grimani, ever the one to advance his fortunes, brightened with an avarice that, to Vito, verged on sickening. "'It is better to learn late than never,'" he said.

The doge grinned. "Ah, wiser words were never uttered. Publilius Syrus of Ancient Rome wrote that, I believe, around 40 B.C."

"You are correct as usual," Grimani replied, "Most Serene, you propose we send an expedition to find the Fountain of Youth?"

"Not a proposal," Memmo said. "A command. And it is I who will be sending the expedition. One comprised of the three men sitting before me."

"Most Serene?" Vito asked, his brain twisting. In all his years as a Protector, he had been sent out of Venice on a single occasion to capture the rogue, Angelo Mascari. A man still at large. The man who murdered his brother. His insides tightened. A mission into an unknown wilderness meant leaving Venice. Leaving Paulina. Then there was the matter of enduring endless hours in her husband's company—a bastard whose unbridled eagerness only deepened Vito's suspicions that hidden motives fueled his every word.

"Yes, Vito." Doge Memmo continued. "Along with a dozen Protectors, you will make port in the town of Santa Marta in the New Kingdom of Grenada. There, our allies will furnish you with supplies and introduce you to a guide who is well-versed in the region and natives. We believe this man is our best chance of interpreting Cáceres's chronicle, navigating the terrain, and finding the Fountain. From there, you are to bottle the waters of the spring."

Grimani sat forward, his face fevered with excitement. "Most Serene, allow me to offer my gratitude. This is indeed a mission of unparalleled significance." He practically purred, unbothered by abandoning his family.

"I am pleased by your enthusiasm," Quattrone said. "For we also request that you stay for a time in Santa Marta. We wish to establish an outpost for the Ancient Order of the Seventh Sun. Once you locate the Fountain, we need to control it. The Protectors will support your mission."

Grimani's eyes lit up. He salivated at the order. "An excellent plan, Exalted Master."

"Forgive me," Vito said, his voice firm, "but does this mission not come with considerable risk? Besides the dangers in the voyage and the undiscovered lands of the New World, we'll be trespassing in Spanish territory."

"An expedition of discovery and exploration, my dear Protector, not one of conquest," Quattrone said. "Moreover, it will not be conducted in secret. We have coordinated with our Spanish brethren so that the Republic of Venice will finance it."

"No doubt a few drops of the spring shared with King Philip?" Grimani asked.

"Right you are," replied the doge. "Italians have worked alongside the Spanish in the Americas for over a century. Cristoforo Colombo, Amerigo Vespucci, just to name two. The Venetian Republic has emissaries throughout the New World. Do you think Colombo was not sending names to the Doge of Genoa? Vito, you will be most intrigued by the guide in Santa Marta."

"Most Serene?" Vito asked.

"A blade for hire. One who claims to be of Genoese descent. Yet we have been told he has a Venetian inflection to his speech."

"A Venetian?" Vito asked. "Do we know who he is?"

"Like I said, he claims to be Genoese. There is more. He's a master swordsman. One who is missing an earlobe. He goes by the name Samuele... Stefanetti."

A fiery rage ran through Vito. Blood roared in his ears. He clenched his fist. A lifetime ago, he had used a broken mirror shard to slice off Angelo Mascari's earlobe, missing his throat by inches. That was shortly after Angelo and his whore had killed her husband, Renzo. The woman's maiden name was Isabella *Stefanetti*. If this 'Samuele Stefanetti' was indeed Mascari, the hunt was renewed.

"It cannot be a coincidence," Vito said. "When do we leave?"

Quattrone grinned. "In a week's time. Make preparations with your family. It will be a dangerous journey."

Vito stood, invigorated by the possibility of finally avenging his brother and Renzo. Against all odds, Mascari may have still been alive. Soon, they'd be on a collision course across the sea in a battle that could lead to either eternal life or brutal death. He bowed to the men.

"And Vito?" said Quattrone.

"Sì, Exalted Master?"

"It is understandable you want Mascari's throat. You shall have it. But do not forget we need him to lead us to the Fountain. I would be remiss to say it is also a golden opportunity to retrieve Doge Cicogna's black book, whether Mascari has it or has knowledge of its whereabouts."

Vito's jaw tightened at the mention of the book—the impetus for all the struggles that started some twenty-five years prior. Memories of secrets, betrayals, and death flooded the surface of his mind.

"I will find Mascari and return him to Venice," he said. "He *will* face judgement."

XXI

Santa Marta, New Kingdom of Granada

6TH of May, 1613

Alarm bells tolled in an incessant rhythm, echoing down the constricted, muddy alleys of Santa Marta. It was an urgent call to arms that could only mean one thing: the seaport town was under attack. Shouts from lookout posts called all able-bodied men to arms.

Angelo Mascari burst out of his small home, still fastening his belt. On it were two wheellock pistols, weapons he kept primed every night. A second belt held two scabbards, a rapier sheathed inside each. As the town defender, the governor had gifted him rent-free lodging at the summit of Calle 22, an ideal central location to be ready for threats should they come from the sea, the jungle, or the town itself.

Twilight and fading stars scantily lit his surroundings, as the sun had yet to rise.

"Papá, wait for me," a youthful voice said in Spanish. Angelo knew its owner all too well.

He spun to find twelve-year-old Francesco in the doorway, wielding a dagger Angelo had given his son five birthdays prior. The blade was short but sharp enough to do damage.

Though time was of the essence, Angelo stepped to the boy. He placed a warm hand on his shoulder and spoke in Spanish, which had long felt like his adopted mother tongue. "Francesco. Franco. Your courage is for the history books. But your place is here."

"I can help, father." His small chest heaved beneath his nightshirt. His eyes were fierce. His chin lifted defiantly. "I know how to fight. You taught me."

"I know, my son." Franco had the spirit of a soldier, no doubt about that, but the boy was ill-prepared to face an onslaught of men. "It's precisely why you need to stay here. Mamá and Juanita need you."

Franco hesitated but nodded, his face flushed with understanding and frustration. He scratched Angelo's thick beard, an action the boy hadn't done since before he started to gray. "I will protect them with my life, Papá. Kill the invaders. Kill them all!"

Angelo exhaled, his heart heavy. "Remember my vow, Francesco." Years earlier, he had sworn to never take another life, no matter the risk. He would keep that promise on this day, as well.

A sharp slap landed on his ass as a burly man sprinted by. "¡Vamos, Samuele!" It was Mateo Vargas, a Spanish captain with a laugh as sharp as his sword. He wasn't wearing a uniform, but everyone in town knew his place, as they did Angelo's. "Let's go before you lose all the glory to me!"

"You only get the glory if you survive, amigo," Angelo called back, his voice loud enough to be heard under the bells. It had been over a year since the town was attacked, and all healthy men raced to its defenses. It had been *twenty-four years* since Angelo adopted the name Samuele Stefanetti, an amalgamation of his Genoese friend's Christian name and his beloved Isabella's maiden name. Now in his forty-fourth year of life, he had used the new moniker for longer than he had used his given name, yet was still unaccustomed to it.

He gave his son a quick kiss on the forehead, then whirled on his heel. Sprinting through mud, he jumped over the legs of a drunkard who slumbered through the chaos. The streets resonated with shouts and the clatter of boots as Spanish soldiers and townsfolk scrambled to defend their homes or the ramparts. Scents of saltwater and impending violence filled the air.

As he reached the hill's apex, he eyed the port. Coasting in the bay was a black, three-mast man-of-war, angling broadside to the port. In the dim light, Angelo couldn't make out any flag or identifying markings. Indigo sails blended with the color of the water. A dozen gunport shutters opened. Cannons stuck their noses out like hungry dogs.

Privateers, licensed by the English crown.

Though they routinely stole for King James, the cutthroats plundered unguarded Spanish ships, not towns. As he continued running, he counted six longboats, each with eight rowers, their faces hidden under broad hats. The lead boats beached. Men jumped out and waded into the water, pistols and blades drawn, bellowing war cries.

A cannonball fired from Santa Marta's lone culverin, positioned on the rampart. Manned by Spanish soldiers on the night shift, the thunderous explosion eclipsed the incessant alarm bells. The iron ball tore through one of the man-of-war's sails, then splashed harmlessly in the water.

Angelo ran past the town's cannon and down the sloping street, the mud slick from morning dew. On the beach, the privateers met the first townsfolk and soldiers, easily cutting them down with pistols and cutlasses.

Soldiers fired harquebuses from the ramparts and reloaded seconds later, but the rifles did little damage. Others shot crossbows, the bolts missing their marks.

A moment later, a dozen cannons fired from the privateers' ship.

Angelo skidded and pivoted toward the town's culverin. "Move!" he shouted to the soldiers manning the long gun.

In the dawn's brightening glow, Angelo watched in horror as a barrage of round shot arced toward the rampart. The soldiers scattered, but far too late. Each cannonball struck the town's defenses with destructive ferocity, shattering stone and bone. One ball landed a direct hit on the culverin's carriage. Unsupported, the iron barrel toppled over, colliding with the cannoneer. His gunpowder bag erupted. Shrapnel eviscerated the soldiers. Others were thrown to the ground.

The carnage was sickening, but worse, the weaponry revealed the true identity of the marauders. Angelo knew these weren't privateers who would've been more merciful. The arc of the round shot was not launched from English cannons, which fired their balls in direct lines. The ship was now fully visible in the morning light. No, it wasn't an English man-of-war, but a Spanish galleon. These were pirates. Though privateers were piratical at heart, they performed their reprehensible jobs for money. Spanish pirates lived for the bounty, along with the thrill of pillaging, killing, kidnapping, and raping.

Screams from the wounded fused with the whistles of the cannonballs in a second volley. One smashed through the torso of the bell ringer, silencing the chime but not the discord.

The air on the beach was thick with billowing smoke and the metallic tang of blood. Pirates released whooping war cries and surged forth, bolstered by their progress and the destruction of the culverin.

Angelo fired at an advancing marauder. The pistol ball ripped through the man's raised palm, taking two fingers and his cutlass. As the pirate gaped in shock at his mangled hand, Angelo holstered his empty gun and drew his rapier. In a flash, he squatted and sliced through the man's heel, sending him sprawling. Without a shred of remorse, Angelo sliced his rapier into the assailant's palms, cutting off his right thumb in the process. Shrieks of pain followed, but Angelo ignored them.

He twisted, his rapier a flash as he fended off another raider. The man hacked his cutlass wildly, but Angelo skirted the blows, using his precision to unarm his opponent. He kicked a boot into the man's chest, plowing him into the sand before severing two fingers. The pirate wailed as he drenched the sand in crimson.

"Samuele! Behind you!" Mateo's alert rose above the chaos.

Angelo rotated, narrowly dodging a cutlass seeking his neck. The pirate, a brute with missing teeth and a wild grin, thrust again. Angelo parried with his rapier. With a deft flick that caught the crossbar, he sent the man's sword into the sand. Angelo pierced his opponent's bicep, then performed the same operation on this man's palms. He hustled behind the pirate and sliced through the back of his knees, then kicked him. The scoundrel howled, his body joining the growing count splayed across the beach.

"I owe you one, amigo," he yelled to Mateo.

"Repay me in wine," his friend called back as he darted to his garrison fighting at the waterline.

All around, soldiers and townsfolk—European and native alike—engaged four dozen bloodthirsty pirates. The thunder of pistol shots and the clash of steel reverberated. Residents fought with desperation and fury, wielding whatever they could: machetes, knives, even clubs fashioned from broken furniture. Spanish soldiers stood out in their tattered but distinct uniforms with red tunics, white breeches, and black stockings. They fired and reloaded their wheellock pistols with mechanical efficiency while others battled with swords and halberds.

Angelo scanned the scene, squinting through the mayhem until he spotted his target: the pirate captain. The man stood tall and barrel-chested, his long coat trailing as he commanded his men. A pistol hung from his belt, and his cutlass gleamed with blood. He gestured sharply to his men before charging up the slope toward the far side of town. Five pirates followed their leader, while another half dozen stormed the town center in a strategic diversion. The remaining crew continued their assault on the beach.

Though Angelo yearned to aid his compatriots in the melee, he eyed the captain, who led his small team to the warehouses. The target could only be one place: a vault containing stockpiled gold and silver to be shipped back to Spain.

Angelo had to make a choice: aid the people and storefronts or stop the gold from falling into pirate hands. Should they get it, it would only enrich and embolden them for the next raid.

"Mateo," he called.

His friend fired a shot, then raced over.

"They're splitting up," Angelo yelled through the noise of the fight. "The warehouses and the town. Meet me at the vault. Have some of your soldiers disable the longboats. Smash the oars. Cut the rigging. The pirates can't leave."

"You know you don't give the orders, right?" Mateo asked with a smile.

"It's just a life-saving suggestion, Capitán."

Mateo snickered before hustling back to his men.

Angelo took off, sprinting for the vault, his boots digging into the sand. The warehouses were short, stone buildings positioned close to the docks for easy transport to and from ships. Angelo wove through the fray, dodging a wild swing.

He trailed the six pirates as they slipped from the harbor to the warehouse district, somehow knowing the vault's location. He crouched on the manure-covered street behind a weathered stone wall of the adjacent building. He'd done unsavory things in his life, but those acts had been performed to accomplish a virtuous goal. These men sought nothing but to plunder, pillage, and destroy the life he had worked so hard to build. He had no formal military training, but years of fighting gave him an edge, one adversaries always underestimated. Mateo scurried up next to him, catching his breath. Ahead, the pirates approached the vault, their captain at the helm. His cutlass flashed as he ordered his men to charge, his voice a low rumble.

In a panic, two Spanish soldiers raised their weapons, but far too late. A flurry of pirate pistol shots cracked the air.

The guards fell where they stood. While two pirates minded the perimeter, others examined the vault doors and their reinforced hinges and locks. It didn't take long before the captain instructed his men to pour out a bag of gunpowder.

"We need a better vantage point," Angelo said.

He tapped Mateo's leg, then used a window ledge and masonry to climb the short building. Crawling on their bellies, they reached the edge of the roof just as a small explosion erupted. Pirates emerged from their cover behind barrels and pallets and approached the now-damaged doors. Using wooden planks for leverage, they pried a door off its hinges. The pirate captain and three of his men entered. Two remained outside to keep guard.

Angelo's gaze landed on a low stone antechamber built into the warehouse's foundation. When he first arrived in Santa Marta in 1590, he took a job in the smokehouse. Some years later, it had been converted to the vault as it was the most fortified building in town. It was used not only to house valuables to be shipped to King Phillip III's court but also to keep certain goods dry, such as cacao beans and vanilla pods. Empty crates and damaged barrels were stored in the antechamber. The cramped space had only one ladder leading up into the main warehouse, and its small chimney, a relic of its previous life, poked through the roof.

As they watched, Angelo and Mateo primed their flintlocks.

The captain barked orders in Spanish, telling his men to take everything they could and load the bounty into waiting carts. A barrel fell and cracked open. Glittering coins spilled from the oak.

"Be careful, you excuse for rancid mutton," the captain snarled.

"Merda," Mateo said. "We're two against six. It's not worth risking our lives to safeguard the king's bounty."

"They'll use it to buy more weapons and ships and to recruit more men," Angelo whispered. "We cannot permit them to strengthen."

"It would help if you could kill them."

"You know my vow."

"Any captured will hang anyway."

"Not by my hand," Angelo replied. He pointed to a chimney protruding from the vault. "The building is the old smokehouse. Unlikely they know that."

Mateo followed Angelo's line of sight. "You're thinking we smoke them out?"

"We light a fire below them, then disable the guards. The smoke will funnel up. They'll think the building is going up in flames."

Mateo grinned. "The other four will rush out."

"And we'll pin them where they stand."

The two climbed down and skulked along the vault's perimeter, staying low and avoiding the pirate guards. They slipped into the shadow of an adjacent storage building, where overgrown shrubs and debris obscured the antechamber entrance of the old smokehouse.

Inside, the air was damp and stale. Faint beams of light seeped through the wooden slats above, the only illumination in the space. Overhead footfalls caused a constant rain of dust. Angelo and Mateo gathered splintered wood from broken barrels and armfuls of burlap sacks placed along the walls.

"This should be enough," Mateo said.

Angelo nodded and tore one of the sacks into kindling strips. "The chimney will pull the smoke upward. We just need to make it copious and fast."

The men worked quickly, laying the wood and burlap into a dense pile. Mateo pulled a piece of flint and a striker from his belt and struck it. The small spark caught hold of the dry fibers. Flames soon licked the base of the chimney, their warmth chasing away the damp chill.

"Perfect," Angelo said, his voice calm despite the urgency. "Now, to ensure the bastards can't escape."

Leaving the fire to grow, they slipped outside, back into the building's shadow. They crept along the side of the smokehouse, careful to stay hidden.

The vault was surrounded by barrels and chests piled high in loosely organized heaps. Slipping through the cargo, he approached the front corner of the building. He pressed his back against the wall and poked his head out.

The two pirates stood guard with their weapons drawn, but their attention was on the commotion at the harbor.

"Now," Angelo whispered.

In a sudden motion, he rushed to the first guard and pierced the man's cheek with the point of his sword. The pirate's eyes expanded in horror. Angelo withdrew the blade and slammed the rapier's butt into his skull, knocking him out.

Ready for a fight, the other pirate straightened, but Mateo severed the man's throat, preventing him from uttering a word. Blood spewed out as the pirate crumpled to the ground. Though Angelo had sworn to never kill again, he carried no compunction nor sympathy when his comrades slayed their enemies.

"Let's slow their escape," Angelo said, gesturing to a stack of barrels.

Together, Angelo and Mateo rolled a barrel against the broken door to hold it in place. They added a pallet to it and propped the dead pirate's body against it, creating a makeshift barricade that bought them precious seconds. Smoke alone wouldn't guarantee their victory. It needed to incapacitate the pirates and drive them straight into their trap.

The fire in the antechamber roared, smoke curling through the chimney and spreading into the former smokehouse.

Muffled shouts filtered through the wooden doors.

"Fire!" a pirate yelled.

Angelo smirked. "They'll bolt any second."

Mateo returned the expression with a nod of readiness.

The pirates' curses turned frantic as the smoke thickened. The chimney vented some fumes, but Angelo had banked on the air currents pushing most of it into the enclosed space. Scrambling boots and coughing fits came from within. The vault door buckled as someone inside slammed into it, attempting to ram it open.

"They've locked us in," came a desperate voice.

"Break it down," replied another.

The barrel shifted. Smoke escaped from the cracks in the doorway. The acrid odor of burning straw spread rapidly.

Barging on the door intensified. The barricade threatened to give way.

Mateo positioned himself at the choke point with two pistols. Angelo waited on the other side. One hand gripped a primed flintlock; the other tightened around his sword hilt.

The fortification broke, and the door flew open.

The first pirate burst through the smoke, coughing and sputtering, his pistol hanging in his fingers.

Mateo fired. The bullet found the pirate's forehead. The man's lifeless body collapsed in a heap.

Two other pirates emerged, eyes wild with panic, like rats fleeing a flood. One tripped over his dead comrade. Angelo quickly disarmed him with his rapier. The other charged, but Mateo raised his unspent pistol, stopping the man in his tracks.

"If you filth do not want to die today," Mateo shouted, "discard your weapons and stand against the wall."

A grizzled pirate glanced at Mateo and Angelo. "You only have two shots between the two of you. There are three of us."

"Which two of you want to die first?" Angelo asked. "Remove your belts."

With a grumble, the men unbuckled their straps and dropped them. They lined up against the wall near Mateo, who kept his pistol and sword trained on them.

"I am Captain Pedro La Tormenta," came a coarse voice. The pirate captain stepped from the building wielding a cutlass, smoke billowing behind him. His eyes swept the scene. Seeing Mateo guarding the men, he approached Angelo.

"I am the storm that demolishes everything in its path," the hulking man continued. "If you desire my cutlass, you'll ought rip it from my fingers."

"I don't care what pompous name you call yourself," Angelo said. "I will be happy to abide by your request." He raised his pistol at the captain's face.

"¡*Guarnición*!" Mateo shouted, calling for his garrison.

A vein bulged in Tormenta's forehead. He growled and lowered his sword an inch.

From behind, something tugged at Angelo's waist.

Without thinking, Angelo spun, bringing the tip of his rapier to his assailant's throat.

"Papá, it's me!"

Angelo's chest tightened at the sight of Francesco, his small, shaking frame silhouetted against the smoke-filled dawn. The boy gripped his dagger with both hands, his stance awkward but defiant.

Angelo pulled his rapier back, realizing he nearly killed his son. That disconcerting notion was replaced with a more urgent, raw fear.

"I told you to stay home," he said, his voice a sharp snap.

A roar of rage erupted as Tormenta surged forth, his cutlass aimed straight for Angelo's chest. Angelo barely parried in time. The strike's force jolted up his arm. He shoved Franco away, who had been inches from the sword.

The pirate captain snarled. "You dare challenge me, *perro*?"

"Dogs defend their brood at any cost," Angelo replied.

Tormenta snickered, then lunged. Angelo blocked the strike, steel ringing against steel.

The pirate pressed the attack, his assault merciless. Angelo feinted left. As Tormenta brought his arm back for another blow, he did so an inch too far. With a sharp thrust, Angelo drove his blade through the pirate's long glove and into his wrist.

Tormenta howled, but he didn't lose his grip on the cutlass. His free hand shot forward, landing a brutal punch to Angelo's cheekbone that sent him staggering. Pain radiated from the strike. His rapier slid from the pirate's wrist. Blood arced through the air, painting Angelo's clothes in crimson.

Francesco took a step forward.

"Stay back," Angelo yelled to the boy, who froze in place.

Angelo turned back to the fight, his adrenaline surging. Tormenta pounced, but Angelo sidestepped the clumsy attack and drove his rapier downward. The steel sliced cleanly through the leather of Tormenta's tall boot, cutting flesh and tendon. The pirate cried out, collapsing to one knee.

Seizing the advantage, Angelo lashed out with a powerful kick to Tormenta's midsection, forcing the larger man onto his back into a pile of gold coins. Angelo drove his heel into the pirate captain's chin. Tormenta's head snapped back, and his body went limp.

"From your fingers it is," Angelo said, snatching the cutlass.

With a foot to the chest, he pinned the man then kicked him across the chin.

Mateo hurried over, his pistol ready, but Angelo stopped him from firing.

"Have your men tie him up. Let the governor deal with him," he said. Breathing hard, he turned to his son. "What are you doing here? You should be with Mamá and Juanita."

"I wanted to help." Tears glistened in the boy's eyes.

There was no time for admonishment. A chilling thought struck him.

"Come, Francesco. Now."

Angelo sprinted back toward his home, ensuring his son was at his heels.

Spanish soldiers in Mateo's garrison raced past them to aid their captain at the vault.

At the top of the hill, Angelo glanced toward the beach, pleased that soldiers had subdued the pirates who remained on the sand. The galleon had retreated. Some pirates would escape, but not for long. With a limited crew, they'd be apprehended. The Spanish fleet would confiscate their ship and everything on it.

In the town, soldiers and townsfolk repelled the invaders, who had smashed windows and sought anything—or anyone—they could find.

As they reached their home, a creeping frost coiled in Angelo's gut and seeped outward, numbing his limbs. The door was ajar. Shouts emanated from inside.

"Stay outside this time," he ordered Francesco. "Do not defy me."

Before he gave the boy a chance to respond, Angelo burst through the doorway to find a towering pirate advancing on his wife. Loredana stood her ground, Angelo's cherished Venetian rapier gripped in her shaking hand. Behind her, little Juanita clutched a broken chair leg, her small face contorted in defiance.

"Stay away from my mama!" Juanita swung the chair leg, but the pirate blocked it and swatted her aside like an insect.

The sight of his family in danger ignited a fire in Angelo. "You picked the wrong house," he said with a growl.

The pirate turned and offered a cruel grin. A red scar traversed his forehead. He sprang forward, but Angelo was faster. He parried the man's blade, sidestepped his charge, and struck the back of his knees. As the pirate stumbled, Angelo disarmed him with a twist of his rapier. The cutlass clattered on the wooden floor. The leprous knave snarled and attacked barehanded, but Angelo struck him with the pommel of his sword, sending the pirate down.

Loredana lowered her blade, her shoulders shaking.

"Angelo..."

"It's over," he whispered, reaching to pull her into an embrace. He glanced at Juanita, who sat upright, tears brimming in her eyes. "You were brave, daughter."

Franco rushed in and hugged his family, wrapping all three in his arms.

The sounds of battle faded, replaced by weary neighbors assessing the damage. Angelo pulled away from his family and stepped outside. Spanish soldiers rounded up the remaining pirates and slapped them in irons, while citizens extinguished the fires. Two town surgeons tended to the wounded, their grim faces illuminated by the morning sun.

Santa Marta had survived the onslaught, but the cost was dear. Angelo sheathed his rapier. This was his home now. He would defend it for as long as he drew breath.

XXII

THE CARAVEL ROLLED OVER the turquoise waters of the Caribbean, its prow slicing through the waves like an axe.

Standing on the quarterdeck, Vito kept one gloved hand on the polished wooden rail, his dark eyes fixed on Santa Marta's hazy silhouette unfurling in the distance beneath the emerald slopes of the Sierra Nevada mountains.

La Miravilla was a sturdy vessel. Its three triangular sails were crafted for speed and its body was built for passengers and cargo. The ship proved invaluable during the eight-week voyage from Cádiz, though its cramped quarters tested the patience of every man aboard as they traveled to the Canary Islands, and then across the Atlantic to the Lesser Antilles.

Liquid heat glazed Vito's body, causing his linen smock and woolen pantaloons to adhere to his skin. The air reeked of pitch and seawater. Wood creaked as sailors scurried across the main deck, while a rigging monkey climbed the mast above Vito's head. The captain called out commands in rapid-fire Spanish to trim canvas and coil ropes. Wind snapped at the lowering sails as the helmsman adjusted course on their approach.

The shoreline drew closer, and Vito let his mind drift over the events of the voyage. Grueling days at sea had been uneventful, yet he had used the time well.

Determined to blend into the colonies, he had learned as much Spanish as possible, finding the language to be surprisingly similar to Venetian. He had practiced with the sailors, dissecting their slang and absorbing their cadences until he could carry a passable conversation. The effort had not gone unnoticed. His companions had remarked on it with grudging respect, and even the crew had begun addressing him with less suspicion.

The voyage had not been short of difficulties. *La Miravilla's* cramped quarters turned every moment with Senator Benito Grimani into a test of endurance. The whiner's incessant complaints about the food, the heat, and the accommodations had grated on every nerve. Worse, his presence was a constant reminder of the life Vito could never have with Paulina.

The senator leaned against the gunwale on the port side of the quarterdeck, shielding his pale complexion from the relentless sun with a wide-brimmed hat. Soft around the edges, Grimani was strikingly out of place amidst the rough-hewn sailors and grim Protectors. The man was a liability—a privileged politician with no stomach for blood or danger.

Vito tightened his grip on the rail and focused on their approaching destination. A patchwork of whitewashed buildings with terracotta roofs clustered around the port and stretched up the foothills. Figures moved like rats on the docks, loading and unloading crates, tending to fishing boats, and shouting over the screeches of gulls circling overhead.

Jagged mountain peaks loomed over the settlement, shrouding the jungle's canopy in mist like sentinels guarding secrets older than time. Somewhere within that wilderness lay the Fountain of Youth, the object of their perilous trek. And somewhere in this town was a man who could've been Angelo Mascari.

The swordsman's betrayal still burned as if it had happened yesterday. Vito had spent years imagining this moment. The confrontation, the satisfaction of avenging his brother. As much as he yearned to jump off the boat and hunt down the villain, the doge's command shackled him, his words replaying in Vito's mind like the refrain of an unrelenting hymn.

Find Mascari. Bring him back to Venice alive. He must stand trial for his crimes against the Order.

Mascari's punishment was not Vito's to deliver, and the thought of tempering his fist when they met ignited a storm of fury in his chest.

"This heat is unbearable." The oily voice broke the air like a sour note.

Vito turned to find Grimani fanning himself with his hat.

"How do they survive in such ungodly conditions?"

"The same way we will, Senator. With grit and purpose."

"It will be Heaven to stand on dry land," Ponte said, climbing the quarterdeck steps to join them. "The men are ready, sior." He straightened his broad shoulders and met Vito's gaze, awaiting any signal from his commander.

"Begin preparations to move the Protectors ashore," Vito said. "Remind them to remain discreet."

"As you instruct, sior." Ponte eyed the port then descended to the main deck to address the men. Twelve Protectors of the Order stood at attention, their discipline contrasting with the crew's hecticness. Dressed in dark cloaks and armed with short swords, crossbows, and pistols, the men's presence on the ship had unnerved even the hardiest sailors, who shunned them as they followed their captain's directives.

"Hold, Sior Ponte." Grimani flushed, his mouth tightening. "The Protectors will stay on the ship."

Vito turned to him with increasing irritation. "Why is that, Senator?"

"Because it's what I ordered."

Grimani's condescending tone made Vito's fingers itch to wrap around the hilt of his sword. "They are *my* men, Senator. I am the Chief Protector."

"Yet I have the seniormost rank on this expedition and am thus its leader, as you well know." He motioned to the town. "Besides, it is a sense most common and as you said to Ponte. The doge's instructions were explicit. Angelo Mascari cannot know the Order is here until the time is right. Any sooner could jeopardize the mission. Thus, you shall stay aboard with the Protectors until after Sior Ponte and I meet with Governor Ruiz, at the least."

Disgust simmered in Vito's chest, but he suppressed it and forced a neutral expression. "You and *Ponte*?"

"It is unusual for a second to convene with a head official, but Mascari has never met Ponte."

"You believe Mascari will wander into the harbor and spot me amidst the throngs of people?"

"It's a risk we cannot take," the senator replied. "Certainly, the Protectors will be noticed. Even if Mascari doesn't see you, word of Venetians could send him scampering to another corner of the Earth. You'll remain on *La Miravilla* with the men until I deem otherwise."

Vito inhaled through his nose as he considered the words. Though he despised taking any instruction from Grimani, he swallowed his pride and conceded the rationale. "Very well. I will wait."

Pivoting back to the railing, Vito raised an eyebrow at the fast-approaching town. Several sections of the rampart were scorched, with piles of rubble speckled at their base. A cannon emplacement had been reduced to a blackened husk, leaving clear vulnerabilities in the town's defenses. He pursed his lips as he considered the implications. Based on the ever-present concerns of the captain and crew, he surmised the damage was remnants of a pirate attack, striking at the heart of Spanish holdings. It was a sign of the turbulence in the colonial province. Another danger he and his men faced.

A clamor drifted over the deck as they entered the harbor—a cacophony of Spanish, Tairona, and African tongues overlapping in the humid air. Indigenous men unloaded goods from small canoes, while Spanish overseers barked directions from shaded positions near the warehouses. Slaves carried crates, their faces carved with exhaustion.

The caravel ground against the dock, large enough to host the mid-sized vessel. The captain called to drop anchor and moor the ship. Gangplanks were lowered.

Movement on the far dock caught Vito's attention. Two Spanish soldiers dragged a Tairona man away, the native shouting curses in the language forced upon him. A crowd gathered. Tairona workers murmured, their voices charged, while Spanish merchants loitered nearby, feigning bemused interest.

The Taironan twisted in the soldiers' grip, his voice escalating. "You come to our land and call it yours! You steal what is not yours to take!"

The butt of the soldier's musket silenced him. The man's legs gave out, and he hit the dock hard. Two other Taironas muttered protests, but the second soldier raised his weapon and muzzled them with a glare.

"Native cretin," Grimani muttered, heading toward the gangplank. "They invite rebellion with their insolence. They should learn to accept defeat with dignity."

Tension in the colonial outpost was a powder keg, a volatile mix of imperial rule and indigenous defiance, and the Spanish soldiers seemed intent on lighting the fuse. For now, Vito needed to maintain a singular focus: Angelo Mascari.

Somewhere beyond the bustling streets and damaged ramparts, the scoundrel lived a deceitful life, unaware his past had rolled in like a hurricane.

Plans and contingencies swam in Vito's thoughts. How long would he have to wait before confronting Mascari? How would he force him to lead them on their quest before clapping him in irons and dragging him back to face his multitude of crimes?

He glanced again toward the primeval jungle, its shadows reaching for the town like creeping fingers. Vito allowed himself a fleeting fantasy: sharing the waters of eternal life with Paulina, so they could be free of Grimani. He considered sending her a letter. He could write it in code, calling her his fig, as he'd done in years past. But it would be impossible with her husband there. In all likelihood, they would return to Venice before the dispatch arrived, and should Grimani discover it, it would be their undoing. He jammed the thought aside and concentrated instead on the tangible task ahead.

Ponte and Grimani's boots clacked against the planks as they disembarked. As soon as they reached the dock, Vito retreated to his cabin, sat at the diminutive desk, and removed his gloves. He sighed at the spots on his sweaty hands. Aging hadn't come easy to him. Though he felt stronger than he did when he was in his twenties, he couldn't deny a loss of energy. These days, he plowed through life more like an ox than an eagle. He dipped his quill into an inkpot and recorded the day's events in a worn leather journal, but his mind dwelled on what lay ahead.

The doge's orders resounded in his thoughts. Mascari had to be returned to Venice alive. Though Vito had never directly defied his leader, in this instance, his own ambitions burned brighter than any command. Waves lapped the ship, and the constant hum of activity wafted in from the harbor. The steady rhythm served to solidify his deliberations. He would play the obedient servant, wait for the right occasion, and ensure that Angelo Mascari's life ended not in Venice, but here, in the New World. He had his own secrets, some of which Mascari may have figured out.

A flicker of amusement crossed Vito's mind. Senator Grimani was ill-suited for the town, let alone a perilous trek.

The jungle loomed as both adversary and ally, holding both dangers and opportunity. A misplaced foot on a cliff, a blade turned just so, a stumble into a venomous snake. Any would guarantee both of his foes never left Santa Marta.

Satisfied, Vito closed the journal and leaned back in his chair.

The Fountain was but a myth, and this expedition was nothing more than their dying doge's fanciful whim, but for Vito, it was a quest that would lead him to a far more satisfying prize.

XXIII

"This." He hummed as he traced her neck from below her ear to her collarbone with faint kisses. "This is my favorite part of you. It's like nuzzling a giant lily petal."

Angelo Mascari glided his lips to her bare shoulder. Her warm skin blushed to a soft pink.

"Or maybe here." His exploration led to a small mole on the top of her left breast, the lone imperfection he'd yet to encounter.

Sprawled together on the bottom of his cousin's white boat, reclining against the bench, Isabella Scalfini propped her right foot on the gunwale. Angelo had lowered the sail, and they bobbed on the mirror-like surface of the Venetian Lagoon beneath an exquisite spring sky. The world was painted in hues, with the faint silhouettes of the city's spires against the horizon. Isabella's presence was as luminous as the sun.

He kissed a path to her right breast and licked a circle around her nipple before sucking it lightly. "Or here. I confess it's difficult to choose."

She stopped him and peered deep into his eyes.

"What troubles you, 'mòre mio?"

"Why do you forever see me at this age?" she whispered, her voice the melody of a memory he could never fully recall. She stroked his graying beard and ran her fingers through his coarse hair, messing it then smoothing it back. "I am but two years younger than you."

She unclasped a silver chain and crucifix from her neck and began to hang it on her lover.

"What are you doing?" he asked, obstructing her movement.

"A gift, my love."

"One I regretfully cannot accept."

She brushed his hand aside and fastened it around his neck. Her eyes smiled, even in somber moments. "You must have something to remember me."

"You are more than memories. You are a part of me."

"Samuele." Her warm accent elongated the second syllable. She shook him gently.

Angelo opened his eyes to his wife sitting beside him on the low straw cot. Loredana's almond-shaped eyes held a quiet warmth, with golden flecks that seemed to catch the light streaming through the mosquito netting. Her sun-bronzed skin, weathered, yet radiant, spoke of thirty-eight years lived close to the land and sea. Her long black hair, tied with a simple band of woven beads as she always wore, draped over her red dress. A delicate spiral carved from fishbone hung from a leather cord on her neck. To him, she was a picture of strength and grace, a reflection of the land that had shaped her spirit and bound her heart to his.

While he would never stop loving Isabella—his soul mate—he had made a life with Loredana and cherished every minute.

Adobe walls, unpainted to retain coolness in Santa Marta's heat, provided more than shelter. They were the unmovable foundation of family. Woven baskets and painted pottery of Taironan design were displayed alongside Spanish crucifixes and candlesticks. Angelo had amassed few belongings and preferred a simple existence. Still, the home was a testament to the life they had built together, a blend of two worlds.

"You dreamed of her again," she said in Spanish, not as an accusation but as a statement of fact. Her voice was steady, but her soft eyes couldn't mask her concern.

Lying had become a part of him, as if his mind had become two books. One was fiction and open for all to read; the other was factual yet sealed under lock and key. He pushed himself upright. Fragments of the dream lingered, like seafoam clinging to the shore after the tide slipped away. He caressed his beard where Isabella had touched it and avoided his wife's gaze. "I dream of many things."

She tilted her head, studying him. "Secrets destroy one's soul, Samuele."

"Some things are best left in the past."

"You let your past weigh on you. One day, it will crush you if you don't share the burden."

"Is that a Tairona proverb?"

Her expression darkened, and her eyes sheened. "No. Every day, our past becomes more of our lives."

Angelo blinked slowly as though each shutter of his lids created a new picture of her words. "And our future gets ever shorter."

"Precisely. You need to speak with Franco."

A deep sigh escaped from Angelo. It had been two days since the attack, and his son had been somber ever since, unnecessarily carrying guilt on his shoulders. "I've spoken to him."

Loredana squeezed his hand. "Not about what he needs to hear."

Laughter and the clattering of dishes preempted his response, much to his relief.

He kissed his wife's forehead and followed her into the adjacent room. Franco and Juanita sat at the small wooden table that dominated their kitchen.

"Papá," Juanita said, her voice bright. Her brown, saucer-sized eyeballs brimmed with curiosity. "You're awake. Did you dream of adventures?"

"Juanita," Loredana said. "Let your father wake properly before you interrogate him." As always, she spoke to the children in an amalgam of Spanish and Chibcha, the language of the Tairona.

"I'm fine," Angelo said, easing into a chair at the table. The aroma of maize tortillas and salted fish seasoned with coriander and chili filled the air. He reached for a wedge of fried yucca root from the platter in the center of the table.

"Did you really kill all the pirates?" Juanita pressed.

Angelo glanced at Franco, but the boy frowned and turned his gaze downward. "I didn't kill *any*. Let that be a lesson. None died by my sword, yet the town"—he glanced at his wife—"and its people were spared."

"Others will carry out justice," Franco said in a mumbled whisper.

"You're the best swordsman in Santa Marta, right?" Juanita asked. "Everyone says so."

Ignoring Franco's comment, Angelo refocused on his daughter. His lips curved in a faint, bittersweet smile. "Strength lies in knowing when to act. And when not to."

His son whipped his eyes at his father for a fleeting instant.

The meal continued in relative quiet. Angelo observed his family with a balance of pride and unease. Franco's eagerness for action worried him; the boy had inherited his sharp reflexes and restless spirit. Juanita, though younger, had a perceptiveness that reminded him uncomfortably of Isabella. And Loredana...

Loredana was his anchor—his safe harbor in a storm he weathered long ago. Yet even she did not know the full truth about the man she had married. He had always deflected questions she had long ceased asking, and he knew she sometimes felt as though she married a ghost, but it was out of necessity. Angelo needed to keep his past locked away, where it could not harm her or the children.

As he helped clear the table, Loredana caught his arm. "You shield them," she said softly. "Do not forget. They are strong. Franco, especially. He will grow into his own, and you must let him."

Angelo nodded, though the thought filled him with dread. "I know. But not while he is still a boy. Especially not if doing so puts you and Juanita at risk."

She squeezed his forearm, her expression unreadable, then released him.

The dream of Isabella persisted as an ever-present shadow on his mind. He touched the gold earring that veiled his missing earlobe. Loredana had fashioned the jewelry, yet it served as a memory of his true soul mate.

After bidding his family goodbye, Angelo walked through the bustling streets of Santa Marta, already baked by the morning sun. With thoughts of how to speak to Franco spinning around him, he needed to gather his wits. Calls of vendors mingled with the clang of hammers, supplanting his inner conversation. Santa

Marta was a boomtown and expanded in population with the arrival of every ship. The town was alive in the wake of the pirate rampage, though its energy carried an edge of tension. Repairs to the palisade and rampart loomed above the market square, with indentured, native, and slave workers sweating under the watchful eyes of Spanish overseers.

Angelo lowered the brim of his hat against the brutality of forced labor. He still had not grown accustomed to it and hoped he never would. A group of mestizo hands hauled timber, their sweat-streaked backs bent beneath the weight of the beams. Beyond them, enslaved Africans carried crates of goods to the marketplace.

Aromas of dried fish and spices mingled with the earthy tang of damp wood. Parrots squawked from rooftops, while stray dogs darted between the stalls, hunting for scraps. Angelo paused by a pottery vendor, drawn to a reddish-brown Tairona vase with intricate patterns and stylized puma motifs.

"Señor Stefanetti!"

A scratchy voice broke Angelo's brief reverie. An elderly mestizo woman hobbled toward him, clutching a basket of woven fabrics.

"*Dios le bendiga*, Señor Stefanetti," she said, bowing deeply, her face lined with gratitude. "For saving us from those devils. My family owes you our lives."

He inclined his head. "Your thanks are misplaced, señora. The men who fought beside me deserve as much praise. I did not fight alone."

"It was you who led them," she insisted, her voice unwavering.

"That was Captain Vargas. I merely lent my sword."

He offered her a faint smile before moving on. Such remarks had become familiar, but they never sat comfortably. Unwanted admiration was another burden, one more layer on an already-laden soul.

The bustling Plaza de Armas opened before him. A makeshift stockade had been erected near the square's center, holding Pedro La Tormenta and his crew. Their sullen faces were streaked with dirt. Their wrists were clasped in irons.

"The dog goes for a walk," called the pirate captain, his voice dripping with mockery despite his predicament. "Come to gloat, have you? Or perhaps you'll beg the governor to spare us? We're not so different, you and I. You'll have a place in my crew."

Angelo didn't look at him as he continued walking. "Enjoy being sun-dried before you swing," he said, devoid of any remorse. His taunt carried the chill of finality, yet the pirate's words pricked at him, like a thorn buried just beneath the skin.

We're not so different.

Near the market edge, Captain Miguel Herrera waited, his boots planted in manure. Though Herrera was Mateo's comrade-at-arms and of equal rank, the two could not have been more different. Herrera's presence always grated on Angelo; the man's distrust was as palpable as the humidity.

"Stefanetti," Herrera said, his tone formal but marked with disdain. "Basking in the town's praise once again, I see."

Angelo stopped a few paces away and adjusted his hat to shade his eyes. "I hear the captain of the guard was absent during the assault. Tell me, *Capitán*, where were you?"

The Spanish captain's brows knitted into a steep slope, shadowing his eyes. "Not that it's of your concern, but I was escorting a caravan carrying the governor's taxes. Pirates don't only strike from the sea. Someone had to ensure the Kingdom's wealth was not plundered."

An insuppressible laugh erupted from Angelo. "A noble task, I'm sure. Though I imagine the men rebuilding the walls might feel differently."

Herrera crossed his arms over a chest gleaming with medals. "Do not presume to lecture me. You have the governor's favor, but that is all. Your Genoese heritage is tolerated, not trusted. And your loyalty? That remains to be seen."

"If my loyalty were in question, *Capitán*, this town would be ash." Angelo stepped closer. "Remember that the next time you wish to question me."

Herrera contorted his face into a mask of controlled anger. After a beat, he turned sharply on his heel and stalked away. Angelo shook off the encounter and continued on to the Cathedral Basilica of Santa Marta. Despite its thatched roof, the church was a refuge of cool stone and muted light, a stark contrast to the outside noise and heat. Angelo crossed himself as he entered. Burning incense saturated the air, mingling with damp stone. Somber notes of Allegri's *Miserere* reverberated off the walls. A choir consisting of twelve Tairona boys sang the hymn, their beatific voices filling Angelo with simultaneous reverence and resentment. For he knew that these boys' parents—like Loredana—were forced into Catholicism.

A White priest conducted the choir, directing them in song, much as he would do in everyday life.

Cardinal Rafael Villalobos sat near the altar in a simple wooden chair, his crimson robes pooled around him like spilled wine. His sharp eyes followed Angelo's approach. His finger moved along with the conductor's baton.

"Samuele," he said. "Can you believe these wretched creatures? Butchering songs for the Lord?"

Genuinely surprised, Angelo said, "I find it most pleasing, Cardinal. I know little of music."

Cardinal Villalobos chuckled. "No, I suspect you don't. So, have you returned to seek absolution or to repeat the sins of old?"

Angelo gazed about the church. Two parishioners sat in the pews, both elderly seamen.

"I come to confess, Your Eminence," Angelo said, his head low.

Villalobos nodded and gestured to the confessional. Angelo followed the cardinal into the booth and knelt.

"Tell me your sins, my son," the cardinal requested.

"The most grievous of all." A familiar weight pressed on Angelo. He had come to the church for guidance on Franco yet couldn't resist broaching a topic that forever haunted him. "I took a life. More than one."

"The pirates?"

"No. I speak of events from years past."

Villalobos exhaled. It was a sorrowful breath, yet Angelo caught a hint of exasperation. "Samuele, the Lord has forgiven you countless times over. You must forgive yourself. What happened in Genoa was years ago. You have proved yourself to be a different man."

Angelo's throat tightened. He stared at the lattice that separated them. In truth, he never confessed to what happened. In all these years, he lied to the priest, a sin in its own right. If he told Villalobos the truth, and it got out despite the man's priestly vows, his life in Santa Marta would be over.

"Guilt is a sign of conscience," the cardinal said, "but not absolution. You must decide if you serve penance for yourself or for those you have wronged."

Angelo looked up, his eyes meeting the cardinal's. "If I cannot?"

"Then your soul will wander, forever seeking what it cannot find." The priest's words were as weighty as the silence that followed. After a minute, he continued. "Samuele, have you told me all there is to tell?"

The question beguiled Angelo; Villalobos had never asked before. "Sí, Padre. Why do you ask?"

"You carry a great weight, my son. You are the only one who can lessen it. You refuse to kill, which is most honorable. The Bible commands it. Yet, you have made your vow out of guilt, not a vow to God."

No reply came from Angelo's lips, as he didn't feel an affirmation to be necessary.

"And yet, though you won't take a life, you lead men to their deaths."

Angelo cocked his head. The comment came off as more than a sanctimonious approach. Still, he needed to keep a cordial, if not diplomatic, relationship with Villalobos. "I defend Santa Marta. Who am I to question our wise governor?"

"Wise he is, indeed. But Angelo, I sense you are imprisoning your own conscience. Only until you reveal yourself to God will you be free. If there is more to tell, it's safe with me. I am our Lord's conduit."

The urge to spill his entire past was great, but Angelo seized. "There is nothing more."

"I see." The cardinal cleared his throat. "How is your beautiful wife? And your children?"

"They are well, Padre. Gratitude."

Angelo made the sign of the cross, left the confessional, and exited the church. Outside, the sun was relentless. A shirtless Tairona boy, no older than ten, approached him, his steps hesitant. The child's arm was twisted unnaturally, evidence of an old injury or birth defect, and his wide, dark eyes reflected both awe and apprehension.

"The governor summons you to the Customs House, señor," the boy said in rudimentary Spanish, his voice trembling.

Angelo crouched to meet the boy's gaze. "He's in Santa Marta? I was unaware of his arrival."

"Arrived on this morn, señor."

"Did he say why I am summoned?"

The boy shook his head.

Angelo reached into his belt, withdrew a *maravedí*, and pressed it into the boy's good hand. "Thank you, *hijo*. Inform his Excellency I am on my way."

The boy hesitated, staring at the copper coin as though it might vanish, then darted off.

Angelo straightened, his mind already turning to the summons. Governor Ruiz was a man of calculated words and hidden motives. Whatever awaited him at the Customs House, Angelo knew it would not be simple.

#

The Customs House stood resolute against the salty breeze, its adobe walls bleached pale, with iron-barred windows that sealed the harbor from the administration housed within. Angelo shoved open the wooden door. Hinges groaned like an old man's joints. The dim interior offered a welcome reprieve from the heat.

The governor's aide led Angelo to the regal executive office, where a familiar smell of parchment, ink, and sweat greeted him. The room was spacious and ornate but functional, with maps and ledgers piled neatly on the governor's oak desk.

His portly frame, fine hose, and embroidered silk exposed his fondness for luxuries, while his powdered face concealed a lifetime in service to the Spanish Crown—equal parts weariness and resolve. Across from the governor sat Mateo Vargas in one of three chairs.

Chatter from the market filtered in through the open shutters.

"Ah, Samuele," the governor said cheerfully, beckoning him forth. "Come, have a seat, my friend."

Angelo settled into the woven-cane chair next to Mateo.

"The man you captured goes by the pathetic moniker Pedro La Tormenta," Ruiz said. "Real name Pedro Grillo. A dark cloud wanted by his majesty for piracy and other crimes. Now, he and his crew will be tried and swinging from the gallows within a fortnight."

The governor opened a small chest and retrieved a handful of gold coins, which he stacked on his desk. He then divided them and slid them in Angelo and Mateo's way. "Four doubloons apiece for your bravery and commitment to Santa Marta and King Philip III of Spain."

Mateo collected his share with a nod of thanks. Angelo stared at them, wondering if the families of those lost would receive any pension.

"A status report, if you will, Captain Vargas."

"Twelve soldiers killed in action, my lord," Mateo said, while pocketing the coins. "Another ten wounded, half of whom will not be able to fight again. The culverin is destroyed, as you know, along with much of the rampart. I am told it will be repaired in three weeks' time."

"Excellent," replied the governor. "Not a single escudo lost. All in all, a successful repelling of vermin. Regale me with tales of the day."

"Twelve men killed," Angelo said. "Five who will never walk again. Who knows how they will provide for their families?" He slid the coins back to Ruiz. "Kindly defer my compensation to them."

The governor perked a bushy eyebrow at the action. "Samuele, your moral rectitude is surpassed only by your valor. Your donation is most appreciated."

Angelo shot a look at Mateo, who rolled his eyes.

"And the king's donation for a new culverin?" his friend asked. "Our measly coins won't help. We need *ten* culverins. This is a town of twenty-seven hundred souls, growing more by the day. We are under constant threat, and now we have only thirty-four in good health."

"I understand your request, Capitán." The governor steepled his stodgy fingers atop his desk. His expression bowled into one of jaded authority. "I shall convey it, but cannons do not materialize overnight. You must make do until new conscripts arrive in a month's time. I shall consult with the colonel then. Perhaps we can consign some weaponry from Cartagena."

As if concluding his statement, he twisted open a small tin and took a pinch of snuff, inhaling the finely ground tobacco in each nostril.

Mateo straightened in his seat. "With all due respect, my lord, there has been a rise in piracy and native attacks."

Governor Ruiz pursed his lips. "Then train your men to be better watchmen."

The comment impelled Mateo into a slouch. There was nothing he could do about it, and he knew it. Angelo respected Governor Ruiz but couldn't understand why he was so reluctant to at least make an effort to bolster the town's defenses. After all, they were guarding the king's bounty.

The door opened, and the secretary entered. He waltzed over to the governor and whispered into his ear.

"Ah, excellent. Captain Vargas, you are dismissed. We shall hear the ballad of your triumph over the marauding knaves at a more opportune hour. Tonight in the tavern?"

"That would be delightful, Governor," Mateo replied. He rose, as did Angelo.

"Not you, Samuele. Please, sit."

Angelo shared a glance with Mateo, who shrugged and left the room. A moment later, the secretary admitted two men. Angelo had never seen them before, but their presence caused a spike in his pulse, for they wore Venetian garb. The visitors approached Angelo with a sense of purpose. One slender, about his height, was impeccably dressed with an aristocratic air and calculating eyes. The other was an imposing figure whose size rivaled any person in Santa Marta. Their cloaks couldn't conceal their rigid, militaristic postures.

He forced his face to retain a neutral expression though his instincts screamed a warning as he stood to greet the men.

"Señor Stefanetti," said Governor Ruiz, "meet our guests from nearby your homeland."

The slender man, whose posture dripped entitlement, offered a tight-lipped smile. He removed his cavalier hat and bowed his head, an act Angelo offered in return.

"Allow me to introduce myself," he said in Venetian, his eyes remaining on Angelo. "I am Senator Benito Grimani of the Most Serene Republic of Venice, and this is my trusted associate, Leonardo Ponte. We have come a great distance to meet you."

The words struck like a blade's edge. Angelo's first reflex was denial. The tongue of his homeland, which he hadn't heard since he left the island city, dragged him backward to buried memories. He calmed the drummer in his chest and crinkled his eyes in mock-confusion.

"Forgive me, gentlemen," he replied in Latin, his tone deliberate. "I do not understand your dialect."

Grimani's smile faltered, replaced by a calculating look. "Latin, then," he said, switching languages without missing a beat. Ruiz nodded, following the exchange with evident interest.

"Please, my friends," said the governor in Latin, motioning to the two empty chairs.

While the two men took the offered seats, Angelo's mind raced. He wondered if they knew who he was, and if so, why the charade? Had they informed Governor Ruiz? If they did, what would become of his status, and Loredana and the children? He swallowed the rising tide of dread.

"What can I do for you, *señores*?" he asked the men, purposefully weaving in Spanish.

Grimani leaned forward, his pale fingers clasped. "Your reputation precedes you, *Domine* Stefanetti. Governor Ruiz says you know these lands better than any Spaniard in Santa Marta. Simply put, we seek a blade for hire. A guide."

"A guide for what?" Angelo asked.

"Not *for* something," Ponte replied. His coarse Latin was tinged with a Venetian accent. "*To* something."

"An expedition," added Grimani. "To the jungle."

Angelo jutted his head back. Could these men truly have traveled from Venice to explore the green hell? Even if they had, he was not the right man for the job. "You'll forgive me, but I have no interest in ever returning to that wretched place. Many men in Santa Marta can serve as your guide."

"Few, if any, who speak Latin," said Ponte. "Fewer still with the reputation of such a skilled swordsman."

Angelo wondered how they knew of him but resisted their bait. If that's what it was. "I have done what is asked of me in service to Santa Marta and the Spanish crown. Nothing more."

"And yet, you've led three expeditions," Ponte said. "One does not venture into the unknown lacking purpose. What were you searching for?"

For a second, Angelo considered if Ponte was a Protector of the Order. He met the man's eyes and replied, "That which we all seek."

The room fell nearly silent, the only sound the din of the market. Grimani chuckled. "A diplomat's answer. Admirable. We are also diplomats, which is why we are willing to employ a Genoan."

A hint of disingenuity revealed itself in the man's voice. Anxiety crawled up Angelo's spine. "How pray, Senator, have my name or deeds reached your ears?"

Grimani's gaze sharpened. "Through our illustrious Doge Marcantonio Memmo, who is friends with King Phillip III. It seems your name and deeds have reached the king's court."

Angelo threw a glance at the governor, who nodded with agreement.

Grimani reached into a satchel and retrieved a leather-bound book. "Tell me, Señor Stefanetti, have you heard of Don Alonso de Cáceres?"

The name was familiar to Angelo, as was the story of the conquistador's ill-fated quest. "I know of him. His expedition ended in tragedy sixty-five years ago. Some say he died in the jungle. Others say he returned alone, unrecognizable, only to die days later in bouts of madness."

"The latter is the truth." Grimani extracted some loose pages from the book. "The conquistador believed he found the path to an infinite future."

The senator's words loomed like a storm cloud. Angelo rested his calloused hands across his lap. He knew what these fools sought and couldn't help laughing. He pinched the bridge of his nose. "You seek the Fountain of Youth?"

"We do."

"As have many before you. And I know the reason none have found it."

"That is?"

Angelo continued laughing and met each man's eyes. "Because it's a myth."

Grimani proffered him the papers. "Perhaps. Perhaps not. You might see something we cannot."

The humor fizzled as Angelo stared at the pages. A whiff of musty parchment hit his nostrils. With a reluctant curiosity, he skimmed through the scribble and sketches. Cáceres's words about twisted trees, impenetrable walls, and indecipherable symbols were desperate, fevered, and laced with a sense of doom.

"These notes," Angelo said, giving the papers back, "say to stay away. Far away."

Ponte frowned. "That's all you have to offer?"

Angelo met Ponte's gaze with an unflinching confidence he had honed over decades. "I offer you truth. The Fountain is a story that consumes men's lives. It lured Cáceres and his crew to their death. It killed many of Juan Ponce de León's a thousand leagues from here, and many others. The jungle does not forgive hubris."

Governor Ruiz cleared his throat, a sound like distant thunder, and leaned forward in his chair. "Senator Grimani, perhaps we should discuss the matter privately?"

Grimani answered with a raised finger. His focus remained on Angelo. "We do not seek myths. We seek opportunity. You dismiss this so easily, yet others would kill for such knowledge."

"I have seen what Amazonia does to men who chase legends," Angelo replied. "The Fountain of Youth is no more real than El Dorado. All you will find is death."

Grimani leaned back, exchanging a glance with Ponte. The broader man's expression was inscrutable, but his fingers drummed once on his chair arm, a subtle sign of impatience.

Ruiz cleared his throat, breaking the tension. "Señor Stefanetti is a pragmatic fellow, Senator. He values caution over folly. Perhaps discuss the fee you are prepared to pay—"

"I will not take your gold," Angelo interrupted, standing. "Nor will I risk my life for a fairytale."

The finality in his tone caught them off guard. Grimani returned a thin smile, exposing a crack in his polished demeanor. "You speak as though you have sought something fantastical in the past." He stared at Angelo, as if probing him. "Would you not want eternal youth? Perhaps to achieve the impossible?"

Angelo's chest tightened, though he kept his expression stony. There was a subtext to the senator's words—if he *was* a senator—that he knew far more than he let on. Had they met elsewhere, Angelo would've disarmed them and forced the truth from their lips. In the governor's presence, he had little choice. He had played such verbal games many times in the past, and this one advanced to a precipice that offered no winning outcome for him. He bowed slightly to Ruiz and switched back to Spanish. "If there is nothing else, Governor, I will take my leave."

"Very well," Ruiz replied with a nod. "Since your schedule is now free, my nephew seeks sword fighting lessons. Let's hope you don't refuse payment for that, as well."

"It would be my honor," Angelo replied. He turned to the Venetians. "Señores, I hope you find your prize. Safe travels."

He strode to the door, his boots striking the wooden floor like a whip on a horse's back.

"Sior Stefanetti?" Grimani called.

Angelo gripped the door handle without looking back.

"'No man was ever wise by chance,'" the senator said. "The Roman philosopher Lucius Annaeus Seneca made that proclamation."

Angelo didn't appreciate the patronizing implication of the quote. "What is your point, señor?"

"A mere observation," Grimani said.

Outside, the sun was blinding, and the market ruckus pressed against Angelo like a tide. His breathing quickened as he walked the cobbled street, his thoughts a jumbled mess, wondering if they knew his true identity. If so, why wait to confront him?

Shadows of the past crept closer, and for the first time in years, Angelo felt hunted again.

His hand drifted to the silver crucifix beneath his tunic, a relic from another life. A cold knot twisted in his stomach. If the Order had sent these men, they would stop at nothing to see him dragged back to Venice. His family's faces flashed in his mind. Loredana, Francesco, Juanita. The answer was as suffocating as the tropical air: he would do whatever was necessary to keep them safe.

To do that, he needed answers.

XXIV

DRUNKEN LAUGHTER, CLINKING PEWTER mugs, and guttural curses met Angelo as he stepped inside *El Ancla Oxidada.* The tavern leaned against the harbor like an old sailor too dogged to fall. A salty breeze from the Magdalena River mingled with the sour odor of ale and unwashed bodies. Angelo only visited the establishment once a month or so, in part because he never had much of a taste for drink but more so because it invariably brought back memories of Venice's *bacari*—wine bars where one could purchase *cicchetti* and *vino* for half a ducat.

But he didn't walk down to *El Ancla Oxidada* to imbibe or take part in anything other than finding the man who had brought him to Santa Marta.

Lantern light bled through clouds of tobacco smoke. Rough wooden floorboards, discolored from all manner of fluids, strained under the weight of the rowdiness. Angelo ignored spirited greetings and scanned the crowd, his gaze darting from person to person. Dockworkers, sailors, and traders filled the room, their weathered faces blending in a tableau of exhaustion and excess.

There was no sign of his target.

At the counter, a broad-shouldered mestizo barkeep dispensed four mugs of ale to the barmaid. She balanced them on a tray and spun around unruly patrons like a circus performer.

"Is Cadamosto here?" Angelo asked.

"Not tonight," the barkeep said while filling other mugs. "Likely on his ship."

"Gracias," Angelo replied, tossing a copper onto the bar before slipping back into the night.

Moored stumbling distance from the tavern, The *San Cristóbal* was a caravel past her prime. Her once-pristine sails were patched, and her hull was lined with barnacles. Still, she floated, as obdurate as her captain. Despite her sorry state, the ship held a place in Angelo's heart, for it was this craft that transported him across the ocean all those years ago. A faint light glimmered through the porthole of the captain's quarters.

Countless hours aboard this ship during the crossing, combined with repeated visits to Cadamosto, provided Angelo an intimate familiarity with the vessel. He also felt like an honorary part of the crew and didn't need permission to board. Still, he walked quietly, not wishing to wake the skeleton crew required to maintain the ship. Five men lounged near the bow, their snores punctuated by the occasional creak of planks. Angelo avoided them and headed straight for the cabin.

He knocked once before entering.

Sebastiano Cadamosto sat slumped at his desk, a half-empty bottle of aguardiente dangling from his fingers. His bare right foot was propped on a pillowed stool, the big toe red and engorged from gout. The captain's gray, grizzled beard glistened with sweat or some other liquid and his eyes, half-lidded, barely registered Angelo's entrance.

"Ah, Angesamueleo," Cadamosto said in a near-incomprehensible garble, setting the bottle on the desk with deliberate care. "What is bringsh you to my humblesh abode at such hour?"

Angelo shut the door and stepped closer. He raised Cadamosto's chin off the desk and recoiled from the stench. "Venetians arrived in Santa Marta today," he whispered.

This got the captain's attention. He straightened as best he could, the haze of alcohol lifting. "Veneshans? What Veneshans?"

"Two men. A senator and another man, possibly a soldier. Benito Grimani and Leonardo Ponte. Do you know them?"

"Not." Cadamosto rubbed his temple. "What businesh have they 'ere?"

"That's what I came to ask you."

"Them names be unknown to me." The captain brought the bottle to his lips, but Angelo pressed his arm down.

Cadamosto shot him a glare but relented.

"Por favor, Capitán. I need you clear-headed." Angelo hesitated, choosing his words carefully. "They claim to be explorers, but I think there's more to it. I don't trust them."

"Paint me a picture," Cadamosto said, his tone sharpening.

Angelo recounted the meeting, detailing their lunatic expedition. As he spoke, the master mariner packed a pipe with tobacco and lit it with the candle. He puffed on it, snorting at the Fountain of Youth, but his frown deepened when Angelo described Grimani's mannerisms and seemingly hidden agenda.

"No. Ain't ne'er heard of them."

"Are you certain?" Angelo's tone carried an edge, surprising even himself. He inched closer, lowering his voice to a hiss. "Because if they know who I am... if they've found me here..."

"Angelo, twenty years and more I've held me tongue. I ne'er showed the letter to no one."

"Not even me."

"Aye. A secret I can keep."

Angelo wished he had opened it when it was in his possession. "Can I see it now?"

The older man's face darkened. "Truth be told, I lost it years ago."

"I need to know what it said."

"'Twas nothing."

"Nothing?" The words were like a rapier to Angelo's gut. "That letter sent me halfway around the world."

Cadamosto continued with a dismissive wave. "Aye, and that was the request. A trip I've made two dozen times over. A favor to repay a debt."

"The nobleman's? Why did he send me here? Who was he?"

"His name matters not, my boy. The letter spoke plain: deliver you to the New World." He took a swig from the bottle. "The New World, eh? Pah! What hubris. What folly, to name a land new when its bones be older than Christendom."

Angelo agreed with Cadamosto's sentiment but he needed to focus on immediate concerns. The answer was plausible, but it opened more questions. The nobleman had also said he'd send for him when the time was right to return to Venice to continue the fight, yet the man perished before his eyes.

"You told no one else about me?" Angelo pressed.

The captain slammed his palm on the desk. "No one. Not a soul. Questionable things I've done in my time, but never have I deceived anyone. On my honor, on my life."

Angelo leaned against the cabin wall, arms crossed, his mind racing with unspoken accusations and persistent doubts. If Cadamosto hadn't betrayed him, then who had? The Venetians hadn't stumbled upon him by chance.

"You're a man most honorable, Captain Cadamosto," Angelo finally said, his voice quieter. "I believe you, mi amigo."

"Good. Because after all these years, I thought we trusted each other."

"We do." Angelo's stomach churned with unease.

Cadamosto sighed, the tension leaving his shoulders. He grabbed the bottle but hesitated before touching it to his lips and set it down instead. "You're better than most, Angelo. Whatever you ran from, for both our sakes, let's hope it hasn't caught up to you."

XXV

"You had me worried," Loredana said, looking up from the dining table.

The sweet scent of crushed herbs filled their home. An oil lamp on the table threw sputtering shadows against the thatched ceiling, contrasting with the rhythmic scrape of stone against stone as Loredana used a pestle to grind a mix of guava and chamomile leaves.

Angelo closed the house door. His gaze settled on his wife, unwilling to break the spell she cast as she toiled with quiet grace. The glow of the lamplight illuminated her dark skin. Her long hair framed her face, where strength and tenderness coexisted in natural beauty. His love for Loredana was true and unwavering. Thoughts of Isabella had distanced with every passing day, but with the arrival of the Venetians, it was as if his soul mate broke through the surface of his mind, huffing for air and in dire need of a lifeline.

"You shan't ever worry about me, my sweet," he said, returning his focus to the here and now. He shrugged off his doublet, unbuckled his scabbard belt, and hung them on pegs near the door.

"What troubles you?" Loredana asked, setting down the pestle.

Her intuition never ceased to amaze him. He often wondered how much she sensed about his former life and how much she chose not to ask.

He walked across the packed-earth floor and kissed her on the mouth, before sitting with a somber exhale. Her brow furrowed, but there was no fear in her expression. Only concern for him.

“There are men in town,” Angelo said, keeping his alarm about his past close to his vest. “They wanted my help for an expedition. I refused. I won’t leave you or the children.”

“Does it pay well?”

“Not well enough if I don’t return.”

Loredana reached for his hand, her touch warm and steady. “You’re a good man, Angelo. A good father. I trust you to shelter us.”

The words struck deep. They were a reminder of her faith and steadfast loyalty, though he could never tell her everything.

Behind them, the children’s sleeping area was curtained off with a woven fabric, one Loredana made using geometric Tairona designs. The faint sound of steady breathing through the thin barrier reassured him. At least they were safe. For now.

A knock on the door shattered the serenity.

Loredana jumped. Her fingers squeezed his hand.

Angelo’s eyes darted to the rapier hanging on the wall. “Go to the children.”

She nodded and retreated behind the curtain. With every muscle coiled tight, Angelo moved to the entrance, unhooked the scabbard, and drew his sword. Perhaps only three times before did they have a visitor at this hour and it was never good news. With the Venetians in Santa Marta, a wave of panic rippled through him, though it could’ve been Cadamosto. He cracked the door open, the blade gripped low behind his back.

Standing in the half-moon light was Cardinal Villalobos. His crimson robes seemed to glow in the quivering torch flame, a marked difference from his calm, unreadable expression.

“Padre,” Angelo said warily, lowering his guard but not stepping aside. “This is a late hour for a visit. Is something wrong?”

“I carry urgent news, Samuele,” Villalobos replied. “May I enter?”

Angelo hesitated before letting him in. The priest stepped inside, his gaze sweeping the room.

As Angelo began to shut the door, more figures emerged from the shadows. Grimani. Ponte. Behind them, men wielded a weapon that confirmed his worst fears: Mongolian short swords. Protectors of the Order.

Angelo's grip on his rapier tightened. He needed to maintain his guise. "What is this?"

"A reunion long overdue."

A hulking man with bird-like features jostled through the other men. Vito Uccello. The rank traitor who caused his demise.

Before Angelo could react, two Protectors surged forward, forcing him to step back.

"You betrayed me," Angelo spat at Villalobos.

The cardinal's expression didn't change. "I serve only our king and the law. Acts of betrayal are yours alone."

Heat ignited in Angelo's veins. He elbowed the Protectors out of the way and propelled himself at Vito, his rapier slicing through the air, his vow to never kill again be damned. But Vito anticipated the attack and sidestepped with ease. The Protectors closed in, their blades flashing in the meager light. Angelo's sword clashed with theirs in a flurry of sparks, but the odds were overwhelming.

Within moments, they restrained and disarmed him.

"Still so predictable, Angelo Mascari," Vito taunted in Venetian. Laughter bubbled through his yellow, crooked teeth. "Or should I call you Samuele Stefanetti?"

Loredana's muffled gasp came from behind the curtain.

Angelo's heart plummeted. Though she didn't understand the Venetian dialect, it was close enough to Spanish that she could've surmised the gist of the statement.

"It's been twenty-four years, but let's try this again." Vito rubbed his hands together as if he were about to feast. "Angelo Mascari, by order of Doge Marcantonio Memmo of the Most Serene Republic of Venice, you are hereby under arrest for murder, adultery, thievery, and treason, for all of which you shall pay."

"To think in all these years," Cardinal Villalobos added in Spanish, "you've deceived your friends, your comrades, your family." He clucked his tongue.

"You're a liar!" Franco called, his voice high and angry.

All eyes turned as the boy stepped into the main room. His dark curls framed a face flushed with rage.

"Franco, no!" Loredana's urgent whisper came too late.

Vito laughed, delighted by the scene. "The boy has spirit. Just like his father."

Franco glared at Angelo. "You lied to us. Even your name isn't real! You've been lying this whole time!"

Angelo's chest constricted. The laceration of his son's accusation—a true one—cut deeper than any blade. "Son, I did it to shield you—"

"Save your excuses." Grimani stepped forward, his tone all business. "We didn't come here for family drama."

He gestured to Ponte and two other Protectors, who seized Angelo's wife and children. Loredana sunk her teeth into a ginger Protector's wrist and reached for Juanita. The man gritted in pain and raised his hand. Grimani caught it, preventing the Protector from striking her.

"Now, now," the senator said. "Just because an animal acts wild doesn't mean you should too."

"Sì, sior," the Protector replied. He clutched Loredana's arms behind her back.

Angelo watched, helpless, as swords gleamed against his family's throats.

"You gamble with your lives." Wrath dripped from Angelo's words. His fingers curled into fists. "Release them!"

"That depends on you," Grimani said smoothly. "You had your chance to accept my offer. Here's the new contract. Guide us to the Fountain. We will release them upon our successful homecoming, and you shall return to Venice. Or... *they die.*"

Heart thumping, Angelo's eyes flickered to his family, who cowered with distrust. "I cannot bring you to something that doesn't exist."

"Myths often have roots in truth," Grimani replied. "As do lies. You know this better than anyone. You, Angelo Mascari, will lead us to it."

"Take me," Franco blurted in Spanish, attempting to wriggle free of Ponte's grasp. "I know where it is."

"Franco!" Loredana's voice cracked.

"It's true. I drank from it." The boy squared his shoulders. His lips curved into a wry smile. "Look at me. I'm seventy-two!"

Even in the suffocating tension, Angelo couldn't smother the pride he felt. The boy was his mother's son—fearless, even in the face of mortal danger.

Vito cracked up then translated the Spanish into Venetian.

"A bold claim," Grimani said with a chuckle. He glanced at the Protectors restraining Angelo. "Kill Angelo. We'll take the boy."

"Leave him out of this," Angelo said in Venetian, his desperation growing exponentially. "If he knows, then so do I. I'll take you."

"A wise decision." Grimani motioned to the Protectors. "Your family stays in town. Under guard."

The men muscled Loredana, Franco, and Juanita to the door.

"How could a man of the cloth do this?" Angelo leered at Villalobos. "You've put a death sentence on them."

The priest scoffed. "I care nothing for your heathen woman or your mestizo brats."

Angelo lunged, but the Protectors held him back.

"Enough," Grimani said, raising his voice. "We leave at first light. Your family will remain safe. So long as you cooperate."

"First light?" Angelo's mind switched to practicalities. "You cannot simply stroll into the jungle. We need plans, equipment, provisions—"

"All prepared." The senator ruffled Franco's hair, much to the boy's chagrin. "We're already outfitted. Porters too. Rest well, Angelo. Tomorrow, we seek immortality."

With that, the Protectors dragged his family from their home. Loredana launched rapid-fire curses in Kogi, the native tongue of the Tairona, but the men stifled her protests. Vito tipped his hat then slammed the door.

"Do not worry, my family," Angelo shouted. "No harm will come to you!"

Four armed Protectors remained in the house, positioning themselves in strategic locations. Angelo collapsed to his knees, the load of the night crushing him.

The Protectors hoisted him up and bound him to a chair.

In the charged silence that followed, Angelo's resolve crystallized like steel forged in a fire. Decades of honed skill with a blade, tempered by cunning and hard-won experience, would serve a singular purpose. He vowed to save his family. No matter the cost, no matter the odds.

XXVI

THE DULL GLOW OF dawn touched the edge of the sky when the Protectors shoved Angelo outside, their boots crunching the dirt. He had only slept a few hours, at first hoping for a chance to escape. Seeing there was none, he conserved his energy while the Protectors stayed awake.

Vito waited in the courtyard. Dark circles etched under his eyes were visible, even in the diffused light. "It's time," he said, his voice gravelly. Two additional Protectors flanked him, their hands resting on the hilts of their short swords.

Any other day this early, his family would still be asleep, or at least pretending to be. His wife would've kissed him once before retreating behind the curtain with the children. Her strength had often steadied him more than his own tenacity, but with them locked away, he couldn't shake the gnawing fear that he might never see them again.

With a heavy sigh, Angelo spared one last glance at his home before Vito and the Protectors frog-marched him to the cathedral.

A layer of incense hung inside the church. The scent took on a new connotation, masking something rotten beneath the surface. It killed him that he never once suspected why Cardinal Villalobos had asked so many questions about his past; the man backstabbed Angelo and broke his holy vows.

Faint light filtering through the stained-glass windows painted fractured patterns on the stone walls. Angelo shivered. In a way, the projected image reminded him of Tintoretto's *Paradise*. Grimani waited near the altar, arms folded, his posture rigid. But it was Cardinal Villalobos who dominated the space, his sanctimonious presence suffocating, as though he wielded the power of divine judgement.

"Ah, our willing guide arrives," Grimani said.

Ignoring him, Angelo scanned the space for his family. He caught sight of Loredana gripping the iron bars of a door in the nave. She stood tall, chin raised, shielding the children behind her like a jaguar guarding her cubs.

Relief and heartbreak warred in Angelo's chest. "My loves," he called to them. "Are you hurt?"

Grimani yanked him away amidst their screams for help.

"They are untouched," said the senator. "I am a man of my word. They will be provided for during our little adventure. It is an honor to spend time in a house of God."

The statement enraged Angelo. "You defile this house, as you defiled my house and everything your feet touch."

The senator stepped closer, his tone hardening. "Remember the consequences of failure. I will also keep my word if you don't deliver."

Angelo's fists clenched at his sides. He smothered the first response that came to his mind and forced himself to speak evenly. "This 'little adventure,' as you put it, is doomed before it begins. You play with my family's lives chasing a phantom."

"That remains to be seen."

Angelo turned to Vito, who stood slightly apart, his arms folded. The Protector had grown haggard. A hat didn't hide his baldness. The years carved hollows into his cheeks and sharpened the cruelty in his eyes, making him look more eagle-like than ever. Yet hesitation, or maybe guilt, blinked in his expression.

"Despite our differences, Vito," Angelo said, his voice low, "I always took you for a man of honor. Whatever vendetta you have against me, it doesn't justify this."

The Protector's gaze faltered before he turned away.

"Coward," Angelo said.

Grimani stepped between them. "You've had your reunion. Let's move. We're burning daylight."

"I'll come back for you," Angelo called to his family, desperation seeping through his pores. "Stay safe."

"Kill them, Samuele!" Loredana screamed. "You must break your vow. You must!"

The plea ransacked Angelo's mind. He would not let harm befall them, yet he needed to remain true to himself. As if chastised from Heaven, the morning sun blinded him when the Protectors forced him from the dark cathedral. Unable to use his arms to shield his eyes, he squinted, tunneling his vision to an unfocused blur.

Townsfolk and merchants muttered and pointed while they traversed the streets. The Protectors marched Angelo like a prisoner. Not one of his neighbors or compatriots came to his aid. Their stares were daggers in his back. Santa Marta was a place where everyone knew everyone else, and Angelo—Samuele to them—had always been the man who kept their homes safe from pirates, quarrels, and native revolts. Now, they looked at him as though he were a criminal.

"Samuele!"

Mateo's voice cut across the commotion. The captain of the watch pushed through the throng, his face flushed with confusion and anger.

"Who are these men? What's going on?" he demanded. His gaze alternated between Angelo and the armed Protectors escorting him.

Before anyone answered, Governor Ruiz appeared, his boots clopping on the ballast cobblestones. "This man is an imposter," Ruiz announced, his voice carrying over his subjects. "He is not Samuele Stefanetti."

A murmur rose from the crowd.

"He is called Angelo Mascari, a fugitive from Venice, long wanted for crimes against the Republic. By order of our illustrious King Phillip, friend to Doge Memmo of Venice, we are cooperating to extradite the criminal to his homeland to face trial."

Mateo's eyes widened as he turned to Angelo. "Is this true?"

The accusation settled like a stone in Angelo's gut. He nodded slowly. "It's true. But everything I've done here—the friendships, the work—was real."

Mateo hesitated, his brow wrinkled. It was the sorrow in his friend's eyes that stung Angelo more than anything.

Grimani stepped forward, his impatience palpable. "Enough. Make haste."

They walked a few paces before Mateo interjected again. "The dock is the other way, sir."

"Discuss with your governor," Grimani said without turning. "He will explain."

Eight Protectors stood at attention outside the town gates, their Mongolian short swords sheathed, their pistols holstered. Each man also had a crossbow strapped across his back, along with a quiver of bolts and a bedroll. Two African men, laden with saddlebags, stood next to a dray mule. Overloaded with supplies, the animal snorted and pawed at the ground.

A better look at the native caused Angelo's breath to catch. It was Loredana's brother, Izel, his drawn. He avoided Angelo at first, but when their eyes met, guilt plastered his expression.

"Izel," Angelo said in a sharp whisper as he stepped closer.

"I didn't have a choice," his brother-in-law replied, his voice trembling. "They threatened to kill Loredana and the children if I refused."

Angelo's nostrils flared with a deliberate exhale. "You believed them?"

"What was I supposed to do? Fight them? They have swords and guns, Samuele."

In his third decade, just a year younger than Loredana, Izel was a short man but muscular and full of boundless energy. Like all Taironan men, he had no facial or body hair. A traditional white tunic hung over his European shirt and pantaloons.

Whether or not Grimani was aware, his cruelest crime in abducting Loredana's brother was that Izel was a *Mamo*, the spiritual leader among the Tairona people. Customary for all *Mamos*, Izel had spent the first nine years of his life in a cave, secluded from the world, learning to listen to the wind threading through the Sierra, to the hush of rivers carving through the valleys, and to the unseen forces that shaped the earth and sky. He emerged as a guardian of Aluna, the force of and behind all nature. Aluna served as a bridge between the living and the spirits that watched over them, man and animal alike.

Grimani shooed invisible flies with a lacy handkerchief. "Touching reunion. Shall we?"

Besides Izel and the slaves' presence, there was another part of the expedition Angelo couldn't stomach.

"Pack animals are ill-suited for the jungle," he said, his tone biting. "A hundred years of exploration have proven that. They'll slip and break their legs. Or worse, they'll attract predators none of us want to face."

Grimani simpered. "Your concern is touching, but the mule comes. She will carry the supplies with the Africans. Move."

Pompous dolt. Grimani's callousness was not a fortuitous start. "We should not bring this mule."

"Will *you* carry everything?"

"Each man should carry their weight."

"We shall use a beast that the Lord created for the sole purpose of hauling things." The senator pointed his flintlock from his hip. "Or should we follow the adage that it's better a journey begin in blood than end in blood?"

"Which philosopher said that?" Angelo asked.

"You're looking at him," Grimani replied as smugly as a person could. "One more thing. If you're lying about the length of the expedition—"

"You'll do what, senator? Kill me? No, you'll follow me into the jungle like lambs to the slaughter, and you'll thank me when you survive the first night."

"You think we'll die in the jungle?" Grimani asked with a nervous chuckle.

"Death is but the first consideration," Angelo replied.

"For you." Grimani raised his pistol to Angelo's head. "Now march."

Angelo surged forth, leading the expedition party toward the mountainous terrain, a wall of green shadows and unknown perils. He glanced back at the cathedral's spire. Inside, his family waited, their lives dependent on him locating a mythical treasure.

Very soon, Angelo promised himself, *their captors will feel a pain far more severe.*

XXVII

THE JUNGLE HAD A way of consuming men. It was an unrelenting adversary with which every man on every expedition grappled. Angelo had seen it before. The wilderness simultaneously united enemies against a common foe and drove friends apart through endless challenges and frustrations. Every step through the undergrowth siphoned away energy and will. The air was so humid it felt like breathing through a wet cloth. The Sierra Madre loomed above them in a mist that clung to the peaks like a funeral shroud, promising nothing but hardship ahead. Roots clawed at their boots, thorny plants snagged their garments, and an incessant whine of relentless mosquitos bombarded their exposed skin like a plague. His captors only gave the lead man a machete, forcing the others to brush aside foliage that often sliced their skin.

The expedition moved as a lumbering beast. Eight Protectors of the Order, their fine doublets sweat-sodden and splattered with mud, flanked the group like restless predators when the terrain allowed them the space. At times, they walked single file, trailing the mule and slaves, always with Vito, Grimani, and Ponte right behind Angelo and Izel. Though Angelo yearned to steal the lead man's machete and turn the blade on his captors, he knew it would've been futile. Machetes had helped the Tairona wage successful—if short-lived—rebellions, but with eleven men carrying short swords, pistols, and crossbows, the machete was good for nothing but cutting vegetation. The slaves trudged along, guiding the mule burdened with sacks of grain, barrels of water, and provisions. Their backs glistened with sweat, and a pang of guilt hit Angelo every time he saw them, knowing they bore the heaviest loads.

They had marched for six days, enduring the jungle's hostility with no inkling if they were closer to the prize Grimani so desperately sought. Terror boiled beneath the surface of Angelo's stoic demeanor. The Venetians needed him and his brother-in-law; without them, they would be consumed by nature. Yet, if Angelo and Izel were injured or killed in an escape attempt, it would lead to his family's death. Grimani had instructed the Protectors who remained in the cathedral to kill them should the expedition not return within fifteen days, allowing a twenty-four-hour margin of error in an arbitrary timeframe. The quagmire was unsolvable. Each step took him farther from Loredana and their children, farther from the life he had built and sworn to defend. This trek was madness, a fool's errand born from greed and obsession. The chronicle offered guidance, but it was vague at best, a collection of Don Alonso de Cáceres's scrawled illustrations and cryptic notes that raised as many questions as they answered.

The scarce clarity Angelo could decipher was a straightforward account. Cáceres and his men had followed the river for a week—or maybe two months—and were plagued by calamities, including snake and spider bites, starvation, and animal attacks. Ultimately, they were besieged by natives who killed them all except Cáceres, who played dead in the muck.

It did not bode well to find a myth.

They'd have more luck using Dante's *Inferno* to find the gates of Hell. Or maybe they had stepped through that gate when they left Santa Marta.

The coarse rope around Angelo's waist pulled taut, jerking him backward. Every jolt chaffed the fabric of his clothes. He stumbled but caught his footing and shot a glare over his shoulder. Izel kept close behind, chewing on coca leaves he stored in a small pouch tied to his belt. Despite being Tairona, the *Mamo* despised this journey as much as Angelo did, but he endured it with the quiet resilience of a man whose knowledge of survival came at birth. Behind Izel, fastened to them by another length of rope, was Vito. His enemy's silence was a welcome reprieve, though Angelo could feel the Protector's eyes drilling into his back.

Meals were meager and fleeting; hunger gnawed at Angelo's gut. Each morning began with a ration of yucca or cassava, hardtack, and salted goat meat they had brought from Santa Marta. He cursed himself for not checking the supplies. The Venetian coxcombs were woefully unprepared in a place as alien to their island city as one could imagine. By midday, the men scavenged what they could from the jungle. Izel scouted clusters of tropical fruit, while others hunted small animals—an iguana, once, and a macaw that had the misfortune of landing too close to a crossbow.

Grimani grumbled the loudest. Unlike the others, who had long abandoned their cloaks and outer garments, leaving them in loose shirts and breeches to endure the heat, he still wore a dark doublet, the fine fabric stained with sweat and mud. Broad-brimmed hats helped shield against the sun when it broke through the canopy, but the shade offered little reprieve. The Venetian senator barked orders, griped about the pace, and launched oaths at the jungle as though it may take offense and part for him. Flush and shiny, he wiped his brow with his kerchief.

A bright blue butterfly, larger than a sparrow, aimed for Grimani's nose. He clapped it as if it were a fly. The insect fell to its death. In disgust, he wiped his palms on his pantaloons.

Low-pitched growls erupted overhead, startling the group.

"Howler monkeys." Angelo pointed to the shaking trees as the unseen animals traversed the canopy.

"That marker," Izel said. He made a beeline for a pile of stones stacked in a deliberate pattern along the path. Each had faint red and black markings, barely visible beneath a layer of grime.

"What does it mean?" Vito asked, his voice breaking the silence for the first time in hours.

The *Mamo* crouched and scrutinized the marker. "It's a boundary. A warning. We are not welcome beyond."

"Or it could mean nothing." Grimani snorted, joining them to peer at the stones with disdain. His Spanish, like Vito's, was surprisingly fluent. "Superstitions," he said dismissively. He kicked the pile, sending it crumbling to the ground.

"You're an adle-brained clodpoll," Angelo snapped, unable to hold back. "These lands are sacred to the Tairona. You desecrate them at your peril."

Grimani turned slowly with curling lips. "I didn't realize you'd become a scholar of native customs, Angelo. Tell me, what else should we fear? Ghosts? Curses? Perhaps the jungle will swallow us whole? The Order knows truths of this world. Truths you couldn't begin to fathom."

A vision of Isabella flashed in Angelo's mind. He stepped closer, his voice seething. "I fathom far more than you know. Yes, you should fear the jungle. More so, the men who guard it."

Grimani didn't reply, his gaze shifting to Vito. It was a fleeting look, sharp and cutting. In that brief glance, there was something... *revealing*: the senator's disdain for the Protector ran deeper than professional hierarchy.

Tension rippled through the group. Grimani held Angelo's gaze before turning with a dismissive wave. "Keep moving," he ordered.

Kill that man.

Angelo's breath hitched at the words whispering in his mind, for they weren't his. He hadn't heard that sweet voice in ages. It was Isabella's. Soft and melodic, just as he remembered, but there was a dark edge to it, like a razor under silk.

The group staggered onward. Angelo joined them, his mind in a fog. The arrival of the Order and now Isabella's reemergence was an unexpected tidal wave that wiped away the life he'd spent years building.

"You'd be wise to pay attention and follow orders," Vito said, walking beside him.

The Protector's odor snapped Angelo from his musings. "Why are you here?" he asked. "Did the doge order you to find me? Or do you serve Grimani?"

Vito didn't turn his head. "You think I wanted to chase you into this hell?"

"You always wanted something from me. First the doge's book, then my life. Now what? Do you really believe in the Fountain of Youth?"

"Why are *you* in Santa Marta, Mascari? Hiding out in the remotest corner of the map? You thought we care that much about you that we'd chase you across the ocean?"

"Yet here you are," Angelo replied, tugging at the rope. "Bound to me."

"Believe me, I wouldn't be here if not ordered. You are nothing more than a coincidental convenience."

"So this *is* about the Fountain of Youth?"

"Let's hope for your sake it exists."

Despair roared through Angelo. His family was doomed. "It doesn't."

Vito threw a glance at Grimani and the Protectors. They were still out of earshot, and the jungle noises drowned out their words. "I told you something. Now a tit for tat. And you? Why *are* you here? You could've disappeared far closer to home."

Angelo gazed at his adversary. It surprised him that Vito didn't know. "I always thought it was to find the artifact."

Vito cocked his head. "Artifact?"

"That's what I call it. Something to free Isabella and the souls."

"I know of no such object. If there's one, perhaps it would be in Cathay."

"Cathay?"

"Sì," Vito replied. "Or Mongolia. Somewhere in the Far East. It's the Order's origins. You're on the wrong side of the earth, my friend."

"I am not your friend." Angelo swatted a mosquito on his cheek. Blood oozed on his fingers. He flicked the insect away. Every word the Protector said caused Angelo's skin to bristle, yet he couldn't let this conversation go. "Then why would the nobleman send me here?"

"Nobleman?" Vito wrinkled his nose. "Ah, you mean Stefanetti."

"Stefanetti?"

The Protector released a raucous laugh. "You took his name, yet you didn't know? The one who aided you was Pietro Stefanetti. Isabella's uncle."

Chilled ripples of shock ran through Angelo's core. No words came to him. For two-and-a-half decades, he had wondered about the nobleman. He had always figured the man was a leader of the Guild, the group fighting the Order. Perhaps that was true, but this new information made perfect sense. The nobleman was his beloved's uncle. He had a vested interest in aiding Angelo—to first free her from her husband's ruthlessness, and then to liberate her from *Paradise*. Desire to do so renewed in Angelo like a spark lighting a powder keg.

"He told you to come here?" Vito asked.

The question was a good one, for Angelo never knew the answer. "Why would he do that?"

"Perhaps it was to escape. I've heard whispers of an artifact that could destroy the Sun Crystal. As I said, it would be in Cathay. It makes no sense for it to be in this jungle..." His voice trailed off as he slipped into thought. "Unless... No, it can't be."

"Tell me."

"Stefanetti was *also* part of the Order. He was quite close friends with Marco Quattrone. It's possible he knew of what the Order sought. What the doge sought. Even back then."

The answer hit Angelo. But like Vito said, it couldn't be. "You mean the Fountain of Youth?"

"It makes sense. If Isabella is locked in *Paradise* for eternity and you drank from the fountain, it would buy you all that time."

The wind dropped from Angelo's sails. As quickly as his desire to free Isabella had renewed again, it vanished with Vito's words. "It's a false tale, Vito. One with only death at the end."

"If it *does* exist?" the Protector asked. "You wouldn't drink from it?"

Angelo laughed. "Your advanced age has rotted your brain with fanciful thoughts. Have you found religion too?"

"You two are getting awfully chummy up there," Grimani called.

Vito offered a grunt to Angelo and dropped back to his place.

As they pushed deeper into the wilderness, the air grew heavier, the jungle darker. Occasional breaks in the canopy offered brief glimpses of the sun, but mostly, the men traveled in shade. The chronicle remained Angelo's constant companion. Though it would surely bring him and his family death, he consulted it frequently and found a depressing camaraderie with its author; Alonso de Cáceres's mission ended in abysmal failure. Angelo prayed that the adventurer's words would save him from the same fate. While walking, he opened the tome and thumbed through the worn pages to study the crude maps and symbols that seemed to be scratched into the pages like warnings from the dead. One drawing of a marker, a swirling design carved into a rock near a stream, caught his attention.

"Do you know what this means?" Angelo asked Izel.

"It is a sign of death," the Tairona man replied, tracing the rune with his finger. "A curse on those who pass."

"Maybe we can lead our friends there."

"Silence," Vito said. "Walk in a single line."

By late afternoon, a disturbing hum settled over them, growing in volume with each step. Angelo snuck a look at the Protectors, who swiveled their heads each way, trying to determine the origin of the noise. As Venetians, they never would've heard such a sound, but he knew what it was. A new plan formed in his mind, one that would lead to a safer outcome for his family.

In his captors' distraction, he stepped next to Izel.

"Follow my lead," he whispered in Kogi.

Izel offered a subdued nod while Angelo dropped back to his position.

The distant drone they'd heard soon grew into a roar. The jungle opened abruptly onto a clearing dominated by a massive waterfall. Water cascaded from a cliff high above and crashed into a pool below. A fine mist-breeze coated everything in its path. As if it were nature's last warning to stay away, the sound was deafening, drowning out the jungle and the Venetians' murmurs of awe. Wet rocks framed the falls on either side.

Angelo nudged Izel.

"This is it," he announced, his voice raised to be heard over the rapids. He spread his arms wide, gesturing to the clear pool at the base of the falls. "The Fountain of Youth."

Several of the Protectors grew wide-eyed. They inched closer to the water's edge.

Grimani sneered, striding forward to the spring ahead of his men. "Do you take me for a simpleton?"

"Look around," Angelo said, stepping beside him. "Do you see any signs of age? Any decay? This place is untouched, preserved by forces beyond your comprehension."

The Venetians exchanged uneasy glances, their skepticism clear. If Angelo could convince them, he could save his family.

"The signs are here," he said firmly, indicating carvings etched into the rocks. The swirling symbols seemed to ripple under the mist, their meaning lost to time. "These are guides. Or perhaps warnings."

An antsy Protector rushed to the pool. He crouched, cupped his hands, and drank. "Delicious," he said, his already ruddy face brightening beneath a mop of red hair. "It must be real. We've found it, sior!"

"Ignoramus," Grimani replied, shaking his head.

"It is true," Izel said from behind them. "There are more markers over here."

The group followed Izel to a cluster of trees near the falls. As they approached, the air grew colder, the mist thicker. Hanging from the branches were intricate constructions of feathers, beads, and bones strung together with strips of leather. Talismans that swayed in the damp breeze.

The mule brayed and heehawed, prancing on her feet. One of the slaves stroked her muzzle. He glanced around the area, as nervous as the beast he tried to calm.

"The mule does not like it here," he said in Spanish.

"Perhaps we should follow the whims of animals," Grimani replied with overt sarcasm.

"Perhaps you should." Izel strode over to the mule. He whispered in her ear and caressed her neck. The animal relaxed but was still rattled.

A Protector yelled in alarm. He shuffled backward and drew his flintlock pistol. A red snake with black and white stripes slinked toward the man. He cocked the hammer and squeezed the trigger. A small spark fizzled in the gunpowder pan.

"Humidity," Angelo said, strutting over.

The Protector drew his sword, but before he could swing, Angelo crouched and picked up the reptile by the neck. "Milk snake," he said. He lobbed it into the brush. "Nonvenomous."

The Protector breathed a sigh of relief and sheathed his blade.

Returning his attention to the talismans, Angelo approached cautiously. The bones were distinctly human-like, carved with the same swirling patterns they'd seen earlier. The feathers were vibrant colors that defied the jungle's greens and muted browns with an air of foreboding.

"I suppose your family made these?" Grimani asked Izel.

"They're markers," the *Mamo* replied, his voice barely audible over the roar. "Protecting something. Or warning us away. We trespass."

"This land was conquered a century ago," Grimani said with a scoff. "It belongs to the Spanish, and they have given us the legal right to explore it. Thus, we do not trespass." He stepped forward to inspect the talismans then snatched the chronicle.

"What are you doing?" Angelo protested, his voice rising.

"Have you been to this place?" Grimani asked, waving his arms around. "To these falls?"

"No," Angelo replied truthfully. "The jungle is many times larger than the whole of the Italian peninsula and Spain combined. I followed the words in that chronicle to the destination."

With impatient hands, Grimani flipped through the worn pages. His lips moved as he read, his eyes darting between Cáceres's scrawled notes and the talismans above them. Finally, he froze. His finger jabbed at a passage.

"Here," he said, his voice taut with excitement. "This is what Cáceres described. 'Guardians of bone and feather.' They marked the path."

He angled the book toward Angelo, who leaned closer to feign re-reading the passage. The words were there, crude and hurried, but unmistakable.

"The *path*, Mascari. Not the destination," the senator said. "Do not play me the fool. Do so again and you will find that our use for you has run its course." He gazed at the top of the waterfall, his face lighting with triumph. "Cáceres wrote that the markers would lead to a sacred place farther up the mountainside."

He shut the chronicle, tucked it under his arm, and surveyed the area.

Angelo knew Grimani was scouting for a way up. Though climbing the sheer cliffs at the falls was impossible, if they circled around to one side, they could ascend a slope. It was steep and muddy, and would be arduous work, but could be done.

Grimani pointed to the precise route Angelo had envisioned. "Gather the supplies. We're going higher."

The Venetians exchanged weary glances but obeyed, hoisting their packs and adjusting their weapons. Frustration surged in Angelo as Grimani strode away, barking commands. The man had no idea what they were walking into and no respect for the dangers the Tairona had warned against.

Izel stepped beside him, his lips grazing Angelo's ear. "We must stop them from going farther."

His brother-in-law filed past. The rope at Angelo's waist pulled taut as he followed. Vito tightened it from behind. The group clambered over rocks, roots, and mud that wound higher up the mountainside.

As they ascended, Grimani's voice rang out from the front of the line, urging them onward with the zeal of a man chasing glory. The mule slipped and struggled. Angelo raced over to help the slaves push her up through the mud and loose rocks until the beast regained its footing. Panting with exhaustion, he couldn't shake the feeling that they were climbing into the jaws of something far greater than any of them understood.

Cresting the ridge, Angelo had envisaged a brief respite. Instead, the cliffside unveiled a river about the width of Venice's Grand Canal. Unlike the placid waters of his hometown's main thoroughfare, this waterway was swollen with recent rains, its currents writhing like serpents in fury. The expedition party stared mouths agape, awestruck by the torrent crashing over jagged rocks. Trees leaned over the water's edge as if barring further entry. The bank on which they stood offered no easy passage, but the fierce power of the white-capped rapids prevented them from crossing to the opposite shore.

His hand involuntarily went to the silver crucifix hanging from his neck.

You must go back, Isabella's voice whispered in his head. *You march toward death.*

XXVIII

"MERDA." ANGELO'S FOOT SANK into a patch of mire. He caught himself against a low-hanging branch, groping its moss-covered surface. They'd covered half a league from the waterfall, and the terrain had grown more difficult to traverse.

"They don't listen," Izel said in Kogi. He tossed his head at Grimani ahead and the Protectors behind. "Men like them believe they conquer the world. Their acts of plunder weaken Aluna. The jungle... it has teeth."

Angelo grunted in agreement while his eyes scanned the riverbank's dense undergrowth. Rain-soaked leaves shimmered under the canopy's filtered light. A sickly sweet stench of decay filled the air. Dampness seeped through his boots, the squelching sound emphasizing the balance and willpower required for each labored step.

He adjusted the rope chafing his waist, but Angelo wasn't alone in his hatred for this so-called expedition. The Venetian Protectors cursed under their breath. Despite being hardened by training and battle, they were city men at heart. Discomfort etched into every grimace and muttered complaint, all echoed by a disgruntled mule.

Grimani had returned Cáceres's chronicle to Angelo and ordered him to continue studying it. Edges of the parchment curled from the humidity. Its crude drawings and haphazard notes offered only vague reassurance. The conquistador had described a series of bends in the river, marked by towering ceiba trees with roots that sprawled like fingers lancing the earth.

"How much farther?" Grimani called over his shoulder.

Angelo was at a loss but needed to appease his captor. "Another league. Maybe less. Maybe more."

Grimani stopped and turned. He wiped his sweat-slicked face, smearing mud across his cheek. "A league more of this hell? You'd better be right, Mascari."

"I'm following a dead man's half-mad ramblings to guide us into the unknown. Or our deaths," Angelo shot back, his tone sharp. He was exhausted. H was tired of Grimani's posturing, tired of the rope, and tired of the jungle itself, which seemed intent on consuming them.

The group pressed on, trudging upstream. Before long, the river split into three estuaries. Angelo consulted the chronicle. For a moment, he thought of leading the group the wrong way—not that there was a correct way—but Grimani would only read Cáceres's writings and discover Angelo's lie. That would be a death sentence for his family.

"Take the estuary on the right," he called to Izel.

The water fanned out, creeping in shallow streams and pools. The ground turned spongy. Water lapped at his calves and rose steadily to his knees as they moved deeper into the flooded jungle. Aquatic plants and trees grew as if birthed from unseen watering cans. Roots and boulders added further obstacles to the murky path, compounded by the risk of lurking crocodiles and snakes.

An hour later, the estuary grew more perplexing. Water braided over obstacles in eddies, mixing then getting caught in sections by natural dams. His skin prickled, not from insect bites, but from the shallow water itself. He stopped, as did the rest of the group, amazed by the sight of dozens of small pools of varying sizes. All connected but at different height levels, their surfaces reflected darkening clouds above them in perfect stillness, only broken by the occasional ripple of a drip from an adjacent pool. The previously ever-present bird calls and animal chitters ceased. The jungle seemed to hold its breath, the air thick and waiting, as if pressing against Angelo's skin like an unseen hand.

"Could this be it?" Vito whispered, stepping next to Angelo. His question broke the peace in a disrespectful yet almost welcome manner. He gestured to the pools, his expression doubtful.

"Drink the water and find out," Angelo replied.

The Protector threw him a sideways glance, surely aware of the illnesses swamp water carried.

Angelo didn't think any of these eddies were the Fountain of Youth. He didn't believe in the Fountain at all. But it didn't matter what *he* believed. He was running out of time. They needed to turn back soon. The chronicle mentioned a place like this, where the water ran slow, amalgamating into small basins before joining the river. There were no markers, no carvings, no signs that this was anything other than a natural formation.

"One of these pools is the Fountain," he announced.

"Again, Mascari?" Grimani said, his tone impatient. "Cáceres spoke of water that shone like the sun. Do you see anything shining here?"

Angelo bit back a retort, choosing instead to focus on the pools, as if convinced they'd found the place. He knelt by one and ran his fingers through the water. It was cool, clear, and utterly ordinary. The jungle, however, was anything but. A shadow moved at the edge of his vision. When he turned, there was nothing but endless trees and vines.

Izel murmured something about spirits in his native tongue, his voice wary.

"Perhaps one *is* the Fountain, sior," Ponte said to Grimani. "Is it not worth inspecting them?"

The senator deliberated the statement, eyeing the dozens of pools. Each had a unique diameter and depth, yet none seemed to stand out from the others. He nodded his agreement.

Though cautious, the group fanned out, each man inspecting the water with a mixture of curiosity and dread. They ventured deeper, needing to step into the basins, as they blanketed the entire river, scattered like circular mirrors across an aquatic landscape.

"*Cavolo!*" Ponte cursed, stumbling forward and landing with a splash. He scrambled to his knees and groped for the offending obstacle that tripped him. "A root," he muttered, lifting a twisted piece of wood. "Nearly broke my leg on it."

The Protector tried to heave it out, but unable to, he dropped it. The wood slapped the pool as if retreating to its home.

Angelo moved closer to find the root gnarled and coated in a slick layer of grime. As Ponte raised another, Angelo spun his head around. They weren't isolated pieces. Roots were everywhere, submerged just below the surface.

"These pools..." The pieces clicked into place. "They're formed by roots."

"Roots for what?" Vito asked, his eyes widening.

Angelo followed his gaze to the riverbanks. The trees' roots could've extended to the river, but why only here? Why so oddly?

"Not roots," Grimani said, his voice tinged with awe as he studied the aquatic topography beneath his feet. "Branches. This whole thing. What we're standing on... it's a *tree*."

The group fell silent, eyeing the pools, the enormity of the discovery sinking in. The leafless branches took on a sinister quality now that they understood their scope.

Along with Angelo, the men scoured the water, trying to find the source of the branches. It made sense that a tree had toppled and landed in the river, but they couldn't locate a broken trunk. Instead, they found an intact trunk lying in the estuary, angling downward into the earth. It was as if the tree *lived* in the water.

"What kind of tree grows like this?" asked a Protector.

Disquiet settled over Angelo. He'd seen wonders and the impossible with his own eyes. He'd heard tales of the fantastic. Never had he heard of a tree that grew horizontally in water. Whatever this place was, it wasn't natural.

Grimani let out a low whistle. "Siori," he said. "None of these pools are the Fountain of Youth. We've been searching for the wrong prize from the start. Mascari, you may have saved your family after all. For we have found something of equal greatness." His eyes beamed with elation. He extended his hands over the branches as if preaching the Sermon on the Mount. "This tree... it's the *Tree of Life*."

Angelo's stomach tightened. The jungle, domineering as it was, palpitated with darkness. Something ancient and malevolent. He glanced at Izel, who quivered his head almost imperceptibly.

"This tree has been buried," the *Mamo* said, his words dripping with contempt. "Look at how the branches burrow deep into the ground."

The men followed his gaze. Angelo had to admit, it appeared the tree was submerged. Yet it seemed to be alive.

"Who buries a tree?" Vito asked.

The question hung in the air like a specter.

"Those who want to keep the Tree of Life for themselves," Grimani replied. He pointed at the concealed branches. "We dig. I want this tree unearthed." The order came swiftly and without room for dispute.

Vito wiped his brow, his eyes blazing with disbelief. "Dig? This is madness, Grimani. It's a dead tree."

"It is very much alive," the senator said. He lifted one of the dark branches and bent it to display the wood's suppleness.

"It's not what the doge sent us to find, let alone do."

The senator turned, his gaze cold and calculating. "The doge sent us to find the key to eternal life, Vito. If you'd like to return to Venice and explain why we failed, feel free to start walking back."

"Is that some sort of threat?"

Grimani said nothing. Instead, he shot his eyes toward Ponte, who nodded in silent understanding. Before Vito could react, Ponte and two Protectors lurched forward, iron shackles glinting in the dim light.

"What the hell are you doing?" Vito barked, shimmying away as their hands grabbed for him. He drove an elbow into Ponte's abdomen, sending the man staggering with a grunt. One Protector caught Vito's wrist, but he ripped free, his boots slipping in the water.

The second Protector came at him from behind. Vito ducked low and smashed his elbow into the man's ribs.

Satisfaction roared through Angelo as the Venetians turned on each other.

Vito lashed out, but Ponte used his crossbow to hammer his wrist away. The Protectors wrenched Vito's wild arms from behind. Ponte slammed the butt of his crossbow into Vito's stomach. His legs buckled as they drove him down with a splash.

In seconds, his right wrist was locked in an iron manacle. The Protectors hauled him up, and while Angelo laughed, they clamped the other end to *his* left wrist, leaving two feet of unyielding iron between him and his nemesis.

Angelo's smirk vanished. His stomach dropped.

"No," Angelo muttered, staring at his exacerbated incarceration. He cursed himself for letting his guard down. "No, no, no."

"What's the meaning of this?" Vito shouted. He tugged the restraint, rattling the chain and yanking Angelo forward.

Grimani stepped closer, his smile razor thin. "'Nothing is more wretched than the mind of a man conscious of guilt.' The Roman playwright Plautus made that observation. You think I didn't know about you and Paulina?" he said, each word laced with venom.

Vito froze. "What?" he spat, his face a combination of shock and anger. "What are you implying?"

Grimani chuckled. "Be careful with your objections, Vito. The doge knows too. He approved this." He gestured to the surrounding jungle. "Consider your sentence to be an Earthly paradise. Be grateful I'm merciful."

He stepped away then turned back, laughing at Angelo shackled to Vito.

"It's quite fitting, isn't it," he continued. "The two of you, intertwined from the start, now forever separated from your loves. The doge adores irony."

"This is a mistake," Vito said with snarled desperation. "Paulina—"

"Paulina is *my* wife. I will deal with her upon my return. As for you, unless you want to be buried with this tree, I suggest you dig."

Vito's hands balled into fists. Angelo, tethered to him, stayed silent, the gears in his brain turning. He hadn't the faintest how he was intertwined with Paulina, but the name felt like the first word of a curse. Maybe she was connected to Isabella and somehow fit into her torturous fate. He studied Vito from the corner of his eye, noting how the man's defiance melted into distress... or regret.

"Bedding a senator's wife, eh?" he asked.

"Shut up," Vito responded.

"Start digging. The rest of you, build a dam."

Grimani's command snapped the group into motion. Vito didn't dissent further, though his movements were reluctant. Protectors forced Vito and Angelo to their knees. Though it was awkward being chained together, they plunged their hands into the wet earth. The mud was dense, making every scoop a battle. Vito and Angelo had to work in a rhythm, scooping out sludge and, together, bringing it to the bank of the estuary.

After the Izel, the slaves, and the Protectors had gathered enough wood from the banks to build a rudimentary dam, they joined in, their collective effort revealing more knotted branches beneath the surface. The Venetians used two shovels they had brought, as well as their swords.

Hours dragged, each moment punctuated by scrapes of metal and grunts of exertion. Sweat dripped into Angelo's eyes, stinging as he wiped it away with a filthy sleeve. The work was punishing, the sediment sucking at their fingers and slowing their progress.

As the last light of day faded, they uncovered what lay beneath. Mud fell away to reveal a sprawling network of branches, all converging toward a trunk that had been completely buried.

Grimani stood in the center of the canopy, his expression triumphant. "Ropes," he commanded. "I want it raised."

The men groaned but obeyed. They secured ropes around the thickest exposed branches and hitched them to the mule. Angelo, Vito, Izel, and the slaves worked in reluctant unison, their movements clumsy but effective. The mule heehawed in displeasure, but a Protector added encouragement with the broad side of his sword. The ropes creaked under the strain as they lugged, hoisting the tree inch by inch from its muddy grave.

A thunderclap concussed the air.

Startled, the mule whinnied and reared on its hind legs. Angelo quickly calmed the animal, stroking her snout.

The sky above them darkened, the first raindrops splattering against their heads.

"Help them," Grimani shouted in the growing downpour. "We cannot lose it in the rain."

The Protectors followed orders. Even Grimani joined in, gripping the ropes and straining with all his might.

Rain drenched them as they struggled to lift the trunk. Silt turned to slick clay beneath their feet, and the ropes slipped despite their best efforts. Angelo's arms burned with exertion, every muscle screaming. Beside him, Vito cursed, his fury redirected at their pointless task.

Slowly, the tree emerged, its trunk rising like some long-forgotten leviathan. Mud cascaded off the branches as they unfurled.

Izel muttered a prayer in Kogi that Angelo couldn't decipher. A chill ran down his spine. This was no ordinary tree. It wasn't just buried. It had been entombed.

With a final desperate heave, the tree rose, its branches clawing for freedom like skeletal talons. It stood like a dark monolith against the stormy sky, stretching upward in defiance of whoever had hidden it.

Lightning illuminated the scene, casting twisted shadows across foliage. Figures lurked in the jungle, their forms outlined in the flash of light. When Angelo blinked, they were gone. He rattled his head, unsure if fatigue played tricks on his mind.

Grimani's manic laughter cut through the rain's volume. "There it is," he said in awe. He patted the exposed bark. "The key to eternity."

Angelo stared at the tree. Unease coiled in his gut. It felt wrong. Everything about it felt wicked.

"You're mad," Vito said, wiping water from his brow. "Your insanity will kill us all. This is a dead tree. Nothing more."

The mule neighed and pranced about nervously, adding to the tension.

"Make shelter!" Grimani snapped, not hiding his agitation. "You will see my discovery in the morning's light."

The group scattered, hastily throwing together makeshift lean-tos. Angelo and Vito worked in silence, already accustomed to being chained together. Rain poured relentlessly, the jungle alive with water and wind, soaking them to the bone. Thunder rumbled in the distance. The tree loomed above them, a presence that seemed to mock—or maybe revel—in their efforts.

XXIX

THE CHILLY DAMPNESS OF the tunnel seeped through Vito's doublet like guilt permeating his soul. The lantern's glow painted fleeting shadows on the ancient stone walls lined with dozens of urns filled with the ashes of those sentenced to *Paradise*. Behind him, a ladder stretched to the quarters of Tintoretto, the man who had vanquished those souls from our Earthly Realm. With the Painter's permission, Vito used the trapdoor to descend to the tunnel, though he told the master it was for official business. This was where he allowed himself to exist outside the rigid confines of duty and morality. Here, in the bowels of the Palazzo Ducale, he could love Paulina devoid of worry, if only for moments stolen from lives they weren't meant to live.

His pulse quickened at her footsteps echoing in the darkness from the opposite end, which could only be accessed from a canal. She came, as she always did, unperturbed by the grave risks, both physical and spiritual. Each meeting, he wondered if it would be their last. Tonight, he was certain it would be.

When she emerged with her lantern's glimmering light, her presence struck him like a first breath, as if he were being reborn. Her veil obscured her hair, but he knew the brown waves cascading down her back, just as they had when they were young. Her navy gown, modest yet elegant, graced her matronly frame. Her gloved hands carried a wicker basket.

"My love," he said softly, the edge in his voice divulging the apprehension he hadn't permitted himself to feel.

In response, she dropped the basket and embraced him. Her ear pressed against his chest as if listening for the heartbeat that raged for her. She brought her lips to his, connecting their bodies, before disengaging.

"I'm sorry I'm late," she said.

"Did something happen?"

She shook her head. "Benito has become more watchful. I told him the maid ruined one of my dresses and that I needed it mended."

Vito raised an eyebrow. Paulina usually created better excuses. "At this time of night?"

She shrugged. "I said it was the dress I wanted to wear for his departure." She offered him a wry smile. "In truth, it's for you. And you? Pray tell, what does your wife think?"

"That I'm finalizing the expedition's inventories. A fitting lie for a man already bound to treachery." Bitterness laced his tone. "No matter. You're here."

She reached out, trembling. Her fingers brushed against his. "I couldn't bear the thought of you leaving without saying goodbye."

He clasped her hand, feeling its warmth even through the silk. "I fear..." His voice faltered; his heart constricted. "I fear this may be the final time."

Paulina flinched as though struck. "Don't say that."

"How can I not? Even if we survive the journey and this absurd expedition, Benito's suspicions have been raised. I know it. I sense it."

"As do I. But he was asking about Leonardo Ponte, not you."

Vito ran his fingers on an urn, tracing the number. The revelation gave him some comfort but didn't settle him. "He has turned my men against me, especially Ponte. Who knows what they may try on this journey."

Paulina arched her back and met his gaze. "Then strike first."

Her uncompromising, domineering nature was one of her traits he cherished. "You mean to kill him?"

"It would solve our problem, would it not?"

"And my wife?"

She glanced at the dirt floor. "We shall discuss her upon your return. This expedition is most opportune, as if heaven-sent. Use the dangers of the jungle to rid us of Benito forever. Then we can be together."

Vito offered her a warm, genuine smile. The thought of being with her was divine, but doubts lingered about his family and his station. "I want nothing more. Our lives... they are cages we can never escape."

Her lip vibrated, and she turned away. "Then why do we keep doing this? Why do we cling to imaginary hope? To something we can never have? It is the worst form of torture."

"Because I love you," Vito said. "Because I have loved you for twenty-five years, through every lie, every sacrifice. I cannot stop. You are my addiction. My opium."

Paulina's eyes filled with tears, though none fell. "And you are mine." She reached down and stroked his crotch. "Especially your pipe."

She rubbed it some more and kissed him, causing every hair on his body to stand on end. Then, she abruptly stopped.

"I wish we had more time," she said. "Benito questions my every move. He confronted the maid about a letter I received from my dimwitted sister. And he made an off comment about deceitful birds."

Vito's stomach dropped. The comment could have only meant one thing. Vito's moniker—the Bird Brother. Still, he needed to reassure Paulina. "We've taken every precaution. He's grasping at straws."

"Have we?" she asked. "Even if it's just suspicions, when it comes to his pride, it matters not. He's ruthless, even when he's wrong."

Benito Grimani was more than a jealous husband. He was a powerful senator, a nobleman with money, influence, and a penchant for revenge. If he truly suspected their affair, there would be no haven for either of them. Paulina was right. Perhaps this expedition was the perfect opportunity to rid themselves of the whoreson dog.

"I won't let him harm you," Vito said. "I swear it."

"You cannot promise that," Paulina replied. "He is a man who destroys what he cannot control. If he knew, he would..."

She didn't finish the thought, but Vito understood. The cost of their love had already been too high, leaving a trail of darkness in its wake. And yet, he would pay any price to keep her. People had died—Renzo, Isabella, Ivan. Paulina never knew the truth that led to their demise. The truth of what Vito did for her and why

Angelo Mascari was being pursued, though the dunce brought all his troubles upon himself.

"There is something you must know," he said, resolved to protect her at any cost. He feared for her safety. And her soul. He would not let her be sentenced to *Paradise*. He paced the area a bit then took her hands again. "Years ago, I took steps to safeguard our love should the worst come to pass."

Paulina's mouth arched upward. Her eyes widened with a blend of trepidation and excitement. "Of what do you speak?"

"It is safer for you not to know, but if anything happens to me, go to my mother. She knows little, but I've left a letter with her that she will give to you. Promise me you'll seek her out."

"She is in the *Convento di Villa San Fermo*, is she not?"

It had been ten years since Vito's elderly mother took her residence in a convent on the mainland. After his father passed, she became a nun and took her vows as a bride of Christ.

"Sì," he replied. "The letter is sealed. Promise me."

"I promise. I love that you took such action, but why speak of such things? You're coming back minus the bastard. You must."

"I will." He wanted to believe his words, but the weight of his choices pressed heavily on his chest, as much as the odds. He could defeat Grimani in a duel, but should Ponte and twelve Protectors side with his adversary, it would be impossible. Even if he survived, the life waiting for him in Venice was not the one he wanted.

"I know," she said. She leaned up and kissed his lips.

The warmth and wetness of her mouth reinvigorated him.

She reached into her basket, revealing a quilted blanket beneath the mended dress. "I brought this... in case we have time. Which I think we do."

Vito's lips curved into a bittersweet smile. "If we do not in the future, then we must in the present."

They spread the blanket on the dirty floor and lay together, their bodies entwined. When they were younger, their clothes would have already been off, but knowing this could be their last time together, they simply held each other. The lantern's glow bathed them in golden light, casting long shadows that danced on the urns. Vito leaned into her neck, inhaling the faint bouquet of lavender on her soft skin. It was an olfactory sense he would never forget.

When the time came to part, Vito escorted her to the skiff. Their kiss was slow and filled with the sorrow of unspoken goodbyes. Paulina pulled away first, her tears spilling over. "Be safe, my true love. Promise me."

"I promise," he said, though the words may have been a lie.

He pushed her off.

She disappeared into the tunnel's shadows, her lantern's glow fading until he was alone once more. The silence was excruciating, a stark reminder of the emptiness that awaited him. He considered sitting next to the urns, where he could wither away with all those souls. But that wasn't him. He'd never given up on anything in his life. If Paulina was in danger, he needed to do everything to ensure her safety, even if that meant utilizing the contents of her father's journal.

With his heart still in the Palazzo's bowels, Vito climbed the ladder back to his life above. He had made a thousand choices in Paulina's name and would make a thousand more if it meant keeping her in his life. As he reached the trapdoor leading to Tintoretto's room, he worried their time had run out.

XXX

"WAKE UP!"

Angelo opened his eyes to Vito's scowl, staring at him. It was possibly the worst image he'd woken to in his life, and with that face in such proximity, his first thought was to reach out and strangle the neck propping it up.

"We need to be vigilant," Vito said. "I dread what this day brings."

"There is no *we*," Angelo replied, his throat dry from the previous night's sleep. He hocked a wad of phlegm then sat up. The shackle linking him to Vito clinked. His wrist ached from the iron cuff, and the raw irritation mirrored the gnawing sense of dread in his chest. Though he yearned to wrap the chain around Vito's neck, the Protector was right and had clearly sensed the same ominous foreboding. "Could this day be worse than the previous six?"

The storm had passed, but its remnants hung over the camp like a second layer. The dam had been washed away, and with the tree's branches no longer a barrier, the river flowed at full strength. The men stirred sluggishly. Muddy clothes and hair adhered to damp bodies.

Angelo glanced toward the tree, draped in mist and silhouetted against dawn's light. It stretched from the water like a waking giant.

A scream shattered the morning stillness.

A Protector flailed his arms, smacking himself. The exposed skin beneath his tunic pulsated red. As Angelo peered closer, he realized bullet ants scrabbled up the man's arms, chest, neck, and face. They bit into his flesh, their tiny mandibles drawing blood. He sprinted for the water, splashing into the shallows as he clawed at his skin, yelping in pain and panic.

The man's wails caused the mule to wake from a rare moment of calm and bray again.

"*Idiota*," Vito muttered, shaking his head. "Should've checked his bedroll."

Two other Protectors rushed to help their comrade, but it was the water that rid him of the insects. He stumbled out of the river, dripping and trembling, his face flush beneath the red welts.

His frantic dash had churned the muddy water around the tree and drew everyone's attention.

"Get up," Vito said, rising and forcing Angelo to join him.

They approached the riverbank. A strange tint in the water became apparent, a faint iridescent sheen swirling around the roots.

"It's beautiful," Grimani said with genuine reverence.

Angelo followed the senator's gaze. The fog lifted to reveal the branches were teeming with oblong, pale orange fruit. Their smooth skin had a shimmering golden hue. They seemed to Angelo like a species of mango but half the size of the typical variety. There had to be six-dozen fruit hanging from the tree, all looking perfectly ripe.

"Is it possible for fruit to grow so fast?" he asked.

"You see wonders with your own eyes," Ponte replied from behind them. "Yet still you do not believe."

"Aluna is angry," Izel said, joining the group. His skin tone had lost its color; his voice edged with desperation. "We must leave this place. Now."

Grimani turned to face him. A mocking smile played on his lips. "You've said that before, native. Yet here we stand, unharmed. You may know the ways of the jungle, but you know nothing of the world. Nothing of worlds unseen. Nothing of the *soul*. What lies have your ancestors passed down to you about this tree?"

"It is not a lie," Izel shot back. "You speak of worlds unseen. This tree belongs to the demon world. That is why it was buried."

"Who buried it?" the senator asked.

"I know not," replied Izel. "Only that it was long ago. Stories have been passed down. I didn't think the tree was real."

"Oh, it's real." Grimani laughed, a harsh sound that carried no humor. "Look at what it bore forth. It is the food of gods!"

He sloshed into the water and reached for a low-hanging fruit.

"No!" Izel lunged forward, but Ponte and another Protector blocked him and manhandled him into the muck.

Grimani plucked the fruit from its branch. The tree seemed to shudder. The air rippled, causing the hair on Angelo's arms to stand on end.

"What was that?" Vito whispered, glancing around.

Either ignoring the reaction or unaware of it, Grimani held the fruit aloft as if in triumph. Its golden-orange surface sparkled in the dappled sunlight. He brought it to his mouth.

"Don't!" Izel called, shuffling to his feet.

Grimani bit into it with audible relish. Juice, golden like honey, dripped down his chin.

"Delicious," he said. "The sweetest thing I've ever tasted." He took another bite and another, ravenous for the flavor. "*Mare de dio*. It is... it is like eating life itself." He licked the fruit and his fingers, savoring every drop.

Angelo watched in stunned silence, his misgivings deepening. Grimani's eyes seemed brighter. His skin radiated. He brought himself to full stature in a pose brimming with confidence.

"You madman," Izel hollered. "You know not what you have done." Kogi curses spewed from his lips.

"Ignore this native cretin," Grimani said. "Come, my friends. Dine with me. 'Rare is the union of beauty and purity.'"

One by one, Ponte and the Protectors followed Grimani's lead, picking fruit from the tree and plunging their teeth into it. They ate ravenously, starved from the rationed provisions. Juices ran down their mouths.

"It is the fruit of the gods," a Protector declared. He reached for a second one.

"No," Grimani shouted. He drew his sword and brought the point to the man's throat.

"Just one more, sior," the Protector begged, his eyes shifting between the blade and the fruit touching his fingers.

"We shall return the remaining fruit to the doge," Grimani said. "Collect them all," he ordered the group.

The Protector nodded and lowered his hand.

"You see?" Grimani declared with authority. "It is indeed the Tree of Life. Its fruit will give us strength, vitality… immortality."

A chasm formed in the bottom of Angelo's stomach. A profound change occurred in the men who had partaken. Their eyes gleamed with frenetic energy. Their movements were erratic with a dangerous aggression to them. They seemed taller, too, though it could've been that they stood with erect postures and their shoulders squared.

"You have doomed us all," Izel said, his voice trembling with rage.

Invigorated by the fruit, the Protectors ignored him. Their expressions glazed with maniacal glee. The senator licked golden juice, his lips curling into a satisfied sneer.

The tree groaned. Its branches drooped with each fruit stolen by a Protector.

"Doomed?" Grimani stepped toward Izel with a bluster. His face was flush, his pupils wide as though drunk on power. "No, native. You are the one who is doomed."

Izel didn't flinch. His dark eyes blazed with defiance. "You do not understand what you have unleashed. What you have ingested. This tree. Its fruit. It belongs to the demons of this land. It will corrupt you."

Grimani took another bite and hawked the pit. Tiny white worms wriggled out of it. He strode closer to Izel, gripping his pistol hilt. "You're jealous, aren't you? That's it. You wanted the fruit for yourself and your tribe."

"Never," Izel shouted. "Bury the tree again. I can find mushrooms to make you vomit. Do this before it's too late!"

"'Fear created the first gods in the world,'" Grimani said. "The Roman poet, Caecilius Statius."

His hand moved in a blur, the pistol drawn and cocked in one smooth motion.

"No," Angelo screamed, registering what was about to happen. He jerked against the chain that bound him to Vito.

The gunshot cracked through the humid air. Birds and animals returned a chorus of frightened calls.

Izel dropped as if the earth had yanked him down. Blood pooled beneath his head.

Angelo froze, his mind reeling in shock from the sudden murder of his wife's brother—another death that stemmed from his actions. Blinding rage coursed through him. He surged forward, yanking Vito with him, but the chain snapped taut, halting his momentum.

"Bastardo!" Angelo shouted.

Grimani turned, his expression a mask of cold indifference. "Spare me your theatrics, Mascari. I've tolerated the insolence of a prisoner long enough."

Angelo balled his fists, his nails biting into his palms. He wanted nothing more than to launch himself at Grimani, to tear the pistol away and make him pay for what he'd done. But that damned chain kept him tethered and powerless.

"Let me at him," he whispered to Vito.

"With pleasure," the Protector replied.

Angelo smiled.

"Enough," Grimani barked. "Guard them," he ordered the two nearest Protectors. Both gripped an arm and drew their swords. "We move," he announced to the group. "Now gather every piece of fruit. Climb the tree if you must."

The slaves hesitated, their gazes combing Izel's lifeless body. Grimani's glare spurred them into motion. Along with the other Protectors, they plucked the golden fruit and stuffed them into leather sacks and burlap pouches they had repurposed from their spent supplies. The slaves were forced to ascend the branches to reach higher fruit. Each time one was taken, the tree quivered, its branches lifting as though the act of harvesting released ballasts.

Grimani paced beneath the tree, barking orders. "Faster! We'll take it all back to Venice. The doge will reward us with riches, and the Republic will gain a power beyond imagination."

Angelo exchanged a glance with Vito, who looked just as pale and horrified as he felt.

"This is madness," Vito said, stepping forward and yanking Angelo with him. "This isn't what the doge wanted. We were sent to find the Fountain. Establish an outpost. Not pillage some cursed tree!"

Grimani's smile faded into a cold, menacing stare. "What the doge wanted?" He sucked his teeth. "What do you, oh wise adulterer and deceiver, know of our Most Serene's wishes?"

More restless than ever, the mule shuffled around, heehawing as if it sensed the coming danger.

The last of the fruit was stuffed into the sacks, the Protectors' movements frantic and jittery. Grimani surveyed the haul with satisfaction. His chest puffed out like a conqueror admiring his spoils.

"Now," Grimani said, turning toward the remaining supplies. "We need speed. Lighten the load. Start with that damn mule."

A murmur rippled through the group. The Protectors' chests heaved up and down, as if out of breath, as if anxious to follow the command.

"Angelo was correct," Grimani said again. "The animal is dead weight on this journey. Do it."

At once, the Protectors drew their pistols and leveled them at the mule's head.

"No," Angelo shouted. He rushed for the animal, yanking Vito with him, but it was too late.

Gunshots rang out. A cloud of black smoke pillowed into the air. The mule staggered once, then tumbled like a felled tree. Angelo's stomach flipped as the Protectors laughed with a guttural, unsettling sound that no longer resembled human mirth.

"There is more dead weight in our ranks," Grimani said. "Cut all weak links," he commanded.

Madness spread like wildfire. With frenzied bloodlust, the Protectors turned on the slaves, Angelo, and Vito. Pistols fired. Short swords sung. The air filled with screams and the sickening sound of metal meeting flesh as the unfortunate slaves were quickly felled.

"Vito, move," Angelo shouted after dodging a Protector's thrust, the blade skimming his good ear. He kicked the man in the thigh.

Another Protector menaced toward them, pistol raised. He pulled the trigger, but the weapon clicked uselessly.

"I adore this humidity," Vito muttered, his eyes flashing a desperate spark.

Seizing the moment, Angelo and Vito moved as one. The chain between them became a weapon, snapping through the air and whacking the pistol from the Protector's hand. They barreled forward. The iron links snagged the man's neck and wrested him to the ground.

The remaining Protectors charged.

"Run!" Angelo yelled.

"Where?" Vito shot back, his breathing ragged, ready to fight.

"Upstream. Go!"

They bolted, the chain jangling between them as they sprinted up the riverbank into the dense jungle. Bullets whizzed past, tearing through leaves, splintering bark, and ricocheting off boulders.

Behind them, Grimani's voice cut through the bedlam like a blade. "Leave them!" he shouted, his words dripping with mockery. "Let the jungle do our work. You will die in *this* paradise, traitors!"

XXXI

SWEAT CLUNG TO ANGELO like a damp shroud as he sprinted upriver, the chain binding him to Vito clinking with every labored step. Jagged rocks and slick roots threatened to trip them, but they pressed on, driven by sheer survival instinct. Babbling water beside them offered no solace, the sound of its rush was a cruel reminder of their predicament. Angelo's muscles burned, and his lungs ached, but he pressed on, his mind alight with a singular thought: save his family.

"Stop dragging your feet, so-called Protector," he said, his chest heaving.

Vito shot him a withering look and spat. "Be thankful I don't wrap this chain around your neck."

Angelo came to an abrupt halt. The sudden slack in the chain caused Vito to stumble. Angelo rounded on him; he kept his voice sharp and low. "This, like everything, all falls on your shoulders."

"If you'd done your job properly and found the doge's book, all of this would've been avoided. You create your problems, Mascari. You always have."

"Problems?" The word incensed Angelo. "You dare say that? You think Isabella's death—no, imprisonment for eternity—is just another 'problem' I could've avoided?" He jabbed a finger into Vito's sternum. "*You* are to blame for her fate. *You* set the wheels in motion. You and Ivan could've prevented her sentence."

Vito smacked his hand away. His lips crimped into a sneer, but his eyes were hollow. "You murdered my brother, Angelo."

Memories Angelo wished he could erase flared in his mind. His chest tightened. He spoke in a lethal whisper. "He would've killed me if I hadn't. He deserved his end, and you know it. Don't pretend his hands were clean."

Turning back, Vito tugged the chain in the direction from which they'd come. "We can't undo the past," he said. "We *can* still stop Grimani. Come. We're going the wrong way."

A single repeated word caused Angelo's breath to hitch, a brief bump in the rhythm of his inner turmoil. "There is no *we*," he said through clenched teeth.

Vito wheeled on him. "You think I care about you? Or me? You saw what happened to Grimani and the Protectors. You saw what he did to your wife's brother. If he delivers the fruit to the Order, or worse, if they plant new trees and propagate it, their power will grow exponentially. You don't know the Order's capabilities or the extent of their reach. That cursed fruit must never reach Venice."

The passion by which Vito spoke stunned Angelo. The Protector had never seemed to be a righteous man. Angelo still had much to learn about Vito, but he had to admit that the prospect of the Order gaining untapped power was frightful. Any embroilment between him and Vito was mere squabble at this point. He'd have to wait for vengeance. Lifting the chain, he spoke to his adversary with a calm voice.

"We need to find something to rid us of this cursed shackle."

"So there is a *we*?"

Angelo swallowed his hatred of the man and worse, the situation. "Until we're detached." He pointed forward. "There are notes in Cáceres's chronicle. Ramblings, unclear thoughts. Grimani dismissed them, but I think he wrote of a lake."

"A lake?" Vito grumbled, his voice strained but laced with sarcasm. "Is there a blacksmith in the middle of it?"

"Perhaps Cáceres left something behind that will help us break the chain. We're powerless like this."

Vito released a tired exhale, then continued their march. The jungle stretched before them, an endless labyrinth of green shadows. Every rustle, every movement put their nerves on edge.

"Grimani means for you to die in this jungle," Angelo said, wiping sweat from his brow. His mouth was parched, but he didn't dare drink the river water.

Vito stopped to catch his breath. "Seven days from civilization, no food, no supplies, no shelter"—he lifted the iron links for effect—"chained to a wretch of man I despise in a Garden of Eden where everything wants to make you suffer? I might just yet."

"Funny what we call Paradise, eh?" Angelo replied. "Who's Paulina?"

"You've always been quick to judge," Vito said with a scowl, his tone half accusation, half exhaustion.

"And you've always been quick to betray," Angelo said.

After a few steps, Vito spoke again. "There was a girl."

Angelo smiled. "There always is." He glanced at Vito, but the Protector stared straight ahead. "Impossible loves," Angelo continued. "An addiction most difficult to break."

"Love is the ruin of us all."

"Unless we can make it work."

"I did what I could."

"For Paulina?"

Vito didn't respond.

"Grimani's wife, isn't she?" Angelo quavered his head. "You're a dirty dog, Vito." His voice softened a fraction. "I suppose I understand. I was also in love with another man's wife, after all."

Vito scanned the area, yanking Angelo's left wrist. "There needs to be a rock or something we can use to smash this thing."

Angelo didn't reply, but he knew a rock would do nothing on the hefty chain binding them together. "So why did you want the doge's book?"

Vito brought his face inches from Angelo's. "I told you when you were lying in the gutter, that's none of your concern."

"Yet it very much became my concern, did it not?"

"You made it your concern. Keep moving."

Angelo didn't respond. Shared guilt hung between them, unspoken yet palpable.

Though they tried to stay beneath the canopy, the sun grilled them as they climbed a steep embankment, their footing precarious on the loose soil. Sweat dripped from Angelo's brow, stinging his eyes as he squinted at the path ahead. It felt as though the jungle was trying to consume them.

"Did you ever find it?" Angelo asked, his curiosity getting the better of him.

"Find what?"

"The doge's book. It must've been easy with Renzo and Isabella out of the way."

Vito fixed him with a hardened stare. "Do you even know where we're going?"

"So it was never in their bedroom?" Angelo pressed. "You used me for naught?"

"Do you have an inkling of this lake's location?"

"Upstream," Angelo replied, pleased he was getting under his companion's skin. "We need to stick to the river, lest we get lost forever. Unless you have a better idea."

The terrain grew steeper, the muddy soil loose beneath their feet. Angelo tested each foothold before shifting his weight. Vito stumbled and swore along with him, his larger frame less adept at navigating the precarious slope.

"Careful," Angelo said. "I don't plan on dying because you can't keep your balance."

"You don't plan to die at all, do you? Not Angelo, the invincible swordsman."

"I've stared death in the face more times than I can count. I don't fear it, but that doesn't mean I'll roll over and let it take me."

Vito grunted, hauling himself up the incline. "Brave talk for someone who's been running since Venice."

Angelo twisted so quickly that the chain snapped taut and yanked Vito forward. "And you've been what? Chasing me? Hounding me? Dragging your guilt and your secrets across continents?" His voice rose, a raw edge cutting through the jungle's racket, which had returned since they left the tree. "What did you think would happen, Vito? That I'd woo a beauty you thought was nothing but a piece of meat, steal from her, and everything would be fine? That Isabella wouldn't—"

The words choked in his throat.

Vito's lips pressed into a thin line. His knuckles whitened as he gripped the chain. "You were a pawn, yes. You know so little of the world. Here you are on the other side of it, and you still know nothing. Know this. I wasn't the only one who made mistakes."

Before Angelo could retort, a sudden hiss froze him in place. The serpent was nearly invisible. Its pale green scales camouflaged perfectly with the foliage. Angelo spotted it—nestled on a low branch, its head raised and poised to strike.

"Don't move," Angelo whispered.

Vito froze, sensing the danger. "Snake?"

"Pit viper," Angelo said through gritted teeth.

"Venomous?"

"Very."

Vito stiffened. His face blanched. "Lovely. What's the plan?"

Angelo's eyes darted around for a stick or rock he could use as a weapon. The snake's pink tongue flicked out, tasting the air, its golden eyes locked onto them.

Vito's eyes widened in alarm as the snake lashed at his face. Angelo's reflexes kicked in. He swung the chain, the iron catching the snake mid-strike. It connected with a thwap. The serpent's body snapped back and tumbled into the underbrush, slithering away with an angry hiss.

Vito exhaled shakily, his face pale. "You could've let it bite me," he said, half-jesting.

"It's the Garden of Eden. We should resist temptation," Angelo replied with a smile.

"You haven't changed," Vito said, a hint of appreciation in his voice.

The trek was grueling as they continued, with roots that seemed to reach out and trip them on purpose, biting insects, and the ever-present threat of unseen creatures.

"What about that?" Vito asked, pointing to a jagged boulder jutting from the ground.

"Maybe." Angelo studied the rough edge, his sharp gaze assessing. "If we can find something to use as a hammer."

He dug up a rock that he could hold with one hand, then looped the chain over the boulder. "Brace it."

Vito complied and held it taut. Angelo slammed the rock down with all his might. The impact sent a jolt through his arms but the links remained intact. The metal refused to give.

"Try harder," Vito growled.

Angelo shot him a glare. "I didn't realize you were an expert on breaking chains."

"I'm an expert on putting people *in* them," Vito said darkly. "People like you."

"To sentence them to a prison of eternity?"

On the next swing, the rock cracked and split down the middle. Angelo tossed the broken pieces aside with a curse.

"This isn't going to work," he said, not hiding his frustration. "We need something stronger."

The jungle closed in as they trudged forward, unable to find anything suitable to break the chain. It felt like an hour. Or maybe five. Angelo relied on the sun but often couldn't see it through the trees.

"We need to turn back," Vito said beneath a rare gap in the canopy. "We'll sneak up on them. Steal some weapons. Succumb to our fate."

Angelo couldn't disagree. The odds were overwhelmingly against them but venturing deeper into the jungle wasn't any better. They were dead men either way. He gazed up at the crack of blue sky above them. He gasped. Three herons flew overhead, gliding downward.

"Come," he said, urging Vito onward.

Dragging the Protector, Angelo pushed aside foliage to follow the herons' path. Never before had he seen such a welcoming sight. By Providence alone, they were delivered from ruin. A shimmering, expansive lake stretched into the distance.

"Cáceres's lake. *Grassie a Dio.*" Vito crouched at the water's edge. He cupped his hands to drink.

Angelo yanked the shackle to stop him. "Don't."

"What now?" Vito asked, clearly exasperated.

"That water feeds the tree. It's poisoned."

Vito raised an eyebrow. "How do you know that?"

Angelo gestured to the lake. A reddish, nebulous haze hung on the water. Beneath the cloudy surface, silhouettes stirred. He squinted, his breath catching as the shapes resolved into outlines of armored figures, their bodies matted in weeds and silt. The water distorted dead men, but there was no mistaking the conquistadors' rusted helmets, breastplates, and decomposing flesh.

Horror plastered the Protector's face. He jerked upright and stumbled backward. "They drank here and died?"

"No. It is they who poison the water," Angelo replied. "They were drowned. The Tairona rebelled against them. I heard stories from Izel, from his parents or grandparents. The Tairona lured their enemies here with tales of gold. They drowned them to defend their sacred land. Not only soldiers. Priests, too. The Spanish were corrupted. Their blood poisoned the water."

Vito stared across the lake, his expression grim. "Do you think these are Cáceres's men?"

"That would be my guess." Angelo peered into the water. "They could be others. The Tairona did not give up their land without a fight."

"Then this place isn't just cursed. It's a graveyard. Grimani wants to drag that damned fruit back to Venice. As if enough blood hasn't been spilled."

"A graveyard it is." Angelo held up the chain. "One that could hold the key to our salvation. Look."

Vito edged closer and followed Angelo's line of vision. In addition to armor, the dead men had been drowned with their weapons.

Together, they waded into the shallows. The stench of rot accosted them, and the water was viscous around their legs. Using a vine to aid their efforts, they hauled a corpse from the depths. The body was a grotesque sight. Its flesh had sloughed away, revealing patches of bone and rusted chainmail. Worms squirmed in the gaping holes where eyes once were. Angelo fought the urge to retch.

"God above," Vito muttered. He gagged as he removed a rusty dagger from the conquistador's belt.

Angelo plunged his fingers into the silt and retrieved a corroded sword strapped to the conquistador's hip. He pried it free and examined the blade. It was a falchion, a lightweight blade that was curved and could double as a machete. This one was dulled and pitted but sturdy enough for their purpose. "This'll do," he said, hefting it.

They worked together, hammering the chain link against a rock while Angelo wedged the dagger into the weakened metal. Each strike sent vibrations up Angelo's arms, the effort draining what little strength remained. Fatigue, hunger, and thirst were taking their toll.

"Keep at it," Vito grunted, sweat pouring down his face.

Finally, with a sharp crack, the sword shattered. Half the blade ricocheted off the rock, just missing Angelo's nose.

"Would've been an improvement if it hit your other ear," Vito remarked with a rare bit of humor.

"Who knew the Order employs jesters? Now we require another sword."

"No. Look."

The center link had fractured beneath the force of the blows. The men pulled apart, a half arm's length of broken chain dangling from their wrists. Elated, Angelo nearly hugged Vito, and it seemed as though the Protector was poised to do the same, but they stopped themselves. Still, the relief of being free was immediate.

"We need weapons," Angelo said, his mind racing. "Even if rusty."

Vito nodded in agreement. Before long, they had fished out two other bodies and retrieved their ancient falchions. They were in a sorry state, and the leather that had wrapped the hilts had long rotted away.

"They'll have to do," Angelo said, rotating the weapon to gauge the balance.

Vito nodded and did the same. "Grimani has to be stopped. But let's not forget we're outnumbered. They seem to have ravenous strength, and we have a seven-day walk in a jungle that wants us dead."

Angelo smirked. "Then it's a fair fight."

A distant howl bellowed through the trees. A shiver skittered down Angelo's spine as they whirled to face the source.

"Make haste," he said.

XXXII

BACKTRACKING DOWNSTREAM FELT AS though time had been wiped from Angelo. It had been mere hours since they traversed the riverbed and already, there were no signs of their footprints. They hadn't found the Fountain of Youth, yet the rapid growth of vegetation, coupled with the pervasive odor of rot, was so extreme, it gave the impression that their lives had regressed. More than once, they questioned if they were traveling along the same estuary.

No river is ever the same, Isabella whispered into his ear. *Nor is the man who steps in it.*

His beloved's words were true. Every move he'd made since they eradicated her vile husband had hardened him, tempering him like steel in fire. Vito seemed changed too—more judicious and composed—but Angelo would never trust him.

It was possible that they got disoriented at the lake. Then again, it could've been thirst and hunger playing tricks on his mind. Not wanting to reveal his thoughts to Vito and fairly confident they were trudging in the right direction, he soldiered on, with his unlikely companion a few steps behind. A forearm's length of broken chain attached to the iron bracelet clamped around his wrist served as a grim reminder of their tenuous alliance. Though unshackled, they were bound by survival and a mission to stop Grimani and the Protectors. Angelo prayed they wouldn't be too late.

"Tell me again why we didn't immediately go straight after Grimani instead of taking this detour?" Vito asked.

"Because, unlike you, I prefer to stay alive," Angelo said, his throat coarse. He swung the falchion into low-rising palm fronds to cut them away. "You want to charge after ten heavily armed men while unarmed? Next time you're chained to someone else, be my guest. Maybe you can try reasoning with Grimani. Assuming he doesn't put a pistol ball between your eyes."

"Six days to Santa Marta," was Vito's reply. "With no food or potable water. Even if we make it, what then? Grimani will already have turned your town into a graveyard. Or worse."

"Shut up," Angelo said, not wishing to hear his prophecy. "We'll make it. We'll collect rainwater. We can drink the water at the bottom of the falls."

"You think it's purified?"

"It makes sense. We drank from the pool on the way up, and we were fine."

"And food?"

Angelo glanced at him over his shoulder. "Dinner is waiting for us."

"Some sort of Tairona riddle?" Vito asked with a snort.

"You don't know where to look." Angelo swept his hand toward the trees. "Venetians think food comes from markets, neatly packed and salted in barrels. Here, it grows, crawls, jumps, or flies."

"Charming," Vito muttered. "Is that how you survived your other expeditions?"

A smile crossed Angelo's face. "I survived those because I knew when to abort."

As they rounded a bend and emerged in a familiar clearing, Angelo stopped in his tracks so suddenly, Vito collided with him. The Protector must've been equally taken aback, as he said nothing about the impact.

The tree—*the Tree of Death*—rose from the river like an ancient weed that didn't belong. It wasn't massive; many of the kapok and açaí palm trees on the riverbank were far taller. It wasn't that Angelo couldn't identify the species. No, it was the tree's form… or *posture*. Leafless and now barren of fruit, it didn't look so much like a tree but rather a countless-handed arm protruding from the water. Gnarly, twisted fingers pointed accusatorially in every direction, even at them.

"At least we went the right way," Vito whispered, reaffirming Angelo's feelings about the path.

Crouching behind foliage, they scoped the area for signs of the enemy.

"See anyone?" Angelo asked.

Vito shook his head. They approached the campsite with caution. The clearing had been trampled in a frenzy—the kind only crazed men could create. Discarded supplies and overturned bedrolls lay scattered.

"They departed in haste," Vito said, kicking aside an empty saddlebag.

"Or left nothing useful to taunt us." Angelo stepped cautiously toward the tree. The air thickened here, laden with more than the jungle's usual humidity. The tree loomed over them, dark and burnished. Its twisted limbs stretched outward and skyward. Part supplicant frozen mid-plea, part predatory statue, it grasped for anything in its reach.

Each time Angelo glanced at it, a different branch pointed at him, reminding him of all his sins. Of all the ills befallen on those because of his actions.

The whiff of death hit them before they saw the bodies. Angelo rushed to Izel, who lay on his back, his lifeless eyes staring in wonder at the sky. A wave of guilt washed over him as if he were treading water in the Atlantic with no rope. He hadn't a clue what he'd tell Loredana. She lost a brother, and the tribe lost their *Mamo*. He glanced back at the tree. Its crooked branch pointed at him as if to say: *Your finger didn't pull the trigger, but your hand guided the outcome.*

He brought his gaze back to Izel and closed his brother-in-law's eyes, then jumped backward.

Tiny vines covered Izel's ears. Angelo tilted the dead man's head. Vines weren't just covering his skin, they grew *through* his ears. Angelo stood and took a closer look at the corpse. It had been less than a day, but it was already decomposing, reclaimed by Aluna.

Stepping over a tangle of smashed undergrowth, he joined Vito, who crouched at the slaves' bodies. "Murderers," the large Protector said, gazing down at the dead men.

Like Izel, the Africans' bodies were also being taken by the jungle. Angelo made the sign of the cross.

Vito did the same and asked, "Should we bury them?"

"No need," Angelo said. "Aluna is reclaiming them."

He whispered a prayer in Latin and Kogi.

Izel's soul would be pleased to see his body returned to the Earth, but Angelo would need to explain his passing to Loredana and her family. The Tairona were a forgiving people, though they'd suffered so many wrongs at the hands of Europeans. The execution of a Mamo may have been a tipping point.

"Grimani took the shovels anyway," Vito said, breaking Angelo's contemplations.

They turned their attention to the dead mule. Angelo's stomach twisted at the carcass. Flies hovered in lazy spirals, buzzing a funeral dirge over the remnants.

"We should eat her," Vito said.

Angelo snapped his head. The very thought of desecrating the mule gave him the urge to bring his fist into Vito's jaw. Controlling himself, he said, "Maggots. The meat is spoiled."

Vito muttered something about cowards and knelt. He gagged as he attempted to move the bloated body. "Give me a hand," he said. "There's another saddlebag under here."

Reluctantly, Angelo went over, though he had no desire to disturb the animal. Memories of his old equine friend, Linguini, rushed into his mind.

They sat with their backs against the hide and planted their feet for leverage.

"What became of Linguini?" Angelo asked.

"Eh?"

"My horse. The one you took in Genoa."

Vito laughed. "Her name was Bellezza, and she was the doge's, not yours."

Angelo grunted, struggling to budge the mule.

"She died peacefully some years back," Vito said.

Boosted by the knowledge of Linguini's fate, he rammed the mule up just enough for Vito to slide out the bag. Opening it revealed the bounty of their efforts: two loaves of stale bread and a pair of water skins.

"Better than nothing," Vito said.

Angelo snatched a water skin, uncorked it, and sniffed. His nose wrinkled at a pungent, vinegar-like odor. "It's foul." He tossed it away and jerked his thumb at the river. "Probably filled with this water."

Vito shrugged, tucking the supplies into the saddlebag and throwing the whole thing over his shoulder. "At least the bread's not moving."

He ripped off a chunk, shoved it into his mouth, and offered it to Angelo, who did the same. Though he desperately needed liquid, food in his stomach invigorated him.

Angelo turned back to the tree. Its malevolence was almost tangible, pulling at him. Stepping closer, he ran his fingers over the bark. Grooves beneath his touch formed distinct carvings he hadn't noticed previously. Spirals and runes mirrored the talismans they'd found at the falls.

"Find something?" Vito asked, standing beside him.

Angelo traced the etchings. His brow furrowed as the story revealed itself. They were Tairona images, carved years, if not decades, earlier. Stylized figures knelt beneath a radiant sun, their arms raised as if in prayer. Jagged lines—rivers, perhaps—cut through the carvings, converging at the tree. Beneath it, outlines of bodies lying prone, their shapes crude but unmistakably lifeless.

"They warned us," Angelo whispered.

"Who?"

"The Tairona," he said, gesturing to the carvings. "This tree, the fruit... Blood of the conquistadors tainted the water, fed the roots, turned it into... this."

Vito crossed his arms, skepticism plain on his face. "You believe that? It sounds like a convenient legend to keep people away."

"They *buried* it, Vito." Angelo narrowed his eyes, irritated that this man who knew of souls and secrets of the world would not believe what he saw. He sloshed out and joined Vito on the riverbank. "You think Grimani's greed simply happened to stumble upon a tree that corrupts everyone that eats its fruit?"

"Grimani's greed is explanation enough. He doesn't need magic or curses. Only power and men willing to follow him."

"And the strength? The bloodlust?" Angelo felt his face flush. He pointed an angry finger at the dead men and mule. "They killed them in cold blood for no reason other than sport."

"Like I said," Vito replied. "Greed and power."

Friction gripped Angelo's body. He screwed his eyes shut, unable to recall the root of their squabble. "The Tairona knew things we don't. They understood the jungle, its dangers, and the curse that had destroyed their people." He pointed to the direction they'd come from. "The evil back in that lake. Whether they corrupted the tree or the tree corrupted them, the Tairona wouldn't have concealed a tree for no reason."

"Or they wanted to scare their enemies," Vito said. "Superstition is a powerful weapon. You were afraid of the Ancient Order of the Seventh Sun before you had an inkling of our secrets and power." He menaced toward Angelo, the tree backdropping his large frame. "You were afraid of *me*. You still are."

The argument seemed to manufacture itself. Though never one to shy away from a fight, Angelo stepped back. He kept his voice steady. "You don't have to believe it. But the tree's fruit grew overnight and turned men into monsters. We watched it happen. If you think that's mere superstition, then you're more of a jester than I thought."

Vito's expression darkened to one of resentment. "We don't have time for your nonsense," he said, rattling his head. "Grimani's not going to wait for us to debate folklore."

"We need to kill this thing."

"How?"

Before Angelo could answer, a gust of wind jangled the tree's branches, the sound like dry bones clattering together. Angelo's unease deepened. The Tairona's secrets belonged deep in the earth.

"Send men out here after we get back," Vito said, his voice breaking the spell. "Bury it again. Or chop it down and dig out the roots. Let's make haste."

Angelo nodded reluctantly. He cast one last glance at the tree, unable to shake the feeling that its shadow clung to them.

They continued along the riverbank, their tension heavier than the heat. Angelo focused on the terrain, scanning for anything edible or useful. The jungle could provide if one had the knowledge—and the will—to accept what it offered.

They reached the falls by late afternoon, its volume overtaking the cacophony of insects and birdcalls. The river cascaded off the cliffside in a shimmering torrent, as if plummeting into an endless nightmare.

The two halted. Angelo quickly realized their shared blunder.

"You brought us to the wrong side," Vito yelled, his voice raised over the roar of the falls downstream. "It's impossible to climb down from here."

"You have eyes and legs. You could've said something."

"Some guide you are."

Angelo ignored the comment. He'd had it with his so-called companion. "We need to cross here. The rocks will hold. If you don't trip over your own feet."

Vito scoffed, his face drawn with the same exhaustion that tugged at Angelo's limbs. He dipped his waterskin into the rapids.

"Don't drink yet," Angelo said.

"You said the falls purify the water."

"That's my guess. If it's correct, it would be the bottom."

Groaning but not arguing, Vito straightened and stepped into the rapids. "I've had it with this cursed jungle."

"I don't remember you complaining quite so much, Vito." Angelo faced the Protector. His conquistador's rusty sword offered a muted glint in a shaft of sunlight. "You think this place is cursed because it's inconvenient for you? You've become a prima donna in your old age. Too bad you didn't find the Fountain of Youth."

Vito chuckled, but Angelo didn't say the words in jest. He rested his falchion on his broad shoulder.

"No, Vito," he continued, the water swirling around his knees. "The jungle is cursed because men like Grimani make it so. Men like you."

"Me?" Vito bristled. "I didn't create this nightmare. If you had done what we paid you to do back in Venice, none of this would've happened."

Rage flared in Angelo's chest. "None of this?" His voice dropped to a dangerous low. He wrapped his fingers tight around the sword hilt. "Isabella wouldn't be in *Paradise*? Ivan wouldn't be dead?" He stepped closer, raising the weapon. "You have the gall to blame me for this when you and your brother coaxed me into your schemes. Paid me to clean up your mess with Paulina."

Vito's face hardened. He stepped closer, the water rising to his thighs. "Ivan died because of you. You killed him, not me."

The words hit like a lash. "Ivan was the last man who died by my hand. Yet here we are," Angelo said, his voice cold. "The two of us, alive, while everyone else pays for our sins. Maybe that's the real curse."

Vito's lips twisted into a bitter smile. "You've always been a self-righteous prick."

"You've always been a selfish dog." Angelo shook his head and raised his sword. "No, that's an insult to dogs."

Vito struck first.

Their swords clashed, the impact sending vibrations up Angelo's arm, and the blow knocked him off balance. Swirls of current threatened to sweep him downstream. He yearned for his rapier, but any weapon to finally end this maggot-fed bastard would do. His promise to never kill another man would end. Justifiably so.

Angelo countered, driving his blade toward Vito's midsection. The larger man parried. Their dull swords locked as they grappled for control. The river splashed around them, the end of the raging rapids a backdrop to their duel.

"You've wanted this fight for years," Vito growled, taunting Angelo like a predator sizing up its prey. "You think you're better than me?"

"I've always been better than you," Angelo snapped, sidestepping a swing that sent water spraying into the air. "In every way."

They circled each other, the current towing their legs. The gripless hilt chafed Angelo's palm, but he swallowed the pain. He feinted then struck low, forcing Vito to block and stumble on the slick rocks beneath his feet.

"You fight like an old man," Angelo said.

"You fight like a drunken thug," Vito said with a sneer, regaining his footing.

Angelo slashed toward his opponent's shoulder. The blow glanced off his blade, giving him the upper hand. But Vito surged forward, his falchion swinging in a brutal arc, that Angelo narrowly dodged.

"You've slowed." Vito's voice edged with bitter amusement. "I remember when you—"

Angelo thrust his sword at Vito's chest. The Protector parried and snagged the blade with his crossbar. Angelo drove it forward, but before the blade reached its mark, Vito let out a guttural noise and pitched back into the water, fully submerged. Angelo froze, his sword where his opponent should've been. Yet he hadn't landed a strike.

For a split second, he thought Vito had slipped on the rocks, but then he saw it: something bulky and sinuous moved beneath the surface. The glint of scales caught the sunlight.

"Vito!" Angelo rushed forward as the water churned around the struggling man.

A colossal anaconda, its thick body rippling with muscle, tightened a coil around Vito's chest and dragged him deeper. Vito thrashed to no avail. His sword slipped from his grasp as the snake constricted.

"Damn it," Angelo muttered, his hatred for the bugger eclipsed by instinct—and by a threat greater than them both.

"Kill it!" Vito choked out, his face reddening as the snake's coils constricted further.

Without a second thought, Angelo dove into the water. The current pulled at him as he closed the distance. The anaconda shifted as it carried Vito farther downstream. Angelo reached the mass and thrust his sword with all his strength.

The blade bit into the snake, the rusted edge drawing blood.

The anaconda recoiled, its tail swinging violently into Angelo, thumping him back.

Angelo popped out of the water, sucked air, and hacked down. The blade carved a shallow gash near the snake's jaw.

The anaconda convulsed and released its grip on Vito.

The reprieve was short-lived. As Vito surfaced, gasping for air, the serpent struck again. Its powerful tail wrapped around Angelo's leg and pulled him under.

The river's force swept them all to the rim of the falls. Angelo fought against the current, slashing at the snake's coils in a cloud of bubbles and sunlight.

Then, the world dropped away.

Angelo barely had time to suck in a breath before he plunged over the falls, the anaconda's body coiling around him like a living vice. He rotated in a chaotic tumble of water and sky and hit the pool below with a bone-jarring impact.

The snake's grip slackened, stunned by the fall. Angelo popped up and coughed out water. Still clutching the sword, he swung it down, severing the snake's head from its body.

Vito emerged from the pool, sputtering and cursing. He clambered onto a rocky outcrop, his breathing labored. Angelo followed and collapsed beside him.

An expression of shock and grudging respect plastered Vito's face. "You... you saved me."

Angelo wiped the water from his face, his chest heaving. "Don't thank me." He choked on the water still in his lungs and pointed to the floating serpent. "We needed dinner."

Vito laughed weakly, his head tipping back against the rock. "You're insane, you know that?"

Angelo didn't answer. Instead, he stared up at the raging falls, which he prayed purified the water. And their souls.

XXXIII

THE DAY'S DWINDLING LIGHT shimmered off the pool beneath the waterfall. Though it looked to Angelo as if it were boiling where the falling water hit, farther out, it became remarkably tranquil, a mirror for the violent cliff towering above. He crouched at the edge and wrung water from his shirt.

Vito, still soaked and panting, sat on a smooth rock nearby, absorbing what sun he could. He peeled the saddlebag off his body and dumped out the disintegrated bread. "At least we can use the waterskins," he said, speaking over the spray and whipping wind produced by the falls.

Though parched, neither rushed to the falls. The anaconda floated limp in the pool, its headless body a testament to their slim escape.

"That thing almost made a meal of you," Angelo said with satisfaction, knowing the inverse would soon be the outcome.

"Would've been an easier death than by your rusty sword," Vito shot back, his lip curling.

"Nearly as honorable."

Angelo's muscles ached, his ribs throbbed, and his stomach gnawed in protest, but they had survived the snake and the fall. And each other. So far. Minor victories, though it had been an eternity since anything had gone his way.

Angelo barked a dry laugh, which Vito joined. He couldn't deny an admiration for the Protector's resilience. "Come." He motioned to the snake. "Help me haul it out."

"Why?" Confusion registered on Vito's face.

"You're hungry, aren't you?"

"I thought you said that in jest."

Shaking his bald scalp, Vito joined him as they gripped the anaconda's body. It was heavier than Angelo expected, its muscle dense even when buoyant. They dragged it onto the muddy bank, where it lay sprawled like some ancient monster from the depths.

Vito trod back into the water and fished around until he found his falchion. He picked it up and frowned. "If this snake lived in that river, wouldn't it stand to reason that it drank the poisoned water?"

"A valid concern." Angelo wiped his hands on his damp trousers. "At this point, my stomach is willing to take the risk. If we cook it, perhaps it'll kill the poison."

"What are you going to burn?" Vito plodded out of the pool and gestured to the jungle. "Everything's wet."

Angelo straightened and scanned the undergrowth. The setting sun cast long shadows across the dense foliage, and the jungle's hum grew louder as nocturnal life stirred. A nearby tree's roots were draped in the telltale red fibers of *pau d'arco*.

"Those roots," he said, gliding his fingers over them. "Strip them. They're dry on the inside."

Vito crossed his arms. "So there is a reason we hired you as our guide."

"Not sure I'd call it 'hired,' but we can iron out my true fee later."

After cocking his head, Vito used his sword to hack at the bark, shaving away strips of fibrous material. Angelo, meanwhile, searched for resinous wood. An *almácigo* tree grew twenty paces away. He pried off a chunk of its hardened sap, a trick he'd learned from the Tairona. Resin would burn even in damp conditions.

Once they gathered enough material, they returned it to a sandy spot next to the waterfall pool, where the expedition had camped. Angelo piled the fibers into a small mound on the previous firepit and layered it with resin. He said a quick prayer and reached into his pocket, relieved the small piece of flint hadn't been lost. A few strikes against his blade sent sparks cascading into the nest of fibers. Angelo coaxed the flames with careful breaths until the fire crackled to life.

"Not something you learned in Venice," Vito admitted as he crouched beside him.

Angelo grinned. "I didn't survive this long by luck."

The anaconda's skin was thick, but they carved it into manageable sections with their blades. Angelo skewered the meat on green reeds and set them over the fire. The aroma was faint at first, but as their dinner roasted, a rich gaminess tempted their palates.

"Who's taking the first bite?" Vito asked.

"Together?"

His companion nodded.

When they sunk their teeth into the snake, the taste was better than Angelo expected—slightly chewy but savory, with a hint of the smoky resin.

"Not bad." Vito tore off a piece with his teeth.

"I think we cooked the toxin out. Consider it Amazonian *bisato su l'ara*," Angelo said, referring to a Venetian method of cooking eel on a flat stone surface.

Vito laughed as he chomped through the meaty snake flesh. "One that was overcooked by a day."

Angelo smiled sadly. The mention of the dish conjured an unusual homesickness within him.

The sun dipped below the horizon, and the jungle darkened. With their stomachs full and their throats quenched by the fresh water of the falls, they were in good spirits. They used rocks to sharpen their decrepit swords. As the shadows grew heavier and bird calls gave way to the rustle of unseen creatures, Angelo scanned for predators in the surrounding trees.

"These shadows remind me of my great-uncle," Vito said, eyeing the trees.

"Your great-uncle lived in the jungle?"

Vito chuckled. "Frankly, I never met him. My father told me of his short life. He was a bell ringer and fell in love with a noblewoman beyond his reach. Much like you, come to think of it."

Angelo raised an eyebrow. "You'd think you would've been more sympathetic."

"It didn't cross my mind till now." The Protector shrugged. "A jealous rival tricked my great-uncle into ringing the bells at midnight to impress the noblewoman. As you know, that's a cursed hour in Venice. An ill omen. By dawn, he was accused of dark rituals and thrown to his death from the *campanile*. Now, on stormy nights, some swear they hear the bells tolling on their own… and see a shadow watching from above."

Angelo stared at his companion in disbelief to assess the sincerity of the tale. Without warning, Angelo burst into laughter. Snake meat flew from his mouth.

"You find the death of my great-uncle humorous?"

"Your father told you that story? It's a folktale. The Bellringer of St. Mark's. Every Venetian learns it from age five?"

"Do you speak truthfully?" Vito looked as though his world had been swept away.

"On my honor," Angelo said. He raised his hand before slapping his knee. He didn't typically find mirth at another's expense, but gladly did with Vito.

"We should move," Vito grumbled. "Grimani is already a day ahead."

Angelo wiped his mouth. The conversation had turned serious again. "Traveling at night is suicide."

Vito looked up from the fire, his dour face half-lit by the flames. "Sitting here while Grimani gets farther ahead could be a death sentence."

"They're burdened with more numbers and supplies. I also know the jungle better than them. We'll make good time in daylight."

"Tell me about *our* numbers. How many fighting men are in town?"

The question surprised Angelo but pleased him. He had been so focused on saving his family, he hadn't considered Mateo and his garrison coming to their aid.

"A recent incursion by buccaneers did major damage," he replied, "but there are thirty-four capable soldiers, plus two captains. One is my best friend. The other, not so much."

"We have a fighting chance then. There are a dozen Protectors, plus Grimani and Ponte."

Bats flew overhead, their erratic flight paths drawing Vito's attention. Though the creatures were unsettling, Angelo silently thanked them for hunting flying insects.

"They have the strength of the fruit and the element of surprise," he said.

"Because they don't expect an attack from the jungle?"

Angelo shook his head. "It happens. There have been two Tairona revolts in my time here. But they wouldn't expect an attack from Europeans. The Venetians could pretend to be friendly."

Vito leaned forward, his expression hard. "Then we need to go now. Grimani won't stop until he's in Venice. Maybe not even then. You think he'll hesitate to spread this... this curse?"

The argument was valid, but they were useless to anyone dead. "This jungle kills fools at night. I've seen it. You want to twist an ankle or get attacked by something worse than that snake? I want to get back as much as you. *More* than you. Remember how you left my family? We'll leave at first light."

They worked in silence to prepare a place to sleep. Angelo searched for large palm fronds, their wide leaves perfect for keeping the damp ground at bay. Not far from the fire, he also found a vine-covered tree with a patch of soft moss beneath. Its roots formed a natural barrier against creeping insects.

"We'll need to stay off the ground," Angelo said, laying the fronds on the moss. "It's not perfect, but it'll help."

Vito worked with Angelo to arrange the makeshift bed, though his movements were reluctant. "Never thought I'd share a bed with the man who killed my brother."

Angelo ignored the jab. He focused on the fire, which he stoked with another piece of resinous wood. Flames would keep the predators at bay, at least for a while.

As they settled in, Angelo sat against the tree trunk, his sword resting across his knees. Sleep wouldn't come easily. Staring into the firelight, the weight of their task settled over him. Grimani was a day ahead and had the fruit, men, weapons, supplies, and the backing of the most powerful men in Santa Marta. Yet Angelo had something the Venetians didn't possess: desperation.

Desperation, he knew, could be a powerful weapon.

Despite his shared predicament with Vito, he still hated the man. But he needed him to defeat a common, stronger enemy.

He lay down next to the Protector, who was turned away from him.

"Truce until we defeat an even bigger snake?"

Vito snickered. He extended his hand over his body, as if a tenuous peace offering.

Angelo gripped it. Then clasped his companion's elbow with his other hand.

XXXIV

SMOKE CURLED INTO THE sky like the specter of death beckoning Angelo to tempt fate yet again. His boots sank into the mud on the path to Santa Marta, each step a reminder of the six grueling days he and Vito had endured. The trek had been relentless through dense foliage, oppressive heat, torrential rain, and ceaseless threats. Nights were spent on broad leaves and meshed vines; days were a haze of hunger and exhaustion. Tropical fruits, roasted insects, and small animals provided enough sustenance to keep them moving. They'd spoken little since the waterfall. It was an uneasy alliance as fragile as the brittle rust of their blades.

He felt as wretched as Vito looked and imagined he was also in a sorry state. Their clothes appeared as though horses had trampled them. Their skin was covered in red welts from mosquito bites. Their hair was clumped and mud-streaked. Each had half a chain manacled to his wrist.

As they crested the final ridge, Angelo wanted his heart to leap for joy at being home—a refuge with his family—but Santa Marta sprawled below them in chaos. Alarm bells tolled. Fires raged across the town, smoke staining the afternoon light. His gut curdled at the sight of bodies scattered in the streets like broken dolls.

They crept as close as possible, staying undetected, and crouched at a vantage point.

Venetian Protectors pillaged the town like a plague—crazed, ruthless, and unnaturally strong. Captain Herrera and several of his soldiers, now just as monstrous, marauded with the wild Protectors in a diabolical alliance.

"Grimani must have given them the fruit," Vito said of the Spaniards bolstering the enemy.

"Their numbers may equal Mateo's now. Maybe more," Angelo replied. On their return, he had expected the Spanish soldiers to be defending the town and fighting the Venetians. It was a bold move by Grimani. One that seemed to be paying off.

"That's if your friend hasn't eaten it," Vito said. Shadows hung on his gaunt face. "Imagine the Order proliferating the fruit. Imagine hundreds, or thousands of soldiers under its spell. If he gets to Venice with that fruit, it's over."

A chill rippled through Angelo like the breath of a stalking jaguar. If Mateo had eaten the fruit, they would be up against impossible odds. A disturbing and previously unknown sensation overtook him—fear.

In the distance, street fires illuminated the cathedral's stone façade. His heart clenched. Loredana. Franco. Juanita. Prisoners of a cardinal who betrayed them all. Seeing the carnage on the streets, he prayed that betrayal was their saving grace.

Conch shell horns rang out, calling for reinforcements.

"We need to aid the town."

"We have to stop Grimani before they reach a ship."

Angelo didn't answer. He recognized the gravity of Vito's statement and didn't disagree, but his focus remained on the cathedral. He'd lost too many loved ones. His grip tightened on the metal hilt of the conquistador's falchion.

Without another word, they descended into his adopted hometown, now a battlefield.

Bodies lay sprawled across cobblestones slick with blood. A metallic tang of iron, ash, and death filled the air. Screams mingled with the rattle of steel and the guttural cries of marauding Protectors. Though the scene was dismal, all was not lost. A squadron of unaffected Spanish soldiers and Tairona warriors fought desperately to hold the evil at bay. Mateo wasn't with them; Angelo prayed his friend was somewhere in the town, fighting valiantly. With their numbers already thinned by the pirate attack and falling quickly to the Venetians, their resistance faltered. Grimani and his Protectors carved through them with feral precision, like predators toying with prey.

Sweat soaked Angelo's filthy, torn tunic as he and Vito sprinted through a wreckage-strewn alleyway. Ahead of them, the melee swelled, as if everyone in the town fought each other.

A high-pitched scream called out, pulling Angelo to a halt. Two of Grimani's Protectors dragged a woman from her home. Her pleas for help sliced through Angelo's chest.

The Protectors' movements were jerky, yet fast, as if invisible strings pulled their limbs. One wielded a bloodied rapier, the other a Venetian short sword. They threw the woman into the opposing alley wall. One set his sights on her, but the other jostled him away.

"Hey!" Angelo called.

They turned their attention, and their eyes lit up. Upon recognizing Angelo and Vito, they bared their teeth in animalistic sneers, almost gleefully.

"They survived the jungle," said the red-headed one to his mate, a brute who ogled in disbelief. "Only to die here."

"Strength and speed they may have," Vito said, "but they're still men."

"We need proper weapons." Angelo raised his ancient blade. "Stay close."

The Protectors charged.

Angelo met the ginger, sidestepping just as the man lunged. He swung, aiming for the chest, but his dull sword glanced off the man's leather doublet. The Protector spun, his rapier arcing for Angelo's gut. Angelo dropped to one knee, drove his shoulder into his opponent's midsection, and slammed him into the wall.

The Protector released a snarl. Spittle flew from his lips. Blood on his faced blended with his complexion.

Angelo grunted and wrenched his sword upward. The chain hindered his movements, but the blade caught the exposed area of the man's right armpit. He ground higher, nearly severing the arm. The crazed Protector froze, trembling, then screamed, as if awoken to the reality of pain. He dropped his weapons and clutched his dangling arm before falling to his knees.

Across the alley, Vito fought like a cornered wolf. His large opponent slashed away, faster than Vito parried. His face strained as he deflected blow after blow with his pitiful falchion. The Protector's short sword struck sparks off the wall, forcing Vito to backstep.

Angelo seized the ginger's rapier.

Vito ducked under a swipe, cursed, then rammed his rusty blade into his opponent's side, only for it to snap clean in half. The man laughed and went for Vito's throat.

"Vito!" Angelo launched the rapier through the air. It pierced the attacker's thigh. The Venetian staggered and dropped to his knees. His sword dragged through the mud.

Unflinching, Vito brought his fist across the Protector's face in a wide arc that knocked him out cold. He then snatched the short sword from the man's stiffening hand, flourished it, and sliced the tip across his throat.

"No!" Angelo cried.

Ignoring the plea, Vito withdrew the bloody blade and kicked the corpse for good measure. "*Bastardo.*" He straightened and wiped his brow, admiring the Mongolian short sword. "At last. A real weapon."

"He was one of your men," Angelo said.

"*Was,*" Vito replied. He flipped the body over and reached for a crossbow strapped to the dead Protector's back. He slung it over his shoulder and found a pistol tucked into the sash.

His face flush, Vito marched over to the wounded ginger, who sat with his back against the wall, trembling as he clutched his arm.

"I pray you, sior," the swine said to Vito with tears in his eyes. "Don't kill me."

Angelo raised an eyebrow, wondering if an injury had broken the fruit's spell. He didn't have the opportunity to find out. Vito slammed the pistol butt into the Protector's temple. The man's face landed in a pile of dung.

Angelo dislodged the rapier from the other Protector's thigh and liberated a pistol. He faced Vito, who leered with satisfaction.

"Imagine," he said. "You and me, side by side, saving the world. You'd have laughed me off the Rialto a year ago."

"I would've pushed you off the instant I saw you." Angelo snorted, checking the pistol's powder. "We'll save the town first. Then we'll talk about the world."

He rose to his feet, the rapier feeling like an extension of his arm. He glanced in the cathedral's direction again.

"Angelo." Vito stepped into his line of sight. "I'll go after Grimani. You save your family."

"This whole town is my responsibility. I can't just—"

"Your family is in that cathedral!" Vito's voice cracked like a whip. "If you want to save this town, start with them. You think Grimani or that crooked priest will spare them?"

The words struck hard. He had sworn to defend Santa Marta, to stand between it and any threat. Could he defend the town while his family remained in danger?

Angelo turned to his newfound compatriot and studied his face. The fires reflected in Vito's eyes, and Angelo saw more than the rat who had taken his beloved and tried to kill him on more than one occasion. He saw a soul who had lost much himself, fighting to claw back a shred of redemption. There was no guile there, just determination, and something Angelo hadn't expected.

Trust.

"I'm going to the docks." Vito cocked the crossbow with a bolt. "I can't let them board a ship. Wrongs shall be righted."

The four short words stunned Angelo. He'd made the same proclamation numerous times, including righting wrongs committed by the man standing before him. Vito *had* changed. A decision cemented in Angelo's mind. "I'll meet you there. Don't die before I do," he said before adding a smile. "Unless it's by my hand."

Vito smirked, a ghost of his old arrogance. "Smooth your hair before you see your wife."

The smell of blood and smoke hung in the air as Angelo sprinted across the war-torn streets of Santa Marta. Fires crackled, their glow turning the town into a hellish inferno. Screams rang from all directions and pierced through the tumult of combat. Angelo needed to reach the cathedral, but he had to secure more weapons first. He cut down an alley, slipping in the mud, and made it to his house at the town crest.

He toed the door open.

"Loredana?" he whispered.

No answer.

He ventured farther in and sent a quick prayer of thanks to find his home intact. He grabbed his belt and strapped it on, added two additional primed pistols and two other swords, including his beloved rapier, then burst back onto the street.

As he ran, the stockade loomed through the haze. Its iron bars were lined with faces both desperate and familiar. The pirates.

"Swordsman!" one of them called, fingers curling through the bars. It was Pedro La Tormenta, the pirate captain. "*Por Dios*, let us out!"

Angelo skidded to a halt. "Why would I do that?" he replied in Spanish.

"Because we can fight," said the pirate, yellowed teeth flashing. "You need us, and we need our freedom. You've seen those devils. You want a chance to stop them? Free us, and you'll have it."

"It's because of you that our ranks are depleted," Angelo replied, anger filling his lungs. "Had you not attacked us, we'd be better prepared to defend ourselves."

"Had your king cared about this settlement, he would've better prepared you to defend yourselves."

Angelo clicked his tongue. The impudence of pouring salt on a wound held no bounds.

"Forgive me," Tormenta said, bowing. "That was out of line. You're right. Let us fight with you to make amends."

Angelo stared at the filthy, unshaven, wild-eyed men who killed and raped for sport. Yet the Protectors and their monstrous allies cut through the trained soldiers like wheat. Pirates weren't men of principle, but they were men of survival.

He pointed to Tormenta's wrist and ankle. "Are you able to fight?"

"You inflicted minor scrapes," he replied with a grin.

"Then minor scrapes bested you," Angelo said. "Swear to fight for Santa Marta. And for King Philip III."

The pirate captain kissed his fingers and touched his heart. "By sea and blade, we swear it."

His comrades did the same, pledging their loyalty.

"Should you break your oath," Angelo said. "The hangman's noose will be waiting. Mark my words. You'll not see another sunrise. But by helping to quell this... incident, I will personally vouch on your behalf."

"Aye," Tormenta said. "We will do right by you."

Drawing the Protector's rapier, Angelo broke through the rusted locks with a series of powerful strikes. The doors burst open, and the pirates spilled out like wolves freed from a cage.

"Stop," Angelo said, raising his pistol. "Only the able-bodied men shall come."

"Señor," Tormenta said. "I need all my men."

"The wounded will only slow us down." He spoke to the others, most of whom sat on the cell's floor. "If you are not fully able-bodied, stay in the cell. I shall secure you pardons."

The men grumbled but uttered their agreement. As the pirates filed out, Angelo lowered his rapier to the chest of one with a scarred forehead—the man who tried to rape his wife.

"Not you."

The villain raised his palms in supplication. "Señor, I swear that future crimes will not be committed by my hand."

"Right you are." With a spontaneous swing, Angelo sliced off four fingers.

The rapist bawled in pain.

"Now you are wounded. Back in the cell."

With the sword tip leveled at his chest, the man complied.

"You're a sick bastard," Tormenta said with a toothless grin. "I like it."

"Stay here," Angelo ordered the wounded. Then he turned to the freed men. "The rest of you, get weapons. Find Captain Vargas. Tell him Angel—er, Samuele—released you. Tell him your pledge."

The pirates scattered into the chaos, hungry for a fight. Angelo didn't wait to watch their actions. It was a risk, but he prayed they'd keep their new allegiance. The cathedral was still his destination.

He sprinted for it, his heart hammering. It loomed ahead, its oak doors cracked open. Haunting strains of *Salve Regina* greeted him from within. Rapier in hand, he kicked in one door and scanned the area for threats. The choir's volume increased as he entered. Unlike the exquisiteness he'd heard before, the boys' voices trembled, laced with fright. Scanning the area, Angelo stepped down the nave. Candles in sconces cast jittering silhouettes against the walls.

"Loredana?" he called out, his volume cutting through the choir in the vast chamber.

No answer.

"Villalobos?" he continued. "Release my family. You've no quarrel with them."

"Father, it's a trap!" Franco's voice splintered the air. A slap and a yelp, followed by the sickening thud of a body hitting the floor.

Angelo surged forward and froze at the scene. His boots skidded on the polished marble floor.

Cardinal Villalobos stood in the center of the nave, a towering figure cloaked in crimson, his presence more demonic than divine. One hand clutched Loredana, forcing her against the altar. Her blouse hung torn at the shoulder, her eyes blazing defiance despite her trembling body. The cardinal ran his tongue along her neck, a grotesque mockery of intimacy.

"Get away from her," Angelo hissed. He advanced cautiously.

Villalobos twisted his face into a wicked grin. He released Loredana to applaud. "The prodigal liar returns. Well done, my son. Only I believed you had the willpower to survive the jungle."

Angelo leveled his rapier at the man's throat and took another step. "Release her at once."

"I wouldn't be so quick to make threats, Angelo," the older man replied with a chuckle. "Have you seen the recent additions to my choir?"

With a lump in his throat, Angelo glanced at the singing boys, who stood twenty paces away. His gut roiled in fury. Two Spanish soldiers held loaded crossbows aimed at the children. The soldiers' eyes were glassy. Their bodies twitched from the fruit's effects. They seemed poised to kill at any moment.

In the middle stood Franco and Juanita, pretending to sing though they didn't know the words.

Angelo's mind raced. He couldn't risk attacking Villalobos outright, not with the soldiers ready to kill the children. He raised his arms in surrender but didn't drop his sword.

"You have me," he said. "Release my family and the others."

An unholy glow illuminated Villalobos's face. His lips twisted, revealing teeth stained by golden juice. "You're too late, Angelo. Watch what I'm going to do to your beautiful Tairona whore."

Before Angelo responded, Loredana snatched a candlestick from the altar. With a cry of fury, she swung it at Villalobos, the heavy brass connecting with his shoulder. The Cardinal staggered but didn't release her. Instead, he lashed out and wrenched the candlestick away. With his free hand, he seized her throat and used his unnatural strength to hurl her to the floor.

"Loredana!" Angelo darted toward her, but a bolt zipped in front of his nose, forcing him back. One of the soldiers had turned his aim against him and was already reloading.

The choir ceased singing. Their hymn was replaced with the echoes of every word and action.

Villalobos laughed. "You've taught your wife bravery, Angelo. Impressive."

"I taught her nothing," Angelo replied. "She was born with more courage and honor than you'll ever know."

"A pity it will cost her life."

Every muscle in Angelo's body ignited. While running, he drew his pistol, cocked it, and pulled the trigger. The weapon erupted in his hand, backfiring. He cursed and dropped it, his fingers singed. Ignoring the searing pain, he drew his second rapier as the soldiers moved to encircle him.

The first soldier hurtled forward. Angelo parried. The clang of their weapons reverberated through the cathedral. The soldier disarmed the rapier from Angelo's left hand, which was weighed down by the broken chain, but he crouched and thrust, his cherished rapier slicing across the man's thigh. The soldier cried out and pitched forward with a dull thud. Angelo neutralized him with a swift kick. The sword slid across the floor. The second soldier pressed forward, his crossbow aimed at Angelo's chest.

"Father!" Franco shouted. The boy burst from the choir and tackled the soldier from behind. The bolt fired wide and shattered a stained-glass window. Light streamed in through the cracks as rainbow shards littered the floor. The soldier jammed his heel into the crossbow's foot stirrup and cocked the string. Angelo charged. He drove his rapier through the soldier's left shoulder, then flicked his left wrist to wrap the chain around his knuckles. He cracked his opponent across the jaw. The man dropped his crossbow as he landed unconscious on the floor.

Angelo whirled to check on Franco, relieved to see him unharmed. "Get the others out," he ordered, before remembering the chaos in the town. "No, bring them to the sacristy."

Franco hesitated but obeyed. He herded the choirboys toward the rear of the altar.

Villalobos moved with inhuman speed. He intercepted Angelo before he could reach Loredana. Using the candlestick, the priest unleashed an assault and backed Angelo against a pillar. The Cardinal's strength was monstrous. Angelo blocked each blow, but fatigue settled in. Villalobos pressed closer, preventing Angelo from effectively using his rapier. The Cardinal's fingers closed around Angelo's wrist, his fingers like iron, forcing the sword down.

"Stop!" Juanita charged from the side, wielding a wooden cross like a club. Villalobos swatted her aside, sending the child sprawling across the stone floor.

"This is Venice's best?" he said to Angelo with a laugh. His breath reeked of rot. "You cannot win. The fruit has made me a god."

Angelo twisted free and angled for a side cut, but Villalobos caught the blade with his bare hand. Blood dripped onto the marble, yet the Cardinal didn't flinch. He shoved Angelo backward, sending him sprawling. Angelo tripped over the Spanish soldier and slammed into the marble floor. Spasms of pain shot up his spine.

Villalobos reached into his robe and withdrew another golden fruit, its surface glistening like oil.

"No!" Angelo scrabbled for the fallen crossbow. The effort was agonizing.

The priest brought the fruit to his mouth and sunk his teeth into the flesh. Juices ran down his chin. He opened his mouth wide to take another bite.

Angelo's fingers lighted on the wooden grip. He snatched the weapon, nocked a bolt from the soldier's quiver, and fired in one fluid motion.

The bolt struck the fruit mid-bite. Pulp spray exploded. The shaft impaled Villalobos in the back of the throat and pinned him to a crucifix mounted on a pillar. The wretched priest's eyes bulged. He floundered for the metal dowel protruding from his mouth. His body convulsed. A growl of rage emanated from his lungs, the only sound he could produce. Blood seeped out of his lips, dark and glutinous.

To Angelo's horror, the Cardinal slid the bolt out. It landed on the floor with a feeble clatter.

Angelo forced his body to rise. His vision swam. With his rapier clutched in his right hand, he staggered to the Cardinal and planted the blade in the man's heart.

Villalobos slumped to the base of the altar, silenced forever.

"Angelo," Loredana called. Franco and Juanita rushed over and embraced their mother with all their might.

Compartmentalizing the pain in his back, Angelo stumbled to his family and hugged them. He stroked their cheeks.

"Are you hurt?" he asked. "Did they feed you?"

Tears welled in Loredana's eyes before she answered. "The cardinal is—was—a pox-marked cur, but things went to hell when he ate the fruit."

Angelo yearned to know more, but Villalobos was dead. The immediate concern was his family's safety. "Take our children. Hide in the sacristy with the others and stay there, come what may what you hear."

"What about you?" she asked, tears rolling.

"I must finish this. The town needs me." He knelt beside her, his hand cupping her cheek. "I'll return. I promise."

"I can help, father," Franco said.

Angelo turned to him. "I know, son. And what's the best way you can?"

The boy gazed at his mother and sister. "I'll defend them always."

Angelo kissed his head.

Loredana's lip trembled, but she nodded. "Be careful."

"I will."

"Father?" Juanita said.

"Yes, my sweet one?" Angelo asked, brushing her cheek.

"You look like a rag doll chewed up by a puma."

The apt description gave everyone a moment of mirth. After one last look at his family, Angelo sprinted from the cathedral, his fury a fire that burned away his fear.

The battle on the docks was a storm of steel. Mateo's men, the pirates, and the Tairona fought shoulder to shoulder, holding off the crazed Protectors and soldiers with sheer determination. Vito stood at the heart of it, contending with the enemy.

Angelo rushed into the conflict. Acrid smoke filled his nose as he emerged onto the dock. Wails of the wounded swelled around him. Wooden planks beneath his boots were slick with seawater and blood. Fires raging in the town cast an orange glow that illuminated the chaos: townsfolk fleeing, soldiers battling, and Grimani and his fevered Protectors cutting through anyone in their path as they marched for their ship. Angelo's muscles burned from a week of relentless travel and what seemed like nonstop fighting. Each step felt like dragging a millstone, but there was no time for rest.

"Vito," he shouted, dodging the swing of a Protector.

Vito whirled toward him, pistol raised at Angelo. For a split second, time froze. Angelo saw the weapon aimed at him.

He means to kill you.

The explosion of the pistol jolted the air. Angelo flinched, then heard a strangled cry behind him. A crazed Protector collapsed, a pistol ball lodged in his forehead.

"Watch your back, amigo," Vito called.

Angelo exhaled sharply. "I owe you one."

"No, you don't." Vito pivoted to engage another Protector.

Smiling, Angelo joined him. The two fell into a rhythm, fighting as if they'd trained together for years. Angelo's rapier flashed, slicing through Protectors' limbs. His vow to never kill again was renewed. Together, they pushed toward the docks where Grimani's ship, *La Miravilla*, loomed like a specter.

"Over there!" Vito shouted, pointing toward corrupted Spanish soldiers led by Captain Herrera, all as wild as Grimani's Protectors. They were locked in combat with the unaffected Tairona warriors and Spanish soldiers.

Amid the fray, Mateo swung a cutlass. Blood streaked his tunic. His face was a mask of exhaustion. Relief at seeing his friend alive and uncorrupted by the fruit warred with dread as Angelo sprinted toward him, his breath hitching.

"Grassie a dio," he said, not hiding the Venetian. "I'm glad you're well, my friend."

Mateo turned. Disbelief froze his features. "Samuele? We thought you were dead—"

"It's Angelo," he corrected, gripping Mateo's shoulder. "No more lies."

Mateo's face hardened, though his eyes exposed a trace of happiness. "I thought—" He shook his head. "You lied to me. I trusted you."

"I'll answer for that later," Angelo said, his gaze sweeping the docks. "Right now, we stop Grimani."

Mateo hesitated then nodded and gripped Angelo's arm. "Don't you dare die on me again."

Before Angelo could reply, Captain Herrera charged, his saber flaring in the sunlight.

"Down!" Angelo shoved Mateo aside, raising his rapier to block the strike. The force jarred his arm to the shoulder, but he held firm. Herrera sneered, his strength unnatural, and plowed Angelo back, sending him skidding across the blood-slick planks.

"Kill the traitor. Governor Ruiz's orders." Herrera pointed his blade at Angelo with a drooling smile. "Though I would've gleefully had done it anyway."

Before the possessed man could strike again, Mateo's cutlass found Herrera's shoulder. The opposing Spanish captain roared, clutching his wound.

Angelo popped to his feet, his chest heaving, and darted forward. Each thrust and parry was a prayer. He aimed his strikes to disarm and maim, not kill.

Behind them, Mateo joined the Tairona, who sparred with Herrera's men.

Herrera swung wildly, his movements erratic and brutal, but Angelo stayed calm, finding openings where none seemed possible. It seemed as though he had no weakness.

Then find a strength and exploit it.

Isabella said the words in his mind, but the advice was from his Genoese friend, Samuele.

Herrera fought like a demon, charging at Angelo, despite his injury. He hacked away, backing Angelo toward the edge of the dock. Just as the Spaniard increased his assault, Angelo dove out of the way. Herrera's momentum carried him off the last plank and into the sea.

Angelo didn't bother to watch the man's fate. Nearby, Governor Ruiz bellowed commands, his face twisted with fury. His ornate armor gleamed, a stark distinction to the chaos around him.

"Governor!" Angelo sprinted the length of the dock to him. "This ends now."

Ruiz turned, his expression darkening. "You! Ends? You are witnessing ascension!"

The governor drew his pistol and leveled it at Angelo. Before he could fire, Mateo's cutlass swept in, striking Ruiz in the neck. His weapon clattered to the planks. Blood spurted from the wound. Ruiz stumbled, clutching his neck, and glared at Mateo.

"You will hang for this!"

"Not before you," Mateo said coldly, delivering a swift kick to Ruiz's chest that sent him sprawling. "You betrayed your people."

Angelo knelt beside the fallen governor. "There's still time for repentance. There must be a way to lift the fruit's curse."

The dock trembled beneath Angelo's feet. He looked up to find the footfalls of Grimani striding toward them, flanked by Ponte and five Protectors, their eyes wide with predatory gazes. They all carried juice-soaked sacks, bulging with what Angelo assumed was the fruit.

"Lo and behold," Grimani called, the derision in his voice cutting through the bedlam. "They survived the Hades that is the jungle. I must say, I'm impressed. You survived long enough to meet your end here."

Angelo rose, tightening his grip on his rapier. "You murdered my wife's brother!"

"And many more," Grimani said with a shrug. He drew his blade. "Come, defender of the damned. Be next on my list."

The fight was a blur of motion and sound. Vito joined Angelo, the two fighting side by side, weapons clashing against the invaders. Angelo's breath came in ragged gasps, his arms weak with the effort of each swing. Every strike was met with unnatural strength that easily parried his blows. Grimani moved like a phantom, his derisory skill offset by his speed and brutality. Constantly on the defensive, Angelo parried, his mind racing for a way to turn the tide. Heeding his old friend's advice, Angelo sought to exploit a strength.

"You're outmatched," Grimani said. His blade sliced through the air.

"The story of my life." Angelo ducked under a strike, rolled, and landed a blow on Grimani's thigh, slicing it clean through.

Blood gurgled from the wound. The senator staggered but maintained his footing. Instead, he stood tall and released a haunting bellow. Angelo took his stance, ready to go on the offensive.

A weight crashed onto his back, throwing him off balance. Filthy fingers jimmied something moist, fleshy, and wrong into his mouth. Grimani cackled with laughter and bolted for his ship.

The realization struck. Some damn Protector had stuffed a fruit between his teeth. Angelo twisted his sword, driving the blade into the man's side. A sharp yelp, then the Protector slid off and sprinted for his comrades.

Angelo clawed the fruit free, gagging. Vito and Mateo rushed to his aid. Without warning, Vito slugged Angelo in the gut, causing him to retch.

"That'll leave a bruise," he said, spitting out remaining morsels. "Thank you."

"I can do it again if you'd like," Vito replied with a smile.

The three of them turned to *La Miravilla*. Grimani and the Protectors had already boarded. They brandished their weapons and barked orders at the captain and crew, who unmoored and hoisted up the ropes.

Angelo, Vito, and Mateo sprinted toward the ship, but two Protectors blocked their path, ready for another fight. On the deck, Grimani waved mockingly. "*Ciao, amighi*. I will give your regards to Venezia," he called down before turning to the captain of *La Miravilla*. "Hoist anchor!"

The captain barked orders to his crew.

"'I am climbing a difficult road, but the glory gives me strength,'" Grimani called, with a taunting gloat and flourish of his hand.

As the three engaged with the two Protectors, the ship's sails opened. It caught a wind and drifted away into the open blue waters.

"We need a ship," Vito said. He parried a blow and landed a strike in the Protector's throat. "So I can cut out that pillock's tongue."

Mateo made a similar move, whisking his cutlass across his attacker's chest. He rammed him off the edge to join Herrera.

Angelo scanned the area and pointed to *San Cristóbal*. "Cadamosto's ship," he said. "With the pirates' help, he can crew it."

"Is that a good idea?" Vito asked.

"Do you have another one? You need to stop Grimani."

"You're not going?" Mateo asked.

Angelo's mind lingered on his family and the town. Though a few soldiers infected by the fruit were still at large, with Grimani and his men gone, most of the incident was subdued. What would be next? As much as he yearned to aid Vito and stop the spread of evil, he was needed here, in Santa Marta.

"This is my home," he said.

Mateo clapped him on the shoulder. "I'll see you at the tavern." He raced off to join the remaining skirmishes.

"Come," Angelo said to Vito. "Let's get your extra hands."

Joining forces, the two combed the docks and adjacent streets. It took some doing, but before long, they had corralled Tormenta and his remaining men and brought them to Cadamosto's ship.

The pirate captain hesitated before boarding the vessel.

"We'd have taken my ship if my treacherous crew hadn't deserted me like mangy curs in heat," he said.

"You'll follow a new captain now," Angelo commanded. "Remember my pledge."

Tormenta released a low growl.

"Are we in accord?"

The now-former pirate captain nodded his head extended his hand, which Angelo clasped.

"Captain Cadamosto is an honest man," Angelo said. "You and your crew follow his orders, and you shall be treated fairly."

"What in blazes are ye dilly-dallyin' about for?" Cadamosto called down from the gunwale. "Stop swingin' yer runnions and get aboard! We've a black-hearted knave to run down!"

The buccaneers tramped up the gangway.

Angelo stopped Vito. "*Bona fortuna*. Good luck, my friend. I never thought I'd say this, but it was an honor fighting by your side."

Vito eyed Angelo's open hand but didn't shake it. Instead, he inhaled deeply. He gazed at the horizon before turning back to his newfound comrade. His expression darkened. "There's a way to stop the Order. To free Isabella."

The words hit Angelo like an anchor dropping onto him. He had resolved to stay in Santa Marta, to be the town defender and, more importantly, his family's defender. If there truly was a way to free Isabella, he could not forgo that obligation—his *first* vow.

The nobleman's words from all those years ago, on the night he left Venice, rang anew.

"I'll send word when it's safe to return. When we can free Isabella and the others."

"How?" Angelo asked his unlikely friend.

"We destroy the Sun Crystal."

Angelo knew Vito wasn't sent to retrieve him to destroy the Order, but how could he refuse Providence?

"Give me ten minutes."

Angelo burst into the cathedral with singular purpose, his boots hammering the stone floor. He reached the sacristy and pounded on the heavy wooden door.

"Loredana," he called, out of breath. "It's me. It's safe. The town is secured."

A heartbeat overtook the moment. Then the lock scraped, the door wrenched open, and his family surged into his arms. The other youths streamed out.

"Go, children," Angelo said. "Run to your parents."

As they left, Franco sobbed as though releasing his father would shatter an unseen enchantment. Juanita clung to his waist, her small hands gripping Angelo's filthy tunic.

Loredana held him just as fiercely, her warm breath against his neck. He didn't speak. He couldn't. The weight of their relief pressed into him. Angelo buried his face in their hair, inhaling her familiar scent. Alive. Safe.

His son pulled back first, wiping his eyes. "I knew you'd come."

Juanita's voice was muffled against his chest. "I prayed for you, Papa."

Angelo kissed the top of her head and smoothed down her tangled locks. "I heard you, little one." He met Franco's gaze, gripping his son's shoulder. "And you. You kept them safe, didn't you?"

His son nodded.

"You did well." Angelo's voice cracked. He reached for Loredana again, drawing her closer. The thought of leaving his family filled him with loathing.

She cupped his face, reaching every line of fatigue, bloodshed, and unfinished business. "Are you hurt?"

"Not enough to matter."

Her fingers tightened, just for a moment, then she nodded. She understood. She always had.

Angelo exhaled, bracing himself. "Children, I need to speak with your mother."

The children nodded in understanding and stepped away. As Angelo led Loredana out of their earshot, he cast a glance at his son and daughter. Franco sat beside his sister, one arm slung protectively over her shoulder. Angelo's chest ached with an unspoken vastness.

Then he turned to his wife, gripping her hand.

"Villalobos, those men," he began. "We found something in the jungle."

Loredana brought her gaze to the dead cardinal. The fruit lay squashed in his hand. "The tree. It is a curse upon these lands."

Angelo wiped his mouth. He disheveled his hair and smoothed it back, a motion he hadn't done in years, but he needed the confidence.

"Izel." His voice hitched. "I'm so sorry. They killed your brother. I couldn't stop them."

Tears filled her eyes, but they didn't fall. "The tree? Does it still stand?"

"It does."

"It needs to be buried again. I will tell my people."

Angelo nodded. "Yes, my love. Tell them to destroy it. The fruit could be a curse upon the world."

"What are you saying? You said the threat was vanquished."

"It's worse. Some men took a ship with the fruit. They mean to propagate it. The evil will spread."

Her face darkened. Anger filled her eyes. But her voice didn't waver. "You mustn't let that happen."

Angelo's heart twisted as he thought of his family. He gazed at his children, hugging each other on the floor in the opposite corner. "I can't leave you."

Loredana grasped his hands in hers. He'd never seen her with such resoluteness in her eyes. "You'll never forgive yourself if you let them get away. Please, my sweet.

"I can't." He again looked at their children, who watched him with trusting eyes.

"Avenge my brother," Loredana said. "Defeat your enemies." She took his chin and forced him to look her in the eye. "Conquer your ghosts. Then come home."

She beckoned Franco and Juanita over and took their hands. "Your father must go on a journey, children. Bid him safe travels."

"No." Angelo bit his fist to force back the tears threatening to fall. Vito and Cadamosto waited for him, but he couldn't bring himself to leave.

Franco gripped his shoulder, prompting Angelo to meet his son's gaze. "Your courage is for the history books," the boy said, repeating his father's words from a fortnight prior. "Use your sword. Vanquish those men. Then come back to Santa Marta, for your place is here."

Whether Franco had overheard his parents' conversation or he was keenly aware of the situation, Angelo knew not. There was one thing he did know—the boy was right. He would not fail him.

"I shall return," he said. "I promise. Over any distance. Over any time."

The children didn't sob. They were stronger than that.

Angelo scrutinized Franco. "The day the pirates assaulted the town. Remember when you joined me at the vault?"

The words caused the boy's eyes to well. "I'm sorry, father. I—"

"It's okay, my son. I would've done the same thing."

"You'd disobey your father's words?"

"If I thought I was helping, yes."

Angelo wiped his son's tears. Franco returned the gesture with a confused smile.

"But," Angelo continued, "a boy may think he's making the right decision when, in fact, his father knows from experience. I need you to be a man now. Defend your mother and sister. Obey orders from authority, so long as it does not conflict with your primary charge. Understood?"

Franco gave a stern nod. "I promise."

After kissing them and saying their final goodbyes, Angelo left the cathedral and sprinted to Cadamosto's caravel, its sails unfurling in the darkening sky. Pirates worked alongside the meager crew, following their new captain's commands.

"Permission for one more to come aboard, Capitán Cadamosto?" Angelo called up.

The old man grinned down at his friend and pulled the pipe from his lips. "Aye. Do it posthaste. It wouldn't be a journey without you, Angelo."

XXXV

As the *San Cristóbal* pulled away from the dock, the wreckage of Santa Marta receded into the distance. The wind carried them away, the sea stretching before them like a reckoning. Angelo didn't know which ship was faster, but if they couldn't catch them at sea, they would at the nearest port.

With the pirates, he liked their odds, though he feared Grimani would feed the fruit to the entire crew of *La Miravilla*. He'd need to strategize with Vito, and perhaps Pedro La Tormenta. He was the wild card.

Isabella's crucifix dangled over his shirt. His hand subconsciously went to it. He kissed it and tucked it back in to keep it close to his heart. Santa Marta receded in the distance. Loredana was a fading warmth he already ached for. He could still hear Juanita's sleepy murmur and feel the growing strength of his son's hands. Leaving them gutted him, but Loredana was right. He needed to avenge Izel, defeat his enemies, and conquer his ghosts. He wouldn't lose sight of the mission. Grimani needed to be stopped. The Order needed to be stopped.

If there's a way...

Isabella's voice was louder than it had been in years.

Providence delivered another chance. He saved his family. Finally, he would save Isabella.

"If there's a way, I will free you," he said to his beloved. "However long it takes."

"We need to stop them before they reach Venice, Angelo."

He turned to find Vito standing next to him, his eyes on the horizon.

"Letting Venice burn isn't the worst thing that could happen," Angelo said.

Vito straightened. "And your friends? Your family? Your *Venetian* family? Allow the Order to win?"

"Never. Come." Angelo crossed the main deck, strode up the quarterdeck, and joined Cadamosto.

"Loosen the halyards. Let those sails breathe, men!" His voice carried above the chaos of the harbor as he pointed to the rigging. The ship's motion was already sobering him up. "You there! Haul on that mainsail. Put your backs into it, or Grimani'll be leagues ahead by sunset!"

The pirates, mingled with Cadamosto's loyal crew, scrambled to obey. One man shimmied up the mast and tied off the lines as the square sails billowed in the wind.

"Anchors aweigh," their new captain shouted. "Brace the yardarms to starboard. I want her bow cutting the water!"

A pirate called down from the crow's nest, "*La Miravilla's* rounding the point, heading north by northeast!"

Cadamosto grinned. "We'll shadow her like a shark. Steady the helm. Keep us tight to the wind." He turned to Angelo and Vito. "Pray the devil doesn't favor her, or we'll be chasing that scurvy rogue to the ends of the earth."

Angelo squinted at the horizon, just making out the silhouette of Grimani's ship.

"If it means him feeling the edge of my blade, I shall do just that."

PART III

AVENGER

"Justice always whirls in equal measure."

- William Shakespeare

XXXVI

Caribbean Sea

17TH OF MAY, 1613

"More sail! We're nearly on them!" Angelo Mascari's voice cut through the salty gusts lashing his face.

The *San Cristóbal* coursed through the chop, sails bellied full. The mainsail strained against the yard, the fore-topsail snapped, and water crashed over the bow. Angelo gripped the quarterdeck rail, eyes locked on the closing silhouette of *La Miravilla*. For the better part of the day, they'd been shadowing Senator Benito Grimani in a desperate pursuit to prevent him from returning to Venice.

Their position was precarious at best—a ship barely armed, a crew stitched from oaths and desperation, and men who'd once tried to kill each other. Not long ago, they all would've slit each other's throats. Now, they sailed beside one another with shared purpose.

"This is our chance," Angelo called again.

Tormenta's pirates winched lines, but the *San Cristóbal's* official crew hesitated.

"Do as he says," yelled Sebastiano Cadamosto. The grizzled captain stalked up behind Angelo, boots pounding across the wet planks. "Let's be clear, Mascari. I command this vessel. You want to spout orders, buy your own damned ship."

Angelo knew his trespass, but in the heat of the chase, only victory mattered. A similarly sized caravel, *La Miravilla's* hull sliced through the sea like a knife. Gray sails against a gray sea and sinking sun. He could almost identify its passengers now. Grimani. Ponte. Other Protectors of the Order of the Seventh Sun. Enemies whose minds and bodies had been poisoned further by a forbidden fruit from the Amazon. If the Protectors weren't stopped, they'd reach Venice and propagate their treasure. The Order would spread its tentacles across the world. His family would be killed, Isabella would be lost, and countless others would be imprisoned in *Paradise*.

"Unfurl the topgallants and brace the yards to starboard," Cadamosto cried. "Tighten every line!"

The captain's old merchant vessel, armed with little more than two cannons, two swivel guns, and a lifetime of stubbornness, reeled onward. She wasn't built for war. Neither was Angelo. Like the ship, he was lean and quick, a master at his vocation. But swordsmanship and soldiering were chalk and cheese.

Yet there he stood. Ready to charge headfirst into the fray.

Angelo squinted through brine-spattered haze at *La Miravilla* as they closed the gap. An erratic Protector waved his arms, then wrenched a Spanish sailor off a mast. The poor man shielded his face, then scampered to wherever the Protector pointed.

"They're running for Española Island," Cadamosto said, eyeing the scene. "They'll seek food and fresh men in Santo Domingo."

"They will not get it," said Vito Uccello as he joined them. "They *cannot* get it."

Unlike Angelo, Vito *was* built for war. Hell, it wouldn't have surprised Angelo if the former Protector was born on a battlefield. His fearlessness was eclipsed only by his solemnity.

The broken iron cuff clamped around Angelo's wrist was a constant reminder of the pain that connected him to the man, both literally and symbolically. Half a chain swung from it like a pendulum. They'd cracked it in the jungle, but in truth, they'd already been tethered for twenty-five years. His eyes flicked to Vito's wrist. A matching shackle. Remnants from a week ago. A world ago.

Cadamosto's men darted about their ship, hands blurring as they fought the clock and sea in an uneasy alliance with ten of Tormenta's buccaneers, spared the noose in Santa Marta, sworn to fight Grimani instead. They had attacked Angelo's home just three weeks prior. The death and destruction they'd caused was severe, but after Grimani and the berserking Protectors raided the colonial town, Angelo had little choice but to recruit the pirates' aid. They'd kept their word and fought valiantly. Now, they were crucial in hunting down the whoreson Venetian senator, working in unison with Cadamosto's skeleton crew.

Tormenta, the pirates' brawler of a captain, demoted to Cadamosto's interim quartermaster, climbed the companionway two steps at a time and paced the quarterdeck. He moved with his shoulders high, as if riding the wind, as if he belonged in the storm. Like Vito, Tormenta was built for war. Perhaps more so.

"We'd have her if you let me lead," he grumbled. "My *Rayo de Sangre* would've torn her in half ten leagues back."

Nobody answered. Tormenta wasn't wrong, but they had no alternative. He was lucky not to be swinging from the gallows.

"Ready the cannons," Vito said. "We strike first whilst we maintain the advantage."

"Not yet," Cadamosto replied. "We have but five rounds."

"Five?" Angelo asked. "That's it?"

"This be a merchant ship. You'd best thank the sea we've got that many. We spent four fending off pirates on our last voyage."

Tormenta innocently cleared his throat. "Not at me." He stopped pacing and slapped his chest. "Let me man the bow chaser."

"It's a moving target," Cadamosto replied. "Not a defenseless, stationary town."

A chortle spat from the large pirate's lips. He slapped Angelo's shoulder. "Hardly defenseless." He turned to his new captain. "And how many ships have you taken, *Capitán*? Eh?"

Cadamosto narrowed his eyes but gave a single nod. "Don't miss."

With a smirk, Tormenta vaulted off the quarterdeck and barked commands to two of his men.

"Come." Angelo beckoned Vito. The two hurried down the companionway and crossed the length of the main deck. "We'll catch them. If not on the sea, then at port."

"Before they kill more," Vito replied. "Certainly, before they bring fruit to others in Santo Domingo."

"Others? You have men there?"

"The Order's reach would surprise you."

Angelo swallowed. He knew Cardinal Villalobos was a spy in Santa Marta, but he didn't consider other towns. "If we clash with them in Santo Domingo without forewarning the governor, we'll find ourselves in irons, no matter how crazed Grimani is. We must take them on the open water."

The swell shifted beneath Angelo's boots as he reached the bow. His hand fell to the hilt of his beloved rapier. He yearned to use it against Grimani but had sworn never to kill again. The world didn't care for promises. Not when monsters sailed free.

A shiver crept down his spine. Grimani fled with blood on his hands, yet the graver threat was a prize that would exponentially increase the Order's power. The cursed fruit he carried was rooted in jungle soil, drawn from the blood of conquistadors and ancient Tairona demons, now infecting the minds of men. The Protectors had torn through Santa Marta like a plague. Faster, stronger, and frenzied with a madness that couldn't be reasoned with. They weren't men. Not anymore.

"Brace the foreyard!" Cadamosto called. "She's pulling wind to larboard!"

Behind him, the helmsman steadied the whipstaff, both arms wrapped around it as if wrestling a caiman. The rigging groaned with tension.

Angelo scanned the horizon at the forward rail, leaning into the spray stinging his face. *La Miravilla* loomed one cable ahead as they closed the gap.

Belowdecks, Tormenta bellowed up through the hatch as the ship dipped on a down roll. "Let their ribs taste iron!"

The bow chaser fired with a thunderclap that reverberated through the ship. Smoke unfurled into the air like an attack flag. The hull trembled. A beat passed before Angelo saw the result: a clean strike below *La Miravilla's* waterline. Canvas thrashed as the enemy vessel faltered.

"Bring her abeam," Cadamosto called out, his command hitting like lightning. "Give them our starboard side. Helm to larboard, quarter point!"

The *San Cristóbal* veered. Deckhands scrambled. Angelo and Vito hustled to midship with the boarding crew while pirates loaded grapeshot into the starboard swivel gun.

Angelo cinched his belt. He glanced at Vito. "You ever done anything like this before?"

The imposing man cocked his pistol and checked the charge. "In the Navy. Lepanto."

"Glad we have experience aboard other than pirates."

"Si," Vito said, then jutted his chin at the opposing caravel. "But every Venetian over there has the same or more. Who do you think recruited them? They won't go down easy."

"And them?" Angelo asked, pointing to the Spanish crew of *La Miravilla*. Kidnapped and forced to sail against their will, they trembled as they performed their tasks.

"Not our concern."

Another boom rocked the deck. Tormenta had fired again, squarely hitting *La Miravilla's* main rigging. The mainsail slipped away like a death shroud. With the helm lost, the ship yawed starboard.

A fusillade of wild swivel shot shrieked over them. Angelo hugged the deck along with the other men. Canvas ripped above. A sailor cried out and clutched his leg. The deck shook, but there didn't appear to be any fatal damage.

Vito crouched beside Angelo. "Their madness is our edge."

"Or our demise."

Tormenta climbed up from the forward hatch, bare to the waist, his face slick with sweat. "Ready grappling hooks! Run out boarding planks!"

Pirates followed orders, while others readied scavenged pistols and swords. Tormenta grinned as he strode across the deck, cutlass in hand. Scars marked his back and chest like tally marks.

"Easy!" Cadamosto called as the helmsman brought them closer. "We'll take her, but not too rough. Slide in like you're bedding your sister."

The *San Cristóbal* aligned parallel, twenty yards out. Pirates dumped buckets of seawater on the coiled hemp grappling lines to strengthen them. As they came alongside their enemy, four hooks arced through the air. Each landed true, digging into *La Miravilla's* gunwale. Pirates grunted and heaved. Wood grumbled as the hulls were drawn together, swaying in the surf.

"Away!" Tormenta roared.

With the ropes knotted tight, his men dropped two boarding planks across the ten-foot chasm between the hulls.

"By the blood of a thousand storms," Tormenta shouted. He led the charge, the plank sagging under his weight.

His men followed. One slipped on the surge. Angelo reached for him but was far too late. The pirate vanished beneath the waves. There was no time to mourn; the fight was already underway. Angelo crossed low, hand gripping his rapier, his breath steady. A wild-eyed Protector appeared the moment his boots hit *La Miravilla's* deck. A crossbow bolt zipped past his ear. The pirate behind him yelped and toppled off the plank.

The forward deck was already slick with blood. A Protector charged with a sword in one hand and an axe in the other. Angelo arched his back, dodging a wild thrust. Shifting his stance, he released a backswing into the man's hand. Four fingers and the axe landed on the deck, just missing his toes. Angelo followed by slashing through the man's thigh. As the Protector tumbled forward, Angelo drove his sword into his chest. The man dropped to the deck. Angelo stood frozen for a moment. His vow lay broken before him.

A scream yanked him from his guilt. Vito fired his flintlock and caught a charging Protector in the chest. The man staggered but kept going, unfazed by the wound. Vito drew his Mongolian short sword and met him, while Angelo joined him to head off another Protector. The two battled in tandem, circling and covering each other, former foes now allied to fight Vito's former men.

"I never knew how you fought with that thing," Angelo said of Vito's sword.

"There's no better weapon in close quarters." Vito swept his blade across a charging Protector's chest, as if demonstrating his point.

"Where's Grimani?" Angelo searched for the bastard senator while dodging another thrust.

"He's mine when we find him," Vito replied.

"Not if I find him first."

"He's mine!" Vito shouted, carving his sword across his opponent's face. "Understood?"

Angelo landed a thrust in his attacker's shoulder, withdrew the blade, and slammed the hilt across the man's jaw, sending him to the deck.

"You can have him."

"Go below," called Tormenta to two pirates. "Find a means to give this coffin a little spark!"

His loyal men disengaged from the fighting and jumped down the hatch.

A war cry split open the chaos. From the quarterdeck, Leonardo Ponte, Grimani's lieutenant, hurled a sword. It impaled a pirate against a mast. Blood smeared Ponte's forehead as he leapt down, grabbed the dead man's saber, and charged.

He came at Angelo with a speed and strength that had intensified since the Amazon. Angelo cemented his feet and parried the first blow that knocked his rapier's pommel into his own head. Fueled by madness, the larger man struck again. Angelo had a second to react. Ponte's saber struck Angelo's manacle, sending sparks into the wet air.

Ponte smiled, drool dripping from the corner of his mouth. Angelo seized the moment, using his speed to stab Ponte through the gut. The man barely flinched. He yanked Angelo's rapier from his hands, impaling himself further. Angelo stumbled backward, shocked by the move. The massive Protector powered forth, the sword still embedded inside him. A swell crashed over the deck. Water smashed into both of them, taking out Angelo's legs. He spat out seawater as Ponte loomed over him, withdrawing the rapier from his abdomen. Before he finished, Angelo snatched a rope and tugged. The coils tightened around Ponte's ankle. It was enough for him to lose his balance. A second jerk caused him to slip. His body tossed halfway over the bulwark, the protruding crossguard catching a cleat.

As the ship lolled, Angelo used the momentum to slide beneath his enemy. He gripped his rapier's hilt, twisted his body, and recoiled upward with both boots. A gurgled grunt came from Ponte as his body slid off the blade and tumbled into the sea. Angelo clambered to his feet, his blood-drenched rapier mercifully still in his hand.

The deck thudded and rocked. Smoke seeped through the slats. Flames licked the aft hatch as the two pirates pulled themselves up and rejoined the fight.

A moment later, Grimani emerged from the fore scuttle, his face smeared with blood and soot. He reached down and hoisted up another man, whom he held at knifepoint. Based on his age and torn officer's coat, Angelo assumed this was the captain of *La Miravilla*, coerced into aiding deranged madmen.

Without hesitation, Vito charged across the slick deck. The stunned captain had scant time to react. Grimani slit his throat and shoved the man at Vito. Vito sidestepped and in a fluid motion, intercepted a vicious swipe. The senator fought like a cornered animal, teeth bared.

Angelo parried a strike from a charging Protector but kept his eye on Vito and Grimani. If they didn't kill the bastard, their mission would be lost.

"You think you can have Paulina?" he said with a snarl.

"She's always been mine," Vito replied.

Grimani released a flurry of strikes that battered Vito onto his back.

Seeing his comrade down, Angelo elbowed the Protector in the nose, splattering blood across his face, and sprinted for Vito, yanking him up. Tormenta and two pirates joined them.

Outnumbered, Grimani grinned and let loose a series of controlled strikes at each man, backing them off. A deafening crack drew everyone's attention as a mast splintered and fractured. Angelo dove out of the way. The mast crashed through the weakened deck, opening a cavern that separated Grimani.

"She'll be yours in hell!" he shouted.

The senator spun and made for the *San Cristóbal*. *La Miravilla* pitched violently. Vito, Tormenta, and the pirates jumped the gap. Angelo threw off a sail that had fallen on his legs and readied himself for the leap, but another Protector grabbed him from behind and tackled him. The two men tumbled toward the stern. Angelo's head snapped against the deck. Pain ricocheted into his neck and sternum. Sucking it up, he shimmied out of the Protector's grasp and booted him in the jaw. Unable to gain purchase on blood-slick timber, the man slid into the water, the waves consuming him like a hungry creature. Angelo braced his foot against a mast and watched helplessly as Grimani raced for their ship.

He jumped onto the gunwale and leapt for the *San Cristóbal*. Angelo launched his rapier at Grimani, glancing the senator's calf. It was just enough. Grimani lost his balance and tripped on a rope, his impetus flinging him into the sea.

"Clock's struck, amigos!" Tormenta bellowed to his men. "Off this ship!"

Flames howled, devouring the aft deck. Smoke thickened like wet wool, stinging Angelo's eyes and lungs. He propelled himself off the mast and caught a cleat, swinging his body to the bulwark.

At the midship deck, *La Miravilla's* surviving Spanish crew fell to their knees, palms raised. "Por favor," one begged, eyes wide with terror.

"Let 'em cross," Cadamosto called from his ship. "Move now!"

The boarding planks shuddered with every lurch of the dying ship. The men rushed across. Angelo tightened his grip as *La Miravilla* descended into the depths. A crazed Protector scrabbled toward the *San Cristóbal*. He made it to the plank, but the awkward angle between the two ships caused it to slip off and vanish into the sea, taking the Protector with it. The enemy ship listed, the stern completely underwater. Smoke fountained from the gunports.

"Haste!" Vito shouted. "She's dragging us under!"

Angelo's eyes snapped to his rapier, skidding across the deck. He kicked, caught the hilt with the arch of his boot, snatched it mid-air, and sheathed it in a single motion. A swell tossed the ship, nearly knocking him flat, but he held tight.

Dorsal fins breached the water's surface.

"The sea has a poisoned supper tonight," Cadamosto said from the *San Cristóbal*.

Grimani's shrieks rose over the chop. The senator flailed in the sea, blood trailing from his leg.

"Bring him up," Vito shouted, the urgency evident over his hoarseness. "I need him alive. Else the doge will think I killed them all."

Grimani thrashed his arms to stay afloat. A fin fast approached, then submerged—a ten-foot shark cruised beneath the senator.

"Do it!" Vito called.

Cadamosto gave a curt nod. Two sailors thrust pole hooks into the water and caught Grimani under his arms. They heaved him up just as the shark breached. Grimani kicked wildly, the beast's nose grazing his heel.

Angelo clawed up the canting deck, boots slipping, hand-over-hand on the bulwark. With no safe way to cross, he swung himself over the side and launched himself for a grappling line.

Rope seared his palms as he caught it, but swung wide, missing his mark with his left hand. Unwavering, he unsheathed his sword and slashed through the tether connecting the ships. The rope split. He slammed hard into the *San Cristóbal's* hull. Hands gripped Angelo's shoulders and yanked him up. He collapsed onto the deck, coughing and soaked.

"Cut the lines!" Cadamosto ordered.

Axes fell. Ropes snapped. The *San Cristóbal* wrenched free.

Catching his breath, Angelo staggered up to find Grimani writhing on the deck, resisting the sailors and pirates pressing him down.

"I will kill Paulina!" the senator shouted to Vito. "And force her tits down your throat."

Vito snatched a pole hook from a sailor's hands and rammed it into Grimani's skull. Bone gave with a sickening crunch. The warped man went limp. Two sailors and two pirates dragged him away.

The senator's silence was a short-lived respite. A blast behind them caused the deck to pitch again as *La Miravilla's* powder hold blew. The explosion lifted the bow like a pot lid boiled over. Debris shot skyward. Fireballs danced on the waves. A remaining Protector, his clothes aflame, hurled himself from the inferno.

The sea welcomed him.

With teeth.

"Raise the mainsail," called Cadamosto.

The *San Cristóbal* caught a breeze and coasted from the vortex of sinking wood and blood.

With the fight over, the crew whooped in celebration.

Angelo leaned against the bulwark, soaked and battered, too fatigued to rejoice. His back ached and his ribs throbbed. Vito, Cadamosto, and Tormenta joined him.

“A victory well earned, Venetian,” Tormenta said, clapping Angelo’s back.

“An alliance forged in hatred.” Angelo held out his own calloused hand, which the pirate captain took with a grip hard as oak.

Vito placed his hand over theirs. “Amen to that.”

The men laughed, but it was short and brittle; it was the type of laughter birthed from borrowed time and desperation.

“Can we find transport to Spain in Santa Marta?” Vito asked.

Cadamosto shook his head. “Sí, but we head for Santo Domingo.”

“But my family,” Angelo said, unnerved by their new course.

“They can wait, amigo. We need to restock. Make repairs. And I won’t let that miserable excuse for feces in the brig bleed on my ship a minute longer than I must.”

Angelo gazed back at the remnants of the battle. Charred wreckage receded in the distance as fire clung to drifting timbers and fins cut through red foam.

Beyond the destruction, Santa Marta waited.

His home.

His family.

Undefended.

XXXVII
Santo Domingo, Española Island

A BRUSQUE, INCREDULOUS BARK of a laugh mushroomed into a rolling howl that left Angelo wondering if it would ever end. Governor Diego Gomez slapped the oak table, rattling the gold buttons straining across his brocade doublet. Years in Santo Domingo's humidity had burnished his skin to the color of pale mahogany. Creases around his eyes sunk deeper as he continued laughing, the noise clashing with an indigenous boy determined to continue playing violin. The music was designed to please the Europeans, yet it heightened the tension.

Along with the governor, Angelo sat with Cadamosto and Vito in the mansion's courtyard. A flower-covered trellis shielded them from the sun. A dark-skinned African boy in formal attire replenished their wine, pickled vegetables, and fried dough cakes.

Governor Gomez's close-trimmed beard, streaked with white, bobbed with his jaw and shoulders. Rings flashed on his fingers as he raised them to the ceiling, as if asking Heaven's residents to join him in this comedy.

"Pedro La Tormenta?" the governor managed, finally corralling his reaction. "The most wanted pirate in the Caribbean? The scum who quite literally took his name from the torment he's caused towns and merchant ships?"

Angelo exchanged glances with his friends, neither of whom was amused. The three men had pleaded their case for their compatriot. They hadn't expected outright agreement, yet they also weren't prepared to be doused in plutocratic spittle.

"The very same, my lord." Cadamosto kept his voice cool and collected, though he wiped beads of sweat from his furrowed brow. He took a swig from his goblet.

"Absolutely not," Gomez replied with a snap. All the mirth vanished as the man turned deadly serious. "I granted you an audience only on your loyalty to the crown, Capitán Cadamosto." He turned to Angelo. "And you, Señor Stefanetti, for your service to Santa Marta. I've heard of your heroism, including protecting the town and His Majesty's gold from Tormenta himself. These tales of the pirate's supposed good deeds do not sway my heart. The man would curse the Lord to dine with the devil."

Angelo massaged his sore wrist. Upon arriving in Santo Domingo three days prior, he and Vito promptly visited a blacksmith to rid themselves of their cursed manacles. It had been Angelo's sole prior disembarkment. Though Cadamosto had urged him to take his leave, he had no desire to do so. From what he'd seen on their walk to the governor's house, the port town was a larger version of Santa Marta. While there were surely superior meals and drink, he was content with what he had on board. The only respite he craved was the knowledge that his family was safe. To achieve that, he needed to go home. And that required safe passage of all their crew.

He shifted in his seat, grimacing at the pain smarting across his ribs. His head throbbed, and his back ached. Though he'd finger-combed his hair before their appointment with the governor, he hadn't seen a mirror in weeks and knew his once-black hair and beard had thinned, matted, and grayed even more. He feared he looked a fool, which supported Gomez's reaction to their request.

The governor took a fried dough and planted his teeth in it, half the cake disappearing in his enormous mouth.

"My lord," Angelo said, bowing slightly. "You are wholly correct that three weeks back, Pedro La Tormenta was at the tip of my blade. Had I not taken an oath, I would've taken his life. Yet now..." He met the governor's steady gaze. "I vouch for every word Capitán Cadamosto has said. Were it not for Tormenta, us three would be dead, as would most of Santa Marta."

"Folly. He did it to save himself from the noose." Crumbs spat from the governor's mouth as he scoffed, chewed, and talked. He looked at Vito. "What say you, Venetian? What part do you play in this rubbish?"

The former Protector removed his hat before speaking. "None, Governor," he replied in passable Spanish. "I hold no quarrel nor love for Tormenta. I care nothing for the fate of him nor his men. I can only tell you what I've seen. He's a valiant warrior. Loyal to his word and of more import, to the men he serves—"

"He serves no one," Gomez said. He finished the cake and washed it down with a hefty serving of wine. The servant boy immediately refilled his cup.

As he backed away, the pitcher slipped from his grasp. Clay shards and red wine splattered across the floor, staining the white tiles. The violinist paused for a moment, then continued playing.

"Imbecile!" the governor roared.

"Apologies, my lord," the boy said. He crouched on the floor and used a towel to clean the mess.

Angelo pushed back his chair and joined him to pick up the pitcher shards.

"What are you doing?" asked the governor, aghast.

"He's but a boy," Angelo replied. "I am merely helping him."

"Get back in your seat," Cadamosto whispered through clenched teeth, his tone brimming with contempt.

Realizing he risked angering the governor further, Angelo handed the boy a shard, offering him a quick glance of pity, then returned to his chair.

A look of amazement passed over Gomez. "You think I treat them ill?"

"No, my lord." Angelo lowered his head. Servitude in any form curdled his blood, yet it was not his place to question it. His own actions disgusted him as much as the scene unfolding around him.

"I provide these boys with employ, sustenance, shelter, civility, and dare I say, family. Their parents are deceased." He gestured to the violinist and the servant. "Now they shall be reared in comfort, learning a proper tongue and customs."

"Please accept my humblest apologies, good Governor," Angelo said. "It has been a trying period of late. I know not what came over me."

The governor tipped his head. "Accepted. Now, where were we? Ah, yes. Your absurd request to pardon Pedro La Tormenta."

“There is no question he transgressed in the past,” Vito said, “but he desires to move past them.”

A mosquito landed on the governor’s cheek. He smacked it, smearing blood on his powdered skin. “I cannot abide by your request. Governor Ruiz would laugh me all the way to Madrid. Where the king would have my head.”

“As it may be,” Angelo said, “Governor Ruiz is in need of replacement.”

“What are you talking about?”

“The man was at the heart of the uprising. Sacking the town and townsfolk.”

“Impossible,” said Governor Gomez.

“If you visit Santa Marta, you will see what’s become of our good governor. And what would have been if it were not for Tormenta and his men.” Cadamosto cracked his knuckles. “Now, I understand your young brother has been positioning himself for a governorship. A good word here… a good word there… I do believe most in Santa Marta would welcome his sage leadership.”

Gomez’s lips formed into a thin smile. “I cannot believe this madness is coming from my tongue, but… I shall issue a temporary stay on Tormenta’s warrant under the condition that he and his crew remain on the *San Cristóbal* and be returned to Santa Marta for trial.”

“Gracias, Governor,” Cadamosto said.

“And,” Gomez continued, “should the warrant be lifted permanently, you will offer one-year contracts to the pirates. Tormenta must relinquish command of his former ship, with which I understand half his original crew has absconded. Those men shall receive no such pardon. Do we have an accord?”

“That we do, my lord,” Cadamosto replied, with a gleam in his eyes that Angelo hadn’t seen in years.

Angelo ducked beneath a beam as he entered Cadamosto’s quarters. The walls creaked with the light roll of the tide. A single lantern bobbed from a bronze hook above the dining table, casting flickers across a trio of men caught between past and future. The smell of brine, tar, and roasted meat clung to the low ceiling of the great cabin. The chamber was spacious for a caravel, nestled beneath the poop deck, where the captain conducted his business and entertained guests when ashore.

Tonight, Cadamosto had pulled out all the stops. Though all the stops for a low-level merchant shipper meant a polished oak table no wider than a barrel top, a pair of pewter candlesticks, and four battered wooden stools.

"I've seen enough ports to know the measure of them," Tormenta said.

"Then you've seen none like mine," Vito replied. "No carriages. None. Every crate of spice, every slab of marble, even the stones for the palaces. All brought in by boat. Gondolas, barges, workboats of every kind."

"Even fishwives row to market," Cadamosto chimed in.

"Courtesans float down canals in gondolas with their legs hanging over the gunwales." Angelo planted his tired ass on the lone free stool. "You'd love it, pirate."

Tormenta took a long swig from his pewter mug, tipped his stool backward, and smiled. "*Former* pirate. Thanks to the three of you. Or no thanks? I've yet to decide."

Angelo poured himself a dose from a flagon of rum and toasted Tormenta. "Better to be sailing under the Spanish flag than swinging from its pole."

"True indeed," Tormenta replied. "My sweet madre would be proud."

A platter of a roast suckling pig, its skin blistered and crisp, sat in the center of the table, surrounded by dishes of fried plantains, cassava bread, pickled onions, and a stew of salt cod, tomatoes, and peppers. A bottle of molasses-thick rum and a ceramic jug of watered wine completed the spread.

Cadamosto carved into the pig with a sailor's dagger. Juices dribbled down the skin. "Gentlemen," he said, tossing a slice onto each man's tin plate, "Santo Domingo may be Spanish, but her pigs are Caribbean. Fat, lazy, and cooked in sunshine."

Tormenta chuckled, reaching for the rum. "Sí, and unlike the Spanish Navy, they don't scream when you gut 'em."

Vito smirked into his wine. "You've got a dark sense of humor."

"You'd too, if you'd seen what I've seen," the pirate replied. His thick hair was tied back with a strip of sailcloth. "I'll say this. After two weeks on nary a ship's biscuit and dried beans, this pig must've fallen from fuckin' Heaven."

The pork was tender, the meat spiced with allspice and clove. Though delicious, Angelo swallowed hard. The memory of Loredana's cooking lingered on his palate.

"You've hardly touched your drink," Cadamosto said, pouring rum into his mug. "You planning to remember tonight?"

"I remember too much already," Angelo replied.

Cadamosto reclined his posture, propping his knees against the table's edge. "Well, I for one am glad we all lived through those buggers. Grimani's lot nearly tore us apart." He raised his cup. "To the mad, the damned, and the barely breathing."

Grimani's screams reverberated from the brig through the ship.

A nervous silence bound them as their eyes darted across each other. They'd been dealing with the madness since he woke. The crew would take turns throwing bread into his cell. Only when he slept—which was never for long—did they have any peace.

Tormenta clinked his mug against the captain's. "To the ones still fighting. New crewmates and all."

The room fell into a lull of chewing. Grimani's shouts died down, replaced by the creak of moorings and the distant calls of sailors in port. Somewhere beyond the bulkhead, gulls shrieked over the shallows.

The men tried to resume their conversation, but Angelo heard none of it.

A path lies before you, 'mòre mio. Isabella's voice whispered in his head, soft as candle smoke. *A path home.*

He pressed his thumb into the side of his bandaged wrist until he felt the dull sting. The blacksmith had cut the manacle free, but the metal had bitten deep. Nearly two weeks of weight had left a permanent mark.

"Drink," Cadamosto said, grinning over the tip of his fork. "It's not every day an honest merchant shares his finest rum with a pirate and a pair of Venetian scoundrels."

"Scoundrels?" Vito snorted. "That's generous."

Angelo lifted his gaze and forced a nod.

Vito slid the mug toward him. "The dead don't drink. You're not dead yet."

For once, he's right, Isabella murmured again. *But you will be someday. Do not die with regret.*

"I never thought I'd be saying this," Cadamosto said, his mouth half-full of cassava, "but you've got fire in you. I'm glad to be having ye and yer crew aboard. Even if only for a year."

Tormenta wiped his mouth with the back of his hand and bowed his head in gratitude. "We'll be good shipmates, each of us."

"I admire loyalty," Vito said. "Even among thieves."

The former pirate shot him a toothy grin. "We're all thieves. Some write laws to allow themselves to do it."

"Then stay on for longer than a year," Cadamosto said. "You're welcome."

"Your offer flatters me, but I've got a debt to settle. And a ship to reclaim."

Angelo arched a brow. "After that? You'll change your ways? Pardons can be revoked. No pillaging or raping the innocent?"

"Not the innocent," Tormenta replied with a dark grin. "You've shown me who the true pirates are."

"And you?" Vito asked, pointing his knife in Angelo's direction. "Are you going to finish the job you started?"

The question was more loaded than Vito had intended. It wasn't Angelo who started the job, but Vito. A different job. Now... he didn't know what he wanted. He poured the rum down his throat. The sweetness of the sugarcane numbed the bitterness of the alcohol and mingled with old blood in his memory.

Grimani's screams pierced the room again.

With a scowl, Vito wiped the wine and grease from his facial hair. He had far more growth on his face than on the top of his head. He stood and clasped Angelo's shoulder. "Let's get air."

They stepped onto the deck. The ship bobbed peacefully, anchored in the bay. The sky overhead was stormless but had bruised to purple and orange. Stars poked through the shroud like soft pinpricks. Though it was an overly sentimental act, Angelo gazed at the horizon, toward his home.

The rigging swayed above them. Despite its age and scars, the *San Cristóbal* was a solid beauty, its taffrail carved with a mermaid whose eyes had long since faded to blankness. She pointed eastward, as if daring Angelo to join her.

"We're heading home," Vito said. "To Venice."

Angelo folded his arms. "You are. I return to my home in Santa Marta."

"You think this ends because that black-hearted squid is in chains?"

Dark waves licked the ship, beckoning Angelo. "Grimani's the last of them. The fruit's at the bottom of the ocean. Your Order's dream died with the ship that carried it."

"You know that's not true." Vito's voice was firm yet held a tender sincerity. "The Doge wants more than strength. He wants control. Power. He wants to extend his life and believes the secret lies in that cursed jungle. Quattrone too. You think they'll stop? That they won't send others? Twice as many? Five times as many? They won't cease unless we burn them to ash."

"I made a vow." Angelo clenched his jaw. "To my wife. My children."

Vito leaned in close. "Of all the people under God's canopy, I'm the last to be saying this, but what of the vow you made to Isabella?"

Angelo met his newfound friend's stare. In all the years he'd known him, it was the first time he saw... remorse.

"The jailer wants to free the innocent?"

"Si. Yes, Angelo. I do. All of them. Even those truly guilty. People change. I have. You have. Yes, you've changed. But I see you when you fight. The fire in your soul that burns for justice. You go back to Santa Marta now, and you'll rot with guilt the remainder of your days."

The wind shifted, snapping across Angelo's face.

"Do you know how many souls have been imprisoned since you left Venice?"

Angelo turned to him and raised an eyebrow.

"*Hundreds.*" Vito rubbed his temples, as if disgusted with himself. "Thousands more will follow if we don't act. The Order must be destroyed."

Cadamosto snorted as he approached. "You two are the most dramatic men I've ever met. He's right, Mascari. You've got one last chance. Don't waste it."

"And if pursuing that chance brings harm to my family?"

"Can you not move them?" Vito asked.

Angelo considered the proposition before snickering to himself. "Loredana would scratch her eyes out before doing so."

"Your friend, Mateo," Cadamosto said. "He'll watch over them while you're gone. He's a good man."

"I made my peace long ago," Angelo said to Vito, shaking his head. "Why would I risk it now?"

"You never made your peace. You fled. Peacefulness doesn't translate to peace of mind or peace of the heart. This will never be over until they're ended."

A long exhale escaped Angelo's nostrils. Vito was right. Peace wasn't peace. Not with Isabella trapped in eternal darkness. Not with the Order lurking in every shadow.

"How will we get there?" Angelo asked Cadamosto, half laughing at himself for entertaining the idea. "One last favor?"

The captain rolled his eyes and laughed. "Doubtful it will be the last, but you know I'll say yes. Are you financing this folly?"

"I have some coin in Venice," Vito said.

Cadamosto scratched his beard and adjusted his hat. He spoke to both men. "Save it. It shan't be difficult to find cargo needing transport to Venice."

"What of our most difficult cargo?" Angelo jerked a finger to the brig beneath the deck.

"We'll keep Grimani bound and gagged," Vito said. "He's our proof. I need him to clear my name, and to get close enough to the Doge and Quattrone to remove them from this Earthly realm."

"You shan't be conspiring against me now, are you?" Tormenta's deep voice resonated across the deck as he joined them.

"It would hardly be a conspiracy without you," Cadamosto replied. "Ready to see the world, Mr. Quartermaster?"

Tormenta released a hearty laugh, took a swig from the rum bottle in his hand, and handed it to his new captain. "How do you think I've been making my living? Where do we be heading?"

"To the floating city of your dreams, quartermaster," Angelo replied.

Grimani's mad laughter echoed from between the bulkheads.

XXXVIII

Port of Mestre, Republic of Venice

14th of October, 1613

The *San Cristóbal* glided into the port of Mestre beneath a gray and brooding sky.

"Strike the tops!" Tormenta bellowed from the quarterdeck. "We moor fore and aft."

The crew leapt into action to secure the lateen-rigged mizzen. Chains rattled as anchors splayed into the murky shallows of the Venetian Lagoon. Sailors buzzed with anticipation as they coiled lines and furled canvas. Despite the work, all eyes, even Tormenta's, were fixed on the island city across the water, mouths agape in wonder.

Angelo stood at the starboard bulwark, one hand clutched around the worn wood, his gaze locked on the silhouette of Venice. The city of his birth shimmered like a mirage. It'd been a figment of dissipating dreams for so long, he questioned if it was real. The domes of San Marco, the spires of San Giorgio Maggiore, and the rigid geometry of the Palazzo Ducale loomed like ghostly memories that flooded his mind. From his vantage point, nothing had changed. Not that he presumed it would, but he also didn't expect it to be the same. Even the lagoon's stench of brine and rot stirred something inside him. Truth was, he didn't know what to anticipate—and still didn't.

Twenty-five years. A lifetime. *His* life.

He'd once imagined he would return triumphant, perhaps in a gilded gondola. Years of exile had turned fire into ash. Then came Loredana and the children, and with them, purpose. A fragile peace. He had long surrendered a homecoming to fantasy.

Now, his return was not as a son of Venice, but as its hidden blade with one purpose: to end the Order and by some means yet known, free Isabella.

The Order dies in its cradle.

His beloved's voice whispered in his head, but now, so close to Venice, so close to *her*, it was as if it rode the wind. Soft at first, then rising over all ambient noise.

He pressed his eyes shut, unsure if it was an attempt to block her out or revel in the beauty of the timbre. Once an undertone of warning, now it carried a tremble of pleading.

"Be quick with those lines," Cadamosto called, snapping Angelo back to reality.

Boots clattered. Ropes wrapped canvas. The ship's deck creaked under nearly two-dozen men, all sallow-eyed, anxious for shore leave, and eager to be rid of the heinous cargo they'd carried for five months.

"Where is she?" came a rasping cry from the hold.

A muffled scream followed before a merciful stillness.

Grimani had descended into complete madness somewhere past Madeira. Vito was alone in his desire to keep the senator alive and bore most of the burden, but it also fell on disgruntled deckhands. Feeding the bastard had become an ordeal. Cleaning him was worse. The madman howled at shadows, struck at everything and nothing, and raved in tongues. Despite his chains, he was a threat to every soul aboard.

Vito emerged from belowdecks, his face pale and his expression grim.

"I've wiped up after drunkards and fools," he muttered, dragging a sleeve across his damp brow and streaking the sweat into his gray beard, "but never before have I scrubbed a senator's shit off my boots."

Angelo returned a humorless snort. "You've been doing it your whole life, my friend. That's what you get for surrounding yourself in aristocratic muck."

The former Protector forced a wry smile and donned his hat. "True. But at least the drunkards had the decency to thank their keeper."

For a beat, the two men held each other's gaze, then laughter rumbled between them, born not of joy but of bitter truth only men scarred by the same fights could share.

Bells rang from the San Marco Campanile. They also hadn't changed. Not their pitch nor their rhythm, drawing Angelo's attention back to his city and his past yet again. "The doge and your Exalted Master. They'll welcome Grimani? In his state?"

"I care not two fucks what they'll do with the senator," Vito replied. "He's proof of a self-induced catastrophe that left a squadron dead. His disgrace is my triumph. A show of loyalty for a dying doge."

"Who is your doge now?"

Vito perked an eyebrow at the lack of awareness. "Our illustrious head of state is Doge Marcantonio Memmo. If he still lives. He had one foot in the grave before I departed."

Angelo scratched his beard, wondering if the former Protector had forgotten a key detail about Memmo's original instruction. "You are aware the Fountain does not exist?"

"Matters not. The myth is as real as wood." Vito winked and tapped his foot. "That despicable miscreant in the brig thwarted our efforts to find it. He killed our men. If it weren't for us, who knows what hell he would've wrought. Doge Memmo clings to life like barnacles to a hull. If I promise him what he wants... he might grant me what we need."

"And that is?"

Vito leveled his gaze. "Your pardon. Your return. Together, we'll destroy the Order. But first, I must be in their good graces. I'll ensure that I remain so and then vouch for you."

Angelo turned to the wharf as the Mestre clocktower bells announced the hour. A few hundred yards off, there was a hive of motion blurred by distance. Dockhands rolled casks, carts rattled over planks, and fishwives haggled with sailors. Shouts carried across the lagoon, rising and falling with the waterfowl, while a flotilla of skiffs and barges ferried cargo between anchored ships and the bustling piers. The smell of tar and salt mingled with smoke from the town's chimneys, as though the shore were leaning out to remind him of how close—or how far—solid ground remained.

He wanted to trust Vito, but too much had transpired over the years. Now that he was back in the Veneto, he itched to charge headfirst, slay the dragon, and return home victorious. He needed something tangible before accepting what was hardly a plan.

"Why would he grant the pardon?" he asked.

"Because you helped me quell Grimani's betrayal. Let's not forget that he and Quattrone also want to establish an outpost in Santa Marta. They could use you."

Angelo's eyes drifted back to the San Marco Campanile. Now silent, it towered over the city like a rigid sentinel.

"And if you still serve them?" Doubt laced his breath.

"How can you ask that?" Vito furrowed his brow. "I serve Venice. I've been the Order's instrument of pain for too long."

The conflict within Angelo raged like a storm tide. He hated this city. What it took. What Vito took. What Venice made of men. Yet there he was again, risking everything to finish what he'd once fled. For vengeance.

For *her*.

Vito squeezed his shoulder. "Stay on the ship, Angelo."

By the time Vito and his Protectors arrived by skiff, the sun had dipped toward dusk. Its muted rays flickered across the lagoon like dying embers. Five men in tabards of dark red climbed aboard, scanning the deck. Each carried a sheathed Mongolian short sword. Vito joined them and made introductions to Cadamosto and Tormenta, exchanging brief eye contact with Angelo, who stepped backward to meld with the crew. Except for one who was about his age, the other four Protectors would've been children when he fled Venice, but it wasn't worth the risk should one of them recognize him from a sketch.

Moments later, Tormenta's men hauled Grimani onto the deck. The sight of the senator, shackled, broken, and bespattered in his own filth, drew gasps from the Protectors. The senator was mercifully in a sluggish and disoriented state, drugged from forced ingestion of a dangerously high dose of mandrake root. His mouth was bound in case he roused.

"*Dios mio*," muttered the Protector of Angelo's age. He had a bronzed complexion, a pitch-black beard, and hair equally dark spilling from his hat. "He lives."

"Si, Zanca," Vito said. "But not as he was. Toss him into the skiff. I wish to speak with the captain."

The Protectors did as instructed. The moment the last man's head dipped below the bulwark, Vito motioned for Angelo, Cadamosto, and Tormenta to join him in the captain's quarters.

"My men have informed me of... rumblings," he said, taking a seat at the table. "The doge and Quattrone may be less pleased than I had previously anticipated."

Angelo disheveled his thinning hair, then smoothed it back. "What are you saying?"

"The situation is complicated."

"Then simplify it, Vito. Kill them. Memmo and Quattrone. Do it today when you deliver Grimani."

Vito shook his head. "The outcome would be a suicide with a new doge and a new exalted master."

"So what do you propose we do?"

"Destroy it from the inside. Sow discord and reveal their wretchedness to the citizens. To do that, I need to assess the doge's health, build allies, test relations. If the cards fall in our favor, I could potentially establish myself as Quattrone's successor. Have him arrested. Then use my position to topple the Order."

"Not a trivial task that can be accomplished overnight," Angelo said.

"Indeed. It will take some days to get in their good graces. Then weeks. Perhaps months. You'll need to stay on the ship until then."

The itch for shore leave didn't gnaw at Angelo as it did the other men. A far heavier burden weighed on him. The thought of his children's faces warred against the darker call of revenge, his yearning to see his family locked in combat with the unyielding vow to shatter the Order and wrest Isabella's soul from its chains.

Cadamosto puffed a smoke cloud from his freshly lit pipe over the table. "Not this ship, amigo. I've already secured cargo for Cádiz. From there, I'll sail on to Santa Marta." His eyes shifted past the walls of his cabin to the direction of the horizon. "We weigh anchor the morn after tomorrow. Best to keep ahead of the season's tempests, before the sea decides she's had her fill of ships."

Find a way.

"'Tis not a problem," Angelo replied. "I've lived a quarter century hunted. I can sneak into the city unseen. Stay with my mother and sisters."

Clearing his throat, Vito rubbed his neck and opened the linen of his doublet. "Your mother passed shortly after you fled Venice," he said, releasing a despondent exhale. "Consumption took her. My sympathies."

Angelo's chest constricted. A cold spike drove into his ribs. His hand instinctively rose to the crucifix at his neck. She'd been sick before he left. It was her deteriorating condition and his increasing debt that led him to take the job with the Bird Brothers. In the years that passed, he had assumed she'd recovered, as unlikely as it was. He muttered a brief, trembling *Ave Maria* under his breath. The memory of his sweet mother pressed at him, burning like an unhealed scar. His father's absence, a shadow that had haunted his boyhood, dwelled closer now.

"Your sisters," Vito continued with a hesitant tone, "they are alive... and well." He paused as if weighing what to reveal next.

"What *aren't* you saying?" Angelo's fists clenched, nails biting into his palms.

"For a time... we had questioned them of your whereabouts."

Anger flushed Angelo's face. Every word peeled opened a wound he had thought scabbed on their voyage. "*Questioned* them? You watched me climb aboard that ship in Genoa. You knew my whereabouts."

"Not your destination."

Tormenta snorted from the side, trying to defuse the tension with a lopsided grin. "Aye, Vito, best not to make a man bleed twice. Once at sea, once in his heart." His laugh cracked the edge of the moment.

"He's right," Cadamosto said. With a wince, he propped his foot on a stool. "Ancient history is oft best left buried."

Angelo clenched his fists, ignoring his friends' good-natured intent. "Did you torture them?"

"No." Vito's eyes fell with his shoulders. His voice was almost a whisper. "What's done is done. They're both married and with children. Grown. Life has carried them forward."

"So you've continued to watch them?"

"Not I and not every day," Vito replied with a nod. "But yes, the Order keeps an eye on them. For you. Which is why you must remain out of the city until the time is right."

Angelo sighed, lamenting internally that it was too risky to visit his sisters, cousins, or any of his kin. His mind turned to alternatives, landing on the town of Mestre. "There's an inn—"

Vito snapped his head at Angelo, his glare an unspoken desire of vengeance.

The words choked in Angelo's throat. He gaze locked with Vito's, two men shackled by sins neither could outrun. That inn was where Angelo had driven steel into his friend's brother's mouth. Though he yearned to gorge himself on the innkeeper's mussels, he couldn't revisit that place. Angelo sensed that Vito reflected on the same night. Surely, he'd recall where Ivan's body was discovered.

Vito's eyes lit up. "You can stay with *my* sister. She lives here in Mestre. She has a workshop. She makes toys and puzzles for children."

"Toys?"

"She's the finest toymaker in the Veneto."

"Finest toymaker, eh?" Tormenta said with a roguish smirk. "I might just have to see her workshop someday. To admire the craft, not her toys, of course."

Vito narrowed his eyes, but Angelo laughed. "An Uccello who makes toys? Was it not your mother who invented the thumbscrews?"

"For when we put our elbows on the dining table," Vito replied.

All the men laughed.

"Perhaps that's why Sofia chose joy." Vito stood and walked over to Cadamosto's desk, where he used the quill to scribble on a sheet of vellum. "She'll take you in."

XXXIX

Venice

TRUMPETS SPLIT THE MORNING.

The fanfare rang bright and brazen from the loggia overlooking the Palazzo Ducale courtyard. Ladies leaned over the rail, waving scarves. From the windows, noblemen tipped their hats and clerks applauded.

Pride swelled within Vito. Despite their expedition to Santa Marta ending in failure, to be welcomed with a display typically reserved for military heroes and heads of state was a moment he'd cherish forever.

Guards opened the gates for the entourage. Zanca kept pace to Vito's right. Of Sicilian ancestry, the Protector was steadfast and loyal, and possibly the only man in the Palace Vito could trust. Years ago, in a moment when Vito prized discretion above all else, it had been Zanca who carried sealed letters meant for Paulina. Vito had never spoken of the affair outright, but Zanca understood. He never asked questions. He delivered every letter. And he returned without judgment.

Behind them marched four Protectors in disciplined formation.

Between them shuffled Senator Grimani.

Chains bound his wrists before him and linked to iron at his ankles. Two Protectors held the restraints tight, forcing him forward, step by step. His hair hung matted against his brow. His mouth chewed the gag, jaw muscles twitching with unnatural energy. Even bound, he radiated ferality.

Musicians, arrayed in crimson and gold beneath the loggia arches, lifted their silver instruments toward the sky and poured the Republic's triumph into the morning. The notes leapt across the stone and marble, bold and jubilant, announcing the return of a successful quest to unknown lands. The ovation and cheers swelled. Even the halberdiers at the Giants' Staircase straightened as if glory itself were ascending toward them.

On the loggia, one of the younger musicians leaned over the rail at the group, curious. His embouchure faltered for a breath before recovering. The other trumpeters pressed on, oblivious.

Vito led the men to the Giants' Staircase.

A second horn wavered. The clapping ebbed.

The prisoner was within eyesight of the nearest guards now. At the top of the steps stood the usher, immaculate in a black doublet stitched with the winged lion, his white gloves pristine, his posture molded from protocol.

His gaze settled first on Vito.

Then moved to Senator Grimani.

Then to the chains.

He did not react at once. Years of service had trained him to absorb shock without expression, but his eyes sharpened.

Below, Grimani jerked against the chains with a guttural half-laugh, half growl. The links snapped taut. Protectors strained to hold him.

The third trumpet cracked. Another fell silent mid-note. The music fractured into ragged strands of uncertain sound.

Contained alarm lined the usher's face. He stepped forward to the balustrade and raised one gloved hand.

The final trumpet cut off.

Gasps replaced the praise before people quickly scattered from view.

Silence fell hard across the courtyard as the ceremony was extinguished. Only the rattle of shackles remained.

Every eye seemed to land on Vito. He adjusted the scabbard at his hip by instinct. Zanca shifted closer so that their shoulders nearly brushed.

Vito had served a doge and the Order his entire adult life. Obedience was bone-deep. He had come here to regain favor, to secure a pardon for Angelo to crush the Order, not break the machinery of the Republic.

He would not betray his friend.

Yet he would not betray Venice.

The conflict tightened inside him like drawn wire as they mounted the first step.

The usher stood waiting at the top of the stairs, clearly attempting to maintain a stoic demeanor, though he winced upon sighting Grimani.

"You will follow me," he said, his tone neither welcoming nor dismissive, but uttered with the exacting neutrality of a man who had escorted senators, criminals, and foreign dignitaries alike.

Vito shifted his weight. The sudden end to the pomp pressed down on him. It was as if not only the musicians but everyone in the palace had vanished. The expedition to find the Fountain of Youth was as unsuccessful as possible, and he would soon learn his fate.

Now, the only sounds were the tap of boots on the marble and Grimani's muttering through his gag.

The usher gestured when they reached the apex. Two of the palace Protectors moved to seize Grimani, while the others fell in behind Vito and his own men. "His Most Serene and the Most Exalted Senator Quattrone await you in the Sala del Collegio."

Vito swallowed hard. The Sala del Collegio was the chamber where the doge and his closest advisors held council. Private ground. *Dangerous* ground. It was almost as if they knew his true motive.

The usher turned on his heel, and the procession followed him beneath the looming arches of the palace.

Grimani shuffled between two Protectors, his mouth twisting with a grotesque grin as he chewed the gag. He gabbled to himself in jagged bursts, then erupted into muffled laughter that bounced along the vaulted ceiling and startled everyone present.

"What is he saying?" the usher asked. "Remove the gag."

"That is most unadvisable," Vito replied. "We shall keep it on."

As Grimani's voice turned into a distorted howl, Vito shoved him forward with a snarl of disgust.

The grandeur of the palace halls was suffocating: glittering mosaics overhead, frescoes of victories, the faint reek of candle smoke and brine. He had been inside the palazzo countless times and always reveled in its beauty and history. His ancestors had built this palace as a monument to their dominion, but now it seemed more like a gilded cage.

He squared his shoulders to project the calm of a Protector returning successfully from duty, but doubt gnawed at him. Still, he followed. What choice did he have?

As they mounted a shallow stair, Grimani hummed in a high, taunting falsetto. A passing clerk stopped and stared. The usher snapped his fingers, and the clerk scurried off, head bowed, as though he'd seen too much.

At last, the usher halted before a pair of carved walnut doors. Gold leaf gleamed along the edges, dulled by time but unmistakable in its authority. Two halberdiers crossed their weapons before the party.

"Your sword," the usher said, his palm out.

Vito stiffened.

"The doge's command. A new law."

While the one at his hip was given to him that morning by Zanca, he couldn't bring himself to relinquish it so soon. "Why only mine?"

"Zanca's, as well," the usher replied. "The other Protectors will remain outside."

Vito exchanged a brief glance with Zanca. The Protector's eyes flickered, also not wishing to be disarmed. Then discipline swallowed it. He handed the usher his sword. Reluctantly, Vito did the same.

"The doge will see you now," the usher said. He inclined his head, and the halberdiers pulled the doors open.

The Sala del Collegio stretched wide and high, its ceiling alive with vignettes of saints and battles, paint glinting in the lamplight like embers in a dying fire.

A carpet of crimson damask ran the length of the floor, worn thin where generations of men had knelt, supplicated, or been condemned.

At the far end, on a raised dais flanked by Protectors in black cloaks, Doge Marcantonio Memmo sat in his high-backed chair, his face sallow beneath his *corno ducale* cap. State robes embroidered with gold thread draped the shell of his body, which to Vito seemed to have aged five years since he last saw him, though it had been less than one. Though clouded by age, his eyes burned with a fury that belied his antiquity. Beside him stood Senator Marco Quattrone, his expression masked behind his gray beard and wrinkled eyes.

Vito bristled. Of the many rooms in the palace, this one had been chosen for its symbolism unique to him. For directly behind the dais was a large painting depicting the coronation of Doge Sebastiano Venier, the doge and Exalted Master of the Order who initiated Vito as a Protector and presented his first Mongolian short sword some thirty-five years prior. He had held that doge in higher regard than all others and would've given his life to protect him. Facing the portrait was a stark reminder of his duty as a Protector and the oath he had taken.

He had new obligations. To Angelo, to innocents yet taken, and to Paulina. Whatever happened here today, this room would be his path to freedom with his love.

The doge's eyes widened. He looked Grimani up and down, then did the same to Vito.

"I am not sure if I should trust my eyes," Doge Memmo said, his voice wheezing. "I had expected you to be holding a vessel. Why is the good senator in chains?"

"For our safety, My Serene," Vito said. "And for his."

Grimani twitched beside him, mercifully silent, though a wet chuckle slid from his throat. The senator looked as though he was a pane of glass ready to shatter. Unable to hold back, a jagged laugh burst from his throat, taking everyone aback.

"What is the meaning of this?" the doge shouted. "Come forward!"

As they approached, Grimani's chains clattered like mock applause. Every step forward seemed to deepen the weight of the portraits, the saints, and the judgment of history.

The guards at Vito's back halted on command, leaving him exposed in the chamber. He glanced up at the winged angels staring down with impassive faces, and for the first time in years, he felt small, as though the room had been designed to reduce men to nothing before the leader of the Republic.

Vito's pulse thudded in his ears. He always thought the expedition was folly but could never have imagined the outcome.

The silence lengthened until it threatened to break him. Then, with a slow lift of his withered hand, the doge leaned forward on his chair.

"Vito Uccello." Memmo's sunken eyes fixed on him, watery yet sharp, as if seeing through the layers of dust, blood, and sea salt carried from his long journey. "You have returned at last. With a prize, no less. Though it is clearly not the elixir I had requested."

The old man's lips tugged into a smile, though it bent more toward mockery or disappointment. "A senator, delivered to us in chains. How... unexpected. Explain what I am seeing. Now." His vision slid lazily toward Grimani, who twitched like a mad dog straining against a leash.

Vito bowed, though the motion felt undeserved. "Your Serenity, Exalted Master Quattrone, if Senator Grimani were unchained, there is no telling what he would do. I brought him before you like this to expose his treachery. Grimani betrayed us all in the jungle. He is poisoned, body and mind, by the cursed juice of the Indies—"

"The elixir." Memmo leaned forward. "So you have brought it."

"Forgive me, Serenity. The juice was from a fruit."

"Fruit," Memmo said, his voice sharper. The tremor of age vanished, replaced by cutting steel. "You speak to me of fruit, when I charged you with locating the Fountain of Youth?" His words cracked through the mask of his frailty. "Do you take me for a fool? You bring me madness when I commanded immortality."

"My lord Doge," Vito said, "No fountain lies in the jungle. There is a tree—"

Grimani writhed, shouting muffled noises through his gag, his eyes bulging with desperation.

Quattrone shifted. "Perhaps we should allow the good senator to speak."

Vito cleared his throat, uneasy with what was sure to happen, but Memmo nodded.

Zanca stepped forward. He crouched and cautiously removed the gag.

A raspy laugh erupted from Grimani. "Lies! He hoarded it! There's a fruit, Most Serene, that much is true. There is no fountain, but there is a tree. The Tree of Life! It will give you immortality and power!"

Memmo's gaze did not move from Grimani. "Pray tell," he asked, "did you return with this fruit? Vito seems unchanged. What really happened to you?"

Grimani's lips curled. With startling speed, he lunged.

Zanca reacted instantly, but Grimani's shackled wrists swung like a mace. Iron struck Zanca's temple. The Protector staggered. Grimani surged upward, chains snapping taut as he seized Zanca's throat and drove him backward into a column.

The chamber erupted.

With grotesque strength, Grimani shoved Zanca aside as if he were a pageboy. He bared his teeth, laughter rising.

"It lives in me!"

The guards advanced with caution, but Grimani raised his hands in surrender, then knelt.

Doge Memmo's lips parted pitifully close to a smile. He spoke to Vito with simmering rage. "We had a path to immortality, and you offer... fruit and madness."

Oil lamps quiver and the hall seemed to shift. Portraits on the walls, once impartial witnesses, now judged Vito. Grimani rattled his chains on the marble floor.

"Despite his affliction," Quattrone said, his voice smooth as obsidian, "Senator Grimani remains noble. We need to learn more about the expedition and this supposed Tree of Life. Restore his honor. Even in chains."

"Unchain me!" Grimani roared, spittle flying. Shackles snapped as he strained against them.

"Keep him bound." The order came from Doge Memmo like a bark. "If he speaks truth, the chains will not offend him."

His gaze cut to Vito.

"And you," the doge said, "expect us to believe this spectacle?"

Quattrone stepped forward, hands folded within his sleeves. "You departed with twelve Protectors," he said evenly. "You return with *one*. Instead of returning Angelo Mascari bound, you insult the Senate itself."

His eyes hardened.

"Why should we trust your account? Are the other Protectors dead? Where is Mascari?"

The words struck Vito harder than any blade. He forced himself to remain still. The path to salvation ran through this chamber with these men. Through restraint. Through reason.

"My lord," he said, bowing. "We were betrayed in the jungle. The fruit poisons the mind, as you can see. The others—"

"Are dead?" Quattrone interrupted.

"Yes, Senator."

"Yet you remain unscathed." He glanced at Grimani. "You managed to subdue the villain who murdered the entire expedition party?"

Vito forced a swallow, unnerved by the line of questioning.

Memmo leaned forward. "You ask us to accept that every man but you succumbed? That no witness remains to confirm your tale? It's your word against a Venetian Senator's?"

The walls tightened around Vito, squeezing him like the python in the river.

"I have served the Republic my entire life," he said firmly. "I have no cause to deceive you."

Grimani released a wet, ugly laugh. "He lies. He hoarded it. He fears what I have become. He and the swordsman killed them all."

Breath seized Vito. His eyes widened at the accusation.

"Curious," Memmo said. "Where is this fruit? I'm quite keen to see it."

"The bottom of the ocean," Vito blurted out, gesturing to Grimani. "Look what it does to men."

"Liar!" the senator screamed.

"I don't have the fruit," Vito said, glancing at the guards stepping forth. "Why would I take it? Most Serene, it's not life. It's poison."

Memmo's eyes flicked between them. Suspicion settled like frost.

"Seize him."

The doge's command cracked through the chamber.

This was no inquiry. They would cage him, question him in darkness, extract what suited them. Imprisoned, he would be useless. Grimani would return to Paulina and do untold harm while Vito rotted in a cell.

He stepped back as Protectors advanced.

"Your Serenity," he tried once more. "If you imprison me, you silence the one man who knows the truth."

"Perhaps," Quattrone said. "Or perhaps we silence a traitor. You will have an opportunity to plead your case."

Steel hissed from scabbards.

Zanca hesitated a fraction of a second before moving with the others.

Vito made his choice. He moved.

Not to the doors but toward the side passage he knew too well. He had patrolled these corridors countless times. He knew which antechambers connected to which galleries, which windows opened toward the canal, and which guards were posted where.

He vaulted the low counsel bench, scattering parchment. A lantern toppled and shattered, oil flaring before guttering out. Shouts erupted.

"Stop him!"

He burst from the Sala del Collegio into the adjoining antechamber, spun through it, and darted into the long corridor leading to the private chancery rooms. Tapestries lining the walls muffled the pursuit for a heartbeat.

Then more boots joined the chase.

"Cut him off at the eastern gallery!"

He reached a second chamber, a records room overlooking the canal between palace and prison. It was a dead end but his only option.

Two guards blocked the opposite door.

Vito grabbed the edge of a heavy walnut table and heaved it sideways, slamming it into them. One stumbled. The other crashed into a cabinet. Scrolls spilled like fish from a barrel.

He sprinted for the window.

Thick velvet curtains hung beside it, tied back with braided cord. He yanked the cord free, looped it around the latch, and kicked the casement open. Warm air slammed into him.

Below lay the narrow canal separating the palace from the prison. The jump was far too high. He risked breaking his legs, if not his neck.

Spanning the gap between the buildings was the enclosed white arch of the Bridge of Sighs. As more guards arrived, he took his chance. Hands seized Vito's cloak as he climbed onto the sill. He twisted free and launched himself outward. His fingers struck the cold marble.

He slipped but hauled himself up onto the curved bridge roof.

Shouts exploded from the window behind him.

The Bridge of Sighs—sealed and windowed with stone lattice—ironically carried prisoners from judgement to cell. He had escorted men across its interior on dozens of occasions. He had watched them breathe their last glimpse of Venice through its carved openings.

Now he stood on its back.

Between palace and prison.

Between loyalty and treason.

A bolt cracked past his ear and ricocheted off marble.

"Hold!" someone shouted. "We need him alive!"

Vito scrambled across the damp curvature, boots sliding on the slick stone. Protectors and guards spilled their heads out from the palace windows.

Another bolt struck near his feet.

At the center of the bridge, where the canal was deepest, he did not hesitate.

He leapt.

The water swallowed him whole, crushing the air from his lungs. Cold hit him like a visceral punishment that served to sharpen his senses.

He kicked hard, rising.

Breaking the surface, he drew the smallest breath and flattened himself against the shadowed wall beneath the bridge.

Voices barked orders.

"Get down there! Search the canal!"

Another bolt splashed wide.

He swam along the stone, then pushed off toward the open sweep of the Grand Canal, arms burning, lungs tight.

His mission lay in ruins. The doge's favor was lost. Absolution and Paulina were further away than ever.

XL

Mestre

"He wouldn't abandon us," Angelo said, lowering his hat against the late-morning light.

Cadamosto rowed with the skill of a man who lived on the sea, his broad shoulders moving like a pendulum. "You say that of a pirate? How rich."

The skiff cut across the distance between the *San Cristóbal* and the wharf, its oars dipping into the water with a steady rhythm. Angelo sat opposite, eyes trained on the low smear of smoke rising from the town. It was nothing like Venice's splendor. Just a hard-edged sprawl of inns, stables, factories, and muddy lanes crouched beneath a gray sky. The last time he'd taken a skiff to Mestre, he rowed with a mangled hand, escaping with his life. He had a single note of guidance: find the man facing him.

The full circle wasn't lost on Angelo. Cadamosto had helped him escape to the New World, and now, the grizzled captain once again aided him to finish the job of destroying the Order. A plan for how he'd do that, without the proper tools and friends in short supply, would hopefully soon reveal itself.

Angelo had offered to row, but Cadamosto refused, needing to burn off some steam. His anger far outweighed any concern for their new comrade, as the former pirate could fend for himself in any circumstance.

"Shore leave ended at dawn," Cadamosto said.

"Cut him some slack. It was a long voyage."

"As quartermaster, he has responsibilities."

"Perhaps he was more lenient when he was captain. The demotion can't be an easy adjustment."

Cadamosto scoffed. "Easier than hanging from the gallows. Stop defending him."

Angelo gazed toward the approaching wharf. Sailors loaded and unloaded cargo on small- and mid-sized vessels. "What of his men? You think he'd betray them?"

"Who knows Tormenta's motives?" asked the captain. "His face is likely in a barrel of ale. Or between a whore's legs. He was given an order, and he defied it."

"You can say a lot about the man, but you can't accuse him of disloyalty. I'd wager my life he wouldn't desert."

"A wager already lost." Cadamosto thrust the oars with a strength Angelo hadn't seen in decades. A vein bulged in his reddening forehead. "It doesn't matter, Angelo. Are you not listening? Whether by forgetfulness, choice, or force, we'll never know. I'll not hold a ship for a man not on board."

If the captain was right, Tormenta's absence would weigh heavier than the coming night. Angelo replayed the possibilities—drunk in an alley, killed in a fight, caught in a whore's bed, or the unthinkable, a betrayal. Each outcome burned. Tormenta had fought beside them, bled beside them. Yet the empty berth on Cadamosto's ship spoke louder than loyalty ever could.

The skiff glided closer to shore. Mestre's tang of tar, fish, and coal smoke thickened the air. Angelo leaned forward. "Well, you've secured your course. What's your cargo?"

"Do you care?"

Angelo shrugged. He didn't.

They said little else as the skiff glided in. Cadamosto brought the oars in with a sweep and reached for the rope.

Angelo gripped his friend's arm. "I owe you more than I can put into words. For bringing me to Santa Marta. Back to Venice. For risking your ship and your men. For everything."

Cadamosto cut a glance at Angelo, hard but not unkind. "Your debt is survival. Nothing more. Nothing less."

Angelo allowed a thin smile. "That's a debt I may fail to pay."

"Then die trying. If you can avenge Pietro Stefanetti in the process, all the better."

Angelo nodded. The nobleman who'd aided his escape twenty-four years prior deserved vengeance.

"A merchant run, since you asked of my cargo," the captain said. "Olive oil, Trebbiano by the cask, spices, and silk enough to clothe a court."

"You need a court of your own, my friend."

The two men held one another's gaze. They were seasoned warriors of sea and fate, both knowing they might never meet again. Neither dared give voice to truth. Angelo knew more than anyone that farewells carried weight, and neither man would be that burden.

"Tell Loredana..." He faltered on the name. "Tell her I'll be back soon. If not in body, then at least in spirit."

Cadamosto's eyes narrowed, the cracks around them sharpening. "You'll return in both. Now go. Venice awaits you. It'll test you more than any storm."

"Travel with God, my friend."

"And to you."

Angelo climbed from the skiff onto the worn planks. He turned and offered a final nod. Not goodbye. Not yet.

The old captain pushed off, the bustle of the port drowning out the rhythm of the skiff's oars.

Ahead, the docks and streets were crowded with life: fishermen gutted eels over stained boards, muleteers wrestled barrels onto carts, a friar picked his way through puddles with his robes held high.

Angelo gripped the slip of paper with directions to Vito's sister's house, but he didn't yet unfold it. Instead, his boots carried him into Mestre's narrow lanes, driven by memory more than map.

Before long, the inn rose before him at the bend of the lane, backed against the woods, its timbers and stone the same crooked bones he remembered from another life. The painted sign swung, the same faded stag pawing the air, its creak as loud as a noose rope.

He stopped.

A man exited the establishment, adjusted his hat, and set out toward the town center. For an instant, Angelo envisioned himself stepping inside. Laughter spilled from the tap room as his transitory friends, the monk and Englishman, exchanged tales over goblets of wine. He could almost picture the innkeepers, older and more rotund now, lines carved deeper into their faces. Would they recognize him? Call him friend?

Or would they see his hands, red with a Protector's blood, and call the authorities?

He shut his eyes. Ivan Uccello's death came back in a flash—desperation mixed with mud and blood. That night, the world had shifted on its axis. He'd crossed from survivor to executioner, a man forever bound to ghosts.

His hand trembled toward the door latch, then curled into a fist. No. To open that door would be to step back into the past, and he had no time for hauntings. Still, the shadows of the street pressed in, whispering Ivan's name as though the man were walking beside him.

Forcing himself to leave, the inn remained at his back like a wound that would not close. He and Vito were forever bound by bad blood.

The streets of Mestre narrowed as Angelo left the bustle of the port district behind. Gone were the bawdy taverns and the smell of tarred rope. Here, the air carried the calmer aura of hearth smoke, tannin from dyers' yards, and flour from nearby mills. The houses were modest, two stories at most, their plaster facades dulled by weather and patched in places with brick. Wooden shutters hung half-closed against the warming air.

Following the scribbled directions, Angelo found the house he sought: a narrow dwelling of rose-colored stucco with a tiled roof that sagged at one corner. Beside it stood a smaller workshop. A wooden trade sign with an engraving of a horse on a wheeled platform hung over the propped-open green door. He rapped on the main entrance.

A servant girl, barely more than sixteen, in a plain woolen gown with her dark hair bound in a kerchief, answered first. She eyed Angelo, then, with a quick dip of her head but nary a question from her lips, said, "You'll be seeking Mistress Sofia. She's in the *bottega*." She stepped aside, pointing him toward the adjacent studio.

"Bondì," Angelo said as he entered.

Inside, a scent of carved pine and paint greeted him. The workshop brimmed with color, craft, and joy. Wooden horses, miniature ships with canvas sails, dolls with jointed limbs, and other toys filled the shelves.

A boy and a girl, each about the ages of Franco and Juanita, greeted him.

"Bondì, sior," said the boy. "How can I help you?"

"Bondì, sior," mimicked the girl, unable to control her giggling. "How can I help you?"

The boy gave her a playful shove. She laughed and plopped onto the floor to play a game Angelo hadn't seen since his youth. It was called *il Gioco della Ruota*—the game of the wheel. Four wooden discs with numerical markings were stacked on a post secured to a wooden base, which was also inscribed with markings. Players would take turns spinning, accruing points by aligning the markings on their disc with those on the base. Angelo smiled sadly at the scene. He'd often wondered what his children's lives would be like had they been reared in the Veneto, though Loredana would hate the lack of nature.

Angelo crouched beside the girl, surprising himself. "Can I play with you?"

She squealed with delight. For a moment, he saw Juanita in her place. A lump caught in his throat, and he stood so abruptly that he knocked over items on the worktable. He scrambled to set them right.

"We have this game in many colors," the boy said, all too eager to make a sale. "Or perhaps a puzzle?"

A woman sat at a workbench, engrossed in smoothing the edges of a small wooden mask. She was handsome rather than beautiful, with flaxen hair streaked with early silver, coiled in a bun, sleeves rolled to her elbows. She wore a modest wool gown with a linen apron streaked with sawdust and paint.

"Marcello," she called without looking up from her work. "Bring our customer back here."

The boy beckoned Angelo to follow. The woman greeted him with brown eyes that could only belong to the sister of Vito Uccello. But where Vito's had a perpetual glare, a warmth permeated from Sofia's gaze.

"How old are your children, sior?"

Though he'd been thinking of them a moment ago, the question took Angelo aback. "Oh, about the same ages as yours, I suppose."

"Does one have an approaching birthday?"

A pang of guilt rippled through him. He had missed Franco's thirteenth and Juanita's ninth.

His gaze landed on a wooden block on the table. He ran his finger over the polished wood, which he guessed was walnut.

"No birthdays," he said. "I would like to get them a gift."

"Looks like you've found the perfect one."

Angelo laughed. "A block?"

Sofia offered a wry grin. She took the box and pressed on it to remove a piece, much like a puzzle. She removed another, and yet another to reveal the final section. Inside that was a tiny knob. He lifted it to find a concealed compartment.

"For your most precious," she said.

"Magnifico," Angelo replied, genuinely impressed. He'd never seen anything like it. A narrow, vertical painting on the wall caught his attention. It hung in the dim light like a vision, no taller than half a man yet vast in its fury. Figures tumbled and strained across the canvas, bodies twisted in terror or rapture, their faces lit by a cold, unearthly glow that seemed to pulse even in stillness. It reminded him of *Il Paradiso.* He'd only seen Tintoretto's masterpiece in its unfinished state and from a hidden nook in the Palazzo wall, but this painting in the workshop had the same violent sweep of heaven and damnation.

"Are you also a painter?" he asked Sofia. "The work is remarkable."

She blushed. "I wish I could take credit. I painted it, but it's a copy of Tintoretto's *Last Judgement*. You should see the real one in the Madonna dell'Orto."

A man with a dark complexion and a darker shock of hair emerged from a back room, wiping wood shavings from his apron.

"Good day, sior," he said. "Luca Rossi at your service. I see you've met my wife and children."

A craftsman of solid build with the rough hands of his trade, Luca wore plain hose and a faded jerkin beneath his apron. He offered Angelo a polite smile and a firm handshake.

Angelo made polite small talk with the family, commenting on their crafts and workshop. Conversing in Venetian was a discombobulating experience. Other than with Vito, he hadn't spoken it in years. Now, here in the Veneto, the land of his youth, it felt like his second language. It was unsettling yet relaxed him in a nostalgic way. His gaze landed on the game on the workshop floor. He yearned to bring one to his children, but given the gravity and uncertainty of his task ahead, he didn't see how he'd be able to carry a toy. An idea hit him.

"Might I be able to purchase just two *Gioco della Ruota* wheels?"

Luca raised a bushy eyebrow. "You don't want the whole set?"

"You can have mine," the little girl blurted out. "We have so many in the back."

She jumped up and brought him two discs. Angelo took them appreciatively and smiled at her. "That is very sweet, signorina. I thank you and my children will thank you."

She beamed and ran off to the back room.

"Forgive me," Angelo said to Sofia and Luca. "Your toys are lovely, but I'm here because your brother sent me."

The couple froze with surprise. They exchanged a quick look before elation consumed Sofia.

"It's been ages since we've heard from Vito," she said. "Has he returned? Is he well?"

"Quite," Angelo replied. "He's meeting with the doge as we speak."

"You're one of his men? A Protector of the Order?"

Before Angelo could answer her assumption, the door banged open. Vito stumbled inside, his damp clothes clinging to him, his breath labored. Sofia gasped. Angelo and Luca joined her in their surprise.

Vito quickly shut the door behind him.

"Vito!" Sofia cried, rushing to him. She caught his shoulders, her hands trembling as they pressed against his sodden clothes. "Months have gone without word, and this is how you return? This man said you were with the doge. Why are you all wet?"

"Sofia, Luca," Vito said, "Marcello, Beatrice. We'll have our reunion, but now is not the time."

"Have you gone to see your family?" Luca asked, his brow knitted with concern. "Your children, your wife, they've feared the worst."

A shadow crossed over Vito's features. "I may not have that chance." His voice cracked on the words as he was stripped of all his usual bravado.

"What happened?" Angelo asked.

Vito gazed at Sofia and her husband. "Forgive me, sister, but I need words with Angelo. Alone."

"This is our workshop," Sofia said. "Can you not speak outside?"

"Please, Sofia. We need to be inside. It's of utmost importance."

Reluctantly, Sofia stepped back, her face etched with a grief and fear she did not utter. She lingered long enough to gather her children. Luca exchanged a glance and a nod with his wife. "Come, children. We must go back to the house."

After a moment of complaint, the family left the men in the shop, where Vito recounted recent events. The news stunned Angelo; despite the Order's penchant for deceit, never would he have considered they'd side with Grimani and turn on their most-trusted Protector.

"Our path is unknown," Vito admitted. "It is the two of us against an army. Against the Republic. Perhaps we must flee to the New World for good."

Returning to Santa Marta, to his family, held tremendous appeal. But what of Isabella? What of the Order's ambitions? He'd never be safe until they were quashed. No, they traveled the ocean to Venice for a purpose. He'd see it through.

"What of a guild?" he asked. "One who fights the Order?"

Vito's head snapped toward him. "You know of the Guild of Silvanus?"

"Stefanetti. Isabella's uncle. The night I fled Venice, he mentioned a guild. They could aid us, could they not? We could join their cause."

Vito shook his head. "They'll never have me."

"I'll vouch for you."

"They don't know you." The unassembled puzzle box caught Vito's attention. He fiddled with the pieces, attempting to fit them together.

Angelo allowed himself a crooked smile. "I'd chance they do."

Vito returned a nod of acceptance. "You're the cause of their patriarch's demise."

The remark gave Angelo a moment of pause, but he let it go. "That's debatable, my friend."

"They may kill me on sight." The former Protector scowled, running a hand across his hatless brow. Almost grudgingly, he added, "I may yet have some men loyal to me."

"Feel them out. Let's you and I pay this Guild a visit. Present our case. Unless you have a better idea."

After a moment, Vito exhaled, his will not wholly extinguished. He fit the final piece into his sister's puzzle box, recreating the solid block.

XLI

THE *SANDOLO* SLID ALONG the Brenta Canal, its oars grazing the water. Angelo sat low, the dusk damp on his clothes, and tried to dispel the apprehension in his chest. He had spent his youth in cramped alleys and his manhood in a backwater colony on the other side of the ocean. Wealth belonged to another world.

Proof of it rose from the darkening water ahead.

Luca was kind enough to lend him and Vito his funeral garb and mourning attire. Angelo's black doublet and leather cloak, treated with linseed oil for waterproofness, were a far cry from his ratty garments that had been torn to shreds by the jungle and ocean crossing. The sweeping brim of his black felt cavalier hat was pulled low. To further retain anonymity, he'd removed the crimson plume and trimmed his unruly beard to a neat goatee. Dressed in similar apparel, Vito and he looked like passable citizens.

The Stefanetti villa loomed like a palace. Perfect symmetry, broad stone steps, and arched loggias that caught the dwindling light bleeding through the clouds. Columns lined the façade, pale and polished. Gardens stretched along the canal with terraces of trimmed hedges and marble statues frozen in time. Even the air smelled different here, with a sweetness from citrus trees mixed with an acidity from burning oil lamps that threw golden light across the water.

What he marveled at most was that this was Isabella's life. The estate was her uncle's—now her cousin's, and while Angelo had never seen her childhood home, he imagined it was similar. He knew Isabella had wealth, but through her husband. Knowing that Isabella grew up in such luxury filled him with a strange sense of pride in that she chose him as her lover. He didn't deceive himself. He never could've had a tiny slice of this dreamland. For a brief moment, he tasted it on his beloved.

"Close your mouth," Vito said. "You look like you're catching flies."

Angelo snapped back to reality. Removing his hat for a moment, he tousled his hair and sleeked it back. Needing to ground himself, he touched the two wooden game discs, which he'd secured to his belt with a leather cord.

"It's impressive, but don't fawn over it," Vito continued, referring to the villa. "The Stefanettis are *vecchie*. Old nobles. Be respectful, not subservient."

Angelo nodded.

"What else did Pietro Stefanetti tell you of the Guild?" Vito asked.

"That I was a liability to it. Nothing more before your men killed him."

Vito brushed the air with his hand. "Another casualty caught in the battle of absurdity. We may be next."

The *sandolo* bumped the dock. A steward, oil lamp in hand, hurried forward to help them disembark. Two guards joined him.

"May I help you, siori?" the steward asked.

"We'd like words with Ludo Stefanetti."

"Is he expecting you?"

"No, but he'll be pleased to see us."

"And you are?"

"Angelo Mascari and friend."

The steward raised an eyebrow, as if recognizing the name. He whispered to one guard, who strode to the villa entrance.

For some minutes, Angelo and Vito sat in their boat in silence, while the steward and guard waited. The other guard finally reappeared from the house and whispered to the steward, who nodded.

"Come," the steward said.

The steps to the villa were wide enough to march an army, which was what Angelo was hoping to see of the Guild. Inside, the great hall opened like a cavern of art and stone.

He froze a moment, absorbing it. Frescoes sprawled across the ceiling, painted figures of gods and saints locked in eternal struggle. Chandeliers flicked with dozens of candles. The floor seemed alive with marble veined in the colors of a sunset, polished so smooth it mirrored the firelight.

"Respectful, not subservient," Vito whispered, again picking up on Angelo's awe.

He kept his face still, though he felt very much an imposter. He thought of his father, who had died before Angelo grew into his strength, and his mother, sent to the grave by consumption. There he was, a man who had slit throats and bled on planks at sea, standing in the home of nobles as if he belonged.

You do, my love. More than anyone.

He swallowed hard. For Isabella. For Loredana. For the fight still ahead.

A man descended the staircase with the measured grace of someone born into privilege. Golden hair had paled to silver at the temples, and the black velvet of his zimarra fell clean over a forest-green doublet stitched with silver thread, the lace of his cuffs immaculate despite the hour. About the same age as Angelo, his clean-shaven face highlighted his handsome features. He carried himself with the self-assurance of old Venetian nobility, yet there was a hardness in his eyes that belonged more to fighters than courtiers.

Angelo knew a version of that face. It was almost like looking at a ghost. Or the kin of a ghost.

Ludo Stefanetti, son of Pietro Stefanetti, the nobleman who died by his own hand rather than be taken by the Order. But Angelo saw more than Pietro in the man standing before him, for he also had the eyes of his beloved—Ludo was Isabella's cousin.

Behind him came a woman. Striking, sharp, and possessing a gaze that measured and judged without apology. Her dark hair spilled over her shoulders in defiance of Venetian fashion, unbound where other noblewomen would have pinned and veiled it. A fitted gown of black velvet clung to her frame, its neckline edged in beading. Black leather gloves hugged her hands despite the warmth of the room. Her bodice was of deep-burgundy silk, laced high and proper, but the dagger riding openly at her hip defied any illusion of courtly grace. Her gaze moved between the two newcomers, lingering on Vito with disdain.

"Madonna mia," Ludo said as he reached the bottom of the stairs, his voice tight with disbelief. "Angelo Mascari walks through my door. My father's ghost must be laughing."

Angelo inclined his head out of deference, as well as to Ludo's late father. "If he's been watching over me, he's been laughing for years."

Vito shifted uncomfortably, but Ludo smiled with appreciation.

As the woman joined them, Angelo bowed again. "Sior e Siora Stefanetti, it is an honor to meet you both. Thank you for receiving us."

He turned to introduce Vito, but Ludo preempted him with a raucous bellow. The woman crossed her arms and frowned. "My wife and children are still at our summer villa in Lago di Garda," he said with a gruff tone that contradicted his station. "This is my associate, the Lady Carmen Ferrante."

"A pleasure, Siora," Angelo said.

"Who is your companion?" Ludo asked.

Vito removed his hat. Carmen recoiled and gasped.

"I know this man," she said. "Vito Uccello. The Bird Brother. Chief Protector of the Order."

Her hand slid to her dagger. In a flash, the blade was on Vito's throat. He raised his hands in defense but did not flinch.

"You bring him?" Ludo asked, his eyes darkening. "You mock us, Mascari."

"If you're going to kill me," Vito said, "at least first hear the reason for my presence."

"I'll spare the city another betrayal. We can hear it from him after I slit your throat," the woman said.

"Agreed," Ludo said. "Do it, Carmen."

"Wait!" Angelo raised his palm and angled his body toward Carmen but didn't intervene for fear of hastening her reaction. "Just listen. Please."

Ludo's jaw clenched. "To what? The reason his family betrayed mine? That he condemned my father to death and my cousin to a purgatorial imprisonment?"

Angelo cut through the tension. "Your father died to save me. For a purpose far greater than my life. The same purpose that's brought us here tonight."

"Purpose?" Carmen hissed. "You mean the Order? The same Order this man serves?"

"I'm no longer theirs," Vito said through gritted teeth. He raised his chin from the dagger. "I've come to help you destroy them."

"You expect us to believe that?" Carmen asked.

"I swear it on my life."

Ludo raised a hand but didn't tell her to stand down. His gaze locked on Angelo. "Is he telling the truth?"

Angelo met his eyes. If they killed Vito, their mission was be doomed before it began. "He is. He's a changed man, and I trust him with my life. He's saved it more than once."

Wind rattled the shutters as Ludo scrutinized them. Then he exhaled a breath that sounded like a mix of disbelief, exasperation, and surrender.

"By the saints, what a cursed night." He gestured toward the corridor. "Come. If you're lying, Mascari, your bodies will be worm food by dawn."

"Hold," Carmen said. "How are we to trust this is Angelo Mascari?"

Ludo stopped in his tracks and turned. "Fair point, my dear. Always thinking for us all. Well, Angelo, how do you validate your claim of identity? There is no one who'd recognize you, other than the man conveniently by your side."

The question was well placed. Angelo threw a quick glance at Vito. His expression held the same thought: they should've prepared for this.

"Your cousin," he said. "Isabella. She was married to Renzo Scalfini."

A snicker escaped Ludo's mouth. "Hardly uncommon knowledge. You'll need to give us more than that."

Angelo brushed back his hair to expose his ear. He folded it forward, showing his missing lobe. "I sustained this while defending her. The day Renzo died." He looked at Vito. "He did it, actually."

"Guilty," Vito said. "With a shard of broken mirror."

Ludo and Carmen smiled.

"Better," she said, approaching Angelo. She peered into his eyes. "Tell us a detail about Isabella. Something only her family would recognize."

Angelo fired a messenger's arrow into his brain. He'd been dreaming of his beloved for a quarter century and remembered everything about her, but most everything was intimate details that her cousin would hopefully not have known.

The crucifix, my love.

Opening his shirt, Angelo pulled out the silver crucifix. "She gave me this."

Carmen scoffed. "As common as the dawn."

"No." Ludo's eyes widened. He stepped forward and held out his palm. "Take it off."

Angelo did as instructed, placing the necklace in the man's open hand. Ludo examined the cross with glistening eyes. He then removed an identical one from his own shirt.

"My grandfather gifted one to all of us children. You see?" He pointed to the intersection of the cross, displaying it to the group.

There, glinting in the light, was something Angelo had never noticed in all these years—a delicate 'S' engraved at the junction.

Ludo returned the keepsake to Angelo and wrapped him in a massive bear hug, before kissing both cheeks. "*Benvenuto a casa*, cousin."

Warmth washed over Angelo's body. He'd never before met Ludo, never been in his residence, but for the first time since returning to the Veneto, he recognized a semblance of home.

After wiping his tears, Ludo said, "My promise still stands about *him*," he said, jabbing a finger at Vito. "Now come."

They followed him through the main hall, lined with portraits of staring ancestors frozen in oil and pigment. Angelo recognized a portrayal of Pietro, Ludo's father. Four paces later, his heart leapt into his throat. He stopped in his tracks. Carmen nearly collided with him, her bare dagger grazing his cloak. Tears welled in Angelo's eyes. Hanging on the wall was a perfect likeness of Isabella, captured at the age he knew her. No, not captured, *preserved*. The last time he saw her, she was strapped to a chair in the Great Council Room in the Palazzo Ducale. Since then, she was only a memory. He wiped his eyes and reached out, touching the canvas, willing for it to be her—to be in the flesh, yet she was flesh no more.

A hand landed on Angelo's shoulder, snapping his reverie.

"A perfect likeness," Ludo said. "Commissioned by Palma il Giovane. She will never be forgotten. Come, my friend."

With a deep exhale, Angelo blew a mental kiss to Isabella and forced himself to disengage.

Along with Vito and Carmen, Ludo led the group down connecting rooms and corridors until he stopped before a painting of Saint Mark the Evangelist. Ubiquitous in Venice, Angelo instantly recognized the subject, for he was depicted holding a book of the gospel, along with an inkwell and quill. At his feet was a winged lion, symbol of the saint and the city. Yet this painting possessed a distinct oddity: St. Mark sat on a tree stump in the middle of a wooded forest. Birds and animals completed the scene. A stag hid behind trees in the distance, giving the impression that the antlers extended from St. Mark's head. While Venice was built on petrified trees piled into the bottom of the lagoon, forest imagery was quite alien to Venetians.

"Seems fortune—or foolhardiness—has brought you to us on this day," Ludo said.

"Or conspiracy," Carmen added.

"Perhaps." Ludo pursed his lips. "The Guild of Silvanus meets tonight."

He ran his hand along the frame's edge, stopping toward the bottom. A click followed. He did the same on the top, which produced a second click. The canvas swung inward to reveal a narrow stairwell.

Following Ludo, with Carmen at the rear, they descended into cooler air that smelled of damp stone. At the base of the steps, Ludo pushed aside a red curtain to reveal a carved wooden panel the size of a small door. He rapped a series of knocks, then pressed against it. The door gave way with a soft groan.

He extended an open palm, indicating for Angelo and Vito to enter. The chamber beyond was modest by the villa's standards but rich in atmosphere. Candelabras sputtered along the walls, their smoke clinging to vaulted beams. A long oak table dominated the space. Around it sat seven men of varying ages and two women, both in their fourth or fifth decade, all in noble finery. Their conversations ceased.

Ludo shut the panel once he and Carmen entered. "We have honored guests, my friends," he said. "Venice's lost son has returned. Angelo Mascari."

Half the group focused on Vito. A gray-haired man pointed an angry finger in his direction. "What is *he* doing here? How could you have brought Vito Uccello? Have you gone mad, Ludo?"

Raising his palms in deferential surrender, Vito spoke softly. "I understand your alarm, but I am not your enemy."

"No?" The man arched a pruned eyebrow. "You serve Quattrone. You've condemned *our* loved ones to Tintoretto's prison."

"Hear him out," Ludo said. "Here *us* out. I am not mad. I do not trust this man, and if he gives us reason, he will not leave here alive tonight." He leered at Vito but turned to Angelo. "I do trust *this* man. He has lost as much as any of us, if not more, and has fought the Order more than any of us, including ridding us of Ivan Uccello. If Angelo vouches for Vito, that is enough for me to listen."

He nodded to the former Protector.

"I am here for the same reason as you." Vito gazed about the room, meeting everyone's eyes. "As all of you. You are all members of the Order, yet here you sit. Conspiring against them. Without success, I might add."

"You lost someone to *Il Paradiso*?" Carmen asked.

"No." Vito hung his head. "To the contrary. I have lost loved ones, but I am also guilty. My eyes have been opened. Fighting ghosts won't unmake them."

"We're here to fight the men who made them," Angelo said, stepping forward. "Together."

Ludo nodded toward the table. "Sit. Let's hear what ghosts have brought us tonight."

They seated themselves at the far end. Candles hissed in the drafts. Shadows bent and unbent across half-lit faces.

Vito broke the tension. "My friends—"

"We are not your friends," Carmen said. She drove her dagger into the table, the knife sticking up like an emphasis on her statement. Its silver hilt was engraved with vines of ivy and oak.

"I understand your distrust," Angelo said to the group. "After all, I was in the same position. We were sworn enemies." He placed his hand on Vito's arm. "How many times did we try to kill each other?"

Vito laughed. "More than once."

Ludo pinched the arch of his nose. "So the Order changes tactics or policy, and you denounce them?"

"No," Vito replied. "The Order hasn't changed. *I* have. I've realized how wrong I was. How blinded I was. I wanted to believe that I was serving a greater good."

While the group seemed to internalize their deliberations, Angelo seized the moment to drive their plea home.

"I see eleven blades before me trying to fight the Order," he said. "We are another two. Not mere blades. Not arrows. We are emblazoned cannonballs that, if launched, will crush our adversaries."

"What do you propose?" Ludo asked.

"Wait." Carmen leaned forward, the ruby pendant at her throat sparkling. "If we speak of anything that may jeopardize the precarious lives we've established, you must swear an oath first. Both of you."

Anticipating the request, Angelo didn't hesitate. "Name it."

Carmen sprang from her seat and pried the dagger from the table. She pointed it at Angelo. "Swear by Silvanus, guardian of the untamed, that you'll give your life to the Guild, to free the lost souls, and to bring ruin to the Ancient Order of the Seventh Sun."

Angelo grasped the blade. Blood welled along his palm. "I swear it."

He released the weapon, and she turned to Vito.

The former Protector's jaw flexed. "I don't swear oaths I can't keep."

"Which part can you not keep?" asked a tall, slender man sitting at the far end of the table.

"All of it," Vito responded. "I will try to do those things, but I cannot promise any of them."

"Then you die here," Carmen said. She raised the knife.

Angelo stood and positioned himself in front of his friend. "He's done more to fight them than you know. Felled former comrades. Risked his life. Saved mine."

"Out of guilt?" she asked.

"Out of purpose," Vito said. "You want to destroy the Order? Then you need me."

"You said it yourself," Ludo spun his body so his legs were sitting on the outside of the table. "We're all members of the Order. Just like you."

"Not just like me. I'm Enforcer of the Charge. Chief Protector."

"Was," Carmen said. "I gather they nearly arrested you."

"Word travels fast. A minor setback. A misunderstanding that can be rectified with influence. You need me. I can go where none of you can."

Ludo scrutinized him. "Where is that?"

"Paulina Grimani's bed."

The reaction of gasps and whispers was instant. Carmen's lips curled into something between amusement and disgust. "You filthy dog."

"Perhaps," Vito said. "But she's my key. Our key. She still holds considerable influence. People confide in her. I can learn plans. I will make amends with Quattrone and Doge Memmo."

"Her husband is a dangerous foe." Ludo said. "Cunning. Connected."

"Skilled with a blade," Carmen added.

"He studied under Salvator Fabris."

Ludo glanced at Angelo, who had perked up at the name, for Fabris was also his fencing master. In Santa Marta and during their sea battle, Angelo had noticed Senator Grimani was an adept swordsman, though erratic, presumably from the fruit's effects.

"Had you stayed," Vito said, "you likely would've sparred with him."

"I have sparred with him," Angelo replied. "And won."

Ludo smiled. "That doesn't change the situation. Grimani is ensconced. He could be doge someday. If he learns of Vito and his wife, Vito won't be long for this world."

"He already knows," Angelo said, unable to keep quiet. "The man's deranged. Poisoned by tainted jungle fruit. It's a good plan, and now's the time to enact it while Grimani is still raving."

Vito snapped his fingers. "Precisely. I also know every Protector, including those who have harbored doubts, especially in light of the failed mission. We take the Order down from the inside."

"Then swear the oath," Carmen said.

"If I do that, then it would hinder my ability to win back Quattrone and Memmo's favor. I cannot let a promise to you impede a promise to them. Though I can swear that my ultimate goal will be to release the souls and crush the Order."

The group nodded at his words.

“Works for me,” Ludo said. “From tonight, we move as one. But mark me, Uccello. If your words prove false, I’ll hang you from the doge’s balcony myself.”

Vito’s smirk was thin. “I’ll give you the rope.”

XLII

The chapel on Giudecca had been forsaken since the last plague. Its bell tower leaned toward the lagoon like a cyclops reaching for salvation, its façade furred with moss and sea salt. Heavy air permeated the inside, damp with the faint essence of old incense and forgotten masses.

Vito ambled through the nave, mindful of the creak of each footfall on the warped floorboards. Moonlight streamed through the broken stained-glass windows, painting shards of gray across the cracked tiles.

The church had long abandoned prayers, but he pleaded that his message had reached his beloved.

Even so, the risk may not have been worth the reward.

He stopped near the altar, where dust-covered melted candles clung to their stands like stubby bones. He wondered if God still listened here, or if even He had turned away.

A whisper of silk stirred behind him.

"You're late. I was waiting outside."

The voice caused a spike in Vito's pulse. He turned to find Paulina, her cloak hooded, her face pale in the dim light. Her beauty struck him like a wound he'd never allowed to heal. Her eyes, large and brown, searched him with more judgment than affection.

"I crossed the canal twice. Just to be certain." He extended his arms and took four long strides to embrace the woman who held his heart. "I missed you so."

Without warning, her hand struck his face with a slap that echoed through the ruins.

"Dio, Paulina..." he murmured, massaging his cheek. "It's been nearly a year, and that's how you greet me? They're watching for me. I had to be safe."

"I don't give a damn about that. You brought him home," she said with a hiss. "Angelo Mascari. You brought him back to Venice."

Her anger was fire. Beautiful and dangerous. He could almost taste it. A flicker of her youth glimmered in her eyes. The passion she'd carried since she was a girl invigorated his senses. Her father had often referred to Paulina as an old soul, but Vito knew the opposite was true; there was no way a person with such vitality could be anything but eternally young. Even now, with forty-one years and three children, she shined from within. He couldn't take it much longer. He grabbed her waist, pulled her in, and planted his lips on hers. She returned the affection like a hungry lioness, squeezing his shoulders and biting his lip. A trickle of blood spread between them, dribbling down his chin.

His hands moved to untie her frock, but she broke free and struck him again, though softer this time, her fingers trembling. Then she caught herself and exhaled sharply. "I should hate you."

He kissed her, their tongues connecting to make them one, even for a fleeting moment. "Maybe you do."

But she didn't move away. She pressed her forehead to his chest, her breath uneven, her body shaking beneath the velvet folds of her cloak.

"Damn you," she whispered. "You'll be the downfall for us both."

He yearned to rip off her garments, to trace every familiar line, but he repressed the urge. Instead, he drew her into his arms and held her, unmoving, breathing in the bouquet of lavender in her hair. The simple contact anchored him even as it unraveled him, steadiness and chaos arriving in the same breath.

This is sin, he thought. *But it's the only thing that feels true.*

"You could be dogaressa some day," he whispered. The words came involuntarily, from a place of guilt, but also from pragmatism and verity. They were at a crossroads. If he walked away, she'd have the future she deserved; if he stayed, he could bring her disgrace.

She jutted her head back with a scoff. "With Benito as doge?"

Vito met her eyes. "As much as it pains me, it's possible."

"He's more a lunatic now than ever."

"Have you seen him? Has his condition worsened?"

She rattled her head. "They won't let me, and that suits me fine. The idea of being in the same room as my so-called husband curdles my stomach."

"Paulina, you've dreamt of being dogaressa your whole life. You were born—"

A finger on his lips silenced him. "I've dreamt of *you* my whole life. I'd give it all away, abandon everything, just for us to be together."

Now it was Vito's turn to chuckle. "*Everything*? The fineries? The servants? The delicacies?"

"You think I enjoy meeting in filthy tunnels and dilapidated chapels?"

When she pulled away, her eyes glistened. Not with tears, but fury suppressed. "They say you've betrayed the doge. That you escaped the Palazzo by attacking your own."

"I survived," he said, fearing that the rumors would soon be worse. "That's crime enough."

"You think survival will save you?"

He didn't answer. Truth was written in the lines on his face and in the bruise-colored bags under his eyes. She watched him, and for the first time that night, her anger gave way to pity. "We shouldn't have come here, Vito. Not now."

"As much as I wanted to see you, woefully, I came for something else."

"For what?"

"Help."

Her lips curled upwards. In all their years together, it was the first time he had asked for any favor. "Of course, my protector. Anything."

Vito surveilled the space again, searching for unwanted ears. When he was certain they were alone, he returned to his love.

"The Order is rotting from the inside," he said. "Memmo's dying, and Quattrone is already feeding on his bones. He talks of expansion, of power. As if he's God himself. That's not what the Order was meant to be. Not originally."

Her voice dropped to a whisper. "What was it meant to be, Vito?"

He exhaled. "A covenant. A brotherhood to preserve truth, to guide men toward light, not drown them in ambition. But Quattrone..." He grimaced, bearing some responsibility for enabling unchecked power. "He's turned it into a kingdom of serpents."

Paulina's face softened. Her still-rosy cheeks accentuated her aquiline nose. "You ask that I help guide it to its original purpose?"

He took her hands and planted tender kisses before speaking. "On the night I left for the New World, I told you that years ago, I took safeguards to protect us."

"You told me that should anything happen to you—" She choked on the words. "Your mother. In the convent. Should I... is now the time?"

"No, no. Not yet, anyway."

Vito tore himself away and paced the chapel while Paulina leaned against a dusty pew. He never meant to endanger her but had always known it would come. Perhaps it had been written from the start—from a single moment in time. He stopped before a headless statue of a saint he couldn't name and studied its fragmented calm, wondering if their fates, like the marble figure before him, had been shaped long ago, only to be broken by unknown hands.

"My sweet," he said, still pacing. "I have a confession."

She cocked her head and arched her eyebrows.

"Do you remember," Vito continued, "years ago, when Angelo Mascari killed Renzo Scalfini?"

"Of course."

"It was believed he stole your father's journal. A black book that contained secrets. One that was in Renzo's possession. You're familiar with this, yes?"

"I am. What are you to tell me, Vito?"

She snatched his hands to stop his motion. He relented, kicking a piece of debris aside.

"The safeguard that I took, what my brother helped me do, was to secure that journal. Your *father's journal*. We paid Mascari to steal it, but he never did."

Her eyes widened. She retreated a step. "What?"

"Things ended most unfortunately, but in the end, perhaps fortuitously, I secured it."

"How could you?"

"I stole it for you."

"Don't insult me." Her eyes flared with dismay. "How could such treachery be for me? Make me understand."

He held her gaze. "I needed leverage, Paulina. *We* needed leverage. If our love was discovered, I'd be a dead man. Your father's book was the only way. If I had it, I could protect you. I could protect both of us."

Four seasons of emotion cycled across her face. She stared at him for a long time, the silence unbearable. Then, the slightest of smiles, proving she understood. "What does my father's ledger contain that could provide such protection?"

"Secrets, 'mòre mio. Proof of corruption. Proof the Church is complicit."

As the words left Vito's lips, he debated internally if now was the time to use it. No, that would be premature. He needed to work with the Guild. They needed strength behind any offensive.

"I took it for us," he went on, "but now it can be used for a greater good. The Church will be forced to act. To bring down the Order. I need your eyes, Paulina. You hear things in those halls no man could."

"You ask me to spy on my husband? On the doge?"

"I'm asking you to save Venice."

Her laugh was hollow. "You always make sins sound like virtue."

"Maybe it is." He stepped closer again. "Maybe God forgives the right kind of sin."

She turned away, bracing herself against a column. Moonlight caught her face. Her beauty. Her anger. Her contemplation. He wanted to reach for her but gave her space. "We need to tread cautiously," he said. "If we expose knowledge that we have the book, we risk it falling into Quattrone's hands. Should that happen, he'll control Venice and Rome. He'll use it to bend the Church, to justify every atrocity."

Paulina looked over her shoulder. "You think he doesn't already?"

Vito hesitated. "He believes himself the instrument of God. I think he's closer to the Devil."

She turned to face him again. "You're no better. You swore yourself to them, Vito. You hunted men for them. Now you want me to help you clean your soul?"

His throat tightened. "No. I only want a future."

Her expression softened. "With me?"

"You know the answer to that question. The book is our key. It will liberate you from Benito's grasp."

"Quattrone's already preparing for Doge Memmo's funeral," Paulina said in a business tone. "He'll use the disorder to take control. He's scheming. He's been meeting with bankers from Paris and Madrid. I'll learn more."

Vito nodded. "That's a start. What do they say about me?"

"Whispers. Doge Memmo is quite distraught."

"I need to get back in their good graces. Will you listen to what they say? Vouch for me when you can? Remind them of my decades of loyalty. I must be able to get close to them."

She stepped closer, brushing her fingers along his jaw. "And when they betray you again?"

"I'll fight."

"What if they go to your mother? Is that where the book is?"

As usual, Paulina was wise beyond her years. She had no strategic training or education but thought like a warrior. Still, he couldn't risk putting her or his mother in even more danger. After a moment of deliberation, he said, "If it comes to it, see my sister, Sofia. In Mestre. I'll leave her with instructions."

Paulina caressed the silver crucifix hanging from her neck. "You're asking me to bear the weight of your war."

"I'm asking you to finish it if I fail."

She studied him for a long moment, then gave him a slow, long kiss. "Very well. I will make you proud. But hear me, Vito Uccello. If the man I love lies to me again, I'll cut out his tongue."

He met her eyes with a mischievous grin. He adored her so. "You'd miss my tongue."

She slapped him again, but this time it was playful.

"We're in a church, you heathen!"

"I'm aware."

"If you lose my father's book, or worse, if Quattrone takes it, you'll damn more than yourself."

"I know that too."

Paulina touched her forehead against his, her breath warm against his lips. "I shall go. Before I change my mind."

Vito lingered, craving to tell her all he didn't say, that he no longer knew which oath mattered more: the one to her, to the Order, or to his own conscience.

Instead, he whispered, "*Grassie.*"

She pulled the hood over her graying hair. "Don't thank me. This is for us. For Venice."

"The Republic owes you a debt. And Paulina, know that Angelo Mascari isn't the villain you think him to be."

"I suspect we'll see his true colors soon."

She slipped out of the church into the night.

Alone again, Vito stood in the dark, the dusty air heavy in his lungs. Every path he'd chosen had led him here. To betrayal, to love, to a gambit that could destroy him.

He wiped the blood from his broken lip.

XLIII

"DO YOU HEAR THAT?"

The physician whispered the question to Quattrone and Doge Memmo as they walked the hallway in a far corner of the Palazzo. Save the tapping of the doge's cane, it was as tranquil as a cathedral before lauds.

"I don't hear anything," the doge said. He threw an inquisitive glance at Quattrone.

"Precisely," the doctor replied.

He stopped at a wooden door flanked by two Protectors standing beside glowing sconces. At the doctor's nod, a guard unlatched a bolt. Since Grimani couldn't go home because of his condition and was too great a risk to stay in an infirmary, the infrequently used storage room had been requisitioned for his convalescence—if such a thing were possible.

The doge's personal doctor had been assigned to the task and assured the council he'd find a cure for Grimani's ailment.

Standing outside the room, Quattrone grasped the question's connotation. Grimani had been stark-raving mad. His screams echoed throughout the palace, which is why they sequestered him as far away as possible. As simple as it was, calm signaled a road to recovery.

The doctor led them into the windowless space, where candles lit a sight that caused Quattrone to retch in his mouth. He wiped spittle from his lips and pressed a kerchief over his nose.

It wasn't Grimani's naked body on the bed that nauseated him, but rather what covered it.

Leeches. Dozens of them.

He made the sign of the cross, gagging as he did so.

Despite his station and fondness for life's fineries, Quattrone considered himself to be a hardened man. Yet every time he encountered the repulsive creatures, his blood chilled.

Small jars had been laid out on a table next to the bed like specimens for a butcher. Dark masses wriggled in each.

The doctor's apprentice, a young man with short, brown hair, removed a bloodsucker with forceps and placed it on Grimani's testicles. He then pried an engorged one off the man's cheek and dropped it in a large jar filled with other leeches.

A wave of nausea rolled through Quattrone. He wanted to rush out but held fast.

Grimani's once-imposing frame had wasted to pallor and sinew. His skin was ashen. His eyes were two bloodshot marbles fixed on nothing. He looked less like the patrician Quattrone remembered and more like a man dredged from a grave.

The physician's assistant pressed a cloth steeped in poppy tincture to Grimani's lips, coaxing him to suck the medication. He swallowed, lips twitching in a half-smile.

"Why have you brought us here?" The words caught in Quattrone's throat.

The doctor's mouth arched into a grin of triumph. "We used more leeches than any other man would dare. One hundred and twenty so far. We drained and drained. The toxins in Grimani, whatever they are, have left their vessel. For the most part."

"Excellent work, *dottore*," the doge said, unbothered by the medical procedure.

"Grassie, My Serene." The doctor smiled and tipped his head. "We bled him until the bile left. Warm wine stayed him from collapsing. Leeches took the darker blood first." He tapped the pot of swollen leeches. The parasites throbbed like a small, obscene pulse. "Taken in time, it worked. The senator is more lucid and quite calm."

"Hello, my friends." Grimani's voice was hoarse, but there was a smoothness to it. "I suppose I owe you an apology."

He lay in a simple bed for a senator's disgrace, held down by leather straps in one of the few Palazzo rooms with bare walls. He carried the visage of a man who'd been unmade and stitched back together wrong. Fat had been drained away from his face, leaving the rigid outline of a skull beneath skin. Yet his eyes were hungry and sharp, practically the only part of his body not feeding a leech.

Quattrone forced himself to meet his gaze.

"Benito," Memmo began, hobbling to his confidante, "we're so pleased you are on the mend. There is nothing for which you need to apologize. Your ailment was a fault not yours."

"'Reject your sense of injury and the injury itself disappears,'" Grimani said.

The doge smiled. "The words of Marcus Aurelius, if I'm not mistaken?"

"Right you are, Most Serene," replied the doctor. "The mind is the most powerful panacea."

"That, and a hundred leeches," Quattrone said. "What do you remember?" he asked, dispensing with formalities and small talk. He wished to stay in that place not one second longer than necessary.

A mournful wail flowed from Grimani, surprising Quattrone into an involuntary flinch. "Remember?" He gazed longingly at the wall, as if able to see the sky. "I bit the sweet thing. It tasted like Heaven. Like the world righted. Then... then blackness."

The doctor hovered. "He's still under the draught, but much improved. Intelligent speech emerges then slips. We also inadvertently discovered the most remarkable thing. Observe." He took a candle from the table and held it over Grimani, then dripped hot wax onto his chest. There was no reaction.

"Does that hurt, senator?"

"Not at all."

It was an unexpected development. The doge's mouth popped open, clearly as surprised as Quattrone. "You feel no pain?"

Grimani shook his head.

The physician swapped the candle for a scalpel. "Forgive me, Most Serene." He made a small incision in Grimani's shoulder between two leeches.

"I feel… nothing at all," he said.

"He should not be conscious," the doctor said. "Yet he clings to wakefulness. He carries no pain. Fascinating."

"Fascinating?" Quattrone turned, sickened by everything and everyone in the room. "We do not employ you for fascination or the obvious, *dottore.* We employ you for answers."

"I only say this is not natural, Senator," the doctor replied with a lowered head.

"Again, stating that which is observable to a monkey. What else is unnatural, *dottore*, is your fondness for your young daughter, as beautiful as she is. Tell us one more thing we already know, and not only shall I tell your wife what she doesn't know, but I'll find the time to enjoy your daughter's luscious flesh."

The doctor cleared his throat and swallowed.

"He aids my recovery," Grimani said.

"Does he?" Quattrone asked, not bothering to shield his continued frustration. "And what of *your* wife?"

Grimani scrunched his face. "What of her?"

Quattrone shrugged. "Has Paulina said anything of your lack of feeling?"

"I have not seen her. Why are you asking?"

The senator's response confirmed Quattrone's suspicions. Still, he pressed, in part to agitate the man. "Oh? She's come to the Palazzo nearly every day for a fortnight. Always inquiring about politics and affairs. Always… overly curious. Yet she hasn't visited you? Odd."

"Now *that* is pain." Grimani's face flushed, accentuated by the flickering candles. "My precious fruit has sapped all feeling but anger. I wanted more and more, and it wouldn't come. They tried to take it. They tried to keep it. You—" He stared at Quattrone and spat before struggling against his binds. He raised his voice. "You craved my power. You envied me."

The doctor shuffled away. Fear glazed his widened eyes. "He may be lapsing into an episode. We must be careful."

Ignoring the warning, Quattrone did not dispute Grimani's accusation. His skin rippled, but he shifted closer to the bed, eager to learn how to capture that power. He tightened his kerchief around his mouth and nose. He met the doge's gaze before turning back to the patient. "Can you locate the tree?"

"You see?" Grimani offered a wicked grin. "It's true, is it not? You also wish to sink your teeth into my fruit."

"Can you retrace your steps?"

The senator's pupils slid like unfocused lenses. "Branches scraped the sky, higher than cathedrals. River of glass. I fed until my mouth could not stop. The trees sang. The people screamed." His fingers twitched as he hollered.

"Where is the Tree of Life?" Quattrone pressed.

With his eyes glazing over, Grimani's head rolled back. "Eden," he said to the ceiling. "Or hell. I bit the fruit. Sweet... sweet as apotheosis. Sweet as Paulina's delicious cunt. Then blackness. Hunger. Always hunger."

"Come, Marco," the doge said. "Let's leave him be."

The doctor scribbled notes furiously, muttering about corrupted blood.

"Speak sense, man!" Quattrone snapped at Grimani. "In the jungle? An ancient city? Give me a detail."

For a moment, Grimani's vision and composure returned to normal. He stared with a pensive brow. "Yes."

The single-word response ruptured Quattrone's expectations, unsettling him further. He rattled his head, exasperated with this person who was once one of the most rational men in the Senate.

"Yes? Yes, what? You'll give me something? A name of a place, perhaps?"

"A name?" Grimani's head snapped forward, a fire lighting his face. "Names burn away. Maps rot. I have tasted the fruit of the gods!" He snarled and flared his body. The leather strap restraining his right hand popped free. "You'll never have it. Never!"

At the flare-up, Zanca burst from a chair in the corner and positioned his body in front of the doge. It was the first time Quattrone noticed the Protector in the room. He cursed himself for allowing worms to cloud his cognizance.

"Vito!" Grimani yelled. "Mascari! They must scream. They must scream! They must scream!"

With his arm untethered, Grimani lunged with feral strength, breaking the left strap, his hand grasping around Quattrone's throat. The sudden violence shattered the chamber. A primal fear roared through him as he met Grimani's gaze.

The man's teeth snapped, desperate for blood, inches from Quattrone's face. As the air vanished from Quattrone's lungs, Zanca fist slammed into Grimani's jaw.

Two other guards raced in. The three men pried Grimani's fingers from Quattrone's neck. He sucked air. Grimani toppled over with the men on top.

The former senator hit the floor, still writhing, spittle flying, laughter twisting. "Roots in blood! Branches in bone! Drink and burn!"

The physician retreated to the wall, clutching his satchel as if it might shield him.

Quattrone backed away from the fight, his fingers instinctively going to his throat. "Subdue him," he managed to shout with a rasp.

As the two guards held Grimani down, Zanca landed blow after blow into the senator's face. Blood drenched his hand and the floor. The doctor rushed over with the poppy tincture.

"Keep his mouth open!"

Zanca squeezed Grimani's cheeks as the doctor and his assistant forced the black liquid into their patient's mouth.

He struggled. A moment later, Grimani's bloodshot eyes rolled into the back of his head. He mumbled to himself, half asleep. The men dragged Grimani back onto the bed, securing and tightening his restraints.

Quattrone straightened, brushing dust from his doublet, attempting to appear unfazed.

"Are you hurt, Senator?" Zanca asked.

Ignoring him, Quattrone lingered at the table, finally allowing himself to inhale. His fingers massaged his throat, mind ablaze. Grimani's reaction was intense, but that's not what dominated the senator's mind. No, it was that the madman had found power in the jungle. The Fountain had been a child's tale, a rumor to bait fools. This tree was something else. Something real. Grimani's madness sharpened the truth; the man had seen it. Touched it. Consumed it.

He clearly had ingested too much, but what if a man were to taste it? Quattrone could harvest it. Control it.

His lips curled into a thin, controlled smile.

"Is it possible he'll recover his memory?" he asked the doctor.

"Anything is possible, Senator."

"Do not attempt to placate me with platitudes, *dottore*. Yes or no?"

The doctor studied Grimani's body. "Considering the progress he's made in such a short time, I think yes."

Quattrone let his eyes close for a fraction, picturing the world like a chessboard. "If we were to obtain more of this fruit, there remains the opportunity of extracting a sample. Preserving it. From that, we may test and perhaps replicate its effects without the ruin. Am I correct?"

The doctor rubbed his chin. "A measured dose of the fruit's poison and a skilled hand... take it as medicine, not gluttony. Control the hunger."

A sudden brightness swept through Quattrone. "If we can harness it," he said to the doge, "isolate the property that binds mind to vigor, then we'd have the world in our hands."

Memmo inhaled a wheezy breath. "You would... make men into gods?"

"No, Serene," Quattrone replied. "I would make *us* into gods. A strength the Order will wield."

"If it makes men monsters?" Zanca asked with a furrowed brow. "If the fruit breaks men the way it did Grimani?"

"He has a point," the doge said. "A strong one."

"Madness often carries truth."

"Or delusion." Zanca averted his eyes.

The Protector overstepped his bounds by voicing his opinion, which was precisely why Quattrone put his trust in him. He humored the man. "Poison corrupts, destroys, kills. No, *power* flows through Grimani. Power always has a source."

The doge's eyes narrowed, weighing the words. "If that source devours those who seek it? The entire party was lost save Grimani and Vito. Now the senator clings to his humanity."

"You think I risk becoming him?" Quattrone gazed at the man on the bed. "No. I think beyond him. Grimani was careless. Greedy. Imagine that fruit in the hands of one who knows how to wield it." He turned to the Protector. "Venice is but a jewel, Zanca. The world is a crown. Tell me. Should we be content to polish one gem while others seize the crown entire?"

The Protector looked to the doge, who nodded his permission. When Zanca responded, he weighed each word carefully. "My duty is to protect, Exalted Master, Most Serene. Sometimes that means guarding against enemies outside these walls. Other times... it means watching what festers within them. I am at your command."

For an instant, their eyes locked. Quattrone's alight with vision, Zanca's with muted suspicion. Then Zanca inclined his head the way a bird stoops to the wind and took two steps backward.

Quattrone studied the Protector, then turned his attention back to Grimani's leech-covered body. He gagged and spat into his kerchief.

"Let us leave this room, Marco," the doge said with genuine concern. "Fresh air shall do us right. *Dottore*, perhaps more leeches are in order. It would seem his mind is not a panacea after all."

Some minutes later, Quattrone helped his doge take small steps in the courtyard. He knew it was difficult for the octogenarian, but the outdoor exercise would do him right. Still, he could not allow a man's well-being to interfere with pressing—or future—designs.

"You promised me a prize," Quattrone said, not hiding his disappointment. "Not fables and fumblings. The doctor believes Grimani's head shall clear. We can return to New Granada and retrieve the fruit of which he speaks. Only a fool would oppose such a plan."

The doge's head snapped to Quattrone. "You overstep, Senator. Be careful with your words."

"Forgive me, Serene." Quattrone bowed in earnest. "That room, the leeches, Grimani. The word slipped from my lips without thinking or conviction. But... why would you oppose seeking the tree?"

"Give me a hand," the doge responded, jutting his chin toward a marble bench.

Quattrone took the man's arm and guided him into the shade. Cracking popped from the leader of the Republic's bones as he sat.

"There is a simple reason." The doge did his best to steady his breathing. "Time. I will be facing our Lord soon. I rolled the dice and took a slim chance to find the Fountain. I fear I will not be for this world long enough for another."

It was the answer Quattrone expected. Frankly, he couldn't fault the man for his hesitation. "Perhaps the fruit can grant you the youth you crave."

"I may be dead before another expedition reaches the shore of Santa Marta. And then? If Grimani's faculties haven't returned, what, blindly searching for a single tree in a sea of millions?" He chuckled. "No, thank you. I prefer to live my remaining days with grace and dignity."

"We don't need to wait for Grimani to remember. There are others who have knowledge, and they are here in Venice."

Memmo's fingers tightened around Quattrone's elbow. "You speak of Vito Uccello and Angelo Mascari."

"You understand why I press, Most Serene," Quattrone said. "The Seventh Sun must be armored against all enemies. These men hold secrets that can reinforce our strength for a thousand years to come."

Memmo tapped his fingers on his thigh. "What can we believe? Our most trusted can no longer be trusted at all. You are trying to catch rain in the wind, my friend."

"If one is dying of thirst, then one must do what one can. Vito is useful," Quattrone continued, "but regrettably, has become unreliable. He is simultaneously a threat and an asset. He must be contained. He must be compelled to reveal the tree's location. If not him, then Mascari."

The sunlight cut Memmo's cheekbones to paper. "Your desire to armor the Order against enemies is well placed. But, my friend, you have your eye on the wrong prize. It is not on the other side of the world, but here in Venice. Doge Cicogna's journal. *That* remains our greatest threat. If Vito has been working with Mascari, he likely knows its whereabouts. I shall place a formal warrant on both. It will flush them. If they run, we'll find the burrow in which they hide."

Quattrone clenched his jaw, trying to maintain an unflappable demeanor. The doge's shift back to the book was not the desired outcome. Still, it could be a means to an end. "You are most wise, My Serene. Though why bother with a warrant? We know who is in the Guild."

The doge nodded his understanding. "There is a precarious balance with the nobles. If we preemptively move against one or two, it will be discovered and lead to revolt."

"Then let's force the Order's hand. Have them move against us."

Memmo turned and raised an eyebrow. The corner of his mouth ticked upward. "Instigate an attack? Then we quash it?"

"Not just quash. We deliver a fatal blow."

The doge nodded his consent. "Make it happen. And Senator, work with Grimani to find the book."

The thought alone curdled Quattrone's stomach. "My Serene?"

"Two minds are better than one. A search for the book will help keep *his* mind out of the literal jungle."

XLIV

ANGELO LEANED AGAINST THE cold stone wall, his arms crossed, taking in each conspirator in the cramped space. Ludo Stefanetti stood at the head of the table with a commanding presence. The steel-gray eyes and stub nose he inherited from his father gave him the calm arrogance of nobility. Beside him, Carmen Ferrante watched everything, her gaze cutting across the room like a scythe.

Candle smoke and tension thickened the air as nine members of the Guild sat around the long oak table littered with wine glasses, bowls of olives, and crude sketches of buildings.

It had been a month since they'd heard from Vito. While he had faith in his friend, Angelo detested being confined to the villa with no action. The grumbles of those around him grew louder each day.

Brightly colored tapestries lined the walls. Forest scenes illustrated Silvanus, god of the woods, luring Angelo into an imaginary world that couldn't exist. Though the trees, foliage, and characters depicted differed dramatically from the jungle, the imagery brought him back to Santa Marta. He was born and raised on a manmade island. Now, the natural world was his home. Yet here he stood, in a secret room, built by a secret group, surrounded by imagery designed to evoke a secret place. His whole life, Angelo had been thrust into places not of his making.

"Then it's settled," announced Tomaso Bruni, a tall, lean man who wore his wealth not in jewels but in posture, with shoulders square, chin high, and an air of entitlement. "Vito Uccello has failed."

The group voiced their agreement.

"I correct myself," the Tomaso continued. "For all we know, he's *succeeded*."

Ludo's broad shoulders bent forward over the table. "Explain your words, Tomaso."

He stood to emphasize his point. "That Uccello has succeeded with his *true* plan of stalling the Guild while the Order gains strength. Waiting another minute is a fool's game. We should strike before sunrise. No warning. No mercy."

Angelo took a free seat and studied the group. He'd been an observer in the Guild's scheming to this point, but that time was over. "You speak as though we've already decided."

Ludo's jaw tightened. "You were the one who said we cannot wait forever. That the Order grows bolder by the day."

"Indeed. That they do," Angelo replied evenly. "I didn't say that we should hand them our throats."

A murmur rippled around the table.

"What's the alternative?" asked Tomaso. "You think prayers will bring down senators and doges?"

"I think reason and planning might," Angelo replied.

"Reason?" Tomaso spat. "We've buried reason with our dead. We've been talking and scheming and talking and scheming for years. Now you appear like a storm cloud and ask us to wait? We've planned enough. Tonight is the night. Why are we listening to him? Why is he even here?"

Ludo struck the table with his palm. "Enough, Tomaso. Let him speak."

"I share your passion. Your desire for vengeance. But now..." Angelo spoke to everyone in the room, then landed on Tomaso. "I'm asking you to be smart."

"You see?" Tomaso said, raising his voice. "He comes here and insults us, yet refuses to take action."

He shot a glare sharp enough to draw blood, as if every misfortune in his life could be laid at Angelo's feet. Tomaso Bruni was the sort of man to whom life had dealt generous cards, but he played every hand as if he were losing. They were near in age, though Tomaso's skin was smoother, his beard neatly trimmed, his clothes finely tailored—the armor of a man accustomed to privilege.

If the Guild were not so desperate for able bodies, Angelo would have ensured that Tomaso be buried in paper and ink, far from any place where fists might be needed.

"Angelo," Ludo said, "You told us what happened in Santa Marta. Who's to say that can't happen here? My father founded the Guild to protect Venice. To protect the innocent. Even if it means risking our own necks."

Angelo leaned back, the old chair creaking beneath him. He thought of Ludo's father. Pietro died for his silence. Isabella waited for his action. It was why he returned to Venice. The Order had stolen from all of them. And yet...

"I care not about risking my neck," he said. "I care that if I lose my head, you won't have another chance."

Before anyone could answer, a familiar pattern rapped on the hidden door. Carmen stood and peered through the peephole. She threw a glance of dismay at Ludo before releasing the lever. Vito stepped in, ducking his head beneath the low archway. His hood was drawn low, and his coat was damp.

He froze at the sight of the group, his brown eyes clocking the room. "You've been busy."

"Where in God's name have you been?" Angelo asked.

"I told you. Trying to win favor of the doge and Quattrone again." The former Protector pulled back his hood, revealing a face rimmed in exhaustion.

Ludo snorted. "Close enough to stab them, I pray."

"Sadly, no. I'm disappointed in the progress, truth be told. I fear they may not welcome me back."

Tomaso rose. "Then your timing is impeccable. We strike tonight."

Vito's jaw clenched. "Then you'll die tonight. All of you."

Ludo shoved his chair back and stood in a single motion. "You think we haven't planned this? We have men in position—"

"You have fools in position," Vito snapped, stepping forward. "They've doubled the guard."

A collective gasp and grumble rose from the group.

"For what purpose?" asked Angelo.

"I know not. My Protectors—"

"*Your* Protectors?" Carmen narrowed her eyes. Her hand fell to the dagger at her side.

"In a manner of speaking," Vito said, calming his tone. "I trained them myself. You'll never reach the inner courtyard before you're cut down."

Ludo approached, his slimmer frame squaring against Vito's broad chest. "Then what would you have us do? Sit here while the doge and Quattrone take more souls and power?"

"Precisely. For now. I've formulated a new plan to bring them down without bloodshed. A better plan."

"What plan is that?"

"I cannot reveal it. Not yet."

"You see?" Tomaso said to Ludo. He stood and spoke with animated hands. "We cannot trust him. It's highly likely that he and Angelo conspire against us!"

The room erupted in agreement and accusations of betrayal.

Vito lifted a hand. When the group settled, he simply said, "Have faith."

"Faith?" Carmen said with a mix of incredulity and fury. "You expect us to trust the man who, a short time ago, would have burned us at the stake with a smile?"

"Things change." Vito lowered his head slightly, as if repenting. "People change."

"Yet your first scheme accomplished nothing, and you refuse to disclose this new grand plan," Ludo said. "Why did you even come here?"

"To tell you to stand down so you don't squander your chance and get yourselves killed in the process." He turned to Carmen. "You spoke the truth a moment ago. It is what I would have done. There are many others who *still* seek to do it."

The room hushed, absorbing the gravity of his words.

"And you?" Ludo said to Angelo. "Have you nothing to add?"

Angelo assessed the situation. Like the men around him, he yearned to storm the Palazzo and kill every last member of the Order. Truth was, they'd never make it past the gate. "No. I have nothing to add because Vito is correct. We're vastly outnumbered, and you wish to launch a full-frontal assault."

Vito nodded to Angelo. "I must go now."

"Where?" Carmen asked.

"It doesn't matter."

"That's it?" Ludo asked. "So you came here to tell us to do nothing?"

"Like the man said, my timing is impeccable." Vito moved for the door but turned to the group. "Once the plan is in motion, it will be too dangerous for me to return. I'll send word when the time is right."

"You have a week," Angelo said in an attempt to placate the Guild.

"I need three," Vito replied. "Most likely four. Delicate things take time."

Ludo crossed his arms. "We'll give you two."

Before anyone could stop him, Vito turned and slipped out the way he came. The secret door closed with a hollow click.

Tomaso was the first to speak. "We're fools if we keep waiting."

A familiar churn boiled in Angelo's gut. Vito's voice of reason solidified his apprehensions. "No. We lie low for now," he said at last.

Ludo twisted to him. "And do what? Wait for Vito to tell us when to breathe?"

"If you want to live long enough to see the Order fall," Angelo said, "then yes."

The fire popped, echoing through the tension.

Ludo muttered and cursed, ripped the door open, and stormed out. The others followed, yet Carmen lingered a moment longer.

"You trust him," she said.

"You've asked me that already."

"Yet he keeps secrets from you."

"If he has reason, then I trust the purpose. He would not betray his friends."

Carmen twisted her face in a repulsed slant. "That you call him friend sickens me."

Without another word, she shook her head and left. Angelo waited until her footsteps faded, then took a candle and slipped into the corridor. The Stefanetti villa loomed silent around him. Marble saints watched from alcoves beneath painted ceilings.

A life that no longer felt entirely his seemed to be slipping from his grasp with every passing hour. He longed for peaceful mornings, the joy of his children playing outside, Loredana's steady presence anchoring their world. He craved the ordinary with a hunger that surprised him. Yet justice gnawed at him as fiercely as any intrinsic desire. He didn't want to wait for Vito; patience had never been his virtue. Still, he knew Vito was right, that some reckonings demanded time. Home on one side. Judgement on the other. The fates pulled him thin until one truth remained clear: this could not be allowed to drag on. One way or another, the fight had to end.

He thought of paying yet another visit to Isabella's portrait, but a sensation he hadn't felt in ages came over him: the urge to pray.

Maybe it was guilt. Or a long-lost habit instilled in him by his parents. Or a whisper from the past reminding him that he was once someone other than a fighter. Or maybe he just needed someone to talk to.

"Pardon," he said to a passing servant, a rotund woman in her sixth decade. "Is there a church nearby? Perhaps between the estate and the nearest town?"

She offered a warm smile that exuded understanding. "If you wish to pray, sior, the family has a private chapel on the estate."

"Perfect," Angelo responded. "Please show me the way."

Using a lantern, the servant led Angelo through the villa to a vestibule that opened to an expansive rear patio. Though the light was faint in the starless sky, he could make out a manicured lawn and pool enclosed by marble columns. A cacophony of chittering and hooting filled the landscape.

"What are those noises?" he asked the servant.

"My lordship's zoo. He's quite fond of the exotic."

Angelo despised the notion of imprisoned birds and beasts but said nothing of it. The Stefanettis had proven themselves to be good people on more than one occasion. Should they defeat the Order—and survive—he would inform Ludo of the inhumanity of caging nature.

A narrow archway opened to a stone path that led past the stables and the orchard, where overripe figs littered the dark ground. Beyond the orchard stood a grove of cypress trees, tall and black in the night.

"Before the war with the Turks, Maestro Pietro's father built a small oratory behind the gardens," the servant said. "He said every noble family needed a place to speak to God without an audience."

The garden stretched downhill toward the Brenta, with narrow paths threading between hedges and low stone walls. There, half-hidden among the trunks, was a chapel.

"The oratory, sior."

The servant lit a half-dozen candles, bowed, and left Angelo alone.

Trembling light revealed a small chapel built of pale Istrian stone, its roof pitched low, like a fisherman's hut that genuflected to Heaven. A faded fresco of Saint Mark's lion guarded the arched doorway. The place was hardly larger than a crypt, clearly meant for private devotion. A single wooden pew. An altar of veined marble. A wooden crucifix scarred by time.

Angelo removed his hat and knelt at the rail, the wood groaning beneath his weight. His sword dug against his thigh, a reminder of who he'd become.

You've killed before. Why stop now?

Isabella's sweet voice filled his head. He knew she was only in his thoughts, but he cherished hearing her. It had been so long.

He bowed. "Because I tire of ghosts."

Am I your ghost?

"No, no, no! My tongue speaks faster than my brain allows. Apologies, 'mòre mio. I'm sorry. I'm so very sorry for so many things. That we've not spoken for so long. Your fate... That I've yet to free you..."

This is not a confessional, my sweet.

Angelo chuckled. "I offer my apologies for outcomes, but you know me. In truth, I've nothing to confess."

Do you speak the truth? Were you not keeping secrets from me? What's done is in the past. I wouldn't change a moment but do not lie to yourself.

"You imply your husband's book?" A great sadness overcame Angelo. "I never meant to deceive you, Isabella. It was not a seduction but true love."

You've proven that time and again. Though if the Bird Brothers hadn't hired you to steal it, then we would have never met.

Angelo smirked at her comment in his head. "So you're saying I owe Vito my gratitude?"

In a sense, but don't lose sight of the Protector's secrets.

"You mean why they desired the book?" Angelo ruminated on his question. "It was not your husband's but the doge's journal, was it not?"

It was never found. Or so they claim.

"Was it in the lockbox? The one I never opened?"

I know not the answer. I do know that after you fled, Vito and his brother would have had some moments alone in the room.

Angelo rubbed his jaw. "You think Vito stole the book? After all this time... he is in possession of it?"

I think you've focused so much on me, you've lost sight of the Order.

"If that were true, then why would he not have acted? If the book is as powerful an instrument as people claim, he could use it to defeat our enemies."

Perhaps he has not been able. Or perhaps the opportunity has not yet presented itself.

Angelo cocked his head at the notion. It explained Vito's surreptitious strategy and clandestine meetings.

You have forgotten that the Order is always lurking behind you.

The muscle between his neck and shoulder blade combusted. Unbearable pain bolted like lightning into his head and chest. Warm liquid sprayed the side of his face and coated his skin.

It took a half second to comprehend the grunt behind him and the shimmer of steel coming down for a second strike.

Suppressing the unrepentant agony, Angelo twisted and caught his assailant's blade, the metal inflicting yet another wound as it carved into his palm.

He released the knife and rolled off the bench. The dagger slammed into the stone. Angelo crashed onto his ass, finally able to catch sight of the attacker.

He scampered backward as Tomaso Bruni lunged again before Angelo had a chance to draw his sword. He caught Bruni's wrist with his good hand. They locked, muscles straining. The intruder's breath stank of wine and fear.

Seizing the advantage of his position, Bruni pressed down on Angelo's weakened left side. The tip of the knife crept toward his throat.

"You should've stayed gone, Mascari," Bruni snarled. "The Order remembers."

Unable to draw his sword, Angelo braced the attack with his right hand, snatched a lit candle with his left, and drove the flame into Bruni's eye.

The turncoat screamed and recoiled, allowing Angelo to pounce to his feet. In a fluid motion, he drew his rapier. The pommel knocked into Bruni's jaw, sending him reeling back.

"So do I," Angelo said through gritted teeth, his anger and adrenaline overtaking his injuries.

He flourished his sword and advanced. Fear swelled in Bruni's face as his eyes flicked between his dagger and Angelo's rapier. He darted behind the pew and burst through the door. Angelo gave chase, boots thudding across the marble and onto the path.

The would-be assassin sprinted through the colonnade and fled into the hedges, his cloak whipping behind him.

Night air bit Angelo's lungs. Each step sent spikes of discomfort up his left side. Bruni vaulted a low wall into the orchard. Angelo sprinted after him, crashing through branches.

Glancing back, Bruni stumbled but regained his footing. Angelo exploited the mistake, catching up and slamming him hard against a tree. The move hurt like he collided with a spiked boulder, but it was worth it. The man's knife landed on the ground.

Angelo slid his rapier's blade beneath Bruni's throat. "Who are you working with? What does the Order know?"

Bruni grinned, blood trickling from his lip. "Does it matter? You think the Guild is safe?"

Angelo swept the pommel of his sword across Bruni's jaw.

The man spat blood into his face, then wrenched free, reaching for another knife hidden in his sleeve.

Twisting aside, Angelo caught the blade on his rapier, metal shrieking as he defended the strike. Pain flared through his left shoulder and hand, the wounds protesting every moment, but he powered through it and smashed his elbow into his opponent's temple. Bruni reeled yet stayed upright by sheer refusal. Snarling, he abandoned any pretense of form or station, hacking, overreaching, swinging with both arms as if wild force might make up for fear. Angelo slipped inside the arcs, reading every clumsy tell. He let Bruni exhaust himself, absorbing the fury and waiting for the moment when desperation outweighed balance.

Angelo needed to subdue him, not kill him. He needed answers.

As Bruni's shoulders sagged, Angelo again brought the tip of his sword to the man's throat, this time keeping his distance.

"Talk now or your next breath will be your last!"

A flash of steel caught the moonlight. His assailant froze. Blood squirted Angelo's face.

Then he saw it: a thin throwing knife jutting from Bruni's throat.

The action registered. Angelo spun to find Carmen striding from the shadows, another blade already between her fingers.

Bruni collapsed, choking on his last breath.

Angelo crouched. He pressed on the knife's entry point, but it was futile.

"Tell me!" Angelo said, shaking the traitor. "What does the Order know?"

Bruni's mouth formed a weak grin as his countenance went cold.

"Merda." Angelo closed the man's eyes and crossed himself.

He rose and staggered, his breath ragged, the world spinning in anguish. He clutched his left shoulder where Bruni's dagger had found its mark. The gash burned hot and deep, slicking his fingers in crimson.

Once a place of solace, the garden now swelled with death and deceit.

Tomaso Bruni lay sprawled at his feet, his fine velvet coat and silk cuffs soaked in blood—half of it Angelo's. The shaft of Carmen's knife protruded from his throat.

She stepped over, chest heaving, eyes burning like coals. "He was a difficult target. You almost got in the way."

For a long, suspended second, Angelo said nothing. His mind refused to reconcile what he saw. A member of the Guild turned traitor, and Carmen, calm as she withdrew the blade and wiped the blood on Bruni's shirt.

"Why?" Angelo asked, cracking the brief silence.

She narrowed her eyes at his drenched doublet and shirt. "You're welcome."

"He was beaten. I could have questioned him."

Carmen didn't flinch. "He was a snake, Angelo. He'd have slit your throat the moment you turned your back."

Without the strength to argue, Angelo stumbled against the tree for balance. "Tell me about him."

Concern filled her eyes. "You need a medico."

"Later. Tell me about him."

"Son of the Bruni trading house," she said coldly. "Respected. Entitled. He asked too many questions. Always keen to stick his nose in the affairs of those among us. I think he wanted us to attack because he was luring us into a trap."

"What did Ludo think?"

"We never discussed it. I had suspicions, not proof. Now I do. Let me help you." She reached for him, but Angelo brushed her hand aside.

Footsteps thundered on the path. Ludo reached them, flanked by two Guild members. "Angelo! We heard shouting—" He stopped cold at the sight. "Madonna..." His eyes went from Tomaso's body to Carmen's weapon to Angelo's injuries. "What in God's name happened?"

"Tomaso attacked him," Carmen said, her defiance steady. "He's been the spy. I warned you."

Ludo's brow furrowed. He crouched over the body. "Impossible. Tomaso's father's money helped fund this Guild. He's been with us for years."

"Who better to betray us," Carmen shot back, "than one who's already inside the walls?"

Angelo exhaled, forcing composure despite the excruciating throbbing that surged through his entire left side. "He came for me in the chapel. He wanted me dead. Plain and simple."

"Why you? Why not any of us?" Ludo rose and glanced at Carmen. "Why not *all* of us?"

"They've wanted me dead for years." Angelo could barely muster the words, the energy draining. "Maybe I was just the start. Get me out of the way. Lure you into an ambush. They know where we are, Ludo. They know this villa isn't only your home."

A chill rippled through the air. Leaves shuddered, as if in agreement.

Carmen screwed her eyes, peering into the dark grounds. "He wouldn't have struck on his own."

Ludo followed her gaze. "You think there are others?"

"It's what I'd do," Angelo said. "Send one to strike, another to watch, a third to report back if the first fails." He winced as the pain surged in his shoulder. "We can't stay here."

Ludo paced the path, running a hand through his hair. "Abandon the Stefanetti estate? You'd have us scatter like thieves?"

"Better thieves than corpses," Angelo snapped. Pain had sharpened his voice.

"Let them come. We face them here. We have the advantage."

"Not the numbers, my friend. What's the most men you've faced at once?"

Ludo didn't answer, but Angelo pressed.

"One? At the academy?"

In his new friend's silence, all was revealed: the Guild was unprepared for a fight, let alone an assault.

"There are three keys to victory, Ludo. Training. Preparation. Providence."

"Providence?" Ludo asked with a raised eyebrow.

"Every time. But we can position ourselves to receive Providence." He gestured to the dark gardens around them. His lungs grew heavy, slowing his words. "Right now, we are lucky we *haven't* been waylaid. We need to go inside. Then go elsewhere to train and plan."

"He's right." Carmen shuffled from foot to foot.

Ludo hesitated, the responsibility of leadership clearly pressing on him. "We can move to my cousin's estate in Mira. It's smaller. Harder to reach."

"No. Not family. A place with no connections," Angelo said. The pain in his shoulder pulsed harder. Black spots threatened his vision. "The Order doesn't stop. They have eyes everywhere. Tomaso proved that."

He looked again at the corpse. The man's features seemed almost peaceful, as though death had stripped him of deceit.

Carmen stepped toward Angelo, her worry padded further. "You require a physician."

They needed to move, but Angelo stared at the dead man a moment longer. What untold promises had the Order made? Or did Tomaso have ulterior motives?

How many spies were among them?

How long before the Order's noose tightened around their necks?

How much longer before trust became a luxury even the nobles could not afford?

Wavering, he met Ludo's eyes, then Carmen's, then gazed up at the sky and made a quick, silent prayer for help. Because the only thing more dangerous than an enemy in the dark was a friend standing beside you, hiding a blade.

The world narrowed to a ringing hum. Edges of Angelo's vision dimmed as if someone were drawing a curtain. He took a step, then another, and the strength fled his legs. The ground rushed up to meet him as blood loss finally claimed what the fight had not.

XLV

FOG DRIFTED IN LOW from the lagoon, rolling across the marshes like breath from a dying world. Vito drew his cloak tighter around his shoulders and pressed Ludo's horse onward, the worn road to San Fermo little more than a pale ribbon beneath her hooves. A convent lay beyond the olive grove, its bell tower rising against a black sky streaked with moonlight. He'd taken this path countless times, yet tonight the steps felt heavier, burdened with an ever-increasing weight.

He wasn't sure how many dawns he had left, how many breaths he'd share with Paulina, if any. He feared their meeting at the ruined chapel was their last. Though he held leverage with Cicogna's book, his ability to use it was a grasp in the wind at best. He had talked a big game to Angelo and Ludo, but it was a last-ditch effort that would most likely fail.

Yet, if he didn't try, he would surely lose.

As he neared his destination, the convent's walls emerged from the mist. Ivy climbed the pale stone arches, scarred by centuries. A fragrance of cypress gusted over the land. The flicker of a lantern moving along the cloister caught his eye, but it disappeared before he could make out the figure. A familiar unease stirred in his gut. Unseen eyes spun a web far beyond the city, even here.

He dismounted and drew a long breath, calming himself before ringing the bell.

A moment later, the heavy door creaked open, revealing an elderly woman with a pale face as smooth as porcelain and an unreadable expression beneath her wimple.

"Vito Uccello," she said with surprise. "It has been some time."

"Mother Superior," he replied. "You look radiant as ever."

She looked him up and down with disdain. "I'd have said the same if you bothered to bathe and clean your garments."

Embarrassed, Vito tucked in his blouse and smoothed his doublet. "Forgive me. I was traveling."

A cloud of disapproval crossed her face. "Too late to be traveling alone."

"I can take care of myself."

"We all can, Vito. But for how long? Your mother prays for you every night. Come. She's in her room."

After bringing the horse to the stable, he followed her through the cloister, their footsteps tapping on the stone. He sensed eyes upon him from behind doorways and curtains. Curious sisters whispered in the dark. He knew it would lead to nothing but nuns gossiping, yet paranoia nipped at his heels, feeding the sense that even sanctity no longer kept the world's corruption at bay.

Though not a pious man, he muttered a prayer under his breath. Not for mercy, but for strength.

Some thirty years prior, within days of his father's passing, his mother decided to join the convent. Vito, Ivan, and Sofia pressed her not to go, but she had insisted. To this day, she had never left its walls. It was a safe space, but on this night, Vito was paying a debt to the devil.

The Mother Superior brought Vito to his mother's room and announced his presence. He found her where she always was, seated near a narrow window, the faint light of a taper tracing the edges of her face. Sister Lucretia Uccello had aged with matronly grace. Lines deepened her cheeks, but her eyes remained the same pale brown. The years had gentled her voice but not her discernment.

When she turned to him, her lips lifted in a weary smile.

"Vito," she said, rising to embrace him. "You look thin."

He rushed over and sat her down. She didn't need to stand on his account.

Her arms lingered around him, as if reluctant to let go. "You've been gone too long." She patted his belly. "Let's take you to the kitchen. You need to eat."

"I'm well fed, Mamma," he said, though in truth he was famished. He glanced around her small chamber. The Spartan room held nothing but a crucifix, a straw cot, a basin of holy water, and an armoire of linens and habits near the wall. A Bible and some books sat on her desk.

Nothing had changed.

"Have you come to tell me you've finally decided to be a servant to God?"

"Mamma, I serve Him in my own way."

She gazed at him in a way that saw beyond words. "I fear this is more than a son visiting his mother. You always come with a shadow behind you."

Her intuition had never failed him. "There are things I must set right."

"Things? Or people?"

He traced an old scar on his palm. "Both, perhaps."

She reached out and touched his cheek with cool fingers. "My son... secrets will kill a man before sin does. You of all people should know that."

Her hands grew bonier and more spotted every time he saw them. Age and death were a fact of life. They didn't bother him, except when he saw it in his mamma. "I do."

The candle sputtered, throwing light across the walls. She sighed, as if surrendering to inevitability.

"You came to retrieve the box you hid in the library."

He blinked, surprised as much by her directness as her knowledge.

"Did you think you inherited your cunning from your father?"

With a grin, she rose, crossed to the corner, and removed a basket of linen from the armoire. From beneath the folds of cloth, she removed a brass lockbox Vito hadn't laid eyes upon in nearly twenty-five years. The brass box was reinforced with steel corners and locked with an iron padlock. Embossed with an ancient Taijitu symbol surrounded by seven sunrays and other emblems, the box flooded him with a wave of memory and emotion.

"You moved it?"

"I wouldn't have let the other sisters find my son's treasure."

"You were always too clever."

"And you, too proud."

She lifted the lid and drew out a small bundle wrapped in plain linen. Vito's breath caught as if she'd unearthed the nails that had crucified Christ.

"Tell me you didn't read it," he said.

Her eyes snapped to him. "Temptation is not the same as sin. There is only one book that I read. Whatever words are within this tome," she said, handing it to him, "they cost you. I can see it in the way you carry yourself."

"It will cost others, not me."

She took the bundle back, placed it in the box, and handed it to him.

"I'll give you a satchel to carry it. Promise me this. When you return again, bring a Bible."

He hesitated, unsure if he'd be returning, then pressed her hands between his, warming them. "I promise. But I have one more request."

By the time Vito reached Mestre, the morning sun bathed the land in an orange hue. His cloak was heavy with dust from the road, his horse sluggish from the long ride. The journey from the convent had taken him along the borders of vineyards and farms, and finally onto a small barge that ferried him down the Brenta.

He had hoped to arrive in the town under cover of darkness. He had pursued people—including Angelo—and knew quite well that the easiest means of tracking was to inquire of the townsfolk. Without fail, they were all too eager to identify the recent presence of a fugitive. As a familiar figure in Venice and Mestre, people would recognize him.

Not daring to rest, he snapped the reins and kicked his heels into the horse's loins. Every bend in the road felt like a set of eyes watching him. Every distant sound pressed at his nerves.

Mestre woke to a hazy fog, barking dogs, and crowing roosters. Smoke from the forges and bakeries hung low over the rooftops.

The contents of his saddlebag seemed to pull against him like guilt. There was no other person with whom he could leave the book. He trusted Paulina but he couldn't leave it with her, not with servants who'd gleefully betray her to Grimani for a ducat. Similarly, he trusted Angelo, but who knew what foolish actions the Guild would take should they discover it? None understood that it needed to remain hidden until the time was right. Only his sister could make that happen and do it quickly. He had no other recourse, despite endangering her and her family. He reassured himself it wouldn't be for long.

"Remind Sofia that her brother still walks in light," his mother had said.

He hadn't the heart to tell her how little light remained in him.

He dismounted across from his sister's home. The shutters were still closed but a faint candle fluttered in the workshop window.

After shielding his face from a man wheeling a cart of produce, Vito surveyed the otherwise empty street and rapped twice.

Footsteps shuffled and the door opened, spilling lamplight into the brisk air. Sofia stood in the doorway, her hair unbound, sleeves rolled up, and streaks of varnish on her forearm, an unbridled look of exasperation plastered on her face.

Wasting no time, Vito took a final glance up and down the street before shuffling in and shutting the door. He peeked through the shutters.

"Has anybody visited you?" he asked.

"Some customers, that's all."

"Did they ask about me? Have you heard anything?"

"No, it's been rather quiet."

Relief washed over Vito. "Good. My horse is outside. Have Marcello water and feed her."

While Sofia did as he asked, Vito paced the floor, glancing out the window. He always prided himself on his nerves and patience, but he couldn't dislodge the unforgiving apprehension that had come over him since he collected the doge's book.

"Where were you? Did you see your family?" his sister asked, reentering the workspace.

Vito cleared his throat, a pang of shame washing over him. On the ride to and from his mother's, he'd been thinking about how and when to see his wife and children. His sons were grown with families of their own, and his wife was surely occupied with her own sisters. Likely, they were unaware of his return. A reunion would not inspire any joy. More importantly, he did not want to put them in any danger. At least that's what he told himself.

"Si," he replied, realizing there was no need to lie. "I saw family."

Sofia read his face. "You went back to Venice?"

Vito lowered his gaze, as if seeing their mother was a cause for guilt. "San Fermo."

His sister raised his chin to meet his eyes. "Vito, you need to go to them. Do they know you're home?"

"Doubtful. And I wish to keep it that way. There's too much risk for me to go there."

She took a step back and scowled. "Yet it's safe to come here? Is your presence putting us in danger? Tell me, Vito."

"I think not," he said with an exhale, praying he was right. "To be safe, I shan't stay long."

"Well, come inside. Are you hungry? How is our dear mother?"

"She sends her love. And this." Vito set the cloth bundle on the worktable.

His sister untied the cloth, revealing the loaf and rosary. Her fingers lingered on the beads, tracing the grain. "You look like you've ridden through hell."

"The ride was fine," he replied. "I fear I've yet to reach hell."

The words came out angrier than he intended. She didn't press him, though she studied his face long enough to see something had shifted. The moment stretched between brother and sister.

Then Sofia noticed the bulky satchel strapped over his chest. She knitted her brow. "What's in that one?"

Vito pulled off the sack and removed the lockbox, setting it on the workbench.

"Have you brought me treasure?"

"Of a sort. Though not one for you." He opened the box to reveal the linen-wrapped book.

Sofia peered at the rectangular contents. "What's inside the wrap?"

"Nothing but a book, sister."

"A book? Wrapped in linen? Secured in a lockbox? What book is it?"

He shook his head. "You're safer not knowing."

"Safe?" she echoed, half-laughing, half-bitter. "You think I don't know what you do? For whom you work? For whom Ivan worked?"

He didn't answer. She was right, of course. But he had nowhere else to turn. His sister crossed her arms, regarding him with the same sharpness their mother used to. "If you're worried about my safety," she continued, "then why bring it here? Why put me or my family in danger, even if you're here but a moment?"

He met her stare. Lamplight carved deep shadows into her face. Silence filled the workshop, save the tick of cooling iron and the faint hiss of a dying flame.

"Because I trust you more than anyone," he replied. "But if you know the contents, you'll be in true danger. I won't have that."

She took a careful breath, as if broaching unsteady ground. "Is it connected... to Ivan?"

"In some manner," Vito said quietly. He wanted to tell her more, but the peril was far too great. "I pray you ask no further."

Finally, Sofia sighed and brushed her hair from her face. "Alright. I won't ask. Keep your secrets. Just keep them out of my house."

Vito sighed. The weight of putting her and her family in jeopardy was almost too much to bear, but he couldn't think of another option. "You've always had a gift for secrets, sister. That's why I came. I need your help in making this disappear for all but a few."

She managed a small, proud smile. "You speak of a puzzle?"

"I suppose I do." He felt the edges of the book in the linen. "Should anything happen to me, there are only two people who should be able to find this. It cannot fall into the wrong hands."

"Why not simply keep it in that box?"

"Too identifiable."

Sofia eyed the bundle, sizing the contents in Vito's hands. Her brow furrowed, but she nodded. "I've a project that might work."

She moved to a corner bench and returned with a wooden box, which she offered to Vito. He placed the black book bundle on a different bench and examined her sister's craftmanship. It appeared to be a solid cube of walnut, the surface smooth as silk, the grain running like ripples over dark water. A combination lock was embedded on the opposite side of the box.

"I've been working on this for weeks. It's meant for a customer's son's name day. A boy in Treviso. He wanted a box with secrets. False sides, hidden catches. I can make another."

She took it back and rolled the combination lock. The sides fell away, revealing an empty interior.

Vito ran his fingers along the edges. The craftsmanship was exquisite. The dovetail joints were so precise, they looked carved from one piece of wood. He placed the open box on top of the bundle and immediately realized the problem.

"It's too small," he murmured.

Sofia frowned, tilting the box. "I can make another. Larger."

"No. I fear we don't have the time."

That landed heavy between them. She stiffened, fear flickering in her eyes.

"Brother, whatever path you tread, it's killing you."

"If I don't walk it, others will die," he said, his fingers tracing the perfect craftsmanship of her wooden box. It would've been perfect if it were larger. He eyed the lockbox, comparing the two. "Your wooden box could fit in the brass lockbox. Maybe... we can hide the book somewhere else. Some obscure place. Your box can contain... a clue."

She smiled. "To its location. Do you remember the hiding games we played as children?"

Before he could answer, a clatter rang out from the end of the workshop. Figurines toppled from a shelf.

Sofia spun around. "Marcello!"

A thirteen-year-old boy emerged from the corner, cheeks flushed and trying to look innocent. His flaxen hair covered his eyes. He was nearly as tall as Vito already, but half his weight. "I wasn't listening," he blurted.

Vito sighed and gave him a hug. "You're a terrible liar, nephew."

"I was hoping to hear stories," the boy said. "Tell me what the New World is like."

Vito wanted to oblige, but today was not the day. He promised himself that if he accomplished his goal, he'd share everything with his nephew. "Another time. Did you tend to my horse?"

"Of course. She was very thirsty. I gave her some carrots too."

"Good boy."

His face darkened. "I'm not a boy, uncle."

Vito arched a brow. "Of course you're not. Tell me, you were hiding to hear stories, but what did you hear?"

Marcello flushed. His gaze landed on the lockbox. "That you need to bury a secret. Please, I want to help. I'm an expert at puzzles, truly." He turned to his mother. "Tell him, Mamma."

"It's true," Sofia said.

Vito's tone softened, but the strength of it remained. "You're to leave this alone, do you understand?"

"I can keep a secret—"

"No."

The word landed like a hammer. Marcello stared at him, searching his face for leniency, but Vito offered none. After a moment, he nodded and disappeared into the next room with heavy shoulders.

When he was gone, Sofia turned back to Vito. "He just wants to be part of your world."

"That's what I'm trying to spare him from."

"He speaks of you all the time. He has carpentry skills but no love for this workshop. He wants to be you."

Vito flapped his coat. "Steer him in the opposite path, sister. A life of mundanity is far better than a life of always looking over your shoulder, never knowing when the day will come."

"So I'm to do this alone?"

The question settled uncomfortably on Vito. He abhorred putting her in danger but there was no one else. If she worked with Angelo, it could increase the risk. Then an idea hit him. "There is a Protector. Zanca. I've confided in him many times. Should anything happen to me, find him. I trust he will aid you, but do not reveal secrets to him.

Sofia set down her tool. Candlelight carved deep lines into her face. "If the contents of that book are so dangerous, then why not burn it?"

"Because it contains the truth. And truth should never be destroyed."

Sofia regarded him with that piercing calm only sisters possess. "Since when do you fight for truth, Vito?"

He wanted to tell her everything—about Paulina, the Order, and the leverage within the doge's book that could bring it all down. Yet each word that came to mind would draw her further into the storm.

"Since I realized that the lies had built a fragile temple of deceit and death."

"Then why not reveal the truth? Why hide it?"

It was a valid question. "Because I'm not prepared to do so yet. I need to establish more allies. More safeguards."

She studied him, then nodded. "Very well. You'll have your hiding place."

He sat on the opposite bench. Then his tone hardened. "The puzzle must be near unsolvable. If someone tampers with the box, the contents should be destroyed."

She frowned. "Destroyed how?"

"You tell me. I trust your hands more than mine."

She ran her finger along the box. "I could fit a mechanism. A spring and a flint. If the wrong code is entered, it sparks. No, that won't do." She pursed her lips and bobbed her head, already seeing the possibilities in her mind. "It could contain a solvent in glass. Yes, the glass could break and dissolve the clue."

"Perfection, Sofia." Pride swelled within Vito. "What should this clue be?"

"That's for you to decide. You said only two people should be able to decipher it."

Unsure of what to do and how to even start, he gazed about her workspace, his eyes sweeping the myriad of toys and boxes on the shelves. He landed on her reproduction of Tintoretto's *Last Judgement*. Many times, he had viewed the original in the Madonna dell'Orto, the church in which the world believed the Painter was entombed... a place nobody would ever think to look. A hiding place in plain sight.

"I could use encoded words," he said.

"Perhaps a poem?" his sister offered.

"I'm not much of a writer. I'm nothing of a poet."

"A thing need not be flawless to be worthy, brother."

"I don't think it will even be good."

"Then don't write it with your brain. Write it with your heart."

XLVI

A LOW, DRY RASP rattled through the marble chamber. Trembling, the doge covered his mouth with a kerchief, then waved it at Zanca to continue.

"We've heard nothing from Tomaso Bruni," said the Protector. An edge of finality framed his declaration. "Not since the night he was supposed to instigate the attack."

Quattrone kept his expression neutral, though he'd expected as much. Bruni had been careless, reckless, or both. Overconfident in his usefulness to both sides. Men like that always thought themselves indispensable right up until a knife reached their ribs.

"We must assume the worst. A pity." Doge Memmo's rheumy stare landed on Quattrone. "And your informants, Senator?"

"Some sightings, Your Serenity." Quattrone clasped his hands behind his back, pacing once before the heat of the hearth before moving to the leaded window. The canal outside was lost in fog. "We've gathered reports from each *sestiere*. Nothing reliable. Vito Uccello and Angelo Mascari remain ghosts."

Grimani leaned forward in his chair, the firelight sharpening the lines in his face. He looked stronger. Color had returned to his cheeks, and a steady focus dwelled in his eyes, but a hint of strain lingered in the way he held his head. It seemed to wobble on his neck, like a broken doll.

"Then we smoke them out," he said, staring into the flames. "They can't hide forever. Doge Cicogna's ledger is all that matters."

"Agreed," Zanca said, pacing at the door.

Disappointment filled Quattrone. They'd been desiring the black book for nearly twenty-five years. He often assumed it had been buried or thrown into a canal. With the knowledge from Santa Marta, it hardly seemed the priority anymore. "Yes, the book," he said absentmindedly. "And whoever knows where it lies."

"Vito knows." Hatred fueled Grimani when he uttered the name. "He knows. You know he knows."

Quattrone had long wondered why Grimani hated the Chief Protector, but he, like many others, suspected the truth had a woman's shape.

The doge cleared his throat. "We cannot upset the nobles. We all reside in a fragile house," he said with as much muster as his faint voice would allow. His hands shivered as he reached for a goblet of watered wine. "Uccello and the swordsman are now working together. We can assume they've told the Guild about Cicogna's ledger. Renzo's home has been searched a dozen times over. Stripped to the beams. You were there with Vito half the time. His home has been searched, as well. Perhaps he's always been colluding with the swordsman, perhaps it's a recent turn of events, but it's only a matter of time before they make their move."

"They won't," Grimani said. "I'll see to that."

Quattrone observed him. There was force in his words again. "You'll have every Protector you need. Proceed carefully. We don't want to spook them into fleeing or worse... force their hand. I need additional information from Mascari since you're unable to provide it."

Grimani slapped the armrest. "*Additional* information? Carefully? What are your true intentions, Exalted Master?"

"Mind your place, Benito. My intent has always been to strengthen the Order."

"Or your own designs?"

Blood swelled in Quattrone's face. "I will say it again, Benito. Mind your place. You are still unwell, and here only by the grace of our doge's hand. If we rush in swords blazing, we risk everything. Just as you did in Amazonia. You had the tree in your grasp and squandered it with your greed." He pointed his manicured fingernail at the senator's forehead. "Now it is lost forever in the jungle of your mind."

"All due respect, Exalted Master," Grimani said through gritted teeth, the veins in his temples throbbing, "but you have no military or strategic experience in these matters. I have fought for Venice. The Protectors were trained under Uccello. He knows our methods. Our signals. Every corner of the city. If we move softly, he'll smell us before we're close. We must bring the hammer down." He pounded his fist into his palm. "We should take their families into custody until Uccello and Mascari have come to us, begging for the pain to cease."

Quattrone's jaw tightened. He always thought Grimani a brute. Now the man was considerably worse since the expedition, as if the heat and madness seeped from his pores. "We shall do no such thing. If Vito knows our methods, then we'll change our methods."

Zanca stepped between them before Grimani could retort. He raised his hands and spoke calmly to the doge. "We'll use civilians. Men who know their families. Men who've signaled interest in joining us. We'll give them that promise. They'll spread the word that the doge offers a pardon to anyone who delivers news of Uccello or the swordsman."

Grimani scoffed. "A pardon? For rats and liars?"

"For bait," Zanca said.

The doge offered a weak nod. "It is a decision most wise. A compromise that molds strategy with strength. Do it. Find them. Then compel the location of the book from their lips."

"As your command, My Serene." Zanca bowed his head.

Quattrone gazed out the window, his thoughts turning inward. They were all fixated on the book. Fools. He had seen the ledger. While it contained potentially damning information, they could control any damage. The promise of the tree—of immortality and unlimited power—surpassed any trivial pages from a quarter century prior. They'd have dominion through the very sap of creation. If he found it, if he became master of the Order or doge of Venice... all would bow.

But now wasn't the time to speak of it. Not while Grimani's rage still permeated the room, threatening Quattrone and his plans. No, instead, he could harness that anger and use it against him. Grimani was a wick already lit. Quattrone could set him off in front of the doge, proving the man's volatility and unreliability. Rumors about Grimani's hatred for Vito had circulated for years, long before the senator took Paulina's hand. Those whispers persisted, and Grimani's outward hatred towards his comrade-in-arms had only intensified.

"Spread word of the pardons to those they love," Quattrone said to Zanca. He threw a glance at Grimani. "Not just their families. It is no secret that Vito Uccello had strayed."

"Strayed?" The senator jumped out of his chair and approached Quattrone with clenched fists. "You speak of my wife?"

Again, Zanca stepped between them, raising his palms up to Grimani. "He didn't say that, sior."

"He didn't need to. Out of my way."

"Do you trust Paulina?" Quattrone asked, peering over the Protector's shoulder.

"My relationship with my wife is none of your concern."

"Enough!" The doge's voice held more power than Quattrone had heard in years. "Squabble on your own time. Find Uccello and the swordsman. I want them alive, and I want the book. Bring it all to me." He coughed into a kerchief before continuing. "I have changed my mind. Time is too precious for your squabbling. Senator Grimani is correct. We've not had word from Bruni because he was discovered. We must assume the Order killed him, which is reason enough to smoke them out, especially now that we no longer have a man embedded."

All three men inclined their heads.

"Alive," the doge said. "I want them both alive. Uccello and the swordsman."

"As you command, Your Serenity," Grimani said.

He turned away, shoulders rigid, with a smug grin consuming his face. Zanca followed him to the door but paused long enough to meet Quattrone's eyes with a shared awareness that neither would state aloud.

When they were gone, Quattrone remained by the window, staring out at the mist curling over the canal. A gondola slid through the vapor like a shadow.

He smiled faintly.

Let them chase ghosts. I'll chase gods.

XLVII

YOU CAN'T SAVE HER.

Juanita's mouth remained closed, but her pure voice whispered the words.

You can't save her.

Franco joined his sister, repeating the words in harmony.

You can't save her.

Then Loredana appeared. Followed by Isabella, the four of them repeated the words together.

You can't save her. You can't save her. You can't save her.

Pain.

It pulsed through Angelo's shoulder like a second heartbeat, dull at first, then sharp enough to drag him into the waking world. The air was thick with charred wood and the faint sweetness of beeswax. Above him, the rafters of the Stefanetti villa loomed in faint darkness. His shirt clung to his chest, stiff where the blood had dried.

He recognized the chamber. On the night of his arrival, Ludo had offered the room to Angelo, yet he didn't recall how he got there. The last thing he remembered was Bruni's body in the dirt. Someone must have brought Angelo to his room to convalesce.

A bolt of agony flared down his arm when he tried to move. His nurse had wrapped his wound well, with tight linen, knotted cleanly up to his neck. In all his years of fighting, this was the most severe injury he'd sustained.

A knife in the back.

He pushed himself upright, dizzy, bracing against the cot. Memories came in fragments. The chapel. Tomaso Bruni's blade plunging into his flesh. Carmen, ending the traitor before answers could be torn from his throat.

Downstairs, voices rose and fell. The house sounded alive, but not in the way a home should. More like a ship battening down before a storm.

Angelo stood, pulling on his doublet, cloak, and hat with one good arm. He managed to fasten his belt and scabbard, then forced himself down the narrow stairway. Each step jarred the wound, but he ignored it. Pain was proof that he was still alive.

In the great hall, disorder reigned. Crates were being sealed, documents fed to the fire, and flintlock rifles were stacked beside the door. Candle smoke curled toward the beams, and pre-dawn light blushed through the tall windows. From what he could tell, the Guild was dismantling itself piece by piece.

"Good, you're awake," said Ludo, turning from a half-packed chest. His fine clothes were rumpled, his eyes sleepless. "We thought you'd sleep another day."

"What's going on?" Angelo sounded like he had swallowed dirt.

"We're leaving," said his friend, gesturing to the turmoil. "The Order knows this place."

"Your family? Are they safe?"

Ludo clasped Angelo's good shoulder, appreciative of his concern. "I've sent word for them to remain at our lake house."

"Where are you going?"

"*We*. To a friend's. Discreet and loyal. I trust you, Angelo, but you'll forgive me if I don't tell you until we arrive. The rest of the Guild is already on their way."

Angelo nodded his understanding of the secrecy, but the tactic didn't sit well with him. "You're retreating."

"Preserving," Ludo said. "You've seen what the Protectors can do. You know better than anyone."

"Precisely. Running won't save you." The burn of helplessness singed his chest. He had come to Venice to destroy the Order, to free Isabella's soul from the prison of that cursed painting. Instead, he was limping through the ashes of yet another failed plan.

Ludo sighed and stepped closer. "We'll strike when the time is right. For now, we survive."

His friend was right, yet Angelo yearned for more. Survival had kept him alive this long, but survival wasn't victory. It wasn't redemption.

Now, beneath it all, was the growing ache for Loredana and his children. Their laughter, the aroma of his wife's hair, the life waiting for him in Santa Marta.

He glanced toward the window. The canal beyond shimmered. Boats waited at the docks, loaded with trunks and barrels, the last shadows of the Guild preparing to vanish.

That was when the door burst open.

Vito filled the threshold, framed by the dim light outside. His eyes swept the room, landing first on Angelo. Color drained from his face.

"*Madre di Dio*," he muttered. "What happened?"

Angelo gave a grim smile. "The Order's spy happened."

Vito crossed the floor in quick strides, his usual composure cracking. "You're wounded."

"I've been worse."

"Have you?" Vito asked, brow knitted.

Angelo shrugged. He winced from the pain ricocheting through his body. "Well, no."

Ludo shut a chest with a heavy thud. "Tomaso Bruni. He tried to kill Angelo."

"Where's Bruni now?" Vito asked.

"Fertilizing my trees," Ludo replied.

Vito froze. For a heartbeat, an unreadable expression flashed across his face. Shock, grief, maybe fear. "Then it's worse than I thought." He turned away. He removed his hat and ran his hand over his scalp. "If Bruni is missing, they'll suspect the worst. The Order will come."

"What words of wisdom, oh great Protector," Carmen said from the doorway, a crossbow slung across her shoulder. Her sleeves were rolled, her braid half undone. "What do you think we're doing here, redecorating?"

"Enough," Ludo said. "We have minutes before the boats leave."

Vito shook his head. "Then I won't waste them. I came to tell you that the first phase of my plan is complete. Now, I'm going back."

Angelo blinked. "Back where?"

"I'll beg forgiveness from the doge, from Quattrone. Earn their trust again. They'll believe me. They must."

Ludo's voice dropped. "That's suicide."

"It's the only way inside," Vito said. His tone remained calm but his eyes burned. "You can't fight them with weapons alone. You must break them from within."

Angelo stepped forward, ignoring the throb in his shoulder. "What happens when they slit your throat for treason?"

"Then at least I'll die trying to make it right."

Angelo had seen that look before. It was the expression of a man who'd already made peace with death.

Vito glanced at Ludo and Carmen before leveling his gaze at Angelo. He drew a slow breath. "You remember the book I asked you to steal from Renzo Scalfini's chamber?"

Memories of everything that led to this moment flashed in his mind. "Do you need to ask?"

"I never told you *why* I wanted that book. It can expose everything. The corruption, the blackmail, the rot at the core of the Order."

This was a revelation. Angelo had asked Vito and his brother why they wanted him to steal it, but they refused to answer. "Do you have it?"

"No."

Angelo studied his friend's face. "You wouldn't lie to me, would you?"

Vito smiled. "You know I would, but I'm not lying to you now."

"Do you speak of Doge Cicogna's journal from twenty-five years ago?" Ludo asked, incredulity in his eyes. "It's real? All this time, I thought it was lore."

"The book may be real," Angelo said. "But its power is lore. Do not let it lead us astray. Our mission is to destroy the Order and free the prisoners of Paradise."

"If the book can make that happen?" Ludo asked.

Angelo gazed out the window. "There is but one book with power and unless our Lord Jesus Christ can rid us of the Order, I see no reason to waste time chasing our tails."

"You are wrong, my friend," Ludo said. "There have been many books that have changed the world. *The Iliad*, *The Republic*, *The Prince*, the Quran, *The Divine Comedy*, to name but a few."

"Precisely," Vito said. "Quattrone and Memmo would kill for this one. We must ensure it ends up in the right hands."

This book had caused Angelo nothing but grief. "Whose hands are those?"

"Someone in the Church. Someone with influence."

"Who?" Ludo asked.

"Truthfully, I don't know yet. That is why I need more time." Vito hesitated, then turned to Angelo. "I need a word. Outside."

Angelo nodded once, wary but willing, and followed him through the rear passage that opened onto the courtyard. Morning air hit him, cool and unmasked, carrying the odor of the canal.

They stopped beneath the overhanging balcony. Neither spoke for a moment. Angelo marveled once again at the notion of two men whose fates had intertwined. Two men who had once sworn to kill one another, now bound together in the frayed alliance of survival.

"You know that love is the reason for this whole mess," Vito said, his voice nearly breaking.

Angelo's jaw tightened. "Paulina? Grimani's wife?"

"Si," his friend said, leveling his gaze. "But you know not her maiden name."

"Pray tell."

"Cicogna."

The surname summoned memories and understanding for Angelo. *Cicogna*. Not because he had a connection, but because everything connected.

Cicogna. Paulina Cicogna, the daughter of Doge Pasquale Cicogna, the ruler of Venice in those days.

Yet there was still a missing piece.

Vito swallowed hard. The words scraped coming out. "When my brother and I asked you to steal the book from Scalfini, it wasn't for the Order. It wasn't for me. It was for Paulina."

"Why in God's name would she want her father's journal?"

"She didn't. She never knew. I needed leverage. In case... in case our affair was discovered."

A flood of rage merged with an equal part of pity in Angelo. His breath left him in a sharp, stunned exhale. All this time. Everything that happened. All the chaos, the bloodshed, the loss. It was not only because Angelo loved Isabella, but before that, Vito loved Paulina.

"So you risked all of this, dragged me into a theft that painted targets on our backs, that drove a living angel into Purgatory, because you needed leverage to defend your adultery?"

Vito didn't flinch. "I was a fool. A selfish one."

He extended his open hand. Angelo gazed at the battle-scarred and aging skin. He hesitated a moment, then clasped it, his own calloused fingers gripping those from the other side of his travails.

"I don't ask for forgiveness, my friend," Vito said. "I don't ask for understanding."

The courtyard settled into a taut silence. Angelo disengaged, then removed his hat and ran his good hand through his hair, tousling it. The old bitterness of every betrayal clawed at him. Years, oceans, and a now-shared enemy had reshaped their lives. The fury ebbed, leaving a steadier tide of understanding and companionship. He smoothed his hair back and donned his hat.

He faced Vito again. "I appreciate you finally telling me the truth."

Relief and shame mingled across the big man's features.

"Do you have the book, Vito?"

"No."

Angelo searched for the lie he feared he'd find. Vito didn't look away, his face raw in its honesty. Maybe he was telling the truth. Maybe not. The day was pushing in. Time was collapsing around them. Bigger battles waited.

He gave a small nod. "Very well."

Tension leaked from Vito's shoulders. "Grassie. Now you know how formidable the contents are, how damaging they can be to the Order and the Republic itself. And why we must find the right people who can act without fear of retribution."

Overhead, a shutter clacked in the wind. Carmen swept past a window. Inside the villa, Ludo issued orders. Birds sang their morning calls. The chirps were ordinary sounds, yet Angelo sensed a shift in the air, like the coming of a storm. And every truth spoken this morn had pushed them closer to it.

"You're a fool," he said. "But a brave one."

"From you, that almost sounds like praise."

Angelo chuckled. "I would never be so bold as to give you praise. Come, they need us."

Vito gripped Angelo's good forearm, firm and steady. "Wrongs will be righted. You'll see."

The words inspired true pride inside Angelo. Not for himself, but for his friend. Vito truly was a changed man. "Not if you get yourself killed."

"It's not death I fear," Vito said, releasing him.

Angelo nodded his understanding, for he felt the same. They could not fail, at least not in this life. It was why they couldn't let themselves fall to the Order. Death would be a better option.

Walking through the estate, they learned that Ludo was with the others loading boats. Angelo and Vito carried a crate to the dock, where heavy mist hung low over the water. They handed the crates to Ludo's men, who lashed them to four *mascarete.* Sleek, light, and narrow, the boats were built to outrun anything short of a full galley.

Carmen paced the terrace with two flintlock pistols ready.

Angelo turned toward Ludo and Vito. "Do you hear that?"

Vito extinguished a lantern hanging on a dock post and listened. "Nothing."

Then came the faintest ripple in the canal. A dark shape slid through the fog, too low and quiet for a merchant's skiff. Another followed. And another.

"Down!" Angelo shouted.

Crossbow bolts hissed through the air, slamming into the wooden balustrade. One struck a lantern, bursting flame across the terrace. Carmen fired back. Her shots disappeared into the white murk.

"Launch the boats!" Ludo shouted.

He wheeled on Vito and grabbed his collar. "You brought them here, *bastardo*!"

Vito smacked his hand away. "Never."

"Then they followed you." Ludo clenched his teeth. His face turned bright red.

"They already knew your location," Vito countered. "You'd been infiltrated."

More crossbow bolts launched overhead. Shouting from the approaching boats increased.

"You could've warned us of that!"

"I would have, had I known."

Angelo shoved them apart. "We don't have time for this!"

Figures burst from the boats, their boots splashing through the shallows. Men in black coats, armed with short swords that gleamed like shards of moons. The Order.

Angelo drew his sword and staggered to meet them. His shoulder screamed in protest, but rage drowned the pain.

The first Protector swung. Angelo parried, the impact jarring his wounds. He drove his knee into the man's gut and finished him with a slash across the throat, his vow to never kill again long abandoned. Warm blood sprayed the stone. Another came from behind. Carmen dropped him with a bolt to the chest.

A broad man with a pitch-black beard charged Vito.

"Your loyalty is misplaced, Zanca," he yelled.

Ignoring him, the Protector launched a series of blows, all of which Vito parried.

"Too many!" she shouted. She shimmied over the terrace balustrade and jumped.

"Cut a path!" Vito's rapier flashed with a fury Angelo had never seen, moving like a man unbound. Every strike was a penance.

A crossbow bolt struck a Guild fighter next to Angelo. The man clutched his wounded thigh. Angelo and another helped the injured man to a *mascareta* as two unfurled their sails and departed in the brightening morning sun.

Through the mayhem, a command broke above the din. "Hold your fire! Bring them alive!"

Angelo froze at the sound of that wretched voice.

Benito Grimani stepped through the haze like an avenging spirit, cloak sweeping, blade already wet with blood. He was stronger now, his affliction apparently gone. His face had hardened to granite. Behind him, more Protectors closed the circle.

"You," Angelo said to Grimani in disbelief.

Grimani smiled without warmth. "You didn't think I'd miss this reunion, did you?"

"I see the rot didn't kill you. I should've when I had the chance."

"You speak of rot," Grimani said, his tone venomous. "Yet you and your friend soil other men's wives."

Raw hatred burned beneath Grimani's words. Not duty. Not loyalty. *Jealousy*.

Paulina.

Everything added up in a split second.

Grimani advanced toward Vito. He shoved the Protecter called Zanca out of the way and raised his blade. "She pitied you, Vito. That was all. You think she loved you? She never loved anyone."

Vito's face twisted. "You would know."

"How right you are," Grimani said, voice cracking under its own weight. "She was *mine*. *My* wife. You defiled her."

He lunged. Their swords met with a clash that echoed across the grass. Sparks flared. Vito ducked a swing and countered, but Grimani's strength drove him back, step by step, toward the villa.

Angelo started forward, but Ludo grabbed his arm. "We must go! Now!"

"Not without him!"

"Angelo," Carmen shouted. "The boats. They're leaving!"

Another volley of bolts sliced through the fog, forcing them down. One whistled past Angelo's ear and embedded in a dock post. He turned. More Protectors poured through the side gate.

He glanced at the Guild's *mascarete* sailing down the canal. One remained. It was their only route of escape.

Ludo drew his pistol, fired, and grabbed Angelo by the collar. "Move!"

They sprinted for the dock. Carmen covered them. She launched another bolt, followed by two throwing knives, all meeting their marks, yet none slowed the onslaught. Behind them, Vito and Grimani's duel raged.

Angelo stumbled, nearly pitching into the canal. Ludo caught him and forced him toward a waiting gondola. "Go!"

"I'm not leaving him!"

"You'll die here!"

Angelo's vision darted back to the fight. Grimani's sword opened a shallow cut across Vito's cheek. Another across his arm. Still, Vito fought on, defiant.

Their blades locked.

"She never wanted you," Grimani hissed.

Vito smiled through the blood. "Then she lied beautifully."

The courtyard erupted into bedlam as Protectors overran the area. Twisting free of Ludo's hold, Angelo planted his feet to meet them head-on, but his injured shoulder screamed. A hot burst of white impeded his vision. Still, he lifted his blade. He'd die before he ran from this fight.

"Angelo, move!" Ludo's voice tore through the clash.

Ignoring him, Angelo slashed at a Protector who lunged too close. Pain lanced up his wounded arm and nearly made him drop the sword. "I can fight—"

"Not today," Ludo replied with a snarl. He seized him under Angelo's good arm and dragged him backward across the dock. "The last *mascareta* is pushing off. We'll regroup!"

Angelo dug his heels in. His vision tunneled on Vito, who fought like a man intent on carving space with every strike. Rage and duty fused into an incandescent battle.

"I'm not leaving him," Angelo hissed through clenched teeth.

A bolt cracked against a post near his head. Ludo wrenched harder, half-hauling him across the planks of the dock. Angelo's boots skidded. His wounded shoulder screamed. Still, he fought to tear free.

"Vito!" he shouted. He couldn't let him fall.

His friend swung toward them for a heartbeat. Blood smeared his face, his jaw clenched, his eyes bright.

"Leave!" Vito disengaged from his fight with Grimani and sprinted for the dock.

Relieved he'd join the escape, Angelo stopped resisting Ludo and jumped into the final *macareta* with Carmen. With Ludo following suit, all the remaining Guild members were safely aboard. They opened the sails as Vito reached them.

Instead of joining them, Vito grabbed a tar-soaked rope coil from atop a supply crate. With his free hand, he snatched a lantern from a hook and smashed it against the dock where the rope lay.

The fire caught instantly.

"No!" Angelo cried, astonished at his friend's actions.

Carmen shoved the boat free of the pier.

Vito kicked the burning coil into a stack of resinous sprigs and pitch barrels beside the dock. Flames roared to life. Hungry sparks licked up the supports and raced along the planks with terrifying speed.

Protectors swarmed him, but the wall of flame was already clawing upward, heat rippling through the air. The nearest of the Protectors' gondolas were blocked as the dock became a curtain of fire. One boat caught, its tar seam bursting into flame.

"*Basta*!" Grimani called out. "Get him!"

"Vito, run!" Angelo strained against Ludo's grip as he struggled to jump from their departing boat.

A Protector slammed into Vito from behind. Another struck him across the jaw. Vito buckled to his knees. Three more descended on him, blades reversed, beating instead of cutting. Grimani drove a fist into his ribs hard enough that Angelo felt the impact in his own bones.

Angelo's *mascareta* lurched with sudden momentum. Carmen and Ludo took up oars, further propelling the craft's speed.

He twisted for one last look.

Fire had devoured the pier. On the shore, barely visible through the smoke, Protectors dragged Vito upright, only to be beaten down again. His body folded with each savage hit.

Angelo gripped the gunwale as the *mascareta* sliced through the water, away from the flames, from the violence, from the man who had once wanted to kill him and who had now given him his life.

XLVIII

He drifted between waking and blackness, hauled by hands to yet another location. Having been those hands one too many times, he was surely being led to a destination of horrors. The world pitched around him in fragments. His cheek dragged along a marble floor cold enough to burn. Every inch of his body was too heavy to lift.

Vito tongued his gums, searching for familiar structure, and found only ragged gaps and loose shards shifting like shells in wet sand. Blood pooled in his mouth. They'd beaten him long past pain and into numbness.

Time had disintegrated under fists, boots, and cold water. It could've been hours, days, or weeks.

When they yanked him upright again, a change in air told him the space was vast. Gold and color glanced the edge of his vision. Murals climbed into shadow. He was in a place in which he'd stood many times before for ceremonies, trials, judgments... and sentences.

The Great Council Room.

The hall within the Palazzo Ducale was meant for the Republic's splendor. Now, it was twisted into a chamber of private punishment. Vito forced himself to lift his head, though it felt like lifting stone. Shapes sharpened, as did the throbbing in his ribs.

In the center council chair beneath Tintoretto's *Paradise* sat Doge Memmo, hunched inside his embroidered robes, his skin as thin as parchment. The man looked as though he might crumble into dust if touched. To his right sat Senator

Quattrone, robes immaculate, sitting with cold authority. Pacing in front of them was Grimani, his flushed face swelling with rageful victory.

Vito knew the dais by feel and sound. He'd escorted prisoners there more than any other Protector. He'd bolted too many hands into the deliverance chair to count.

Now, the same shackles would gnaw his own limbs.

The Protectors wrenched him into the heavy seat, his back to the men watching the proceeding. Cold iron locked over his wrists. Another clamp tightened around his ankles. Pain shot through him so bright, vomit spewed from his gut and trickled over his lips.

He sagged. There was only one ending for him.

He had failed. He prayed that Sofia would finish her work. He prayed Paulina would be safe. He prayed Angelo would avenge him, free his soul, and destroy the Order.

A figure stepped into view, cutting his line of sight. A familiar large silhouette in black Protector garb.

Zanca.

For a moment, Vito's breath stuttered in his chest. Zanca didn't speak, but his eyes tightened with a downward twitch of the corner of his mouth.

"Do your duty," Vito managed to whisper.

The Protector didn't answer.

Quattrone stepped in front of Vito, nudging Zanca aside.

"Vito Uccello," the Exalted Master said, his voice serene. "Over the last two days, you have refused to answer remarkably simple questions. This is your final chance. Where is Doge's Cicogna's journal? Tell us, and we shall be merciful."

Vito lifted his bruised face. "Merciful to who?" he managed through wheezed breaths.

"To you, of course." Quattrone raised an eyebrow, as if the question were as obvious as the sun.

"That means?"

"We shall cease any torture and deliver your sentence forthwith."

Vito snickered. An offer of pain relief wouldn't sway him to do anything.

The senator heeded him a moment longer, as if silence were a challenge. He released an exhale of disappointment.

Grimani strode forward, breath hot with rage. "Where is the traitor, Angelo Mascari? Speak now. Where is he hiding?"

This was an easy question for Vito to ignore, for he did not know the answer. He stared past them both, letting his gaze rest on the chamber's artwork. Anything to keep his mind from slipping.

Quattrone's tone sharpened. "The tree? How can we find it?"

"The tree is lost!" Grimani snapped. "We need Mascari. We need the book."

Vito's mouth felt glued shut by dried blood. He gave nothing in return.

At the base of the dais, Zanca shifted. It was only an inch, barely noticeable, but Vito caught the moment. A tightened jaw. Eyes lowered. His friend was uncomfortable with the proceedings and torture of the once Chief Protector.

"You refuse to answer," Quattrone said. "Very well."

Vito's eyelids drooped, heavy with swelling. He let them half close, not in defiance but because the load of his own body was too great.

Grimani smiled, like a man knowing he'd just won a game of *Bassetta*. He nodded to a Protector.

The doors to Vito's left groaned open.

A woman shrieked. "Unhand me! You bastards! Release me now!"

Vito's heart slammed violently against his ribs.

Paulina.

Two Protectors wrested her forward, her hair half-loose, skirts torn where she'd struggled. She kicked, twisted, and clawed. The Protectors brought her before her husband, who seized Paulina's arm and dragged her in front of Vito.

Vito strained against his shackles, his body coming alive with rage. Metal bit into bone.

"Are you hurt?" he asked.

"DO NOT SPEAK TO HER!" Grimani's roar echoed off the walls.

Paulina cowered, whimpering as Vito had never seen. She used to be so strong. He prayed Grimani hadn't been beating her.

"I will ask you one last time," her bastard husband said, saliva dribbling down his chin. "Where is the book?"

Torture and physical agony could be endured. But the thought of Paulina's pain eclipsed any notion of tenacity. Grimani had played his hand and played it well.

A great sigh escaped Vito's lungs. He'd lost. He'd tell them to save her. He inhaled again to summon the courage to betray all others.

Impatient, Grimani slapped Paulina hard across the face. She took the wallop then returned a wad of spit in her husband's eyes. He wiped his face, then threw his fist into her gut.

"No!" Vito struggled to free himself, yearning to wrap his fingers around Grimani's throat.

She heaved a silent cry and crumpled to the floor.

"Speak now," Grimani said, his voice juddering with fury. "Where's the book, Uccello? Where is Mascari? Tell us, and she walks out of here alive."

Breath rattled across Vito's broken teeth. "She's the mother of your children."

"And for that," Grimani replied with a sneer, "her adultery should be ignored?"

Vito tried to speak, but his throat spasmed.

Grimani yanked Paulina's arm, twisting it behind her back until she screamed. "Answer!"

Blood pooled in Vito's mouth. He forced air into ruined lungs.

"Don't," Paulina whispered.

Her moment of doggedness was an inspiration. He loved knowing that a fire still burned within, yet it also revealed a hard truth: if Vito gave the Order the book, it would make things worse for Paulina and countless others.

From somewhere beneath agony and terror, he dredged up words.

"I... gave it... to Angelo," he rasped, voice barely human. "Mascari has it."

It was a lie. A desperate, impossible lie. But a plausible one they'd believe.

The only lie that could save her.

Paulina met his eyes. Her resistance melted into broken rawness. The bonds clamped over his limbs felt as if they had tightened around his heart instead.

Grimani absorbed Vito's strained confession with a slow inhale, shoulders loosening, eyes narrowing as if he'd hoped the defiance would drag on forever.

Quattrone, however, looked at Vito the way a butcher examines a cut of meat, checking for rot, weakness, and truth.

"Where is Mascari, pray tell?" the Exalted Master asked.

"I... don't know."

"You gave him the book," Grimani snapped. "You expect us to believe you know nothing of his destination?"

"I speak the truth," Vito said. "He vanished. He didn't tell me where."

"Lies." Quattrone's gaze chilled. "Most unfortunate."

He flipped his fingers toward a Protector. "Bring the others."

The command rippled through Vito's spine. *Others?*

The door on the far end of the hall creaked open.

Vito's heart collapsed inside him.

Sofia stumbled into the room, jostled by a Protector behind her. She straightened, her head held high, her graying blond hair braided tight, face pale but composed. Behind her was Marcello, his palpable fear seeping through his attempt at a stony demeanor. Upon seeing Vito, their eyes went wide.

A Protector shoved them forward. Vito nearly tore the armrests from the chair, straining to rise.

"I'll kill you! Leave them alone—"

Grimani flashed out, silencing him with a backhand blow across the mouth that split lips already torn open. Vito's head snapped sideways. The room swung.

"Brother!" Sofia's voice pierced the haze.

The Protectors brought the new prisoners forward. They stood in line with Paulina.

Quattrone gestured impatiently. "We were going to leave your family alone, but we caught them creeping out of the Church of the Madonna dell'Orto. At night."

Grimani gazed at the massive painting over Doge Memmo and the council chairs, then leaned into Sofia's ear, his eyes gleaming at Vito with a fanatic's hunger. "*Tintoretto's* church. Has your brother been whispering secrets? Secrets that carry severe penalties if revealed? Should we also question his wife and children?"

"Why were you there?" Quattrone asked.

Sofia's eyes snapped to Vito. So fast that anyone else would have missed it. Behind that glint revealed something astonishing: Cleverness. Resolve. She crafted a perfectly blank expression for her inquisitors. "Because we pray, siori," she said. "It was our family's church."

A hollow laugh echoed from Grimani's throat. "At night?"

Sofia angled her chin, as if offended. "We are free to worship wherever and whenever we wish. I was concerned for my brother. We went to pray for him. I see my concern was quite valid. I am not the one who has committed a crime here."

Once more, Sofia glanced at Vito. It was more than cleverness and resolve behind her eyes. It was satisfaction.

Accomplishment.

She'd finished the puzzles and must have placed them in certain spots, including in the Madonna dell'Orto. Vito marveled at his sister's cunning. The plan was risky, but genius. The Order loved to hide things in plain sight. She hid their prize in the last place they'd think to look. If only she and Marcello could maintain the ruse.

Quattrone's nostrils flared. "If you will not speak," he said, "perhaps the boy will."

A Protector seized Marcello and pinned his arms back. He gritted his teeth, impressing Vito with his inner strength, but he wasn't nearly as strong in the moment.

"Stop!"

They ignored Sofia's plea. A second Protector struck Marcello across the cheek.

"I swear it!" Vito rasped. "I gave Angelo the book. I haven't an inkling where he went. He didn't tell me for this very reason. All I know is that he left Venice."

The Protector clenched the back of Marcello's neck.

"Please, Senator," Sofia cried, struggling against her own captor, her plea pained with desperation. "Our family has been friend and loyal servant to you and six doges. We've sacrificed so much. We lost our brother, Ivan, in service to the Republic and your Order."

A cackle sprouted from Grimani. "Ivan was weak. He let himself fall to the Swordsman's blade."

"Enough," Quattrone snapped. "Let the boy be."

Grimani shot him an impatient look, but Quattrone stood firm, raising his palm to the Protector restraining Marcello.

"I said release him," Quattrone shouted, exerting his authority. "Expel them both from the palace."

Marcello shuffled free and embraced his mother.

"Thank you," Sofia whimpered. She gazed at Vito for the final time. It was sorrowful, yet her eyes burned unbroken with a look that seemed to say: *this is not over*.

Vito exhaled a heavy sigh of relief as two Protectors escorted his sister and nephew to the door.

"I am a merciful man, Sofia," Quattrone said as they reached the threshold. "The Order is merciful. I shall permit you to watch the cremation of your brother's corporeal vessel."

Sofia halted the exit, allowing herself to absorb the morbid invitation. Then they ushered her out.

In five long strides, Quattrone climbed the dais and approached Vito. His face was a storm cloud ready to break. "Mascari would not abandon Venice without telling you. Without a plan."

"That is the plan," Vito shouted, spittle dropping down his chin. "He left the Republic entirely. Until it is safe to return, as he did years ago."

Quattrone stilled. "To Santa Marta?"

"Somewhere else." Vito swallowed hard. "Somewhere no one will find him. The New World is more immense than you could begin to imagine. Ten, no, one hundred times greater than the whole of the Italian peninsula. It dwarfs Europe, and only a sliver has been explored."

Quattrone and Grimani exchanged blank expressions, as if unsure what to do with this new knowledge.

Then an exhale of relief wheezed from behind Vito.

"Then the book is gone," Doge Memmo said. "Out of Venice. Out of reach of our enemies. This is... acceptable."

Quattrone wheeled on him. "Acceptable? Are you mad? The book is nothing more than a loose end. The Tree of Life—"

"Enough of that fantasy," Grimani snapped. "My head is clear now. You, senator, may need the leeches yourself. The Tree, the Fountain, these are nothing but legend."

The Exalted Master's rage boiled over. "You dare call it legend? You are proof—"

"I am proof that consuming rotten fruit diseases the mind," Grimani yelled back. "We have a crisis. A traitor. A fugitive with information that could destroy us. He must be hunted."

Quattrone stepped so close to Vito that their breath mingled. He whispered in his ear. "How do I reach the tree?"

Vito's vision blurred. "Grimani speaks the truth. It's poison and death, not life."

A long, trembling pause stretched between them.

Then Quattrone's face hardened into lethality. "Very well. You have served the Order for the final time." He straightened and addressed the room. "Vito Uccello is branded a traitor to the Order evermore. He endangers us all. By the authority bestowed upon me as the Exalted Master of the Ancient Order of the Seventh Sun, I levy the ultimate sentence upon him. Remove Paulina from this hall."

Through salt-drenched eyes, Vito watched as men who'd previously been under his command dragged his beloved from the Great Council Room.

Other Protectors drew the curtains and lit candles, while others carried in a candleholder wielding the Sun Crystal. A prism was lowered from the ceiling. As Quattrone commenced the ceremony, a sense of peace washed over Vito.

He would pay a price.

But he had *saved* them.

It was his last thought before unimaginable pain engulfed his body.

XLIX

"NO," ANGELO SAID, PARRYING Ludo with enough force to propel the weapon from his friend's hand. The trainer landed with a clack and slid across the marble floor.

Ludo gaped at his open palm. "I executed the *imbroccata* exactly as you instructed."

To Angelo's left, Carmen lowered her own wooden practice sword and stared wide-eyed at Ludo's on the other side of the room.

"Your *imbroccata* was adequate," Angelo said, referring to Ludo's thrust. "I meant I'm not hiding here another night. Two days, Ludo. Two days since they took him. Since *we let* them take him."

He returned his two training swords to the rack and strode across the *fortezza's* massive dining hall. Niccolò Riva had been kind enough to allow the Guild to convert the space into a training area and war room. For hours each day, Angelo had been instructing the group. The Guild's swordsmanship was far from ready, but Vito was running out of time. He balled his fists and pressed them against the map table, where comrades drew sketches of the Palazzo Ducale from memory.

"You can best me in training, but look at you," Ludo said. "Your bandage is half-soaked. You're still bleeding."

A maroon patch had spread through the linen binding Angelo's shoulder. He hadn't felt the fresh bleed through the haze of anger. He ignored the throbbing. "Then wrap it tighter."

Carmen stepped over, her jaw set with a resolve Angelo had once mistaken for coldness. “Recklessness won’t bring Vito back,” she said. “Not from the fate that has befallen him.”

“He could still be alive.”

Neither responded.

Angelo drew a breath in a futile attempt to steady the fire burning through him. The great hall pressed around them: thick stone walls, a vaulted ceiling reinforced with iron ribs, and narrow windows set deep enough that no arrow could find a line through them. A perfect fortress. A perfect prison.

“We should never have come here,” he muttered under his breath. He said it about the *fortezza* but realized that internally, he meant Venice.

Ludo gestured broadly. “This place is the only reason the Order hasn’t found us yet. Riva lives like a man the world forgot. Even the doge has forgotten his name. No one would think to look for us here.

“That helps *him*,” Angelo snapped. “Not Vito.”

Other Guild members busying themselves in the hall slowed but didn’t halt their tasks. They all heard. None intervened.

Carmen lowered her voice. “Angelo... we know what he means to you.”

“It’s more than friendship.” He clenched his teeth. “You don’t realize how much his loss affects us.”

Vito’s face rose unbidden in Angelo’s mind’s eye. Bloodied, defiant, swallowed by a swarm of Protectors on the burning dock. What kind of friend sails away while the other is beaten half to death?

He closed his eyes briefly. Behind them were other faces. Loredana’s. Franco’s. Juanita’s. Waiting for him in Santa Marta.

What kind of husband leaves?

What kind of lover fails twice?

What kind of man runs?

Were they his words or Isabella’s? He didn’t know anymore. He forced the musings down, pushing them behind the immediate need to move.

An image of Sofia and her family flashed before him. He wondered how far retribution would go. He prayed they were safe.

Trust your heart, 'mòre mio. Your instinct.

"We can't stay here," Angelo said again, quieter but no less fierce.

"The Order has the entire city under its thumb," Ludo said. "They wanted Vito alive, and they want you more. You heard what the scouts said. The Protectors are sweeping the canals every night."

"Then we hit them when they're not sweeping," Angelo replied. "Strike at dawn. Or midnight. Or—"

"With what force?" Carmen swept her arm over the room. "You can't raise your right arm above your ribs."

A muscle twitched in Angelo's jaw. She was right, but that didn't ease the burning within.

"Think like the man who has survived all these years," Ludo said from across the table. "Not like a wounded bull."

Angelo shot him a glare. Ludo held it.

"You're a strategist. One of the best. Vito trusted you. Maybe more than he trusted anyone. If he could speak now, he'd tell you to use your head. Just as he did before when he told us to stand down, and you agreed."

Carmen approached more softly this time. "Don't let grief make decisions you'd never make otherwise."

"He saved us," Angelo said with a deep exhale. "All of us."

"We will avenge him," Carmen said. "Save him if he still yet lives. But not today."

Angelo turned and stared out the narrow window slit. Beyond it, a sliver of courtyard could be seen. When they first arrived, Ludo had explained that Niccolò Riva was a reclusive noble scholar and a distant relation of Ludo's deceased mother. Riva owed the Stefanetti family an old debt, but it would be impossible for the Order to make the connection. Riva had built his home like a man expecting a siege, which was beneficial for the Guild. Infuriating for Angelo. He could sharpen his sword only so many times before the metal was gone.

A chair scraped. A younger Guild member, a man as thin as a mast rope, looked up from a sheaf of parchment.

Ludo nodded, then turned back to Angelo. "We need you," he said. "We need your mind, your strength, and when the time comes... your fury."

Angelo inhaled, letting the air settle the tremor in his thoughts. He faced the others. A dozen people stood scattered about the room. Nobles, exiles, craftsmen, all carrying the same weary fire in their expressions, all of them looking at him.

"The Order thinks they're untouchable," one woman said. "We should drag their secrets into the open. Let all Venice see them for what they are."

A few murmured in agreement.

"That's been the Guild's purpose since we began," Carmen said. "Expose them. Tear away the ritual and intimidation. Show the city what they truly do to the condemned."

Vexation tightened Angelo's stomach. "We have what, twelve people?"

"Sixteen," Carmen said. "Others will join our cause."

An involuntary laugh escaped from Angelo's mouth. "They infiltrated you, not the other way around. You think you can restart recruitment? I do not have a lifetime to waste here. You also miss the Guild's *true* purpose."

"Which is what?" Ludo asked.

"We must destroy them. We must release Isabella and the others from *Paradise.*" Angelo pointed a finger at each person in the room to drive home his point. "I will find a way. *That* remains my path."

"Earlier, you said my *imbroccata* was adequate," Ludo said. "Not excellent?"

The question surprised Angelo. He turned to his friend. "No."

"How can I improve?"

Without answering, Angelo drew his rapier and selected three dates from a bowl. He tossed all three into the air. Tracking the motion of each, he flicked his wrist. Six halves landed on the marble.

Ludo and other Guild members gaped at the move.

"With precision," Angelo said. His old master's admonishment returned to him. "Right now, we're hacking away like Turkish street rats. This entire operation needs to be more precise."

"Like this?" Carmen asked. She twirled, drew a knife from her bodice, and flung it into a date on the floor, impaling it.

Angelo smiled at her grace and skill, but it didn't assuage the angst rippling around him like a current.

Ludo straightened. "Va bene. Then what do you suggest?"

"We smuggle ourselves into the Palazzo," Angelo said. "Disguised as servants."

"Too many checkpoints," Ludo responded. "They know their staff. Anyone with access to the Great Council Room is watched."

Angelo stood and paced the room, letting the movement stimulate his brain.

"We bribe a Protector. A low-ranking one."

"If he talks?" Carmen asked. "Risky and unreliable. He could betray us."

"We ignite a public riot to distract the Order. Attack then."

"Too uncontrollable," Ludo said. "They'll lock the Palazzo down, and innocent people may die. Angelo, please understand we've considered everything. None of this will work."

"Vito was right about one thing," Carmen said. "We need leverage."

"They have the advantage," Ludo added. "Plain and simple."

"Then let's change that."

Before Ludo responded, heavy footsteps echoed down the corridor.

The Guild turned as Riva appeared in the doorway. His eyes appeared more sunken than usual. He scratched his bushy gray beard and looked straight at Ludo before speaking, his expression stiff with concern.

"I've heard from my longtime retainer," he said. "Word spreads through the streets. Criers near Rialto. Lantern-bearers in the northern *sestiere*. The bells at San Zanipolo are tolling."

Ludo shot up. "For us?"

"Hardly." Riva snickered. "This morning... Doge Marcantonio Memmo was pronounced dead."

The room stilled. Even the air seemed to pause.

Angelo glanced from Ludo to Carmen, then back to Riva. In the quiet that followed, a realization slid through him.

"*That* is our leverage," he said.

A dead doge meant power shifting hands.

Power shifting hands meant chaos.

Chaos meant opportunity.

Chaos could destroy the Order.

L

JANUARY 2, 1614

QUATTRONE MOVED THROUGH THE Arsenal's inner corridors with the certainty of one who believed Venice bowed under his will. Of late, he questioned not only that notion, but if the Republic itself remained the force it had been for centuries. An intense heat smote him before he reached the ruined doorway. The stone passage opened into the *Segreta Fornace*, the secret foundry reserved for the Order's most delicate work, and the air shimmered with scorched iron and wet ash. The breath of the furnace lingered like a slain dragon.

The damage made his jaw clench.

A steel door lay twisted like softened wax, torn from its hinges and hurled across the floor. Smoke drifted from the blackened edges of the breach, curling upward into the ceiling. Two Protectors carried away a gurney. The occupant was barely conscious, with a mangled arm and face streaked with soot. Others swept debris and shoveled embers into water barrels that hissed in protest.

The Guild had struck again. Their fifth time in as many weeks. Each had grown more brazen. Molds for Mongolian short swords had been destroyed, along with two dozen of the weapons and a new holder for the Sun Crystal, one which Quattrone had intended to ship to Spain.

A curse slipped from his breath. He would not show fear. Not in this place. Not after weeks of being mocked by shadows.

Grimani waited near the largest furnace, his expression drawn tight by frustration. Zanca stood behind him, stiff as a ramrod, eyes fixed on the destruction. When he saw Quattrone, Zanca's Sicilian complexion and beard weren't dark enough to hide his face flushing with embarrassment. He was a man who walked with dignity and never sought to shift blame. When he was promoted to Enforcer of the Charge after Vito's betrayal, Zanca embraced his role as head Protector of the Order wholeheartedly. It was no wonder he'd taken full responsibility for failing to nullify the insurrection. Quattrone had been wondering if he'd made a mistake.

"Report," he said.

Zanca opened his mouth to speak, but Grimani intercepted him, gesturing toward the shattered doorway. "The blast came from inside the antechamber. They breached during a shift change, moved quickly, avoided the main patrol routes. Minimal footprints. No witnesses."

No witnesses. No mistakes. No mercy.

It was a dramatic shift in the Guild's tactics. For years, they had done nothing but talk amongst themselves. Now, it was the group's signature.

Quattrone stepped carefully through the rubble, examining the scorched smear along the stone floor. The explosive had been small yet purposeful. Not designed to kill, but rather to embarrass. The Order's private foundry was infiltrated like a common merchant's storehouse.

"What did they take?" Quattrone asked.

"Weapons. Short swords, crossbows, rapiers," Grimani answered, his voice laced with bitterness. "And an incendiary mixture we've been developing. They left nothing intact."

Quattrone's fingers curled around the ridge of a fallen beam. The heat bit into his skin, but he held it anyway, forcing himself to feel the humiliation.

"The city teeters without a doge," he murmured. "In the disarray, thieves of conscience strike at us with impunity."

"We've searched every district, Exalted Master," Zanca said. "Interrogated half the city's smugglers and informants. No sightings. No leads."

"No *successes*," Quattrone corrected. "Be precise."

Zanca stiffened, shame hardening his features.

Outside, a hammer clanged against a die, the echo reverberating through the ruined foundry like a heartbeat in a metal coffin.

"The Republic can't elect a new doge," Grimani said, overly eager to shift the subject. "The councils argue day and night, and nothing moves. The unrest grows worse. Riots last night near San Marco. People cry out for stability."

"We will give it to them," Quattrone replied. "If they elect Giovanni Bembo."

"Bembo has support," Grimani said. He picked up a busted sword, gliding his finger over an unfinished blade, now split in half. He tossed it into the rubble heap. "The patricians want a unifying figure. We can guide him."

We can control him, Quattrone thought. "Is he aware of the attack?"

"Yes. He was here earlier this morning." Zanca hesitated. "He was... concerned."

Concerned. Not outraged. Not startled. Just concerned.

It was promising. A man who hid his true emotions was worth cultivating.

Quattrone paced the perimeter of the blast zone, inspecting every scorch mark, every splintered edge. The Guild grew bolder. Their attacks had struck supply caches, informants' homes, and staging points across the city. Each strike was coordinated. Calculated. A message.

To Quattrone, the message was clear: *We are not finished.*

Needing to escape the stifling, poisoned air, he headed outside without a word, knowing Grimani and Zanca would follow. The arsenal's smoke had thinned enough to reveal the bruised sky above the lagoon. Quattrone stepped to the elevated walkway overlooking the dry docks. Cold, salty wind threaded through the massive timber frames of half-built galleys. Sparks leapt from a row of smithing stalls. Rhythmic hammering echoed across the water.

"One Protector was badly injured," Grimani said, his breath visible in the chill. "He won't hold a sword again."

"Did he identify the perpetrators?"

"Not by face. Our men tried to fight them off, but it was no contest. Among them was a master swordsman. His rapier moved like a hurricane."

A master swordsman whose rapier moved like a hurricane. A sharp change in tactics. It could only have been one man: Angelo Mascari. Quattrone suspected Vito had lied about the swordsman's retreat. It didn't make sense that the man would've returned to Venice only to turn around again at the slightest danger. It had to be Angelo.

"Whatever you think you've done these five weeks, Zanca," Quattrone said, "it isn't enough. I expect more from the Enforcer of the Charge."

The chief Protector bowed his head with shame and humiliation.

"A wounded dog only forgets its fear when you force it to recognize the chain around its neck."

Quattrone turned to watch a barge drift through the canal. Even here, the unrest showed. Too few workers. Too many shadows at the edges of the docks. Whispers traveled like rats along mooring lines. Venice was restless. Venice was afraid.

Perfect.

"The Guild can't hide forever," Grimani said, his tone brittle.

"They've done it successfully for five weeks," Quattrone replied. "Need I remind you that their success is your failure?"

Grimani bristled. "Need I remind you that I am also a senator? An equal under the doge?"

The question triggered a smile in Quattrone. He'd been waiting for it. "Need I remind you I am the Order's Exalted Master and that this is Order business?" Not waiting for a response, he turned to Zanca. "You served Vito for many years."

The Protector swallowed. "Si, sior."

"You knew him better than anyone."

"Si."

"Yet you remain loyal to the Order."

"Si, sior." Hesitation betrayed Zanca's response. Barely perceptible, but enough. "I serve the Order, and you are the Order. That which is rancid should be cut out."

Quattrone nodded his agreement and leaned closer. "I need someone who understands Vito. Someone who can understand why he'd befriend an enemy."

Zanca raised an eyebrow. "You speak of Angelo Mascari?"

"There is only one reason why the Guild has become emboldened," Quattrone continued. "I need an emissary. Someone to whom the Guild will listen rather than attack. Someone who can make Mascari listen."

"Assuming he's still in Venice," Grimani said.

"He is," Quattrone replied.

Zanca's brow creased. "You want to send a message?"

"A truce," Quattrone said, though the word felt venomous on his tongue. "An opportunity for Mascari to stop risking the lives of innocents. To meet. To talk. Perhaps to get a concession."

"If he refuses?"

Quattrone's smile was thin as a blade.

"Then he reveals himself."

He let the gravity of the plan hang in the air, watching the men consider it.

"Vito lied about Mascari," Quattrone said with conviction he truly held. "He never left Venice. The swordsman is behind these attacks. He will not stop until he is put down like the rabid animal he's become."

A crane rattled nearby as the workers hoisted a stripped mast from the lower slip. Quattrone watched the motion of ropes and pulleys, his mind assembling the city's unrest much like the mechanisms before him.

"Find the Guild," Quattrone said. "Find Angelo Mascari. I don't care what walls must be torn down."

Zanca nodded. "Si, Exalted Master."

"If Bembo wishes to sit in the doge's chair," Quattrone said to Grimani, "he must understand who truly governs Venice."

The smoke from the foundry rose and swirled around Quattrone as if pulled inward by his voice.

"This city is a tinderbox. I will decide where the spark falls."

LI

THE *SANDOLO'S* OARLOCKS CREAKED as Zanca rowed away from the cemetery island, the craft's lantern slipping into the dark channel's fog. Only then did they dare speak.

"We should have killed him." Carmen kept her voice low, but her tone was sharp enough to cut the headstones that surrounded them. She tugged on her dark-brown wool gown and fitted bodice. The heavy clothing was unusual for her but suitable for the winter damp—and anonymity.

Angelo fixed his gaze on the water where Zanca had disappeared, anticipating the Protector to reemerge with two-dozen comrades. Yet the cemetery remained still. Moonlight cast long shadows from the tombs and rows of cypress. An ominous sense of discomfort crept through him, which could've been from a possible ambush or from the place itself, yet he held no fear of ghosts.

"That would've accomplished nothing." Ludo tightened his gray cloak against the chill and leaned against a mausoleum. "Quattrone must have an ulterior motive."

"Si," Carmen answered without looking at him. "To kill us."

Angelo rationalized that his unease was caused by the burial ground—a modern break from Venetian tradition. When he lived in the floating city, most bodies were interred under church paving stones. He rattled his head, scattering errant nerves, then exhaled a cloud of winter's smoke. He, too, turned up the collar of his leather cloak to shield himself from cold lagoon air. Life in the tropics had thinned his blood to watered wine. "Or something else altogether," he said to his friends. "Even if he means harm, it's worth hearing him out. Zanca is but a messenger. No doubt Quattrone has an ulterior motive, but he takes equal risk in meeting us. We could kill him."

Carmen's head snapped toward him. Her lips curled upward. "*That is* a plan. Why squander the progress we've made? Now is the time to press, to cut off the head."

Ludo raised a finger, but she preempted his argument.

"We have them on their heels, Ludo. You think it benevolent they want to chat?"

"They seek a parley. To negotiate a truce."

She threw her hands up in frustration. "To what end? They cannot be trusted. Do you not remember what they did to Vito? He was their chief Protector!"

"Oh, now you care for him?" Angelo smiled and winked. "You wanted to slit his throat when you first met the man."

"I was wrong." Carmen's gaze fell to the ground. "And now what of his family? They are as much victim as I."

Her anger was a match strike in the dark, bright enough to highlight the tension in her jaw. She paced a few steps away, her ankle boots crunching on frozen gravel. Angelo shared her rage. No, his was a fury that eclipsed all others. He, too, longed to deliver a devastating blow, yet he found himself rethinking his words.

"Ludo's right," he said. "We need to hear them out."

"You just said we should kill Quattrone." Carmen seethed with confusion.

"Killing him won't be fatal to the Order. Worse, failing to kill the Exalted Master—or succeeding—may thwart our ability to release any souls. The Order will replace him, tighten their security, enlist more Protectors, and launch an all-out offensive against the Guild."

Ludo crossed his arms. "Precisely. I am no fool, Carmen. Quattrone does nothing without expecting power, coin, or blood in return."

"That's why we stay careful," Angelo said.

Carmen released a harsh breath. "Careful won't protect us."

"He wouldn't bargain unless we had something he needs." Ludo shifted his weight and lowered his felt cap. "If Quattrone genuinely intends to free people from *Paradiso*, we must consider it."

"He believes every rumor," Carmen said. "Especially those that promise power."

They both turned to Angelo.

"It gives us leverage," he said. "If Quattrone wants what he *thinks* we have, he may talk."

Carmen stepped closer, her face lit by the weak glow of her lantern propped on a headstone. "What if he's luring us into a corner?"

"Then we stay out of corners," Angelo replied. "We set the terms."

Ludo nodded. "If he keeps his word... if he'll truly release the prisoners... I cannot ignore that. Neither can either of you."

His friend's eyes were weighted by the grief of family unjustly condemned.

And for Angelo... *Isabella*.

The three of them stood in the island's silence, save the rustle of cypress trees.

"You both yearn for something this isn't," Carmen said.

Angelo spun to her. "I want it to end. If a parley gets us closer, then we use it to our advantage. We exploit our position."

She paced between the headstones. "You're both fools. If Quattrone wants to speak, it's because he's found a way to bury us without lifting a blade." She jabbed her finger towards the dirt. "We may as well lie down here and never leave this island."

"Death is but the first consideration." Angelo looked toward the lagoon, toward his past and future. "It's worth the risk."

"You both risk erasing all the gains we've made," Carmen said.

"They're desperate," Ludo said. "Desperation can be used."

"They're desperate because of our success!"

"You overestimate our achievements." Angelo placed a warm hand on Carmen's shoulder to halt her pacing. "We're mosquitoes biting a lion."

Ludo paced the area, then turned to Angelo. "Zanca mentioned maps of the New World. Something about a tree. What was he talking about?"

A gust of wind rolled through the boneyard, gnawing at Angelo's injuries. Fresh aches layered themselves atop old wounds. The reality of it all settled on him like an unwelcome frost.

"Quattrone believes in legends," Angelo said. "The doge, too. They think wonders are hidden in the jungle. Remedies. Maybe even immortality. He speaks of the Tree of Life."

Ludo and Carmen widened their eyes. Their mouths popped open.

"Is this a farce?" she asked. "You cannot be serious."

Angelo nodded with solemn displeasure. "I wish I jested. They previously sought the Fountain of Youth."

"How do you know this?" Ludo asked.

"Because they forced me to help them find it."

Ludo stared at him in a moment of disbelief. "Did you?"

"We found poison, betrayal, and death. Myths. Fantasy. Nothing more. Whatever he suspects, it's built on lies and fragments from madmen."

"Does it matter?" Ludo asked. "Belief is a powerful leash."

Carmen released a low, guttural sigh. "So you think Quattrone wants to trade prisoners for stories?"

"For the promise of power," Angelo said, shaking his head. "Control. An expansion beyond Venice."

Ludo's voice grew rough. "If it's truly a myth, then let's give him what he wants. I could see my sister again. Carmen, your father and husband. Angelo, your beloved."

She turned away, blinking hard. Her anger was washed away with a softer expression triggered by Ludo's reminders.

"I don't trust them." Her words quivered but were still sharp. "I won't. But I... understand why you want to try."

Angelo drew a long breath through his nose, bringing an essence of moss and damp stone. When Zanca had offered a truce in exchange for maps to the tree, the request had caught him off guard. In the minutes since, the reason for the compromise sharpened into focus. It seemed inconceivable that Vito would reveal the tree's location, no matter the torture. Senator Grimani was clearly unable to recall the route.

Quattrone had no other recourse.

It was a plea that Angelo would use to his advantage—one they could use to turn the tables.

He deplored the idea of the Order returning to Santa Marta, but this time, he'd be prepared and ready. He could protect the town and his family, and deliver the victory he craved on his own turf.

"The jungle is the most unforgiving place on Earth," he said. "I can lead Quattrone and the Order to a demise of their own making."

"Fake maps?" Ludo asked with a growing smile.

"They would never discern the difference," Angelo replied.

"It's risky," Carmen added. "They'd demand assurances."

Angelo shrugged. "So long as they honor our requests first."

"It can lead to the best possible outcomes," Ludo said.

Carmen narrowed her eyes. "If we do this, we do it our way. Not theirs. We dictate the terms. When we give them Angelo's maps, we control the place. The hour. The exits."

Angelo nodded. "Agreed."

"If they try anything," she said, her tone steady, "I'll cut out Quattrone's heart before he can blink."

"That is precisely why you must stay behind," Angelo said.

Carmen snorted a laugh. "Now *that* must certainly be a jest."

"If the three of us are killed," Angelo said, "all is lost. You must stay with the others and prepare for the worst."

"He's right," Ludo added.

Carmen threw her hands to the sky, released a heated exhale, and stormed off to their waiting gondola. She didn't need to respond further; she was their only hope should the meeting end in disaster.

"Send a message to Zanca," Angelo said to Ludo. "We'll provide a list of prisoners. Set the terms and location. Tell Quattrone he can have his precious maps."

LII

TWENTY-FIVE YEARS. TWENTY-FIVE YEARS since Angelo was forced to flee Venice. Twenty-five years since he traversed Europe and the ocean. Twenty-five years filled with unimaginable wonders... including new purpose, friends, and *family*.

Loredana, Franco, and Juanita had given him a new life, one to which he yearned to return. No, it was more than yearning. It was an obligation. He had been away for far too long.

Back in the city proper for the first time since his return, he stood in the unsteady gondola with Ludo and two soldiers of the Guild. Though he'd known these men a relatively short period, he also called them friends and trusted them with his life. He had responsibilities to them too. An obligation to Isabella. A promise he had made so long ago.

While it was Vito and his brother who had set him on this course, he often felt another hand guided him. For what reason, he knew not. Conflicting commitments warred within, but he sensed that one way or another, it would all be over soon.

A late January breeze cut through him, stilling his nerves. Canal water lapped the *fondamenta*. A crescent moon scantily lit their surroundings, for they had snuffed their lanterns upon arrival.

He wished he could've seen more of his city, that he could see his sisters, cousins, and friends, and even lay eyes on his beloved Isabella in *Paradise*. Sadly, the warrant on his head rendered his wishes impossible. Even being on the outskirts of Venice to meet his enemy presented significant risk. Their plan was rife with danger but had the potential for them to reap the reward they pursued.

After discussing locations with Ludo and Carmen, Angelo's preference was deemed the best for its seclusion and means of escape to the Venetian Lagoon. Angelo had also chosen the Rio di San Girolamo because it was the last place in the city he'd seen when he left all those years ago. Though that moment was brief and also at night, he recalled every potential hiding spot, should they be ambushed.

"He's late." Ludo whispered the words in his gruff voice.

"He'll come. The temptation is too great for Quattrone." Angelo kept his eyes fixed on the canal corner, though he shared his friend's concern.

Another memory from a quarter century prior graced Angelo's mind, one he didn't wish to disclose to Ludo. Around the corner from where their gondola now bobbed, Ludo's father—his identity then unknown—was murdered when he aided Angelo's escape.

That nobleman, Pietro Stefanetti, Isabella's uncle, gave his life for the cause. He had instructed Angelo to flee until it was safe to return to liberate Isabella and the others. Angelo never imagined it would take so long. In that time, Tintoretto imprisoned hundreds of other souls, and Quattrone had set his sights on far greater designs. Angelo would give the man whatever he wanted, if only he could free Isabella and return home.

"There," one of the two Guild soldiers whispered. He pointed to the canal corner.

The glow of a dim lantern hanging on a gondola's bow appeared like a lost star set adrift on the water.

Angelo and his men readied their crossbows. They had two-dozen bolts prepared at their feet, and each had a sheathed rapier. Though Angelo's prowess with a blade was unmatched, he knew the Order's methods. They, too, would carry swords but would no doubt use crossbows as their initial weapons. The unprepared never won battles.

The enemy gondola made its silent approach.

"Who goes there?" Ludo asked. "Quattrone, is that you?"

"Keep your voice down," came an angry whisper.

The gondolier steered their craft broadside to the Guild's.

Four men stood in the boat in the muted light. As expected, Zanca and two other Protectors wielded crossbows. Mongolian short swords hung at their hips. A bearded man, in his middle-sixth decade, positioned himself in the center of the gondola.

"Which one of you is Angelo Mascari?" he asked. His tone was deep, and he spoke with confidence.

"Are you Quattrone?" Angelo replied.

"Address me as Exalted Master."

Heat roared through Angelo's veins. "I shall do no such thing."

"Very well," Quattrone replied. "Then 'Senator' will suffice. You are still a Venetian, are you not?"

If the senator was asking questions designed to provoke a reaction, Angelo had to admit it was working. He took a breath before speaking calmly. "I have always been and always will be. I left only because I was forced to leave. By your hand."

"Hardly. Your hand turned the dials of fate."

"I was thrust into a machination not of my making."

"Yet you embraced it wholeheartedly."

Unable to control his temper, Angelo raised his crossbow. Quattrone's Protectors matched his stance. Angelo's forefinger rested on the metal trigger. How he longed to squeeze it and release a bolt into Quattrone's throat. If he did, the same would happen to him. He had no fear of death, but it would accomplish nothing. The Order would instate a new Exalted Master, all the souls would remain in *Paradise*, Loredana would lose a husband, and Franco and Juanita would lose a father.

"With all due respect, Senator," Ludo said. "Did we come out here at this time of night to discuss Angelo's history or our proposal? Do you agree to our terms?"

Quattrone nodded at his men to lower their weapons. They did as instructed. Angelo relaxed his grip and lowered his. Ludo and their compatriots followed suit.

"Tell me about Vito Uccello," Quattrone said.

The request surprised Angelo. Surely, the senator knew Vito well. Angelo raised an eyebrow, realizing the question was designed to set him off balance.

"He's your man," Angelo replied.

"You were with him in the New World. Things changed between the two of you. Why?"

Angelo exhaled through his nose. He had no interest in rehashing past events and less in providing the senator with any information outside their terms, even if it was mundane.

"Will you release Isabella and the others we requested?" He phrased the statement as a question but uttered it as a demand.

"Provide me with the information and maps you claim to have," Quattrone replied, "and they shall be released immediately."

"Release them first. I need to witness. Then, and only then, shall I provide you with the promised information. You shall have your path to the Tree of Life. You can eat until your heart is content. Which it never will be."

Quattrone snickered. "Very well. It will happen by week's end. We will make arrangements with your envoy."

Angelo glanced at Ludo, who nodded back with a slight smile.

"Then we have an agreement," Angelo said to Quattrone, before motioning to depart.

Not relinquishing his crossbow, a Guild soldier pushed them off with the gondola pole using his free hand.

Angelo never moved his eyes from his enemies.

"If you don't honor your word," he said, "the Guild will never cease fighting the Order. We shall release all the souls and banish the Order to hell."

"I'd like to see you try," replied Quattrone, his voice skimming across the water.

LIII

BEDAZZLING LIGHT FILTERED THROUGH the tall windows of the Sala del Collegio, cutting thin bars of shadow across the packed chamber buzzing with shifting voices. Patricians moved between benches. Envoys whispered in corners. Scribes waited with quills half-raised. The Great Council's latest session had ended without a result, and disappointment hung in the room like stale air.

From the opposite end, Grimani spoke at the top of his lungs, pleading his case for Bembo.

Quattrone stood near the hearth, warming his hands more out of habit than need. Three weeks of inconclusive voting had drained everyone's patience, his own most of all. Bembo should have been elected by now. On that, he and Grimani agreed. Every day without him meant more uncertainty for Venice, less control for the Order, and delayed inevitability for the Guild.

He'd considered sending a message, but letting them wait and squirm played into his hand. Angelo's maps were most desirable—and he'd acquire them—but he had no intention of releasing a single soul. In fact, after Bembo's election, *Il Paradiso* would soon see its borders swell.

He kept his posture calm, though the delays were tightening around his plans. He needed the Republic still, not drifting. A city without a doge was a ship with slack rigging, and foreign winds were already pushing at the sails.

Three patricians nearest him debated the latest ballot, but their words melded together. They didn't see the danger of inaction. Or they did, and preferred anarchy to a doge aligned with him.

Either way, time no longer cooperated.

The crowd of senators thinned as men filed into the adjacent hall, leaving Quattrone with a handful of others.

"Senator Quattrone," called a liquid voice. "A moment."

He shifted to find his fellow senator, a man Quattrone had appointed as an Inquisitor of the Order.

"Antonio," Quattrone said, shaking his friend's hand. "Delighted to see you. How's the family?"

"Spending my money," Antonio replied with a chuckle.

Beside him was another senator Quattrone knew well—a man who served as a Lord of the Night of the Order.

Both men carried the polite stiffness of people who were about to ask the kind of question no one wanted answered in public.

Antonio scrutinized him with the calm of someone who rarely wasted words. "The Council will adjourn this afternoon. No consensus."

"Their hesitation serves no one," Quattrone replied.

"Mm." Antonio put his hands behind his back. "Speaking of hesitation... I understand you had business near the glassworks on Murano a fortnight ago. In the Matins hours."

The question surprised Quattrone, but he comported himself with the propriety of a senator being unduly questioned.

"Murano? No. You've been misinformed."

"Strange," Antonio said. "Someone was certain they saw movement there. A lantern on the water. Perhaps they mistook another for you."

Quattrone measured his answer. "Then they mistook someone, yes. I haven't been to Murano in at least two years. What of it? Why are you inquiring about my affairs?"

The younger patrician watched him, more interested in Quattrone's reaction than the exchange.

"These are brittle days," Antonio said. "People notice comings and goings. Even small ones in the Matins hours on Rio di San Girolamo or outside the ghetto walls."

The specific location revealed the subtext behind Antonio's inquisition. They weren't asking about Murano. No, they knew precisely where he was, and the message was clear: *We're paying attention. You're moving pieces without sanction.*

Quattrone forced himself to maintain a stoic composure. "As I said, it's been years since I was on Murano, and my business is my own."

Antonio's expression said otherwise.

A prickle of unease seized Quattrone's spine. Not panic, only the recognition that someone had revealed his meeting with Mascari and the Guild. If the rat divulged their late-night encounter, they likely also told the Lords of the Night of Quattrone's desire for details of the New World. He trusted his Protectors, but he'd have words with them, as well as the boatman.

"We must go," Antonio said.

"To where?" Quattrone asked, seeking to turn the tables. "These are brittle days, and people notice comings and goings."

Antonio offered a crooked smile. "A meeting with Ambassador Bedmar, if you must know."

The name carried weight. The Spanish ambassador. That two senators would be meeting with him during ducal deliberations added concern to Quattrone's plate. Bedmar was the kind of man who thrived in political uncertainty. Quattrone had already secured the support of many of Spain's most influential, from nobility to their preeminent artist. The Spanish unanimously favored the Order's expansion, yet Bedmar was the last man Quattrone wanted involved in any way.

"Pray tell, why would you be meeting with the Spanish ambassador during such brittle times?"

Antonio held his gaze a heartbeat too long, then said with a toothy smile, "In such times, it's best to keep our allies close and apprised of any news. It is but a simple diplomatic courtesy."

With that, the two men bowed their heads and left Quattrone standing alone.

Cold air slipped through the arches as he crossed into the loggia. The buzz of the Great Council Room faded behind him, replaced by the muted hum of the courtyard below. He walked slowly, keeping his pace measured so anyone watching would see a man lost in routine after a long session.

Yet his thoughts were anything but steady.

Antonio's questioning replayed itself with unwelcome persistence. The man had probed yet knew of the meeting. Antonio was far from careless. He was deliberate and loyal to an older vision of the Order that had no room for greatness. The conversation unsettled Quattrone. While they were equals as senators of the Republic, he was the leader of the Order. Those two men were of judicial rank.

Gripping the cold stone balustrade, he scanned the courtyard to catch them walking toward the palazzo gate.

The questions weren't a warning; they were a marker. A note slid across the table. The Lords of the Night were consorting with the Spanish ambassador... and Antonio collected secrets the way other men collected coin.

If Quattrone were to enact his vision of finding the Tree of Life and expanding the Order, he would need to do it immediately. For that, he needed Angelo Mascari's knowledge of its location.

His jaw tightened. He pushed off the balustrade and continued down the loggia. A servant approached from the opposite end, quick in his movements but trying not to appear rushed. When he reached Quattrone, he bowed.

"Senator," the young man said, "you are needed at once. The Council requests your presence."

"Very well," he said, and followed the servant back inside.

LIV

THE MORNING CROWD SWALLOWED them as they stepped off the narrow *fondamenta* and into the churn of Venice. Angelo kept his head low beneath the broad hood of a pilgrim's cloak. The wool was coarse against his neck. The disguise wasn't uncommon. Pilgrims came and went from shrines across the lagoon, so it was enough to hide his features. Ludo wore the same, his beard tucked into his collar. Though Carmen had a dozen throwing knives secured to her bodice, she had cloaked herself in a faded nun's habit, the veil obscuring her face. It was the best way to move unseen in daylight: anonymity through reverence.

Angelo pushed deeper into the *calle*, letting the city absorb them. Merchants shouted over each other, competing for morning business or arguing over tariffs. In a quarter century, nothing had changed. It was good to be home, though Angelo felt a bit like a visitor—or worse, an outsider. While business-as-usual flowed around them, tensions simmered. Subtle agitation clung to the air like brine.

But that wasn't why he had convinced Ludo and Carmen to reconnoiter the palace.

It was the silence from Quattrone.

Three weeks. Not a summons. Not a whisper. Nothing.

Gondoliers cursed at one another as their boats scraped under a low bridge.

"We knew he'd need time," Ludo said from behind Angelo and Carmen on the narrow *fondamenta*. "The nobles are tearing at each other over the election. No doge means no peace. I've also learned Quattrone has been meeting with Spanish emissaries."

"To what end?" Angelo asked.

"He's planting seeds. Earning favor. I believe he wishes to expand the Order."

The news sent warning bells through Angelo's brain. He exchanged a look with Carmen, who appeared equally concerned.

"Another reason why we must crush them now. Quattrone's an opportunist. He's using this prolonged election to his advantage."

The trio stepped around a toppled fruit cart blocking the street. A small knot of men argued nearby, sleeves rolled, faces flushed. Two patricians' servants accused the other of sabotage. Carmen slipped around them, keeping her pace steady, then slipped past two women haggling over spinach heads that were already wilting.

"If he were true to his word," she continued, "he would've sent a messenger, even if to tell us he needs more time."

Angelo nodded. That part gnawed at him. Quattrone hadn't simply delayed the release of the souls; he hadn't made contact at all. Not even a coded scrap of parchment passed through one of the safe channels they'd arranged. Angelo couldn't decide whether the Order was too occupied to reach out... or deliberately ignoring them.

Every day without word from Quattrone was another day Isabella remained trapped in that prison of pigment and memory. Another day the Order could be plotting the Guild's demise, maps or no maps. Another day before a reckoning.

A group of soldiers marched past them toward the square, halberds on their shoulders. Carmen stiffened until they'd turned the corner.

"That's twice we've seen patrols," she said.

"It's the election," Ludo said. "Every faction is desperate to show strength. They need to keep the peace as best they can."

He led them down a wide *calle*, letting the noise of the morning swallow their conversation. "If the noble families are still at each other's throats, Quattrone may be stuck in Senate chambers or private councils. If the streets have calmed, then he's out of excuses."

"If he's out of excuses," Carmen said, "then he's lying."

"That's what we're here to learn," Angelo said.

He didn't disagree with Carmen. As much as he wanted a diplomatic solution, they couldn't risk losing their advantage… if they still had one.

If Quattrone was waiting for a doge to be elected, it could happen any day.

If not, then Carmen was right. They would need to act—and soon.

Adjusting his hood, he followed Ludo toward Piazza San Marco. His pulse quickened, not from fear of discovery, but from what he might learn. Or perhaps it was because with every step, he neared Isabella.

The moment they reached the square, the first bell tolled like a pummel to the ribs, a deep iron herald announcing itself to the city. Hundreds of pigeons scattered into the sky.

One heavy, resonant note rolled across the rooftops from the Campanile. Another toll followed from the belltower, and another, slow and deliberate, each one carrying the load of a decision that would shape every person in Venice. Ludo stopped mid-stride. Around them, merchants, sailors, and ladies froze as if the lagoon had turned to ice. Then smaller church bells answered, chiming in uneven bursts across the *sestieri*, a spreading wave of echoing bronze. Other bells followed until the square shook with a layered chorus cascading down from the *campanile*. The meaning was unmistakable. Venice had elected a new doge.

Whatever advantage the Guild had drawn from the city's prior disarray was gone in an instant.

It seemed all of Venice had ceased its activities and rushed toward the square. The three of them let the crowd pull them forward like a tide. More people poured from side streets—tradesmen, servants, sailors smelling of bilge, noblewomen with their attendants, cheesemongers, fishmongers, and every other Venetian with healthy legs.

They reached the edge of Piazza San Marco, where the sun climbed above the basilica's domes, turning the gold mosaics to molten light. A platform had been erected near the *logetta*, flanked by officials in crimson and black.

Carmen drifted close and lowered her veil. "We have our answer."

The crowd surged toward the base of the *campanile* as the last peal rolled across the square. A herald in crimson stepped onto the small wooden dais beneath the belltower and lifted a parchment high above his head. His voice cut through the winter air.

"By order of the Great Council," he cried, "let it be proclaimed: the Most Serene Prince Giovanni Bembo is elected Doge of the Republic of Venice!"

A wave of excitement swept the square. Banners unfurled from upper windows. San Marco's bells thundered again, sending the news across the city.

"The city has its anchor again," Angelo said.

That anchor would calm the ship in rocky seas. The window of tumult had closed, along with their opportunity.

Ludo rubbed a thumb along his hood. "The doge's election will steady the Senate. Quattrone will be freer to move now." He hesitated. "Or he may feel safer turning against us."

Carmen faced them both. "Which means we need to act. Soon. Quattrone was merely buying time."

The crowd moved like a wave toward the basilica, people eager to witness the beginning of a new reign. Voices rose in celebration. Venice, for all its cracks and fractures, was binding itself back together again.

And that was the problem.

"Carmen is right," Angelo said. "Let's strike before they do."

He cast one long look at the basilica as Doge Bembo stepped out to greet the crowd. Bells rang again, and the square erupted.

The stones of the Riva *fortezza* still held the morning chill as Angelo stepped inside with Ludo and Carmen. Guild members moved with tightly wound purpose, crossing between outbuildings, carrying crates of gear, bundles of rope, and rolled cloth that concealed weapons.

They wove through the courtyard toward the eastern workshop where Angelo had installed the cartographer. Bright light spilled through the open doorway and caught the room full-on, illuminating boards, quills, and scrolls as if the workshop were a lantern set in stone.

Master Orfeo bent low over a stretched vellum sheet, his fingers stained with charcoal dust, his quill slicing thin lines. He barely glanced up as the three entered.

To keep the ruse, Ludo had hired a Venetian cartographer famous for mapping the whole of the Mediterranean in his younger days. He'd since drifted into obscurity—someone who was respected yet would be far from Quattrone's mind.

"May I suggest chorographia more in keeping with the Portuguese reports, sior?" Orfeo asked, already reaching for the quill. "The curvature of the Rio Negro. It needs a wider bend."

Angelo stepped closer, studying the emerging map. Orfeo was good. *Too* good. The man had a gift for shaping a world he'd only heard about and seen in his contemporaries' discoveries, drawing the jungle as if the trees whispered their geometry to him. It was Angelo's goal to steer the Order far away from the tree's location and instead, lead them deep into the jungle, where they'd get lost and meet their timely demise by the Tairona, other tribes, or nature's teeth. But a balance was needed; some partial maps existed. Should Orfeo suspect Angelo's accounts were deceitful, the man could relay his concerns to others. Those words could eventually reach Quattrone's ears.

"To the contrary," Angelo said. "You've done excellent work. Continue as you have." He tapped the page with his finger. "Maintain the direction of the tributary here. The ridgeline, too. Both are essential."

Orfeo nodded. To Angelo's knowledge, the cartographer never suspected a thing. How could he? Other than Grimani, Angelo was the only living European who had traversed that impossible path on the far side of the world. If Providence cooperated, the senator would never regain his memory.

Carmen leaned her hip against a beam, arms folded, eyes fixed on Angelo more than the map. "This is folly."

Orfeo cleared his throat softly, sensing the shift in tone but wisely keeping his eyes on the parchment. Angelo turned away from the table and gestured for Ludo and Carmen to follow him back into the courtyard.

She threw her hands in the air. "What is the point of creating the maps if Quattrone has no intention of honoring his pact?"

"Because we hired Orfeo." Angelo scanned the battlements out of habit. "Let's maintain the ruse."

"What if Quattrone obtains the maps? Or employs your mapmaker?"

"Then he'll march to his death."

A breeze tussled Carmen's unbound hair. She made no attempt to hide her disdain. "Every day the Order sits untouched, they regain footing. If we attack them directly, we can cut off the head. Force a surrender."

Silence stretched like a rope pulled taut.

"We can't simply storm the palazzo." Angelo softened his timbre but maintained his intensity, joining Carmen's course but taking a different tack. "Not a surrender. A capture."

Carmen nodded. "Yes. We take the bastard at Bembo's coronation."

Ludo shot a glance at her. "The courtyard of the Palazzo Ducale will be packed. Militia, guards, nobles, clergy—"

"All eyes will be on Bembo," Carmen cut in. "Not us."

"It's madness," Ludo said.

"No, it's brilliant." Angelo tipped his hat to Carmen.

"If only you'd listen to me about everything." She winked at him.

"It's the edge we need. They'd never suspect it. My concern is if our plan fails. We'll be trapped with every Protector and guard in the city. It's safer to abduct him later, maybe at a party, then bring him back to the Palazzo Ducale when it's quiet." Angelo turned to Ludo. "You've attended a coronation ball, haven't you?"

"All of them since my birth," he replied. "At least a dozen. Maybe fourteen or fifteen."

"I've been to some as well," Carmen added. "They've all be masquerades."

"Even better," Angelo said. "Largely peaceful, joyous affairs, are they not?"

Ludo shrugged and rubbed his jaw. "To my knowledge, there has never been so much as a drunken skirmish."

The corner of Angelo's mouth rose involuntarily. "All things are ripe for change."

LV

THE BELLS BEGAN BEFORE sunrise, their iron voices rolling across the city in long, methodical strokes. February's damp air carried the sound as if it were a summons issued directly to every citizen in Venice. By the first sheen of orange on the horizon, the Doge's Palace was alive with movement. Servants hauled banners and scribes bustled across arcades with sealed documents. Lesser nobles fastened cloaks against the chill as they filed toward the courtyard for Giovanni Bembo's long-awaited coronation rites.

Senator Marco Quattrone stood at the highest of the west-facing windows in the *Procuratie vecchie*, watching bodies accumulate in the great square. The scene should've filled him with satisfaction. The Republic had endured quarrels, accusations, and midnight meetings, but at last the Great Council had been beaten into consensus. Predictable, dutiful Bembo was to be crowned. Now that the day had arrived, satisfaction felt thin. Quattrone sensed too much motion beneath the surface of things, like a shifting sandbank waiting to ensnare a ship.

He drew back from the window as a page approached, breathless with haste, announcing that the first procession had departed San Marco's sacristy. Quattrone dismissed him with a nod. He smoothed the front of his black robe and headed toward the stairs. Pride swelled through him. Putting a doge on the throne was a momentous achievement for him. Perhaps his most consequential in his six-and-a-half decades of life—more than becoming a senator or even the Order's Exalted Master. He looked toward the future, one he'd shape to his will, one that would bring far greater achievements. Yet a faint instinct he had learned not to ignore resisted. The city felt different this morning. It was weighted and expectant, as if Venice, herself, was holding her breath.

Corridors leading to the palace were already choked with people of rank, each eager to claim proximity to the new duke as he entered public office. Quattrone drifted among them with the ease of a man accustomed to being overlooked when he wished. Conversations floated past: the usual gossip, boasts, strategic business arrangements disguised as pleasantries. Threading through it, he caught resentful glances from a few who'd backed alternatives to Bembo. He reminded himself it meant nothing. Every election bred suspicion. Every rise in influence casts shadows.

The palace gates opened with ceremonial resplendence, admitting the early dignitaries to the courtyard. Trumpets sounded a fanfare announcing Bembo's approach. The rising sun kissed the red and gold of the great banners unfurling from the surrounding arcades and over the platform erected for the investiture.

Quattrone paused before stepping forward with the others, taking in the knot of guards—all Order Protectors led by Zanca—stationed at three corners. Seeing them now, he wondered if the increase was too much. It was a ceremonial precaution. In Venice's history, there had never been an assault during a coronation. Should the Guild attack, it would be suicide.

The herald's voice cracked across the square, announcing the arrival of the new doge. Cheers erupted as Bembo's crimson-robed figure emerged.

Quattrone's earlier doubt dissipated like fog clearing in the late-morning sun. He'd done it. The cheers weren't for Bembo. They were for *him*.

The coronation had finished hours earlier but bells throughout the city still rang. Festivities continued through Venice in a jubilation that refused to end. like smoke. Lanterns burned across canals large and small, casting a golden light over the entire city. Gondolas slid past one another, prows dipping under the weight of passengers draped in silk and velvet, the water black and calm as ink.

From the roof of an adjacent building across a side canal, along with Ludo and Carmen, Angelo watched *Ca' Corner della Ca' Granda* glow across the canal. Light spilled from its *piano nobile* windows in warm bands, catching on the water and breaking apart. The measured rhythm of harpsichord and strings carried to him beneath a starry sky. This was not Carnival excess. This was power honoring itself. Masks were expected tonight, even encouraged, though these were restrained. No grotesques. No feathers. Respect for the office, even in celebration.

They'd chosen this vantage point to afford them a bird's-eye view of the interior, the main entrance on the Grand Canal, and the side foot entrance on the *fondamenta*. The owner of the building was well paid for his silence.

Angelo tucked his hair and adjusted his cavalier hat to obscure his face. He decided against a costume, opting to wear the clothes Sofia's husband had donated. The black leather cloak, cut to fall clean from the shoulder, enabled him to move easily with his stride. On his hands were a gift from Ludo—leather riding gloves that would serve as protection for blade work. Carmen braced herself against the tiles, slick from mist, her face uncovered. She, too, had refused a disguise. "Let them see me," she'd said. "It'll be a reckoning."

The remaining Guild members of fighting capability were stationed outside the Palazzo Ducale, awaiting their arrival with their prize.

A gondola nosed in toward the water entrance of the freestanding, monumental noble's palace that exuded more wealth than half the city would earn in their collective lifetimes. Footmen moved to steady it. A woman stepped out, her mask chased with silver filigree. Angelo tracked the movements of the guards on the docks and foot entrance—how many, where they stood, how often their attention drifted back toward the doors.

The woman's laugh and auburn hair brought a glimpse of Isabella to the forefront of his mind. He had come too far to let this slip away because of political squabbling.

Inside, the fête was in full bloom. The ballroom on the *piano nobile* breathed heat and perfume. Tapestries muffled sound along the walls. Servants threaded through the crowd with trays held high, masks hiding their fatigue.

Quattrone stepped from his gondola as if the night had parted for him, flanked by two maskless ducal guards in dark cloaks. He paused at the top of the steps, surveyed the entrance, then passed inside.

"There," Carmen whispered. "That's our window."

"Not yet," Angelo said. "Stick to the plan."

The music softened and somewhere inside, a toast was raised. Angelo could make out a few words and pieced together the rest—Venice eternal, Venice unbroken, Venice chosen by God. A lifetime of conflicting emotions boiled within him.

Then a figure hurried to the side entrance. Young. Clean-shaven. Dressed as a minor chancery clerk, no mask, his posture confident without arrogance... just as instructed. Ludo's sixteen-year-old cousin carried no papers, but he didn't need to. He spoke to the guards who refused entry at the threshold. Two minutes later, Quattrone arrived, clearly irritated by the interruption.

Angelo watched the senator tilt his head and narrow his eyes at the fake clerk's face, then the clerk's fingers trembling like a jib not tied down. Ludo had instructed his cousin to say that the archivist found a discrepancy in the coronation documents requiring Quattrone's immediate presence.

He quickly put his hands behind his back and spoke. Quattrone motioned as if questioning. The exchange lasted only moments, but tension coiled tight in Angelo's chest. If Ludo's cousin forgot his lines, or if Quattrone suspected even the slightest hint of shenanigans, all would be lost.

The senator stared at the fake clerk for an eternity.

An attendant handed a drink to Quattrone. He sipped the beverage, then shooed Ludo's cousin with a dismissive wave.

"Playtime is over," Carmen whispered. "Let's go down there and take him at the door while we have the chance."

A rock plummeted to the pit of Angelo's gut. All the effort, all the loss, all the years... like ash in the wind. Was it the boy's mannerisms? A single word he uttered?

The boy gazed up to the sky. He seemed to plead for help, but then abruptly spun on his heel and caught Quattrone just as the senator was returning to the revelry. The boy did not bow too deeply. He did not rush his words. He spoke as if he belonged there. At that moment, he did.

Quattrone stopped.

That alone was something.

He turned slowly, again measuring the boy. He questioned him further.

Ludo's cousin didn't hesitate. If following direction, he was telling Quattrone there was a missing signature, that if the wrong document was entered into the registers, it would be noticed by nightfall by the wrong people.

Quattrone studied him for a long moment. He seemed to ask short, sharp questions. The boy answered each in rapid-fire response. The senator's mannerisms shifted from suspicion to calculation. Scandal was a blade that cut both ways. Quattrone understood that better than most.

He gazed at the main dock entrance, then glanced in the direction of the Palazzo Ducale. He knew the distance—how long it would take to walk there, handle the documents, and return to the party. Perhaps twenty-five minutes. Thirty at most. Forty-five by gondola. Music swelled, then dipped. For a heartbeat, Angelo thought Quattrone might summon a guard to apprehend the fake clerk.

Instead, the senator gestured inside, and two ducal guards joined him. They were surely skilled and armed with *schiavona* swords, a double-edged broadsword designed for cutting and thrusting, but it was only two men.

It looked like confidence. It might have been haste. Either way, the Guild's entire strategy hinged on this opening.

Leaving the gala, Quattrone led the boy and the ducal guardsmen down the *fondamenta* and toward the darker streets. The hook went in cleanly, yet unease bubbled in Angelo's chest, one colder than fear. It was a sense that once a thing was set in motion, it no longer belonged to the creator of the action.

Whatever fate awaited them, they would meet it moving forward.

"Now," he said.

The three scrambled to their feet and raced for the roof access door. They hurried down the stairs in time to spy the men crossing the small footbridge that traversed the side canal.

They followed Quattrone, Ludo's cousin, and the two guardsmen deeper into the cut of the city, away from the glow and noise, onto a *calle* that led toward the Palazzo Ducale. Lantern light glistened off the mist-slick stones.

Inching closer as they stayed in the shadows, Angelo counted steps. Counted breaths. His pulse had climbed, not from danger but from possibility. Isabella's release had felt abstract for so long. A task out of reach. Now, it narrowed to a singular point: Quattrone standing before *Paradise*, forced to open the way for his beloved's liberation.

He didn't know what that looked like or what he'd do, but it didn't matter.

He was so close. So close.

One of the ducal guards slowed. "This is not the way."

He looked back a hair of a second after Angelo and Carmen yanked Ludo behind a corner.

The boy didn't stop. "It's a shortcut, sior."

"He's right," Quattrone said. "Do try to keep up. I don't want to spend one extra moment on this nonsense."

The instant they continued, the trio followed.

Carmen opened her coat to access her throwing knives.

When they crossed the next bridge, she made her move. With cat-like grace, she bounded down the stairs and whipped a knife at the nearest guardsman. He turned at the last second and the blade merely bounced off the man's helmet. Cursing, Carmen's boots scraped stone as she sprinted for him and drove her shoulder into his back. The guardsman slammed face-first into the bricks with a crack of teeth. He shouted once before she hooked his knee with her foot and dragged him down hard.

The second guardsman spun, *schiavona* sword half-clear.

Steel rang as Angelo's rapier caught the draw and knocked it aside. The guardsman swore and pressed again, pushing Angelo back two steps before he slid closer and slammed his pommel into the man's cheek. Bone popped. Blood sprayed. The guardsman staggered, but didn't fall.

Ahead of them, Quattrone turned at the commotion, stunned. "What—?"

Ludo hit him from behind, wrapping an arm around his throat and driving him into the wall. Quattrone clawed at Ludo's forearm, gasping, heels grinding stone.

The first guardsman scrambled to his feet and lunged for Carmen. She ducked under the swing, took the hit on her shoulder, and snarled as she rammed a knife under his ribs. He screamed and grabbed at her wrist. She headbutted him until his grip loosened. He sagged against her.

Recovering, Angelo's opponent charged. Angelo braced himself, twisted, and let the man's weight carry past. He slashed low, feeling the rapier bite into the guardsman's thigh. The man howled and went down, clutching the wound.

Not hesitating, Angelo kicked the sword away and drove the point of his rapier down, stopping short of the throat. "Stay down. Not a word, lest you wish it to be your last."

There was reluctance, but the man glanced at his fallen comrade and nodded acquiescence. Mid-nod, he scrambled to his knees. Angelo swept his boot across the guardsman's jaw. The man collapsed cold on the cobbles.

Confident the guardsman was unconscious, Angelo rushed over to Quattrone and Ludo. The senator fought back like a cornered dog. He bucked hard, elbowing backward. Ludo grunted as the surprise move caught him in the ribs.

"How dare you?" Quattrone said, facing his would-be abductor. "Do you know who I—?" His mouth popped open. He swiveled his head to Angelo and Carmen, then back to Ludo. "Stefanetti? The insolence! You'd defile our pact?"

"A pact you never intended to keep," Ludo replied.

"What do you want?" Quattrone asked, spittle flying from his lips.

"You know what we want." No longer could Angelo suppress the rage burning within.

The senator laughed. "Then honor your side of the bargain. Bring me my maps."

"It's too late for that. Release my beloved. All the souls."

"So many years," Quattrone went on, shaking his head, his tenor calm and assured. "So much grief. Vito. Ivan. Your Genoese friend, I reckon. Isabella. How many others died because of you?"

Angelo's hand tightened until his knuckles ached.

"Say her name again," he said evenly, "and I will forget why you're still breathing."

"We're losing time," Carmen said. She pulled out a cloth already soaked with enough laudanum to pacify Quattrone but keep him lucid. She shoved the rag into his mouth.

The senator bit down, eyes wild, shaking his head as she forced it in. His words turned to muffled fury.

Angelo seized him by the collar and slammed him back against the wall, forearm across his chest. "Move again and I sever your hands. That is our new pact," Angelo hissed into the Exalted Master's ear. "Nod if you understand."

Quattrone glared. Then slowly, he nodded.

They bound his wrists behind him, rope biting into flesh. He struggled all the while, shoulders straining, breath hissing through his nose.

Footsteps echoed at the mouth of the alley. Laughter. Men sang a drunk song. Angelo held still, counting again.

The sounds passed.

Ludo crouched and stripped a fallen ducal guard of cloak and helmet, hands quick despite the blood. "Help me."

Angelo followed suit, shrugging into the heavy maroon cloak. He unbuckled the *schiavona* sword from the dead man's belt and let its distinctive, forward-sloping basket hilt settle around his knuckles. It was a weapon designed for killing in tight places. To complete the disguise, he scooped up the guard's helmet, though he carried it in his free hand as he didn't want to dull his senses.

They hauled Quattrone upright between them. To anyone watching, it would look as if they were transporting a prisoner.

For a heartbeat, the night held its breath.

Then they moved in a steady formation.

"I'm coming, 'mòre mio," Angelo whispered.

I know. I can feel you.

"Run home, cousin," Ludo said, squeezing the boy's shoulder. "You did an exemplary job here today."

"Let me go with you, Ludo. I can help."

"You already have. You've made your grandfather proud, rest his soul. Now go."

The boy nodded and sprinted down a side alley.

With Carmen leading, they angled toward a wider street. They'd be exposed for ten minutes, especially at Campo San Moisè, but it was the most direct path to the Palazzo Ducale. As they approached, the celebration, lanterns, and banners increased in number, but at this hour, the city had returned to stone and damp air rising off the canals, with music dissolving into a resonant hymn.

Bound, drugged, and gagged, Quattrone stumbled between Angelo and Ludo, yet he held his head high, his eyes raging defiance. He tilted his head, as if listening to something only he could hear, and tried to speak with garbled words.

"Shut up," Angelo said, tightening his grip on the man's arm. "You put yourself in this predicament. You broke our accord, not us."

As they reached the *calle larga*, Angelo halted the group and surveyed the street, one of the longest stretches in the city. A few stragglers and drunkards roamed the area, but it was otherwise clear. Satisfied, he motioned for them to continue.

They picked up the pace, relieved at the uneventfulness. Soon, they crossed the stone footbridge that opened onto Campo San Moisè, an unobstructed square dominated by its namesake cathedral, a baroque structure that loomed over them like a sentinel. Even at Piazza San Marco, they could stick to the shadows of the arcade. Here, if snipers were positioned in one of the buildings enclosing the square, it would be a death sentence.

Quattrone mumbled something.

Nearly running, Ludo and Angelo hauled him across the piazza.

Angelo's heartbeat matched their pace. Every three steps, he'd check behind them.

Hooking around the cathedral, the narrower alley was a direct arrow to the arcade that encircled Piazza San Marco on three sides. They were nearly there. If they made it into the colonnade, they'd be able to stick to the shadows almost the entire way to the palace. They'd reunite with their Guild comrades outside the gates, storm their way in, bring Quattrone to the Great Council Room, and compel him to perform the ritual that would release Isabella and the others.

He tossed his cavalier hat aside and donned the guard's helmet. It muffled his hearing and obscured his peripheral vision, stultified sensations to which Angelo wasn't accustomed and detested, but as they neared the Palazzo, it was a necessary accoutrement.

He was so close.

The passage brought them beneath the darkened arcade between the Church of San Geminiano and the Procuratie Nuove. The mouthpoint to Piazza San Marco.

So close.

The square opened beyond, vast and pale in the night. The campanile rose like a black pillar against the clouds. The domes of the basilica floated in darkness. At the far edge, the corner of the Palazzo Ducale revealed itself, beckoning them like a forbidden prize. It was as if Isabella watched over him, guiding him safely to her. A few paces ahead, Carmen looked back with a rare smile. He exchanged a glance with Ludo. They'd do it.

The prize captured his attention for a second too long.

LVI

BOOTS STOMPED FROM BEHIND. Ahead, Protectors emerged from dozens of columns, steel glinting off drawn swords. Others stepped out of the deeper darkness of the colonnade wall.

This was no rush. No scramble. It was a net drawing tight.

"Swordsman," said a voice slicing through the low mist. "You've been expected."

A figure stepped forward from Piazza San Marco, tall, unhurried, rapier resting easy in his hand. His face caught what little light there was.

Grimani.

Angelo shifted his stance, rapier in its scabbard, his right hand gripping Quattrone's arm, the *schiavona* sword heavy in his left. Carmen and Ludo backed closer, instinctively forming a gauntlet.

Protectors closed in.

"Release him," one ordered.

Quattrone shouted through the gag, twisting violently.

"Make a path," Angelo said.

Grimani smirked and nodded to Zanca, who had emerged at his side.

"Cut them down," Zanca said.

Steel rang.

A Protector lunged. Angelo met the blade with his *schiavona*, the impact jolting up his shoulder. He drove forward, forcing the man back while keeping his body between the circle and Quattrone.

"Move," he shouted. "Take him to the Palazzo. We'll barricade ourselves in."

He released the senator and drew his rapier, comfortable with a sword in each hand.

Ludo and Carmen tried to drag Quattrone past the column line, but two Protectors cut them off.

Angelo charged for Grimani and Zanca, but three Protectors converged on him. He parried high, turned low, then brought the *schiavona* across a brutal backhand that split a man's guard and drove him to his knees. Another blade slid past his rapier and tore his sleeve. The warmth of blood sprayed across his jaw.

He spun to aid his friends just as Quattrone wrenched free of Ludo's grip.

"Now," Grimani said.

Zanca and four Protectors charged for Quattrone. Two others attacked Angelo. He fended them off as he managed to see a Protector strike Ludo across the jaw. Carmen held her own, defending herself against two men twice her size. Zanca caught Quattrone under the arms and dragged him backward.

"Protectors!" Zanca said. "With me. Now!"

They joined him and carried Quattrone away, disappearing back into the alley from which Angelo and his friends had emerged.

"After them!" Angelo shouted. "We need Quattrone!"

He drove forward hard, rapier and *schiavona* sweeping wide to keep the approaching Protectors at a distance. "Go!"

"Angelo—" Ludo began.

"I'll hold them!"

Carmen pulled Ludo away to chase after the Protectors and Quattrone.

Angelo gave ground slowly, blades flashing, forcing the Protectors to respect the reach of steel. One rushed him. He slipped inside the cut and drove the pommel into the man's face. Another lunged low. Angelo kicked his knee sideways and finished the exchange with a thrust that dropped him.

More appeared from the columns in seemingly infinite numbers. If only Angelo could get word to his comrades waiting at the Palazzo gates. Cavalry would be most welcome, but for all he knew, they were already compromised. He shuddered at the thought of another mole.

From above, a shutter slammed. Angelo used the noise as cover, vaulting off a stone ledge to shift behind a Protector. He lashed out with both swords in a whirlwind of motion. The *schiavona* bit into the attacker's shoulder. The rapier thrust under the chin of another, forcing him back.

With the numbers overwhelming and his strength already waning, Angelo broke contact, turned, and ran, chucking the helmet and replacing it with his discarded cavalier hat.

He caught up with Carmen and Ludo two streets later, their breath ragged, their faces distressed.

"Where is he?" Angelo managed through panting breaths.

"We lost him." Carmen shook her head. She seemed angrier with herself than anyone.

Shouts echoed behind them.

Protectors poured onto the street from the arcade.

"Let's go," Angelo said. "This way!"

They sprinted the way they had come, back to Campo San Moisè. Lanterns strung across the square revealed what waited for them: Protectors were already there.

"This was a trap from the start," Ludo said.

"Form on me," Angelo said, exhaling his agreement. Whether Quattrone's cunning or another traitor, he knew not. At this point, it mattered not.

The first wave rushed them. Angelo stepped forward to meet it.

Rapier and *schiavona* moved as a single instrument of death connected to his body. Precise thrusts of the rapier drove men backward, with the heavier blade clearing space when they pressed too close. He turned a strike meant for Ludo and riposted through a throat. Another man tried to flank. Angelo pivoted and smashed the *schiavona* into his jaw.

Ludo and Carmen fought against the onslaught in the center of the square, but the Protectors broke their ranks, separating them.

Fighting like a storm, Carmen launched her remaining throwing knives, all meeting their marks, but doing little to quell the tide. Her dagger flashed in tight arcs. She cut one man across the face, then crouched and drove the blade into his groin. He cried out and collapsed. Another Protector raised his short sword and stepped in for the killing blow.

Unprepared, her eyes widened, ready to accept her fate.

Angelo did not think.

He hurled the *schiavona*.

The heavy weapon spun, hilt over tip, and struck the man full in the back with a sickening thud, hammering him to the stones. Carmen slid under the blade and returned the strike of another Protector before nodding her thanks.

Angelo raced over to fight by her side.

"Get out of here, Mascari," she said.

The request shocked him; she knew he was the best fighter there.

"You need to live another day," she implored, blocking a cutting slice.

He did the same, then thrust his rapier into the man's abdomen. "You need me here."

"Go!" she yelled. She disengaged from her adversary and shoved Angelo away, luring the nearest Protectors to the steps of the church.

Two men closed on her from either side. She ducked a swing and slammed the dagger into one's throat.

The other lunged, driving his short sword through her corset and into her ribs.

She staggered but remained on her feet, swinging and slashing until she fell on her knees, weapon in hand, unyielding. Angelo's stomach knotted.

He parried swings from three Protectors, desperate to reach her.

A crossbow bolt pierced her shoulder.

She cried out in pain. Another one embedded in her thigh. She sank to her knees at the foot of the church steps, black velvet spreading dark against the stone. Unyielding, she continued to swing and slash.

"Carmen!" Angelo started forward, his stomach knotted.

Crossbows snapped up. Bolts struck the slick cobbles at Angelo's feet.

Protectors kicked her down and pried the daggers from her hands. Others took positions in front of her, standing guard.

He turned to find Ludo, fighting off three converging Protectors. He fought like a desperate man, wild but fearless, propelling one back, then another.

"Return to your family," his friend called.

"What of yours?" Angelo yelled back.

"Go!"

A blade slid under Ludo's guard and drove into his side. He gasped but didn't fall.

Instead, he wrapped his arms around the man who struck him, dragging him down.

Two more Protectors fell on Ludo, wrenching his arms back, forcing him to his knees as blood darkened his cloak.

"Ludo!" Angelo shouted. Enraged, he slashed his opponent's sword away, kicked the man in the gut, then pivoted and raced for his friend.

A wall of steel drove him back.

Ludo knelt, defeated. Drenched in blood, Carmen attempted to drag herself to the church door.

The odds were overwhelming.

Realization settled in Angelo: *they intended to capture them alive.*

Muscles aching, he focused on defensive footwork to conserve arm strength. He backed up, leading the Protectors away from Ludo. As he did, a miracle unfolded. Ludo's cousin appeared through the side alley with the six Guild fighters who'd been awaiting them at the Palazzo gates. The boy had done it.

While three felled the men holding Ludo, the other three set up a defensive perimeter.

"Live your life, Angelo!" Ludo called as his comrades hauled him into the night.

With their backs to his friend, the Protectors missed his escape. Some gave chase, but Angelo used the opportunity to goad others to the center of the square.

Protectors surged forth, forcing him back toward the narrow bridge that fed into the square.

He retreated step by step onto the bridge, breath burning, shoulder screaming, his rapier the last line between himself and the men advancing to finish it. Though he abhorred running from a fight yet again, he had no choice. The odds were overwhelming. He also did not want to be cut down in a chase. If he turned and ran, crossbow bolts would be launched into non-lethal body parts. The only possible escape would be if he could make his way to an alley corner.

A ruckus shuffled behind him before he took another step. He peered over his shoulder.

Six ducal guards, dressed like those from the party, trotted up to the other side, blocking his egress.

He glanced at the canal. If he leaped, it would provide some cover, but Protectors would surely jump in after him. Without a boat, it was pointless.

Angelo remained alone on the bridge, surrounded, breathing hard. Streets behind him were filled with Protectors and palace guards, moving in disciplined formation. Quattrone had escaped. Carmen was captured. Vito gone. Ludo severely wounded. The Guild had failed. And *Paradise*—Isabella—slipped further away.

Please, 'mòre mio. No more death on my account.

He loosened his grip on his rapier. Never in his life had he surrendered.

Energy depleted, he dropped to his knees. Cold stones and cool air rising off the canal below chilled his body. He had tried his best. For what? To deprive his wife of a husband? To steal a father from their children? In the end, neither victory nor defeat was worth the sacrifice.

"There he is," boomed an all-too-familiar voice.

Protectors parted as Senator Benito Grimani sauntered forth, unharmed, unbothered. A drawn rapier was gripped in his right hand.

"Angelo Mascari, the infamous swordsman. Returned home for his dramatic defeat." He reached the base of the bridge. "'The victor is not victorious if the vanquished does not consider himself so.' Quintus Ennius said that. A poet, no less. Will you finally consider yourself vanquished when my sword is in your heart?"

Protectors around him laughed, egging him on.

Angelo refused to take the bait.

"Tell me, Mascari. Did you lose your honor in the jungle, or did you spend it here in Venice, one dead friend at a time?"

It was the taunt Angelo needed. His muscles coiled like spring wire. His fingers wrapped around the hilt.

One path yet remained: Grimani.

Ignoring his beloved's plea, he pounced to his feet and thrusted. The senator parried and stepped into a defensive position.

"Yes!" he bellowed, the word echoing off the surrounding buildings.

Lanterns swung overhead with Grimani's revelry, throwing long, wavering shadows that further mocked Angelo.

The air shuddered around them as the two men faced each other, chest to chest with barely a span of stone between them. Angelo's rapier gleamed in the lantern light. Across from him, Grimani's eyes were coals, his own rapier twitching in his grip.

Grimani struck first, a savage arc aimed to split Angelo from shoulder to hip. Angelo blocked with the rapier. The impact rattled his forearm and drove the air from his lungs. Grimani pressed, elbows jabbing, kicks snapping off, aiming not to wound but to destroy.

Angelo countered with renewed purpose that fueled his energy. The clang of metal echoed across the canal below. A vision flashed before him with each clash. Loredana. Franco. Juanita. Vito. Tormenta. Samuele. And then—Isabella. He angled, pivoted, and leveraged his rapier in a vicious jab into his foe's ribs. Grimani snarled, then smiled as he gazed at the blood trickling down his doublet, as if the wound didn't faze him in the slightest. He stepped backward to free himself of the incision and knocked Angelo's sword away. Catching him off guard, Grimani forced Angelo to twist and dodge. The senator snared behind Angelo's crossguard, slicing open the back of his right hand—an old wound ripped open.

He tossed the sword to his left hand and parried yet another vicious strike.

"You think you can best me, Mascari?" Grimani said, spittle flying from his mouth. "You're a cretin from the street. Filth who helped shield my wife's adultery."

They circled, boots dancing on the slick cobblestones. Angelo's chest ached with grief and fury. He would die here, alone, never feeling the warmth of the Santa Marta sun. Never holding Loredana. Never hearing Juanita's giggles. Never teaching Franco the art of fencing. Every motion Grimani made was a hammer against his soul. A reminder that he had failed.

"A gutter rat who squandered the one chance in life he was given."

The senator feinted, drove low, then twisted, striking a glancing blow across Angelo's good shoulder. Pain bloomed. Blood slicked his sleeve. Grimani spat venom.

"You dishonored Master Fabris. He never forgave himself after you fled Venice. He died knowing you were a traitor to the Republic."

The words hit their mark.

"You speak of traitors," Angelo said, loud enough for all the Protectors to hear. "Yet Quattrone met with me under cover of night! He yearns to seize control. To expand your Order. Where were you? Part of this conspiracy? Or betrayed from within?"

Grimani's eyes widened.

A murmur rose from the Protectors.

Angelo seized the opportunity. He moved like water, vaulting off the edge of the bridge, his rapier snapping upward into Grimani's jaw. He staggered back, then charged in a fury, trying to pin Angelo against the railing. The fight was brutal, but for all his training, wealth, and position, Grimani lacked the one thing Angelo maintained.

Control.

He shimmied away, and using the slick cobblestones, slid as he feinted a low thrust. Grimani moved to parry, but Angelo pivoted hard, taking his momentum to drive the rapier into his opponent's exposed side.

The man gasped and spun to counter. Angelo followed with a crushing downward thrust of the rapier, slicing across the senator's forehead. He tried to twist, but the cuts were precise. Angelo found his foe's throat.

Grimani's knees buckled. Blood spilled across his clothes, wetting the stone beneath him. He stumbled into the railing, eyes in disbelief. Angelo dropped to one knee, chest heaving, muscles screaming from exertion, body trembling with grief and rage.

He had vanquished Grimani. If this man hadn't induced his wife into the arms of her lover, that wouldn't have led Vito to bribe Angelo to steal the doge's book. He wouldn't have met Isabella, and he wouldn't have met Loredana. Grimani was the catalyst for everything that had happened in Angelo's life, good and bad. And he lay dead at his feet.

The bridge quieted, save the flow of water below and Angelo's ragged breath. As the Protectors realized what transpired, they closed in. Ducal guards did the same from the other side. He had survived the duel, but Angelo was still surrounded. The city had become a cage, and the night had only just begun.

The Protectors leveled their blades at Angelo. He counted three dozen men, maybe more. Far too many for him to fight.

He straightened with effort. His arms trembled. His wounds burned. His rapier felt heavier than it ever had. He wondered if they'd kill him, throw him in prison, or sentence him to *Paradise*. There were no good outcomes. He'd never see his family again. He'd be remembered as the traitor who failed in an attempted coup. Almost like muscle memory, he straightened his stance, blade up, rapier ready, showing them he would not yield.

The men hesitated. They knew his skill.

One stepped forward. Then another.

A lantern shattered at their feet, sending shards of glass and oil into the Protectors' boots.

A second one landed and exploded. Fire bloomed. Smoke rolled thick and low, biting the eyes. Shouts broke formation as the Protectors glanced upward to find the source. Someone cursed. Another lantern went down, aimed for the Ducal guards, then another, flames licking up celebratory ribbons strung along the bridge.

Angelo spun, disoriented, lungs burning—

—to find a man swing out of the smoke on a length of cloth torn from a coronation banner. He landed hard, boots skidding, cutlass already moving.

"By the blood of a thousand storms!"

Tormenta.

He greeted Angelo with a feral grin and a new gold tooth. His beard was braided with a strip of red cloth.

"You're a hard man to find," the pirate said, and drove his blade across the nearest Protector's throat. The man crumpled into the flames.

"Where the hell have you been?" Angelo asked, stunned.

"Looking for you." Tormenta blocked a Ducal guard who charged through the fire. "But first I had to find the exit of a courtesan parlor."

His friend's arrival reinvigorated his strength. He flourished his rapier and thrusted it into the guard's exposed side, piercing his heart. The man folded and rolled down the bridge. Flames caught their clothes, creating a small wall on both sides of the bridge, buying them precious seconds to regroup. They braced themselves for the coming onslaught, Angelo facing the Protectors. Tormenta facing the Ducal guards.

"When will you learn not to fight armies by yourself?" the pirate asked.

"I wasn't alone." Angelo wiped the sweat glazing his brow. "We failed. I failed."

"No, my friend. You succeeded."

"How's that?"

"You'll go home and see your family. There's a ship waiting in Mestre if we can escape this bilge box."

Crossbow bolts ricocheted around them. One tore Angelo's cavalier hat from his head. Another skimmed off Tormenta's cutlass.

Their enemies released a war cry and charged through the flames.

Tormenta moved with short, violent bursts. He hadn't lost a step. With newfound energy, Angelo's rapier cut through any bodies that pressed too close.

Reinforcements quickly arrived through the thinning smoke. Far too many.

Tormenta grabbed Angelo's collar and hauled him to the balustrade as bolts clattered off stone.

"This is done!"

Angelo shook him off. "Isabella. I can still—"

"Do you want to die fighting for a love you lost?" Tormenta snapped. "Or live for loves you've saved?"

Angelo gazed at him, then at the men coming for their throats. Then at the city surrounding them. His free hand subconsciously went to the two wooden game discs tied to his belt. Loredana. Franco. Juanita. They waited for him. They needed him.

The pirate softened his grip a fraction. "Your fight isn't finished. But it isn't here. Not like this."

Another bolt cracked the stone inches from Angelo's hip.

Tormenta pointed over the railing. Below, a narrow cargo skiff drifted loose, its handler slumped unconscious in the stern, rope already cut. The canal was dark, choked with reflections and smoke.

Go, my love.

"Jump," Tormenta said. "Or I throw you off."

Angelo glanced once more at the men closing in, at the city that had taken everything from him, yet gave him so much more.

Then he listened to Isabella and vaulted the rail. In his peripheral vision, Tormenta followed.

Cold punched the breath from Angelo's chest as he hit the water. He surfaced once, long enough to see Tormenta climb aboard the skiff. Angelo swam over as the pirate drove a pole into the water, propelling them hard into the shadow.

Shouts rang out above. A bolt hissed past. Another struck the skiff, inches away from impaling his hand.

Smoke and echoing shouts swallowed them as Tormenta swiftly navigated them into the Grand Canal.

Angelo collapsed on the boards, shaking, staring up at the night sky broken by firelight and falling ash. Venice slid away, still beautiful, still indifferent.

Isabella was still trapped. The Guild was shattered.

But his family was alive.

LVII

DAWN CAME THIN AND colorless over Chioggia, a pale seam of light stitched between sea and sky. The gloomy morning felt more like winter's tail than the approaching season of rebirth.

It had taken all night for Angelo and Tormenta to row from Venice to the relative safety of the quaint fishing town. By the time they stood on the damp planks of the brigantine, Angelo was sleeping on his feet. Tormenta's ship had more life in her than he had in him, but he needed to keep his eyes open for a little longer.

The two-masted craft was disguised as a fishing boat but was truly built to run. A half-dozen lanterns burned low along her rail as the crew, dressed as fishermen, moved in silence. Everything about the vessel spoke of speed and departure.

"Quiet now," Tormenta murmured somewhere behind him, his voice low but carrying. "Make her ready. No songs. No shouting."

Men answered with nods and hand signs. Lines were coiled. A yard was walked up. The mainsail hung slack, waiting.

Angelo flexed his right hand slowly. Sharp pain answered, but his bones and muscles obeyed. That was something. He had learned to take comfort where he could find it.

All he needed to do was slip out on this brigantine.

That was it. No more fighting. No more heroics.

One more destination: home.

He leaned a shoulder against a stack of tarred crates and let the magnitude of the night settle into him. Carmen's last stand, Ludo dragged away, Grimani's breath leaving him on the stones. The promise of *Paradise*, of Isabella—so close he had almost touched her.

Almost.

Gazing back at the city, he willed her to speak to him.

She remained silent.

He closed his eyes and envisioned his beloved's face as he remembered it, as he always did. Alive. Laughing on his cousin's skiff beneath a perfect Venetian sky.

Loredana rose unbidden, replacing that image, steady and real, with Franco and Juanita standing tall and strong beside her. Two paths, pulling him in opposite directions. One, futile. The other, his future.

He had failed the dead.

He had survived for the living.

Tormenta walked over, boots scuffing on the planks. He looked no worse for the night's work—dark hair tied back, coat open, cutlass sheathed at his hip.

"Told you Chioggia would do," he said.

Angelo glanced at the sailors making final preparations. He gazed out toward the Venetian lagoon. There were no ships heading toward them, yet he couldn't shake the feeling of dread. Perhaps he'd lose it once they set foot in Santa Marta. Though he knew the war was far from over. "You were prepared."

His pirate friend shrugged. "Always am." Then, after a beat, "Took some effort. Courtesans cost money. But they listen. And gold opens doors men think are locked."

Angelo threw him a sideways look.

"Do you think I'd travel without it?" Tormenta asked, as if discussing the weather. "Venetian courtesans know how to keep their mouths shut. Santa Marta whores yap like gulls over a carcass."

Angelo would've laughed if he had the strength.

The pirate squeezed his elbow and gazed at him, as if attempting to read his mind. "You did not fail, amigo," he said with a softness that belied his personage. "You defeated Grimani. As you said, Quattrone never got his maps. Santa Marta will be safe."

"If they come? Will you help defend her?"

"Aye. By your side."

Angelo sighed. He hadn't won the war, but in the scheme of things, what seemed like minor victories may have been enough to turn the tide.

A muffled shout came from the deck. The bosun raised a hand as lines were cast off.

As the two men headed toward the bow, the crew hoisted the gangplank.

All they had to do now was leave Chioggia without raising an alarm.

And pray that the sea, at least, would let them pass.

"Captain!" said a breathless sailor, racing to Tormenta and Angelo.

"What is it?" Tormenta asked.

"A skiff, sior," said the man, alarm permeating his voice. "They row with fury."

"A skiff? How many men?"

"Only two. And a woman."

The word captured Angelo. "Woman?"

They rushed to the stern to find two men rowing with purpose toward the brigantine. A woman, dressed in a black cloak and bonnet, stood at the bow, frantically waving her arms.

"One of your courtesans?" Angelo asked.

"I think one of yours," Tormenta replied with a snort.

"Sior Mascari," called the woman as the small craft approached within earshot. "A word before you depart, if you please."

Angelo squinted. He didn't recognize her rosy cheeks and aquiline nose yet sensed a strange familiarity.

"And you are?"

"The Lady Paulina Grimani."

The name caused all the blood in Angelo's body to run cold.

He exchanged an uneasy glance with Tormenta.

"Want me to send a bolt through her forehead?" the pirate asked.

Of all the people to find their ship moments before their departure, Paulina Grimani was not on the list. Given the effort she made to reach them, it seemed worth hearing her words, at least in Vito's memory.

"Do we have time?" Angelo asked.

"Takes but a second to fire a crossbow."

"No. Time to talk?"

The pirate scowled and grumbled under his breath. He scanned the horizon, which remained clear of threats, then waved his hand. "If it's a trap, I'm leaving without you."

Moments later, Angelo stood on the quay with the widow of the man he'd slayed less than twelve hours prior. He scanned the area on both land and sea, still wary of the lady's intentions.

"I assure you, Sior Mascari, nobody other than my boatmen knows I'm here."

"Then people will be looking for you."

"Which is why we only have a moment."

"How did you find me?"

Paulina smiled. "Have you seen your companion?"

Angelo glanced at the ship, where Tormenta pretended not to be watching.

"He's the storm that demolishes everything in its path."

"You're a bit of a tempest yourself," she said with a wink.

"I'm more of a spring rain," Angelo replied, an involuntary reaction to inject levity into their discourse.

"Maybe we should swap names!" Tormenta called from the ship before disappearing.

Angelo and Paulina chuckled. A quiet passed between them, neither sure what to say.

"Why have you risked coming here?" He finally asked. "You're noble. A senator's wife. A doge's daughter."

She nodded. "I am all that. I am also a victim, like you. A victim of a vicious system and a victim of the brutality of men. Quattrone killed the man I loved."

Her heartbreak was palpable and touched Angelo's core. It was as if they were opposing forces in the same struggle, never realizing until now how intertwined they were. They had both sacrificed so much for love. They had lost so much to *forbidden* loves.

"The man you loved killed the woman I loved. Though in the end, Vito was a good man. A good friend."

"I know." She lowered her head a moment before meeting his eye. "I fear I bear some responsibility for Isabella's demise."

"You came here to tell me that?"

"I came here to tell you that you do not need to fear the Order pursuing you further."

He studied her face. "How can you be certain?"

"Because with Doge Memmo and my husband gone, Senator Quattrone is alone in his belief in the folly of the Fountain of Youth or the Tree of Life."

"That won't stop him from seeking it. He's the Exalted Master."

"Quattrone is finished. His ambition, his desire to own the world, is his undoing. One day, it will be the downfall of the Order itself." Paulina gazed out at the ocean, as if contemplating the intricacies of fate. Gentle waves lapped the brigantine as a waddling of loons swam by.

"You have a family now in the New World, yes?"

"A beautiful one."

"Trust me." She placed a hand on his chest. "Enjoy what you have in this world. Live in the moment for the loves you have now and realize how lucky you are. Do not take them for granted. Do not leave them again."

It was as if she spoke not only to Angelo's heart, but from it. Yet his mind refused to stray from his eternal beloved.

"Did you know Isabella?" he asked.

She removed her hand and wiped a tear from her eye.

"We had met a handful of times. She had a beautiful soul. It should not have been taken."

"I feel as though it was severed from mine. I will never stop fighting for her."

"Then do so in the next life. Soul mates aren't always destined to be together." She embraced him and kissed both of his cheeks, the warmth from her lips sending an unexpected wave of emotion through Angelo. "Safe travels, Sior Mascari."

Her oarsman helped her board the skiff, then revealed his face. It was the Protector known as Zanca. Fear rippled through Angelo, but the man spoke calmly.

"Vito Uccello had a purpose," the man said. "A secret. If there's one last thing I do in this world, it will be to help keep it. Seeds of an empire's collapse are always sown within its bones."

Without another word, he tipped his head and stepped into the boat.

Angelo watched them row away until Paulina was but a dot that vanished into the lagoon.

Senator Marco Quattrone tapped his cane on the brick bridge and whistled an upbeat ditty. A pigeon cooed, seemingly in time. The last sunrays of the day twinkled off the peaceful canal water. A perfect evening, for the recent turn of events proved he would join the Council of Ten at the next opening.

He couldn't have written a better script himself. Mascari had unwittingly helped to rid Venice of Grimani, unfaithful Protectors, and the Guild. With no remaining enemies, Quattrone would ascend to heights of power never seen. He would embrace apotheosis.

The swordsman's maps were unnecessary. There were other ways to get what he desired. He'd expand the Order around the world. It was only a matter of time.

The punch to the skull came without warning. A ringing detonated between his ears. A kick to his calf sent him to the ground. His head smacked against the stone balustrade. Large hands lifted him and spun him around. He came face to face with Zanca, whose smug grin reeked of misplaced satisfaction.

"You've become rancid, Exalted Master," he said. "You shall witness the Order's glory forevermore from *Paradise*." Another man with an unruly brown beard forced a sack over his head. The strike to the gut impelled a saliva gob from his lips into the cloth.

EPILOGO

SANTA MARTA

21ST OF JULY, 1614

THAT SWEET SMELL OF tropical humidity had caressed Angelo's nostrils since they sighted land. He hadn't realized how much he'd missed it. How much he longed for it.

A bliss he'd never known overwhelmed him the moment he stepped on Santa Marta soil. When he had returned to Venice, he had thought he'd returned home. Now he realized it was a fantasy. A fleeting moment. *Now* he was home.

"Papá!"

The word was the most beautiful he'd ever heard. He brought his gaze to the speaker of the words to find Juanita, nearly bouncing. Next to her stood Franco, and of course their radiant mother, Loredana.

"It has been a journey, my friend." A hand rested on Angelo's shoulder.

He turned to Tormenta.

Without words, they clasped forearms. The wild pirate kissed Angelo's cheeks, then strode the dock, tipping his hat to Angelo's family.

The children and their mother ran to him. He knelt to receive their hug. Warmth radiated from their bodies, washing him in love and relief.

"You returned," Loredana said. It was the first time Angelo had ever seen her eyes glisten.

He kissed her tenderly, then did the same to Franco and Juanita's heads.

"You've both grown so much."

"You have more gray in your hair," Juanita said.

Angelo kissed her again. "That I do."

"Are you Angelo or Samuele?" Franco asked.

The question was a spike in his gut, more painful than any injury he'd sustained. With all that had happened, he'd forgotten his deception. He would need to answer for his lies, but they were his family. They'd understand. He'd make amends. If they didn't forgive him, he'd try again. And again. And again. Earning their trust and love was his new mission. He would not fail.

"Angelo. No more lies. I'm your father. Your husband. I will never leave you again. I shall protect you until I'm in the ground and one with Aluna."

"We are not punished for our sins," Loredana said, "but by them."

Angelo nodded. She spoke the truth—one he finally understood.

"I have a gift for you, my son." He unbuckled his scabbard belt and handed it and the rapier to Franco.

His eyes widened. "Really? You're giving me your sword?"

"Use it well." Pride swelled within Angelo as he gazed at his son.

Franco beamed. He drew the sword, then frowned. "There are so many notches on it."

Angelo laughed and ruffled his son's hair. "Then grind and polish them out. You can make your own."

"What are those?" Juanita asked, pointing to the discs tied to his belt.

The question brought a smile to his lips. "Those are for you and Franco. It's a game but first I need to carve the other parts. When I'm finished, we'll play every day until you're a grown woman."

"Even then!" Juanita replied, beaming.

"Even then."

"Come, my love," Loredana said. "Let's go home."

Angelo stood and joined his family as they walked toward town. He paused a moment and gazed at the sea, back toward Venice.

"I will never forget you, 'mòre mio," he whispered to Isabella. "I will never forgive those who wronged you. My soul will not fail you."

I know, Isabella said in his mind. *But live* this *life*.

Soft fingers clasped his hand and tugged at it. He looked down to find Juanita pulling him away. "I don't care what anybody calls you. To me, you'll always be Papá."

He kissed her head, and they joined Franco and Loredana.

THE SWORDSMAN OF VENICE

Thank You

Thank you for reading THE SWORDSMAN OF VENICE. If you enjoyed it, please consider adding a review on your place of purchase, Goodreads, and BookBub. Nothing helps an author more. Your review will encourage readers to pick up a copy of this and other books by Rob Samborn.

FOLLOW ROB SAMBORN ON SOCIAL MEDIA

www.robsamborn.com (sign up for his newsletter here)

Goodreads

BookBub

Facebook

Instagram

Threads

TikTok

Time Has No End

For more of the Painted Souls saga, read how Angelo's journey connects to the present in ***THE PRISONER OF PARADISE***, ***PAINTER OF THE DAMNED,*** and ***MASTER OF THE ABYSS***.

Bonus content is available at the end of this book.

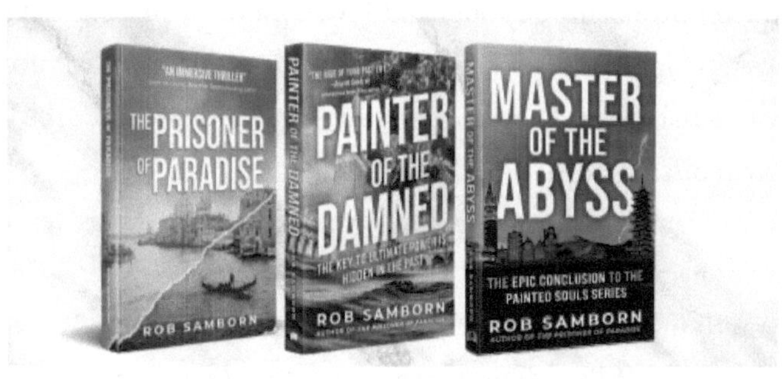

ACKNOWLEDGEMENTS AND AUTHOR'S NOTE

I could not have written the Swordsman of Venice without the support of numerous people.

First and foremost, thank you to my wife, Tiffani, and my two children. Without your uncompromising support and love, I never would have finished this book. I know I've lost a great deal of family time, but I will make it up to you.

My phenomenal editor, L.A. Mitchell, has been with me since the beginning, and once again offered unparalleled edits and notes.

The team at Damonza did an absolutely stunning job on the cover. Every time I look at it, I'm inspired.

Thank you to my agent, Kimberly Brower, and former agent, Aimee Ashcraft (you're very missed!) of Park, Fine & Brower Literary Management, for providing unyielding support and guidance along this long, rocky journey that often feels like one of my characters'. You could say they've supplied the swords and maps.

Thanks to my fellow author and writer friends. You know who you are and you're in my thoughts. My parents, brother, extended family, and friends—you all provided everlasting support. You're not named here but you also know who you are. I am forever grateful.

Finally, I want to express my undying gratitude to all my readers. Thank you for letting me share my stories with you.

The Swordsman of Venice was borne from characters in the Painted Souls series who insisted on their stories continuing. Who am I to refuse such a request?

Little did I know that a request would morph into a quest.

Why did I choose to set Part II in northern South America? Well, that requires some backstory and a confession of sorts.

The Swordsman of Venice is the continuation of Angelo Mascari's journey following his hasty departure from Venice, which occurs in the prologue of book one, *The Prisoner of Paradise*. Over the course of the Painted Souls trilogy, all but one scene takes place chronologically *before* the prologue. In that prologue, a mysterious nobleman (who we now know is Pietro Stefanetti, Isabella's uncle), tells Angelo to flee to New Spain. I confess I wrote that simply because I thought it sounded cool and was a challenge of immense proportions. Imagine in 1589, needing to travel to the other side of the planet. He had no friends, very little money, and had never left his home. Here's the passage:

> From under his gold-embroidered, hip-length linen cloak, the nobleman removed a pouch of coins and a sealed letter, which he offered to Angelo. "Take these and this skiff. Make your way to Palos in Spain and find Sebastiano Cadamosto. Give him the letter. He'll provide you passage to New Spain."
>
> "*New Spain*? What about our next move?"
>
> "This *is* your next move. It's your *only* move. At least for some time."
>
> "It's the other side of the world." Angelo abhorred the desperation in his voice, like a punished boy sent away when a man's work had to be done.
>
> "At present, you're a liability to the Guild, to the cause at large. You'll be caught here, anywhere in the Republic, perhaps anywhere in Europe. Go, posthaste.

Eagle-eyed observers and history buffs will note that Angelo never made it to New Spain. Instead, he landed in the New Kingdom of Granada.

Three books, two novellas, and years later, what seemed like a cool idea turned out to be an immense challenge not only for Angelo, but also for me. Why?

Because quite simply, there is precious little material about the time period and region (at least in English). I relied on what few books there are, old maps, and conquistadors' journals that had been translated. Many of these sources were off by dozens of years and hundreds of miles, but I had to make due.

Americans learn disgracefully little about the lives and cultures of native North Americans, and near zero about native South or Central Americans. There are small exceptions and snippets, but for the most part, we are lied to from a very young age about the true history of the United States. The history of the annihilation of the pre-Colombian Western Hemisphere is completely whitewashed and shielded from us. While the conquest of the Americas represented a turning point in world history, and many positive things have come from it, it is also quite possibly the greatest crime ever committed.

How many of us are aware that in 1492, the largest city in the world was Tenochtitlan, the capital of the Aztec Empire?

Ever wonder why there are so few surviving Aztec, Mayan, or Incan relics? It's because the conquistadors either destroyed it all or, if made of gold or silver, melted it down into ingots.

Why aren't we taught that an estimated *55 million people* were killed in the conquest of the Americas? That's the estimated equivalent of the number of casualties in World War Two. Yet we rarely hear about it, if ever.

Nothing can change the past.

But perhaps we can use our knowledge of it to improve our future.

After all, every day, our past becomes more of our lives.

I encourage readers to learn more about the history of Latin America. A starter list of books include:

Open Veins of Latin America by Eduardo Galeano

River of Darkness by Buddy Levy

Born in Blood and Fire by John Charles Chasteen

I also recommend watching the classic film, *The Mission*, starring Robert DeNiro, Jeremy Irons, and Liam Neeson.

BONUS CONTENT

From The Prisoner of Paradise

1589 A.D.
Republic of Venice

"Were you followed?"

Angelo Mascari struggled to catch his breath, panting from his twenty-minute sprint through serpentine streets in oppressive summer humidity, not yet able to answer the tall nobleman glaring at him with steady, pale blue eyes.

Unfamiliar with this district of Venice, Angelo's nerves demanded his senses be at full attention. They stood on the *fondamenta* of a narrow canal at a corner outside the Jewish Ghetto. No torches or lanterns lit the footbridge, the wall's porticos, or a dozen other potential hiding spots on either side of the waterway. Silently, he thanked the moon for its fullness, as its light would provide precious seconds of reaction time should a lurker reveal himself. A black skiff bobbed next to them. Other than retreating the way he'd come, the boat was his only option for escape.

He was hesitant to trust the nobleman, but with friends in short supply and a warrant on his head, Angelo had little choice. That the man had yet to kill or arrest him was a promising sign. He slowed his breathing and leaned against the wall, the stucco's mildew finer than wet velvet.

"You spoke the truth," Angelo said between inhalations. "I should not have gone." The heavy sea air left a salty tang on his lips.

"Were you followed?" his contact asked with a clipped whisper. Though the windows in the four-story buildings looming over them were shuttered, voices carried in the cramped neighborhood.

"No, impossible." Angelo scanned the alley and glanced over his shoulder, more concerned with potential pursuers than prying ears. His words betrayed his confidence. No one was aware of his attendance at his beloved's sentencing—but anything was possible.

I know that now.

His unnamed collaborator narrowed his eyes, seemingly reading Angelo's doubt. Six or seven decades of lines etched themselves into the man's face, framed by chin-length, oyster-gray hair. A snub nose lay in waiting over a trimmed beard of tarnished silver.

"Your childish endeavor accomplished nothing and nearly ended your life."

Angelo did not appreciate this near-stranger chastising him, but he held his tongue. During their lone prior meeting, the man declined to disclose how he knew of Angelo's predicament. He had also refused to divulge his identity, though his precise, modulated diction and distinct, upper-class air exposed his nobility.

"And you ruined your garments." He scowled at Angelo's lacerated hemp doublet and bloodstained white wool shirt, a stark contrast from the man's all-black, posh attire. "That may pose a problem," he said.

Angelo scratched at the squalid bandage that wrapped his left ear. Having neither bathed nor seen a mirror in many days, grime coated his bruised face and matted his curly, dark hair, but he cared not about his appearance.

The incredible sight he witnessed less than an hour earlier dominated his thoughts, though he'd yet to process it. He loathed to trust his eyes. From a concealed alcove in perhaps the largest room in Venice, he had watched, helpless. As his enemies concluded their ritual, it appeared as though they had drained Isabella's very life essence from her body. In the flesh, yet flesh no more. *The unimaginable agony she endured.* His final vision of the once-beautiful girl, wilted and shackled, would be engraved in his brain for the remainder of his days, however few they may be.

He blamed himself for the whole of the affair. How could he not? Though only twenty, Angelo strove to live a virtuous life despite the widespread vice in his city. In the end, he succumbed to the greatest addiction of all—*love.*

Now, with no foreseeable way to rescue her, he felt no justification for standing unscathed. He should have been in her place. With his dreams quashed and his well-being an afterthought, he had two goals: avenge his beloved and—*by some means yet known*—save her from the torturous fate that befell her.

"Be truthful," Angelo said, a humble demand. "What has become of Isabella? What? What did I witness?" He hung his head at the hopelessness.

"Mourn later. She's not lost forever."

A breeze skittered moonlight across the canal, bringing with it an acrid, fishy odor, though Angelo found it refreshing on his sweat-drenched skin. Hope swelled within.

From under his gold-embroidered, hip-length linen cloak, the nobleman removed a pouch of coins and a sealed letter, which he offered to Angelo. "Take these and this skiff. Make your way to Palos in Spain and find Sebastiano Cadamosto. Give him the letter. He'll provide you passage to New Spain."

"*New Spain*? What about our next move?"

"This *is* your next move. It's your *only* move. At least for some time."

"It's the other side of the world." Angelo abhorred the desperation in his voice, like a punished boy sent away when a man's work had to be done.

"At present, you're a liability to the Guild, to the cause at large. You'll be caught here, anywhere in the Republic, perhaps anywhere in Europe. Go, posthaste. The ceremony has surely ended by now."

Angelo eyed the boat. He had already been forced to flee danger twice in three days. The mere notion of abandoning Venice without so much as a goodbye to his friends and family grated his core. He'd never set foot on the mainland and was now told to traverse it. A most uncertain future lay beyond the horizon. How could he help Isabella from across the oceans, idling for years with a handful of ducats to his name?

"No," Angelo said. "I cannot leave my home."

"You should have considered that before seducing a married woman."

Angelo seethed. "She's the love of my life. Not some wanton mistress. I'll join your cause and fight them here." He grasped the rapier at his hip.

"Your prowess with the blade is well known." The nobleman laid a gentle hand over Angelo's and guided the sword into its sheath. "But how will you fare against a hundred men?"

"I shall die fighting."

"Death is but the first consideration. And *then* your beloved will indeed be lost forever."

Angelo conceded and released the hilt. He accepted the letter and coin purse, tucking them into his doublet. "To what purpose do you aid me? Answer that, I pray you."

"Mutual adversaries. You may be the key to their demise. I'll send word when it's safe to return. When we can free Isabella and the others. Now go."

With a reluctant nod, Angelo untied the small boat, then clasped his collaborator's hand. "Thank you, sir. Tell me. How can I save her?"

"We need to—"

A whiz through the air was followed by the sickening thud of penetrated flesh and bone. The nobleman gazed at the blood pooling around the tip of the arrow jutting from his right shoulder, then at Angelo, with a mouth agape and befuddled eyes.

A second arrow embedded itself in his collaborator's thigh. Cries of anguish slipped from the old man's sagging lips. He dropped to his knees. The sight of yet another person's blood inches away was too much for Angelo to bear. Like all Venetians, he was accustomed to injury and death, but never like what he'd witnessed recently. Never so *sadistically*.

"Go," the man ordered, straining to utter the command. "You've seen what happens if they catch you alive."

Angelo crouched and examined the arrow.

"There's nothing you can do."

Shifting to the wall, Angelo peeked around the corner. Two hulking men dressed in dark garb—one winding a crossbow, the other loading a bolt into his, stood thirty paces away.

"How? How can I save her?" Angelo asked in a whisper, crouching close to his collaborator. If he didn't learn now, he'd likely never learn.

"Love of God, Mascari." The man gripped Angelo's collar. "What are you waiting for?"

Footsteps ambushed them.

Angelo squeezed the nobleman's uninjured shoulder, then drew his rapier. "Wrongs shall be righted. Starting now."

The attackers reached the corner. Both wore hoods obscuring much of their faces. A scar spread from the larger one's eye to his mouth. The shorter of the two, though taller than Angelo, had an unruly brown beard.

"Run, you fool," the nobleman shouted as he slunk into the canal, just below the bearded man's swipe. The nobleman struggled to swim away, but the assailant caught his cloak and hauled him back onto the ledge.

The larger attacker charged. Angelo was ready. He lunged his rapier at the man's crossbow, inducing an errant shot. The arrow ricocheted off the wall. In a flash, the man dropped the weapon, drew a short sword, and unleashed an assault. He pressed Angelo without remorse, driving the bout down the length of the narrow *fondamenta*.

The strikes were relentless and crushing, but the attacker's shoddy technique exposed a weakness—his arm remained stiff, his wrist lacked rotation. Angelo parried the hacks, anticipating the right moment to riposte. It soon arrived. He angled for a side-cutting stroke, but an arrow flew through the flesh between his knuckles, cleaving a lump of skin from the back of his hand and spraying his arm with blood. The bearded assailant, while kneeing the nobleman to the ground, had shot with remarkable aim. Angelo gritted his teeth; his scorching right hand would be useless in this contest.

In one fluid motion, Angelo parried a wild swing from the attacker, tossed his rapier to his weaker left hand, and pivoted, dodging another blow. The switch drove his opponent off balance. His blade scraped the wall.

Angelo circled the man's short sword with his rapier and squatted, completing his move with a slice through both thighs. The man dropped to his knees, writhing in agony. Angelo kicked his chin, then booted him into the canal.

Isabella was not yet lost.

He rushed to aid his collaborator but stopped short. From the alley, the commotion of an untold number of men, yelling and running toward him, reverberated off the adjacent walls.

At the corner, the nobleman's eyes grew wide at the fast-approaching mob. "Go," he screamed to Angelo with his remaining strength.

Death is but the first consideration. His collaborator's words tolled in Angelo's mind.

He spun, stomped on the scarred man's fingers gripping the *fondamenta* edge, and raced for the skiff. An arrow zipped over Angelo's head as his horsehide boots met the boat's bottom, his impetus propelling the craft forward. He thrust the oars into the murky water.

Half a dozen men, all in black, rounded the corner. The first gave chase, dashing along the canal edge. Angelo paddled with all his strength, an excruciating task with a mangled hand.

At the canal's edge, the pursuer tossed his empty crossbow on the cobblestones and dove for the boat. He caught the gunwale, nearly capsizing it.

"The Order *will* take you," he cried as he climbed in.

Angelo yanked an oar from its rowlock and swung it into the attacker's cheek, knocking the man into the water. Resuming his frantic paddling, he glimpsed the far end of the *fondamenta*. As the bearded assailant pressed the nobleman to the ground, the old man stretched for his boot, retrieved a dagger… and slid the blade across his own throat.

Stunned, Angelo rested an oar to cross himself.

An arrow struck the skiff. Another flew past from his ear. As more arrows landed in the water, Angelo hunkered and rowed furiously to the wider Rio di San Girolamo canal, which led to the open waters of the Venetian Lagoon.

Guilt roared through him—his collaborator's death was on his hands. A vision of Isabella flashed in his mind. *'Mòre mio. I failed you.*

One day, he vowed. *One day, her captors will feel a pain far more severe.*

I

Present Day

Salvatore della Porta slid his rectangular Gucci eyeglasses higher up the bridge of his Roman nose and allowed the irritated voice on the other end of the phone to ramble on. The Commissioner of the Venice Biennale had been complaining for five minutes without a single pause. Della Porta combed his fingers through his salt-and-pepper hair, parted to the side and brushed back with the slightest amount of hair tonic. Though not a classically handsome man, he was keenly aware that looks could be improved with an appropriate fashion sense and proper grooming techniques.

"You and your pathetic hubris probably cut attendance in half," the Commissioner screamed into della Porta's ear. The man's Italian was flawless, but his Swiss accent and heavy-handed cadence made him sound like a dubbed version of a dopey cartoon dog.

"It has nothing to do with hubris, signore," della Porta said in Italian, maintaining an even keel.

"Then what? Enlighten me."

"With all due respect, you may've been a bigwig in Basel, but you're unfamiliar with certain sensitivities here in Venice."

The braggadocio continued to berate him for declining an interview with the London *Times's* art critic, but his voice trailed off to a place that hovered behind della Porta's ears. Switching the call to speakerphone, della Porta stepped over to a bookshelf where rows of long-cherished manuscripts made their home. He traced his finger through a layer of dust on the shelf and made a mental note to reprimand the cleaning crew.

This office was his home and, in this case, truly a palace. He glanced about the spacious room, bedecked with early baroque-era furniture, 19th-century seascapes, and a collection of antique telescopes, sextants, and compasses that would make historians dizzy with glee. Of course, one would expect nothing less in the office of the Director of the famed *Musei Civici di Venezia*, an august foundation of eleven museums in Venice. His workspace was the beating heart of the *Palazzo Ducale*, or Doge's Palace—the foundation's touristic highlight and cultural crowning star.

Della Porta turned his attention out the window to the Venetian Lagoon. Hundreds of vessels of all sizes entered or departed the city in a fluid tapestry.

This used to be the seat of government for the wealthiest maritime power in the world, he thought. *Now it's a museum for tourists.*

He sneered at a cruise ship. Needing to take control of this conversation, della Porta sat at his desk and picked up the phone's receiver.

"We have nothing to hide, but that's not the point," he said. "Lionel Benton may be a prominent art critic, but he also loves shining the spotlight on himself with his outrageous conspiracy theories. Every two years he attempts to damage my reputation or the Palazzo's with accusatorial nonsense that could tear down everything we built."

The Commissioner's rant rose in volume as he continued.

Della Porta suppressed a sigh and shut his gray eyes for a moment. At times, many times, he could not believe he held this position. He wasn't a man to dwell on the past, but would his authority be questioned so frequently had he come from more prestigious means? Raised modestly in a coastal suburb outside of Venice, he developed an early appreciation for the arts on his first school trip to the city and learned his business acumen in his teens, when he ran his father's apparel company in the summer months. His four younger siblings didn't inherit the ambition gene and inexplicably still lived in Chioggia. Though only fifty minutes away, he limited visits to two or three times per year, either for Christmas or to dine at his brother's *trattoria*, which della Porta had bailed out financially some years back.

In comparison to those whose shoulders he now brushed, his middle-class upbringing left him somewhat unrefined—a half step above his family and schoolmates, yet a half step out of his current circles. In situations like these, insecurities revealed themselves with less than professional manners.

"I don't care if his review castigates the Biennale and exposes the trash you think passes for art," della Porta cut in. "If you don't like my decision, take it up with the mayor." He slammed the phone down with a clenched hand.

The skirmish would have ramifications, but della Porta reassured himself he acted with reason. He wouldn't let an outsider jeopardize all that he wanted—no, *needed*—to accomplish. He'd worked too hard professionally and sacrificed too much personally to reach this point, even leaving his fiancée twenty years earlier to focus on his career. He hadn't dated since and had no regrets. As a priest is married to the Church, della Porta was married to the art of his museums—*eternal* art that transcended the mundane.

His anger toward the Commissioner and the man's fugacious taste gave him a jolt of unexpected energy. Della Porta raised his slight frame from behind the ornately chiseled desk and smoothed his custom charcoal gray wool suit before shutting down his computer and pocketing his smartphone.

As it was after hours and the Palazzo was devoid of visitors, he strolled the expansive hallways, passing through rooms that were time capsules of Venice's heyday, and entered the Great Council Room, his footsteps echoing in the chamber. Still the city's largest room, it had once been the assembly hall for the Senators of the Republic, and their impassioned ghosts empowered him.

He groped the ever-present pendant hanging from his neck beneath his shirt.

The room's air tasted of history, of centuries-old incense. The heaviness scuttled past his tongue to the far reaches of his lungs and calmed his pulse.

Della Porta sat on one of the permanent red oak benches encircling the room. With the walls and ceiling covered in masterworks depicting Venetian history by Veronese, Tintoretto, Palma the Younger, and other Renaissance masters, the space never ceased to inspire him.

Tintoretto's *Paradise* spanned the entire main wall. A somber yet groundbreaking work, the painting depicted Jesus coronating Mary as Queen of Heaven, enveloped by hundreds of adoring souls. Lining the top of the three other walls were portraits of the seventy-six *doges*, the dukes who governed the Republic for eleven hundred years.

Della Porta gazed meekly at the artwork. All the people in the paintings seemed to mock him: *You're not the right man for the enormity of the task at hand.*

The rear wall held the portrait of Doge Marino Faliero, though a black shroud had been painted over his face to commemorate his brief rule. Della Porta had memorized the story at an early age. The traitorous duke was decapitated after an unsuccessful coup d'état. Faliero not only lost his head, but the people mutilated his body and burned many records of his existence.

A chill bristled della Porta's skin. He shook it off. Where the duke failed, he would not. This was *his* time for ascension, for reviving past glory.

Composing himself with three quick exhalations, he strode toward *Paradise.*

"Remember who you are," he whispered.

When he arrived at the wall, he crouched, reached under a seat, and twisted the lever that unlocked the hidden door.

II

FUCK, THAT HURTS.

Nick O'Connor couldn't recall getting hit in the back of the head with a baseball bat, but it was the only explanation he could muster in his hazy state. A thick cloud capped the collateral pain streaming to his frontal lobe. He moistened his lips and shifted, mentally scanning his body for additional signs of trauma. His lower back ached, and his quadriceps screamed, but they were nothing compared to his head.

A distinct, sterile odor mixed with the stench of dried blood wafted into his nostrils. A steady dripping floated into his ears like drops of water hitting an empty metal pan.

"Doctor, he's waking up."

A young woman's voice hovering over him sounded anxious, but the allure of her tone coaxed his mouth into an involuntary smile. Soft hands clasped his, comforting him. He knew that voice and touch, perhaps intimately, but the throbbing in his skull prevented him from placing their owner.

Footsteps rushed near. "Excuse me, Mrs. O'Connor," another woman said with a rough, battle-weary voice.

Upon hearing, 'Mrs. O'Connor,' Nick smiled. The young voice and touch belonged to his wife, Julia. His contentment dissolved to dismay. Even without seeing her, he should've been able to recognize the love of his life.

Julia's fingertips lingered, connected to him a second longer before releasing her grip. "He's gonna be okay, right?"

Nobody answered.

A cold palm rested on Nick's forehead. A finger lifted his eyelid. Intense light cut through the dark, flooding his vision.

Nick recoiled and swatted the hand away.

"Let the doctor do her job, Nick," said a male voice he recognized instantly. It belonged to Wade, his older brother.

The light invaded his space, and again, Nick shoved it off.

He opened his eyes completely to find an auburn-haired woman in her sixties wearing glasses and a doctor's coat. She gripped a penlight between claret-red fingernails. Next to her stood Wade, a few days shy of his thirtieth birthday. He wore an amateur hockey jersey, and his wavy brown hair had the marked look of sweaty helmet-head.

"I'm fine," Nick said, his hoarse words clawing over parched vocal cords. "I just wanna know what happened."

Fuck, my head hurts. He didn't have a clue as to why he outright lied to a physician. He was far from fine.

Julia watched behind Wade, her hand pressed to her mouth. Nick gazed beyond his brother and smiled warmly at her. The bronze specks in her emerald eyes shimmered beneath the harsh, fluorescent ceiling fixtures. Typically, one glance at any inch of his wife was a cure-all, but admiring her now offered little consolation. Never had his brain experienced such an acute beating or disorientation. Determined to get his bearings, he assessed his surroundings further. He lay on a narrow bed with crisp white sheets in a small room. He attempted to raise his hands but felt his arms chained to the bed.

Alarmed, he lifted his head. He only glimpsed the same amateur hockey jersey on his torso before an invisible mallet whacked his cranium back onto the pillow.

"What's the last thing you remember?" the doctor asked.

"Why am I in a hospital?" Nick winced. Every word was like a piledriver pendulating from ear to ear.

The doctor tucked the penlight back in her pocket. "You're at Mass General. You were body-checked, and your helmet came off. Your head hit the ice."

Snippets of a hockey game trickled into Nick's memory. Rushing the goal... the clock ticking down... readying his stick for the shot... nothing.

"Out cold for thirty-three minutes," his brother added. "In and out of consciousness for another hundred and forty-four."

"But why am I chained to this bed?" Nick asked, still unable to move his arms.

In unison, Julia and Wade furrowed their brows and turned to the physician for an answer.

"That's the morphine talking," she said. Lifting Nick's left arm, she showed him an IV needle stuck in his vein. The dripping sound evaporated, replaced by the steady beeping of an EKG machine.

Nick sighed, though a part of him wished he was healthy and under arrest for some mysterious crime.

Julia squeezed past Wade to Nick's side. She took his hand again and kissed it. Nick gasped at the marble-size, spherical diamond on her engagement ring. "I was so scared," she said. "Seeing you laying there... You haven't even touched that. Hello ...? Nick—?"

Nick O'Connor woke with a start.

Beads of sweat rolled down his back.

"You okay, babe?" Julia placed her iPad on the table, staring at him with a grave look of concern.

He blinked and glanced around. The sights, smells, and sounds of his present location blitzed his brain like a tsunami flooding his subconscious. They were in Venice, on a side of St. Mark's Square, sitting at a round, white linen-covered two-top table outside of Caffè Lavena. A paid bill and an untouched cup of espresso sat in front of him. Julia's empty cappuccino mug sat next to her iPad.

"Yeah, yeah. I'm fine," he muttered.

Exhaling, Nick felt more mystified than relieved. The memory was so lifelike, yet it faded as he checked out the throng of international tourists parading through the plaza, large enough to hold three football fields and lined with hundreds of arched windows set above an arcade of overpriced restaurants and gift shops on the ground level. Two young boys raced past their table flapping their arms, scattering a flock of pigeons into the air. A tour group followed, led by a college-aged woman wielding a yellow umbrella like a marching baton. The three dozen other tables at their café were occupied with the same thing as theirs: tourists eating an overpriced breakfast, looking at their phones, or people-watching.

Though the sky was overcast, the dawn's rain had left a sheen on the geometrically-patterned stone floor, so he shielded the glare battering his sleep-deprived eyes.

"You look like you hit a wall," his wife said. "You gonna drink that or what?" She pointed to his espresso. Gone was the sphere on her ring, replaced by the one-carat, princess-cut diamond he bought her nearly five years ago.

"Sorry, I... got lost in the moment a sec. I'm just jet-lagged."

Frowning, she turned her gaze across the vibrant square.

Nick took a sip of his coffee and caressed the gash on the back of his still-sore head, a most unwanted trophy from the hockey game. He wished he'd worn a hat to cover the stitches.

It had been two weeks since the accident. *Well, not an accident.* He still resented the opposing player in his community league who decided a blind cross-check was a shrewd tactic. He'd recollected everything by the following day. Amazingly, it wasn't the hit or the pain he couldn't shake, but that image of Julia and Wade gaping down at him in the hospital.

He felt terrible being such an inconvenience to everyone. Even the rink janitor had complained about the amount of blood. But what really ground Nick's gears was his doctor prohibiting him from playing when the game resumed a few days later. He'd led the Boston Pilgrims to three city championships in a row and was pissed to hell he had to watch this final from the bench. They lost.

Nick sighed. *What's another year?*

Julia eyed him feeling his head wound. "Does it still hurt?"

"Nah, solid as a rock." He knocked on his skull, aggravating the discomfort.

Though he hated all the attention over a stupid injury, Julia's compassion never failed to imbue warmth in his soul. She was his rock and his heart. They were both only twenty-eight, but he never once questioned his decision to tie the knot young. Her sunny outlook, profound intelligence, and genuine empathy for all living creatures added up to a marriage their single friends envied.

He didn't blame her for still worrying about his injury, but other than a wicked headache and the occasional mind-wander, he felt fine. Or, at least, that's what he told the doctor. And his wife. The doc cleared him for the trip, though Julia had wanted to cancel the entire thing. Nick had none of it. Even if he had severed a limb, he'd take her to Venice and help her realize her dream.

He threw her a smile that stretched into an irrepressible yawn. She smiled back and returned her attention to her iPad.

Not yet adjusted to the time change, Nick woke before dawn in their room at the Bauer Hotel, a beautiful five-star, where Julia had managed to find an unbeatable last-minute rate. Realizing she was also awake, without a word, their spooning segued to a lazy lovemaking session, a departure from their typically vivacious sex. Although he could've stayed in the king-size bed with her forever, she reveled in the early start. With one more free day until she needed to work, she had a full itinerary of sightseeing planned.

After checking in the previous evening, they explored a small slice of the maze-like city and ate dinner at a quaint restaurant near their hotel, which Nick surmised served the best mussels in Italy, if not the universe. Venice's food and scenery had already blown him away, but later he realized that on the walk back, he had criticized the city's government for permitting motorboats in the canals. It wasn't how he'd imagined their first night out. An unexplained funk had rolled into Nick's head like a New England fog, and dispelling it proved to be difficult.

He despised his current mindset and had been trying to return to his old self all morning. His wife, on the other hand, exuded full vacation mode, despite the fast-approaching, most important meeting of her career. Reclining a bit, she crossed her legs, her tight white jeans getting even snugger. He loved her rocking yoga body, but in the moment envied her comfort level. Nick regretted choosing dark blue Levi's over shorts. The Mediterranean humidity made the denim stick to his thighs, and his most cherished article of clothing, a wide black and brown leather belt with a matte chrome buckle Julia had bought him two birthdays ago, suffocated his body.

Loosening his belt a notch, he inhaled the woody and roasted citrus notes of the espresso. He swigged a shot, swished the deliciousness around his mouth, swallowed, and shook his head to disperse the caffeine. More awake, he reflexively grabbed his cell to check his social media accounts and political news, but curiously felt zero desire to do so—which he didn't mind. He'd been trying to kick the masochistic addiction for two years. Going cold turkey wasn't in the cards, but perhaps this trip would be the diversion he needed. Pocketing his phone, he leaned across the table to view Julia's iPad.

The screen displayed a dinner party from a seemingly impossible perspective of multiple angles from the ceiling corner, stitched together in a mosaic. Stark walls dominated the shot, and the people were saturated in vivid color. The photo showed much of the dining room yet offered no indication of who held the camera, giving the surreal impression of a spider's eight eyes observing the routine event of humans eating dinner. The upper-left of the screen showed the logo for the Venice Biennale Art Exhibition.

"There's too much red," Julia said, perturbed. She pulled her shoulder-length, honey blonde hair into a ponytail, wrapping it with a hairband from her wrist.

"Right. *That's* what the judges were thinking. That gallery in New York, too. Come on, Jules, it's literally an award-winner." Beneath the table, Nick gave her a playful nudge, an attempt to convince her—*or himself*—he'd returned to normal. "When's your meeting again?"

"Tomorrow at two." She picked up the tablet and opened the email app. "Speaking of which, I finally heard from Delta's inflight magazine."

"You're a rock star, babe. So that means a fully expensed trip? Tuscan steaks every night from here on out?"

"Hilarious. They agreed to *look* at the article. I haven't even written it yet."

"Still great news. It'll be awesome, and they'll run it. What about the others?"

"Nothing yet. Anyway, point is, I'll need another three hours or so at the Biennale to interview some people. There's lots you can do. The art's gonna be amazing, or I read there are beautiful gardens there, or you can take a tour, or there are boat—"

"Babe, babe, I'll find something to do. Venice was always your trip. I'm just along for the ride. And the pasta. And the wine. Actually, that's not a bad idea. I'll find a bar and wait it out. Mingle with the locals."

Chuckling, she rolled her eyes, knowing he was half-serious.

Sure, the sights or a boat tour would be cool, but they wouldn't be the same without Julia. Nick meant every word about it being her trip. After her photo took first place in the Biennale's amateur entry competition, he used his banked PTO and booked a three-week vacation, including four days in Venice. The cost exceeded their budget, but the joy on his wife's face was worth every penny.

A New York gallery owner had reached out to meet her at the exhibition, so the trip was already paying off for her career. The Delta article was gravy. He didn't care he brought in 90% of their income as a fintech software architect. Julia's freelance journalism helped pay for some stuff, but Nick cared far more about her real passion—photography. With her talent, it was only a matter of time before she hit a home run.

Nick downed his remaining espresso and turned to her. "Hey, what do you call people in Venice who can't see?"

"What?"

"Venetian blinds."

"Is that supposed to be funny?"

"Not even a little bit." Nick stood. "Come on, let's go see some sights."

"Now you're talking," Julia said, tucking her iPad into her leather purse that doubled as a camera bag. She pulled out her DSLR and rose.

He reached into his pocket and dropped a few euros on the table.

"You don't need to tip here," Julia said.

"It's not gonna bankrupt us." Nick knew his habit of tipping generously annoyed her. He appreciated her concern since they only had one full-time salary, but he wished she'd trust him with their finances. It was the one thing about her that bothered him. *Well, maybe not the one, but the list is damn short.* They both let it go and joined the teeming masses in the square.

He scowled at the tourists. "Is it wrong to wish we came here during Covid? Remember all those pics of deserted squares? Dolphins in the canals?"

Julia widened her eyes. "Beyond morbid. Painful too."

"Sorry."

"I love that everything is back to normal"—she sidestepped a woman hauling six shopping bags—"but I get your point. I pity the locals. How many plagues has Venice lived through?"

Nick shivered. Her question struck an odd, personal chord. He intertwined her silky fingers with his. "At least we're finally in Europe together. Eight years later..."

"Eight? Wait, are you still beating yourself up over that?" she asked, picking up on his tone of regret.

"Missing out on a week in Paris with my girlfriend? Yeah."

"And miss a week of the season?"

"*College* season. And it's not like I got drafted."

Julia motioned to Nick's head. "Can't say I'm too upset about that."

He knitted his brow. "Either way, I should've visited you."

"Honey, it's the *now* that matters. And the future." She kissed his hand. "We have the rest of our lives to travel. Including this trip, which is already epic, and I can't thank you enough for it."

He prayed she was being sincere. Like an answer from above, sunrays penetrated the thick cloud layer.

"I don't know why I've been so salty since we got here," he said, "but I promise I'll turn it around. Prepare yourself for the happiest tourist Venice has ever seen. Hey, get a shot of me with the tower in the background." He ran a few feet and brandished two thumbs up, his double-wide grin making Julia laugh.

She positioned herself to get the best angle, crouched, and raised the camera. "The light's perfect right now," she said. "Love those dark eyes and gorgeous smile. This might be the next cover of *Hot Husbands Magazine*."

Nick replied by turning around and wiggling his butt.

With his back to Julia, he glanced up at St. Mark's Campanile, which he'd read about on their flight. The thirty-two-story brick bell tower reached for the sky and was adorned with a giant pyramidal cap. Directly below the pyramid, a six-foot-tall, gravity-defying stone chimera sculpture soared over the city. Saint Mark's winged lion was the ubiquitous symbol of Venice, its image gracing everything from doors and tiles to umbrellas and bags of souvenir pasta.

As the lion flapped its wings and took flight, the ground shifted beneath Nick.

The monster swiveled its face toward him, exposing a row of sharp teeth. The piazza slanted, and the tower elongated. His equilibrium slipped. The chimera banked and flew away, aiming for a crack in the clouds.

The bustling sounds of the square vanished. Blood pounded his eardrums. Faint church bells rang. Distraught women cried in the distance.

"Turn around," Julia called.

His heart rate quickened. His breath popped in short spurts.

He turned back to his wife. Her green eyes morphed to brown, and her fair skin took on a more olive, glowing complexion. Nick offered a weary grin, unsure of what was real in the moment.

Keep it together, buddy. Don't ruin this for her.

Julia snapped the picture and hung the camera strap across her chest before walking over.

Relief washed over him as he realized she hadn't noticed the episode. His heart resumed its normal pulse, and the clamminess encompassing him dissipated.

"Ready?" She linked her arm through his.

Her touch calmed him back to reality and hopefully… *normality.*

He cleared his throat. "For what?"

"The Palazzo."

"The whatzo?"

"Babe, it's right there. I told you at the café."

She pointed to a large, elaborate building fifty yards away. "The Palazzo Ducale. I'm dying to see it."

"Impressive," Nick said, perking his eyebrows as he turned to look. Every square inch of the four-story peaches-and-cream-colored façade was ornamented with statues, columns, capitals, arches, and tiles.

The Palazzo was situated on the edge of St. Mark's Square, at the corner of the *Riva degli Schiavoni*, the wide waterfront promenade along the Grand Canal. The river-size canal was the biggest in Venice—a major water thoroughfare winding through the city from end to end.

Nick inhaled through his nose. Though he lived in a coastal city, the air here seemed more… settled.

"What is it again?" he asked.

Julia flashed him a look as if he'd said the most unreasonable thing she'd ever heard.

"I was listening to you, babe. I don't know. The caffeine hasn't kicked in yet. Tell me again."

She groaned but pulled out her iPad.

"Though it shares a wall with St. Mark's Basilica," she read aloud from the TripAdvisor app, "the Palazzo Ducale's design casts a mismatched juxtaposition with the mushrooming onion-bulb architecture of the cathedral. Since 1923, the imposing Venetian Gothic landmark has been a museum, housing hundreds of the world's most important Renaissance artworks. Built, damaged, and rebuilt since the twelfth century, the compound encompasses a mix of architectural styles." She smiled at the building. "It's the Doge's Palace."

"What's a doge?"

"A duke. They were the leaders of the 'Most Serene Republic of Venice' for over a thousand years. It's a top sight in Venice."

"It *does* look like it's calling our name. Or... we could use the gray weather as an excuse to cozy up with a bottle of wine in our room."

"Come on. We're seeing it now," she said, clearly peeved Nick was trying to weasel his way out of something on her must-do list. "We'll have wine tonight."

"All night?" he asked with a smirk, pulling her body into his.

She kissed him. "Can you think of a better use for jet lag?"

"I like it."

Julia pulled away and tucked the iPad into her bag. "I know you do. And I promise you'll love this place. It's the kind of art that'll change your life. See you there."

Before he replied, Julia made a mad dash toward the Palazzo. He gave his wife a few more seconds, then took off, slapping her butt as he ran past.

For a moment, he could've sworn soft strands of auburn hair brushed across his face. Hair that smelled of cinnamon and rose. Hair that smelled...*familiar.*

www.ingramcontent.com/pod-product-compliance
Lightning Source LLC
LaVergne TN
LVHW091246150826
845673LV00006B/1336

* 9 7 8 1 9 6 5 9 4 6 7 8 7 *